ACKNOWLEDGMENTS

With thanks to Haden, Brett, Sue, Frank, Leland, David, Shelly, Evan, the Mount Lawley Mafia, and my wonderful wife, Amanda, as always.

D1585510

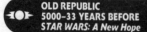

OLD REPUBLIC
5000-33 YEARS BEFORE
STAR WARS: A New Hope

*Lost Tribe of the Sith**
Precipice
Skyborn
Paragon
Savior

3650 *YEARS BEFORE STAR WARS: A New Hope*

The Old Republic
Fatal Alliance

1020 *YEARS BEFORE STAR WARS: A New Hope*

Darth Bane: Path of Destruction
Darth Bane: Rule of Two
Darth Bane: Dynasty of Evil

RISE OF THE EMPIRE
33-0 YEARS BEFORE
STAR WARS: A New Hope

Darth Maul: Saboteur*
Cloak of Deception
Darth Maul: Shadow Hunter

32 *YEARS BEFORE STAR WARS: A New Hope*

> ### *STAR WARS:* EPISODE I
> #### THE PHANTOM MENACE

Rogue Planet
Outbound Flight
The Approaching Storm

22 *YEARS BEFORE STAR WARS: A New Hope*

> ### *STAR WARS:* EPISODE II
> #### ATTACK OF THE CLONES

22-19 *YEARS BEFORE STAR WARS: A New Hope*

The Clone Wars
The Clone Wars: Wild Space
The Clone Wars: No Prisoners

Clone Wars Gambit
Stealth
Siege

Republic Commando
Hard Contact
Triple Zero
True Colors
Order 66

Shatterpoint
The Cestus Deception
The Hive*
MedStar I: Battle Surgeons
MedStar II: Jedi Healer
Jedi Trial

Yoda: Dark Rendezvous
Labyrinth of Evil

19 *YEARS BEFORE STAR WARS: A New Hope*

> ### *STAR WARS:* EPISODE III
> #### REVENGE OF THE SITH

Dark Lord: The Rise of Darth Vader

Coruscant Nights
Jedi Twilight
Street of Shadows
Patterns of Force

Imperial Commando
501st

The Han Solo Trilogy
The Paradise Snare
The Hutt Gambit
Rebel Dawn

The Adventures of Lando Calrissian
The Han Solo Adventures
The Force Unleashed
The Force Unleashed II
Death Troopers

REBELLION
0-5 YEARS AFTER
STAR WARS: A New Hope

Death Star

0

> ### *STAR WARS:* EPISODE IV
> #### A NEW HOPE

Tales from the Mos Eisley Cantina
Allegiance
Galaxies: The Ruins of Dantooine
Splinter of the Mind's Eye

3 *YEARS AFTER STAR WARS: A New Hope*

> ### *STAR WARS:* EPISODE V
> #### THE EMPIRE STRIKES BACK

Tales of the Bounty Hunters
Shadows of the Empire

4 *YEARS AFTER STAR WARS: A New Hope*

> ### *STAR WARS:* EPISODE VI
> #### RETURN OF THE JEDI

Tales from Jabba's Palace
Tales from the Empire
Tales from the New Republic

The Bounty Hunter Wars
The Mandalorian Armor
Slave Ship
Hard Merchandise

The Truce at Bakura
Luke Skywalker and the Shadows of
Mindor

STAR WARS
THE FORCE UNLEASHED
II

SEAN WILLIAMS

BASED ON THE STORY BY
HADEN BLACKMAN

LUCAS BOOKS

TITAN BOOKS

STAR WARS: THE FORCE UNLEASHED II
ISBN: 9780857680945

Published by
Titan Books
A division of Titan Publishing Group Ltd.
144 Southwark Street
London
SE1 0UP

First edition August 2011
2 4 6 8 10 9 7 5 3 1

This edition published by arrangement with LucasBooks, an imprint of
Random House Publishing Group, a division of Random House, Inc.

www.starwars.com
www.starwarstheoldrepublic.com
www.titanbooks.com

Did you enjoy this book? We love to hear from our readers.
Please email us at readerfeedback@titanemail.com or write
to us at Reader Feedback at the above address.

To receive advance information, news, competitions,
and exclusive offers online, please sign up for the Titan
newsletter on our website: www.titanbooks.com

A CIP catalogue record for this title is available from the British Library.

Printed and bound in Great Britain by CPI Group UK Ltd.

For Robin Potanin,
fellow lover of
champagne and good sci-fi

DRAMATIS PERSONAE

ACKBAR; Rebel leader (*Mon Calamari male*)

BAIL PRESTOR ORGANA; Senator and Rebel leader (*human male*)

BERKELIUM SHYRE; repairman (*human male*)

BOBA FETT; Mandalorian bounty hunter (*human male*)

DARTH VADER; Sith Lord (*human male*)

GARM BEL IBLIS, Garm; Rebel leader (*human male*)

JUNO ECLIPSE; Rebel captain, *Salvation* (*human female*)

LEIA ORGANA; Princess and Rebel leader (*human female*)

MON MOTHMA; Senator and Rebel leader (*human female*)

PROXY; droid

RAHM KOTA; Rebel general and Jedi Master (*human male*)

STARKILLER; Rebel and apprentice to Darth Vader (*human male*)

YAT-DE VIEDAS; Rebel leader (*Rodian male*)

YODA; Supreme Master of the Jedi (*nonhuman male*)

A long time ago in a galaxy far, far away. . . .

PROLOGUE: Cato Neimoidia

JUNO ECLIPSE STOOD with her hands behind her back and stared down at Cato Neimoidia. From the bridge of the *Salvation*, the densely forested world shone a brilliant green against the star-dusted black, and she was keenly reminded of other forest worlds she had visited during her career as an Imperial pilot.

Callos was the first. There she had obeyed orders that had resulted in the death of the entire planet's biosphere.

Felucia was next, and that world, too, had been left poisoned in her wake.

Kashyyyk, the last and most difficult to recall, had not been damaged at all. In fact, the prospects for its forests' continued survival had taken a sharp turn for the better following the destruction of the skyhook that had threatened to enslave every last Wookiee and to ensure the planet remained part of the Empire forever. The resolution made in the ruins of a jungle hut, where a handful of people had vowed to rebel against the

Emperor and free the galaxy's tormented trillions, was bound to help, too.

Given luck, then, the forests of Kashyyyk would survive, but Juno remembered wondering how she herself possibly could. The pain she felt had been too great, the sense of loss too deep. Every living thing reminded her of the part of her that had unexpectedly wakened within her and then died just as suddenly. Her heart beat with a heaviness that hadn't been there before—not even when she'd been held captive for months in the *Empirical*, expecting to be executed at any moment.

Sometimes she woke in the night, still feeling *his* lips against hers. They had kissed just once, but the memory of it was burned in her brain. He had died, and she lived on. It had taken a year before she finally felt as though she might be over him. So why was she letting a bunch of trees bother her now?

She told herself to get it together. Juno Eclipse had bigger things to worry about.

"Excuse me, Captain," barked a voice at her elbow. "Our probe droids are picking up an atmospheric disturbance in the vicinity of the target."

She turned away from the view to face her Bothan second in command. "What kind of disturbance, Nitram?"

"Explosions."

"Show me."

The circular display screen in the center of the bridge zoomed in tight on the city closest to the Imperial stronghold. Secondary screens flashed infrared images conveyed by heavily encrypted transmissions from the droids on the ground. The bridge city hung like a vast urban hammock from its overarching stone spire. Several thick supporting cables were glowing red. One was actually burning.

"Looks to me like nothing more than local insurrection," she said. "If it keeps Baron Tarko off our backs, all the better."

"Uh, yes, sir." Nitram cleared his throat.

Juno studied his long face. "Speak your mind. That's an order."

"Well, there were some unusual heat readings immediately prior to the blasts. You can see them here, and here." He pointed to a recording time-stamped an hour earlier. "It looks like a ship's exhaust."

"So where's the ship? I can't see it."

"That's exactly my point, sir." He looked around the bridge, then leaned in closer to whisper, "I think it might be General Kota."

Juno didn't know whether to be annoyed or amused. For such a young officer, Nitram was good: he had, in fact, stumbled across the truth of their mission with impressive and inconvenient speed. Fortunately, Juno had learned fast under her Imperial masters to keep every emotion well concealed.

"You've been listening to too many stories, Nitram," she said, clearing the incriminating secondary screens. "Wherever Kota is, he's not slumming here with us."

That was a lie, of course: She would recognize the signature of the *Rogue Shadow* anywhere, even when it was fully cloaked.

"Yes, sir."

Nitram had no choice but to accept it as the truth. She was, after all, his superior officer. But that didn't have to be the end of it.

"Sound the alert. I want twelve fighters strafing that city in the next five minutes. Let's take the chance to strike while the Baron is busy."

Nitram saluted. "Yes, sir." He swiveled briskly on one heel and snapped out a string of orders.

Juno turned back to the window, hiding a smile. The EF76 Nebulon-B frigate *Salvation* was a valuable part of the growing Alliance navy, and she had no intention of putting her inexperienced crew in serious harm's way. But it *was* a training run, she told herself, and what better way to learn than in the thick of combat? She was sure, anyway, that the infamous Baron Tarko would soon have more to worry about than her green hotshots.

Sirens wailed through the ship. Feet thundered on bulkheads. With a string of distant thuds, a dozen Y-wings launched and, wobbling only slightly against the starscape, grouped in two six-ship formations rocketing down into the atmosphere.

"Take us out," she told Nitram. "No point hiding now."

The *Salvation*'s seven ion engines roared into life, thrusting it from its redoubt behind the planetary system's smaller moon. The deflector shield generator was running at full capacity, ready for immediate reprisal. Baron Tarko's facility on the ground wasn't heavily enforced. It consisted of a slave processing plant with a number of ancillary buildings, including barracks, laser batteries, and TIE fighter launchpads, all suspended from the bridge city over a giant sinkhole. A constant stream of freighters came and went from the world, redistributing the Empire's ill-gotten prisoners. Intelligence made very clear that the Baron thrived on bribes from high-ranking Imperial officers keen to obtain the best "stock," while at the same time selling excess numbers to the Hutts and other criminals. What he did with his wealth, exactly, no one knew. But all could guess at the suffering he was responsible for. If someone *were* to put an end to his brutal regime, they would be doing the entire galaxy a favor.

That wasn't the *Salvation*'s job, however. Juno's orders were strict: Prick the Baron's defenses and see how strong they were; shake her young crew into battle readiness; and under no circumstances risk the integrity of the ship. The official line was that resources were more valuable to the Rebellion than tiny victories—at least at the moment. When the navy was big enough and the lines of supply more secure, *then* the fight could begin in earnest.

Not everyone agreed with the official line, though. Some thought the fight had already begun and could be pursued by a small force as readily as by something larger and therefore less defensible. Take out the right target, the naysayers said, and entire star systems could be disrupted. Like the ripples that spread across a pond's surface at the drop of a single stone, every Imperial facility and process that relied on slave labor would be slowed down by a successful attack on Cato Neimoidia.

Juno had heard the argument a thousand times. She

knew just how much difference even a single person could make. The newly formed Rebel Alliance wouldn't exist at all, most likely, but for *him*.

She shook her head, annoyed at letting herself be distracted again. Kota needed her. She wouldn't let him down.

News of the frigate's presence spread fast through the freighters orbiting the plant. Many vanished into hyperspace, taking their slaves with them. Others broke orbit and began to descend dirtside. Her fighters dodged among them, increasing the chaos of the skylanes. Red dots on the display screen signaled the launch of a TIE defense squad: ten ships, exactly as expected. Laser batteries swiveled to track the Rebel squadron.

She tuned half an ear to the star pilot chatter even as she monitored Nitram's handling of the crew.

"Watch that tower, Green Six."

"On your tail, Blue Four."

"Arm turbolasers. Target those batteries."

"Keep it tight, Green Two. Keep it tight!"

"Fire at will."

The *Salvation* rocked as its powerful lasers unleashed their deadly energies onto the planet below. Juno felt a rush of cautious pride. Her people were nervous, excited, and occasionally frightened—as was perfectly appropriate. Cato Neimoidia might be an outpost, but it was fundamentally connected to the Empire as a whole. Stick around too long and the whole weight of the enemy would come to bear on them. Everyone understood that they had to be in and out fast, or they'd never get out at all.

The turbolasers missed, but someone else didn't. The ground-based lasers exploded into a million pieces, destroyed by unknown fire.

Juno gave silent thanks to Kota and his invisible militia, and readied herself for Nitram's excited announcement that his theory had been confirmed. Kota was indeed active in the galaxy, striking hard and fast against the Alliance leadership's express orders. They couldn't stop him, and they had many reasons to be grateful for his activities. Baron Tarko would soon regret ever coming to his attention.

Instead of gloating, Nitram said in a worried tone, "Launches—ten more TIEs!"

"That can't be right," Juno said, leaning closer to check the data. It was all too right, unfortunately; intelligence had gotten the fighter strength wrong. Worse still, the TIE fighters were coming their way. "Launch all remaining Y-wings. And put someone else on turbolaser control. I want the roof of the barracks in flames in the next two minutes if I have to come down there and press the button myself."

"Yes, sir!"

The crew's energy level ramped up a notch. There was no time to hold back out of nerves or uncertainty. Intel flooded through the ship like an invisible gas. Within moments, they would be under attack, and all were aware of the frigate's strategic disadvantages. It was well armed and well shielded for a vessel of its size, but the slender midsection connecting the engineering and crew quarters could be ruptured by concentrated enemy fire. Were that to happen, the atmosphere would vent immediately, killing everyone aboard.

The turbolasers fired again. Targets on the ground burst into brilliant balls of fire. Juno caught glimpses of the cloaked *Rogue Shadow* ducking and weaving among the TIE fighters below. It looked like the general was trying to find a place to land. Once he and his commandos were on the ground, the ship could automatically retreat to a safe location and wait for a signal to collect them when the mission was over.

Juno hadn't flown the *Rogue Shadow* since the events on the Death Star, but she still knew its specifications by heart. Better than she knew the *Salvation*'s, in fact. Here she was just the commander. In the *Rogue Shadow* she had been captain *and* crew. There was an important difference.

Rebel and Imperial starfighters met in the vacuum between the frigate and the planet. Energy weapons flashed and ricocheted. The screens were full of light. She wished she was out there with the pilots, breathing acrid cockpit air, thumb growing tired on the firing stud. Her heart beat faster for them even as she reminded herself of her new duties. War was simpler in a starfighter, but it wasn't better. The bigger picture was what mattered. Winning the war, not the battle.

In that sense, she had some sympathy for those who opposed Kota's way of thinking. Going in too hard, too fast was a sure way to be encircled and wiped out. A degree of caution never went astray. That was why she surreptitiously helped him—to keep him in check as much as to watch his back. Someone needed to make sure he didn't go AWOL as he had before. The Rebellion needed him.

Thinking of the downsides of Kota's campaign made her frown. What was taking him so long? The *Rogue Shadow* should have been on its way ages ago.

"Nitram, concentrate fire on those cannon emplacements there and there." She indicated two locations near the barracks. The fire coming from both was much greater than intelligence had indicated it should be. Maybe that was the problem.

"Yes, sir."

Rebel starfighters changed course to attack the targets. The exchange of weapons fire intensified.

Juno squinted at the data, worrying at the inconsistencies between the intelligence gathered from Imperial sources and what lay evident before her. "Get those probe droids closer to the barracks. Something doesn't look right to me."

Finely balanced forces jockeyed for position on the ground and in orbit as she waited for the data to trickle in. From a distance, the Imperial installation looked perfectly normal. It possessed a spaceport, shield generators, security compound, and so on—all the same as on any occupied world. But it was better defended than most, and the spaceport was crowded. Why land so many ships on commercial territory when there was plenty of space over by the slaving compound? More important, why were Imperial records on Cato Neimoidia so wildly different from what was actually here?

There was little to tell from the data, so she turned her attention to the starscape around them. No sign of Imperial reinforcements.

"Why hasn't the Baron called for help yet?" she asked Nitram.

"I don't know, sir. We've been monitoring signals closely."

She cupped her chin and thought hard. It was only a matter of time before the Imperial fleet showed up, whether Baron Tarko called for it or not. All it took was just one fleeing freighter to sound the alarm and the Emperor's boot would descend to crush the Rebels. Really, with forces evenly matched and Kota dragging his heels, she should already have sounded the retreat rather than risk the *Salvation*.

"Give me the comm," she said. "Don't listen."

Nitram's ears went up and then flattened down against his skull. "Whatever you say, sir."

She selected a little-used channel. "Blackout to Blackguard. Respond, please."

The line crackled for a moment, and then Kota's gruff voice came on. "I don't have time to talk."

"Bad luck. This is taking too long. You need to pull out."

"Negative, Blackout. Leave if you want to. I'm staying to finish the job."

She ignored the implied reproach in his words. "How? You're never going to get close enough to the barracks to get Baron Tarko. It's too well defended."

"That's no barracks," he said.

"Then what is it?"

"I don't know, but it won't be anything by the time I—"

Kota's signal disappeared into static in time with a bright flash of light from below. Two of the probe droids winked out. The *Rogue Shadow*'s heat signature disappeared into an expanding ball of fire. Someone had dropped something big on Cato Neimoidia, taking out several Rebel and Imperial starfighters at once. Fire licked at the walls of the Imperial compound, making them glow bright red.

The crackle over the comm intensified.

"Respond, Blackguard. This is Blackout. Do you need help down there, Blackguard?"

Nothing.

Juno tried again, forcing herself to speak calmly. Nitram was watching.

"Blackguard to Blackout. Respond immediately!"

Nothing. The bridge was silent.

She stood, frozen, with one question echoing in her mind: What would the man she had loved have done now?

She knew the answer. He would do everything in his power to rescue his friend and Jedi Master. He would fight with every drop of energy in his body. He would let nothing stand in his way.

But she wasn't him. She didn't have his powers and she did have responsibilities he never had to consider. Besides, *he* was dead, and now there was no sign of Kota, either. What was she supposed to do—rescue a ghost? If she knew how to do that, she would have done it a year ago.

An alarm sounded. The bridge came to life around her.

"We've got company," said Nitram, gaze dancing across the rapidly filling display screen. "Two frigates, a cruiser, and—yes, a Star Destroyer, *Imperial*-class. Could be the *Adjudicator*. It's launching fighters. Captain?"

Everyone on the bridge was looking at her.

"Recall our pilots," she said in a clear and level voice, knowing that her hand was being forced. There was only one responsible decision open to her now. "Bring everyone aboard, then get us out of here, fast."

"At once, sir."

Juno stepped back from the display screen in order to let her officers go about their work. Tiny dots converged on the *Salvation* as its starfighters broke off their engagements with their enemy and raced for safe harbor. She counted eighteen, which meant six pilots wouldn't be going home. In exchange for what?

Again, the answer lay before her. Her crew was functioning perfectly well, and they knew through hard experience that Cato Neimoidia was better defended than they had expected. The *Salvation* had pricked the Empire and forced it to respond. Someone, somewhere, would be grateful for the *Adjudicator*'s unexpected absence from their skies.

But where did that leave her?

"Take us the long way to the rendezvous," she told Nitram. "We don't want anyone on our tail."

"Yes, sir."

Nitram didn't question her order, even though the reason she had given him was meaningless. The truth was that she needed time to think.

Kota was gone. How was she going to explain *that* to the alliance leadership?

Farewell, old friend, she thought. *What kind of mess have you landed me in this time?*

"Calculations complete," said Nitram.

"Ready the hyperdrive," she responded automatically. The shields were taking a heavy pounding, making the floor sway beneath her. Just two starfighters remained outside. When they were aboard, she gave the order.

"Jump."

The *Salvation* rushed into hyperspace, leaving the ill-fated world, its mysteries and its ghosts, far behind.

Part 1

REVOLUTION

CHAPTER 1

Present day . . .

FROM THE DEPTHS OF MEDITATION came a man's voice.

"You're running out of executioners, Baron!"

Starkiller opened his eyes. He knew that voice. It tugged at parts of him that had lain dormant for a long time—or never genuinely existed at all, depending on one's viewpoint.

He shied away from both memory and contemplation. There was no point wasting energy on either when his very survival was at stake. How many days he had been down the pit he no longer knew, but in that time he had neither eaten nor slept. His enemy wasn't physical in the sense of a foe he could strike down or manipulate. It was himself—his fallible body, his weak mind, his faltering spirit. He would endure and emerge whole, or never emerge at all.

Such was the life of Darth Vader's secret apprentice.

"He is dead."

"Then he is now more powerful than ever."

More voices. He closed his eyes and shook his head.

Kneeling, he placed his manacled hands on the slick metal surface below him and concentrated on hearing the world outside.

Long stretches of isolation had attuned him to the cloning facility's many moods. Through the metal he heard a relentless hiss that could only be rain. Sharp cracking sounds were lightning, coming and going in staccato waves. Rolling rumbles were thunder, and a deeper note still was the song of seabed-hugging currents that circled the world.

He was on Kamino. Starkiller was sure of that much. He had been reborn on the distant waterworld, where a significant percentage of the Emperor's stormtroopers were grown. Here it was that he would live and grow strong, or die weak and unmourned. Every hardship, every hurdle, was one step closer to full mastery of his fate. That was the lesson underlying all lessons.

A new note entered the planet's endless song: the scream of a TIE advanced prototype starfighter. Angular and fleet, with bent vanes, it entered the atmosphere with a whip-crack sonic boom and descended on a bold, high-energy descent toward the facility.

Starkiller tensed. He knew that ship's sound and could sense the well-practiced hand behind its controls. He heard stormtroopers marching quickly in response to their master's electronic summons, calling orders to one another as they went. Blast doors opened and closed with booming thuds. The facility woke from its unattended slumber.

He didn't move as the TIE fighter landed. He didn't open his eyes as two heavy, booted feet dropped onto the platform and began the long walk through the facility. He breathed at a steady pace through the whine of the turbolift and the hiss of doors opening. A ring of red lights at the top of the pit came on, and although he felt the light against his hunched back, he didn't look up.

He heard breathing, mechanical and regular. Heavy footsteps came to the very lip of the pit, and stopped.

"You're alive," said Darth Vader.

At the voice of his former Master, Starkiller looked up, blinking against the light. Vader's boots were three meters above him, barely visible behind the lights and the grate that separated the pit from the dark room beyond. The Dark Lord loomed like a shadow, a black hole in the shape of a robed man.

Starkiller's throat worked. It was so dry he could barely talk at all.

"How long this time?"

"Thirteen days. Impressive."

The compliment was hard-won. It ground out of the triangular grille covering Vader's mouth and fell on Starkiller's ears like dust.

"The Force gives me all I need."

"The Force?"

The hint of praise turned to warning, as it did so often.

Starkiller lowered his head. He knew what was required. The weeks of training and isolation he had endured made that exceedingly clear.

"The dark side, I mean, *my Master*."

One gloved hand moved. The grate flew open.

"Come," said the dark figure above him.

The metal floor beneath Starkiller lurched and began to ascend. He forced his leg muscles to unlock from their long kneeling position, and stood to meet Darth Vader upright and unbowed.

The room above was sparsely furnished, with no windows, just one exit—the turbolift—and little light. Shadows cast by terminals and floor lamps made its very dimensions ambiguous, but Starkiller knew from long training exercises that the room was circular and its walls were impenetrable. He flexed his fingers, yearning for a lightsaber to hold. Muscle memory was keener than any other kind. Even with the new skills Darth Vader had taught him, his hands wanted to fight the way he knew best.

At the very edge of his vision stood several skeletal PROXY droids, awaiting activation. If he was lucky, he would be unshackled and allowed to duel some of them. If not . . .

The lift ground to a halt. Vader stepped back to study him. Starkiller felt the keen eye of the Sith Lord on his gaunt form even through the layers of durasteel, obsidian, and plasteel that covered the man's face. Something was different. Although nothing had been said, he could tell that this was no ordinary training session.

He waited. There was no hurrying Darth Vader.

"I have a mission for you."

"Yes, my Master."

"Starkiller's former conspirator has been captured."

He experienced a moment of confusion. Then his memories stirred, providing a name. The name of the one who had lured him away from the dark side and to his death.

The same voice that had disturbed him from his meditation . . .

"Vader thinks he's turned you. But I can sense your future, and Vader isn't part of it. I sense only . . . me?"

"General Kota," he said, struggling to keep himself anchored to the present.

"Yes. You will travel to Cato Neimoidia and execute him."

"And then will my training be complete, Master?"

"You will not be ready to face the Emperor until you have faced a true Jedi Master."

The voice was Darth Vader's, but again from another time, another memory. The present-day Darth Vader hadn't spoken at all.

Starkiller put his manacled hands to his head and turned away, lest his disconcertion be exposed. No matter how he tried, no matter how he concentrated, the past simply wouldn't leave him alone.

Vader's close attention hadn't ebbed. "You are still haunted by visions."

"Yes." There was no point denying it. "Yes, my Master."

"Tell me what you see."

He didn't know where to start. Thirteen days, this time, he had stayed motionless in the pit, subjected to visions and hallucinations through all his senses: strange odors, fleeting touches, voices calling him, sights he could never have imagined. He tried to ignore them, and when he couldn't ignore them, he tried to piece them together instead. Neither was entirely possible, and every attempt hurt so badly he despaired of it ever ending.

"Sometimes," he said, falteringly, "I smell a forest on fire."

"Continue."

"I see the general falling, and feel the ground shake as a starship crashes around me. And I hear a woman—a woman's voice—when I try to sleep." He swallowed. This was the most painful recollection of all. "I can't understand what she's saying. Do you know who she is?"

A pleading note had entered his voice, and he hated himself for it.

"They are the memories of a dead man." Vader came closer, his physical presence lending weight to his words. "A side effect of the accelerated cloning process and the memory flashes used to train you. They will fade."

"What if they don't?"

"Then you will be of no use to me."

Starkiller straightened. For the first time, that fact had been said aloud. He had always known it was so; Darth Vader wasn't renowned for his charity. But to hear it stated so baldly—that this Starkiller, this clone, would be disposed of like some faulty droid if he didn't pull himself together soon—had a profoundly focusing effect.

Not for long.

"Try the Corellian razor hounds."

That was a new voice, one he hadn't heard before. He winced, and knew that by wincing he had effectively doomed himself.

"Starkiller's emotions made him weak," the Dark Lord

said. "If you are to serve me, you must be strong."

What form of service that might take, Darth Vader had never said. To take the former Starkiller's place, he presumed, as a weapon that could be aimed at the Emperor then Vader's enemies whenever he commanded. From treacherous commanders to perhaps the Emperor himself—that was how it had been, and how he assumed it would be now. For the moment, however, that didn't matter. The new Starkiller wanted only to live.

"I am strong, my Master, and I am getting stronger."

Vader stepped behind him and waved a hand. Metal complained as the manacles dropped from Starkiller's wrists and hit the floor with a boom.

"Show me."

Numerous pairs of eyes lit up in the shadows. The PROXY droids were activating. Starkiller's fists balled in readiness. He had defeated their training programs over and over again. There wasn't a Jedi simulation that could beat him.

But this was different. Even as Darth Vader provided him with his weapons—two lightsabers with matched crystals, producing identical red blades—he saw that he wouldn't be fighting Jedi Knights this time. The targets stepping out of the shadows wore uniforms not dissimilar in color to the Sith's ancient enemy, but these were ordinary men armed with nothing more than blasters.

He had seen such armor before, in the memories of the original Starkiller's life. Men like this had fought him in a TIE fighter factory high above Nar Shaddaa. They had been on Corellia, too. He remembered the places clearly, even if he couldn't put them in context. The uniforms weren't Imperial. That was the only thing he could be sure of.

More voices came to him, a veritable babble of overlapping statements that went some way to filling one hole in his memory.

"We'll join your alliance."

"All we needed was someone to take the initiative."

"Let this be an official Declaration of Rebellion."

And he did remember now. The PROXY droids were wearing the uniform of Kota's militia, later adopted by the Rebellion—the Rebellion the original Starkiller had brought into being through a mixture of deceit and something that felt, through the obscuring veils of the cloning process, remarkably like sincerity.

"You must destroy what he created," Darth Vader intoned.

Starkiller ground his teeth together. If he was going to survive the coming minutes, he had to concentrate. He wasn't really destroying the Rebellion, just an imitation of it. And what did the Rebellion matter now, anyway? It existed. The original Starkiller was dead. He needed to move on.

The troopers rushed him from all sides. Twin red blades flashed as he met their advance, spinning and slashing with an easy grace that belied the strength behind it. Mastery of the Jar'Kai dual-lightsaber fighting style hadn't come easily, even given his inherited knowledge of the Niman and Ataru techniques. Using two blades came with both advantages and disadvantages. Although he could attack or defend himself against more than one opponent at once, he could only wield his lightsabers one-handed, reducing the power of his blows.

Building up his physical strength had therefore been a key part of his training on Kamino, starting with simple weights and graduating to combat training with droids like these. Dueling the Dark Lord himself had come last of all, and he had clung to that ultimate challenge even as his mind played games with him. He might not know who he was, but he could learn—and had learned—how to *fight*.

Fight he did, deflecting every attack the faux-Rebels dealt against him, singly or in pairs and trios. Holographic limbs and blasters were no match for his blades. Sparks flew. Droids fell in pieces. Brown uniforms turned red with illusory blood.

More droids issued from the wall, crowding him, coming at him in waves of four or more. Starkiller went into a fighting trance, stabbing and sweeping complex arcs through the air. His nostrils were full of smoke. The stink cleared his head. No more voices assailed him, and no doubts, either. He was who he was. Born to kill, he killed.

With a roar he forced his way through a wall of Rebels, slashing and hacking as he went. They fell apart on either side, leaving just one standing before him. He raised both blades to strike him down.

Not him. *Her.* She was a slender, blond woman in an officer's uniform clutching a blaster in both hands.

Starkiller froze.

He knew that face.

He took a step toward the woman.

"You're still loyal to Vader! After all he did to us—branding me a traitor and trying to kill you—"

"No," he said.

The words in his head wouldn't be drowned out.

"I saw you die. But you've come back."

"No," he repeated, raising his blades.

"Don't make me leave another life behind."

"No!"

The woman cowered before him. "Wait," she said in a voice identical to the one in his head. "Don't!"

"Now the fate of this Alliance rests only with you."

He lowered his blades, stunned out of his fighting trance. The voices were the same!

Memories stirred in his mind. Images of the woman before him came in a bewildering rush. Vader wanted him to destroy everyone the original Starkiller had fought with, and that meant this woman, this Rebel officer, this . . .

"Juno?"

"Yes," she said.

"Strike her down" came the command from Vader.

"I—I can't."

"You must learn to hate what he loved," said Vader, and suddenly it was just the three of them in the center of the droid-strewn training ground. Starkiller, the Sith who had created him, and a woman from the first Starkiller's past.

Conflicting impulses warred within him, triggered by the ongoing cascade of recollections. Juno was Juno Eclipse, the woman Starkiller had, yes, loved. But he wasn't Starkiller, so what did he owe her? He was just a clone, and she was only a droid, an illusion fashioned to test him. What did it matter if he did as he was told, as he had been bred to do?

His hands trembled. The twin red blades wavered. They grew steadier as he drew his elbows back, preparing to strike.

"I guess I'll never need to live this down."

He remembered a tender pressure against his lips, the feel of her body against his, a heat he had never experienced before, in this life or any other . . .

He couldn't do it. He couldn't kill her.

With a double click, he deactivated his blades. His arms came down and hung at his sides.

"It is as I feared."

Darth Vader lashed out, channeling the dark side with practiced ease. Starkiller winced, but it was the training droid the Dark Lord had targeted. His lightsaber sliced it neatly in two. The image of Juno Eclipse vanished in a shower of sparks.

Starkiller held his ground. No more *my Master*. No more pretense. "What will you do with me?"

Darth Vader strode to face his former apprentice, kicking the body of the droid out of his path.

"You will receive the same treatment as the others."

"What others?"

"Those who came before you went mad within months, tormented by emotional imprints I was unable to erase. Some would not kill their father, others their younger self. With you, it is this woman. Now you will suffer the fate they did."

Starkiller bowed his head, rocked by the revelation that he wasn't the only Starkiller Darth Vader had re-created. This he had never been told. The possibility hadn't even been insinuated—although he should have guessed.

How many had come before him? How many had died before they had ever truly lived? Could his creator possibly be telling the truth about their stubborn emotional imprints? He spared no feelings for the father he could no longer remember or the boy he had stopped being long ago. It didn't seem remotely possible that any version of Starkiller could do anything other than share that love for Juno Eclipse.

Another vivid memory tore through him.

Staring down in shock at the sight of his Master's lightsaber protruding from his stomach. Unbearable pain. Falling heavily to his knees with a choked scream.

And another woman's voice, the dying words of a Jedi Master he had killed.

"The Sith always betray one another—but I'm sure you'll learn that soon enough."

His mind cleared, and he stared in new understanding at the Dark Lord before him.

Vader was lying. There had been no other clones—or, if there had been, they had felt the same way as him. The original Starkiller had loved Juno Eclipse, and so did he. He was sure of it. He felt it in his bones, in the genetic machinery of his cells. It was the one thing he was sure of.

Vader wanted to weaken that certainty, to turn him back into a weapon, by implying that this feeling was spurious.

And worse—the act of killing Juno Eclipse was symbolic only, here in the Vader's secret cloning laboratory. How long until that became Juno's *actual* slaughter? Would that have been the next stage in his training?

The hum of the Dark Lord's lightsaber changed pitch slightly as Vader shifted position.

Before Vader could strike, Starkiller turned. He didn't activate his own lightsabers. Vader would expect be expecting that—a defensive pose, or at best a halfhearted attack. Starkiller would surprise him with the one weapon Vader couldn't wield in return.

A burst of lightning arced from Starkiller's fingers. Too late, the Dark Lord raised his lightsaber to catch the attack. Lightning crawled up and down his chest plate and helmet, provoking a painful whine from his breathing apparatus. The servomotors in his right arm strained.

Starkiller had only a split second before his former Master repelled the attack. The Force flowed through him. Droid parts and debris rose up and spun around the room. With a harsh rending sound, the metal wall burst outward, letting in the fury of the storm.

But even in the grip of his passions he knew that there was a difference. He was intimately familiar with what being driven by negative emotions felt like. His original had been a slave to the dark side until Juno and Kota had shown him how to be free. That legacy remained even now. He would choose the emotions that ruled him. He would not be a slave to them.

The dark side tugged at Starkiller, and it was hard to resist. He hated his former Master. He feared for Juno. He doubted the very fact of his existence. Killing the man who had created him would go some way to solving at least two of those problems. The temptation was very strong.

Vader's blade caught the edge of the lightning. The Dark Lord began to straighten.

Starkiller leapt for the hole he had torn through the wall and entered the storm. He jumped high and long, aiming for the landing platform he had located by hearing alone, weeks ago.

He came down with a solid thud on the slick metal platform, just meters from Vader's TIE fighter. Lightning split the sky into a thousand pieces. Thunder boomed. Far below, and all around, the sea raged.

The rain and wind scoured him clean. He opened his mouth and felt moisture on his tongue for the first time in thirteen days. After so long in the pit, it tasted like freedom itself.

His arrival took the squadron of stormtroopers guarding the facility by surprise, but they reacted quickly enough. Sirens sounded. Blaster rifles came up to target him. Three AT-STs standing guard over the landing platform clanked and began to turn.

Starkiller bared his teeth. His heart beat with an excitement he hadn't felt since his awakening in Vader's laboratory. This was why he had been made. This was why he existed.

He reached out with his hands and flexed his will. The Force responded, swelling and rising in him like an invisible muscle. A nearby communications tower groaned and twisted. Sparks flew. He wrenched the tower down and sideways, sweeping it over the platform, knocking the AT-STs into the ocean and crushing the stormtroopers gathering to rush him.

Something exploded—a generator, pushed far beyond its capacity. Through the exploding shell of shrapnel stalked a black figure holding a red lightsaber. Vader was moving with surprising speed.

Starkiller almost smiled. Vader's rage was not so easily escaped. But he had done it once before. He would do it again.

The starfighter behind him was unharmed by the devastation he had wrought. Starkiller ran to it and leapt inside. He worked its familiar controls with confident speed, activating systems still warm from its last flight. Its ion engines snarled.

An invisible fist gripped the starfighter. Starkiller increased the thrust. His determination met Darth Vader's rage, and for an instant he was unsure which would win.

Then all resistance fell away, and the TIE fighter leapt for the sky. He fell back into the seat and watched the black storm clouds approach him. Electrical discharges danced around the cockpit. Darkness briefly shrouded him.

Then he was through and above the clouds and rocketing high into the atmosphere. The planetary shield surrounding Kamino was designed to keep ships out, not in, so he passed easily through their visible barrier. Stars appeared, and Vader was far behind.

Now what?

He didn't dare believe that he was entirely free, or that Juno was entirely safe. He had to find her before Vader did. He had to be with her.

Every breath he took filled him with the certainty of that fact. This was the emotion that would rule him, not revenge or bloodlust or despair. But how to pursue this mission? Where did he start looking for one woman in an entire galaxy?

"Starkiller's former conspirator has been captured."

General Kota. If anyone knew where she was, it would be him.

As the cloud-racked face of Kamino receded behind him, Starkiller locked in a course for Cato Neimoidia.

CHAPTER 2

Four days earlier . . .

THE *SOLIDARITY* SHONE like a miniature star in the
reflected light of Athega system's blazing primary. The
streamlined, organic-looking star cruiser, a recent Mon
Calamari model, hung in the shadow of volcanic Nkllon,
a small world about as inhospitable as any Juno could
imagine. There the *Solidarity* and its small flotilla of
attendant vessels were simultaneously hidden from any
passing gaze and shielded from the blazing, hull-stripping
light of the deadly sun.

"Your request to come aboard has been granted,"
Juno's second in command said. Nitram spoke cautiously,
as though reluctant to intrude on her mood. "The shuttle
is ready to launch."

Juno didn't blame him. Knowing what she faced, she
had been tense throughout the journey, and her crew had
left her alone, which was exactly what she had needed.
She had a lot to consider where the Alliance leadership
was concerned.

"Thank you, Nitram. You have the helm until I return."

He saluted, touching his left ear with the tip of one paw-like hand. "Yes, sir."

She strode unhesitatingly from the bridge, keen to give the impression that she had no doubts at all about her return, when in fact there were no certainties at all. She had put her ship at risk to assist Kota on one of his unauthorized missions. In the past, the success of Kota's missions had protected her from disciplinary action. This time, she had no such recourse. Officers had been demoted for much less.

The short hop in the shuttle seemed to pass in seconds. She saluted the escort awaiting her at the other end, keeping the fear that it was there to take her prisoner deeply concealed.

"Welcome aboard, Captain. Commodore Viedas is expecting you. This way, please."

The detail fell in around her, and she matched their pace step for step. Around them, the ship hummed with industry and discipline, its white fittings clean and well maintained. Her ship, the *Salvation,* seemed old and clunky by comparison. It had been liberated from the Empire during a skirmish over Ylesia and renamed in the style of the fledgling Rebellion. The *Salvation* still bore the scars of battle, unlike the *Solidarity,* which looked brand new.

The issue of the ships making up the Alliance's fleet occupied more than her own mind, as she discovered on being admitted into the commodore's secure conference room.

Yat-de Viedas was a Rodian, and a natural for

enlistment with the Rebel forces, given the Empire's xenophobic stance on non-humans. A privateer of some standing, he had risen quickly through the ranks of the Corellian Resistance, ultimately to be handpicked by Garm Bel Iblis to lead the attack group Juno belonged to. He was short, and his Basic became increasingly accented under stress, but he was liked and respected by his officers. Juno had served with him briefly after the birth of the Rebel Alliance on Kashyyyk, and she knew that, whatever came next, it wouldn't be born from maliciousness or ill feeling on his part.

"I'll hear nothing bad said about the MC-Eighty." Viedas was pacing from one end of the conference room to the other, addressing the rest of the small gathering. Present via hologram were Mon Mothma and Garm Bel Iblis, presumably from their respective homeworlds. The Senators looked stressed and didn't notice Juno's entry. Princess Leia Organa attended in person. She returned Juno's salute with a respectful nod.

So far, thought Juno, *so good.*

"The redundancy of its shield system is of prime advantage," Viedas was saying. "I cannot overemphasize how important this is in conflicts against the Empire. We will always be outweaponed, so defense should always be our first priority."

"I understand, Commodore," said Mon Mothma. "But the simple fact is that we can't afford any more of them. Not at the moment. Our resources are stretched too far as it is."

"If the Mon Calamari won't give them to us," said Bel

Iblis, "then we must take them."

"We're not pirates," said Leia. "My father would not agree to this."

"Your father isn't here. Perhaps if we had greater access to *his* resources—"

Juno cleared her throat, and the commodore turned to face her.

"Ah, good. Captain Eclipse, would you care to report the outcome of your mission to Cato Neimoidia?"

"Of course, sir." She came deeper into the room, trying to take the measure of the meeting. Clearly something had leaked. Someone on her bridge, or perhaps in the starfighter squadrons, had let slip what had happened, so the people before her already knew part of it. The question was: Would they give her a fair hearing, or had they already made up their minds?

"My orders were explicit," she said, deciding to draw the picture in black and white herself and thereby disallow any enemies she might have the advantage. "Gather intelligence, shake up my crew. That's all. When the opportunity came to assist General Kota in his mission to kill the Imperial administrator on Cato Neimoidia, I decided to do so."

"What kind of assistance did you provide?" Bel Iblis asked without any sign of prejudgment. She knew that he would be interested, first and foremost, in the military angle.

"We acted as a distraction for the ground forces, primarily by launching starfighters, but also by making the frigate's presence known. We jammed signals in and out, inasmuch as we could. The *Salvation* engaged directly with the enemy only when it became clear that General Kota required our active support."

"Did he know you were going to be there?" asked Mon Mothma, who no doubt cared less about the tactical details than the circumstances under which the brief alliance had come about.

"He did, Senator," Juno said.

"And how did he come to be privy to this information?"

"Because I told him two days in advance."

"I see." Mon Mothma's lips tightened. "Would you care to explain why?"

"I wasn't aware that I was required to keep secrets from a general in the Rebel Alliance."

"But you *are* aware, no doubt, that the general's actions are not always sanctioned by the Alliance."

"Yes, Senator."

"Do you consider yourself to be part of his renegade campaign?"

"No, Senator."

"Yet you disobey orders in order to help him. How do you explain that?"

Juno felt as though the deck were slipping out from beneath her. She wondered again who had sold her out, and if she would get the chance to find out why before she was decommissioned, maybe worse. "Permission to speak freely, Senator."

"Granted," said Garm Bel Iblis.

Mon Mothma glanced at him in surprise and some annoyance, but didn't countermand him.

"I have helped General Kota before," Juno said, "on Druckenwell, Selonia, and Kuat. Each time, his missions were successful in helping the Alliance. Each time, my assistance cost the Alliance nothing. I took no orders from him, and he accepted the limitations of our arrangement. He knew that the responsibilities of my command took precedence over the success of his mission." *At least I hope he did,* she added silently to herself. "We were on the same side, Senator, and I am not ashamed of helping him. I would help him again, in a heartbeat." *If I could.*

Everyone started to speak at once, but it was Mon Mothma's voice that carried the moment.

"Did you know about this, Commodore?"

"No, Senator, but I take full responsibility." Viedas's green skin had turned faintly purple around the edges. Juno hoped that didn't mean *anger* among his species.

"Commodore Viedas couldn't have known," she said. "I was careful to keep it a secret from him, because I knew that he would not approve."

"Did you take any losses, Captain?" asked Mon Mothma.

"Six starfighters," she said. "That's less than our last official mission, which was considered a success."

"I want more details," said Bel Iblis, leaning forward in the hologram to steeple his fingers. "What did your collaboration with Kota gain us?"

"Well, we know that Cato Neimoidia is better defended than we initially thought. It's taken some hits and brought in reinforcements. The Empire knows we're watching the slave industry now. Baron Tarko will be more cautious in how he mistreats his 'stock.'"

"So he's still alive?"

"I'm afraid so."

"You said *were*," put in Leia. "You and Kota *were* on the same side."

Juno couldn't meet the Princess's observant eye. It was she who worried Juno more than the others. Her father had been an old friend of the general. They had known each other longer than Juno had been alive.

"Kota fell on Cato Neimoidia," Juno said. "His end of our joint mission was not successful."

The air in the conference room seemed to solidify as the news sank in.

"Did you *try*—" Bel Iblis began, but cut himself off. The thought didn't need to be finished.

"You were constrained by your orders," said Mon Mothma, nodding. "That I understand. But do you see where you have left us? By assisting Kota—by actively *encouraging* him in his reckless solo campaign against the Empire—you have cost the Rebel Alliance our most experienced general. Can you honestly say that we have benefited from this outcome?"

Juno met the Senator's accusatory stare without flinching. "I believe he would have died anyway— perhaps long before now—without my help. You know his history as well as I do. He was never going to sit around and watch as opportunities came and went."

"She's right," said Bel Iblis. "The longer we wait, the more people like Kota we're going to lose."

"But if we attack now, we might lose *everything*." The passion in Mon Mothma's voice was naked. Even by hologram, the mixture of grief and determination could not be mistaken. "Renegades like Kota would have us die by degrees or burn in one final conflagration. There must be another way!"

"There is," said Juno.

All eyes turned back to her.

This was the moment she had prepared for all the way from Cato Neimoidia. She wasn't going to let it slip through her fingers.

"We've lost a general," she said, "and we must mourn him. But we can't let a setback like this knock us off course." She said the words with a faint sense of déjà vu, remembering the traumatic times after the agreement on Kashyyyk—except then they had been Kota's words, not hers. "We must find a replacement for him—a military leader who will rally people to our cause—someone who comes with his own resources, as Kota did, but someone who also captures the perfect balance of action and caution we need to embody, if we're going to win this war."

"Do you have someone in mind, Captain?" asked Mon Mothma.

She was ready for this, too. "I've been hearing about a Mon Calamari called Ackbar, a slave we rescued from the Eriadu system—"

"Captain Ackbar has pledged his support of the Alliance. We already have him on our side."

"But we don't have his people," Juno persisted. "They were among the slaves Kota tried to free on Cato Neimoidia. If we can earn the support of the Mon Calamarians, then we get their soldiers and their ships with them. Didn't I just hear you talking about the MC-Eighty star cruisers as I came in? Imagine if we had the resources of the entire Mon Cal shipyards at our disposal! Wouldn't the Emperor have to sit up and take notice of us then?"

Viedas nodded, and so did Bel Iblis. "He would have no choice," said the Senator from Corellia.

"There are no guarantees the Dac resistance movement will ever join our cause," said Mon Mothma. "We've approached them several times. They remain unconvinced we mean business."

"Actions speak louder than words," said Bel Iblis.

"I agree," said Juno. "A decisive strike against the Empire on Dac, with the support of Captain Ackbar, and they'll come around for sure. It's exactly the opportunity we need."

"And what if it goes wrong?" asked Mon Mothma. "What if this mission fails, as Kota's did, and we lose Ackbar, as well? Then we'd be even worse off than we are now."

Juno felt some of the frustration that must have boiled inside Kota, ever since the optimistic early days of the Alliance. She wasn't afraid for herself and the fate of her career. The Alliance itself was at stake now, bound up in endless bickering and disputes.

"Princess," she said, "you're very quiet."

Leia looked up at her. "I don't feel that I can offer an opinion without further consultation."

"But your father has the deciding vote, and you represent him, so—"

"So I would like to consult with him before I cast that vote, if you don't mind."

The firmness of the rebuff took Juno by surprise. She had felt sure that Leia's opinion would be the same as hers. It was she, after all, who had cemented the agreement on Kashyyyk, she who had chosen *his* family's crest to represent the hope they all had felt, then, for the future.

It didn't help that Bel Iblis looked as frustrated as Juno felt.

"We mustn't rush in, Juno," said Mon Mothma, her tone ameliorating now that it was clear she had the upper hand. "Kota has barely been gone a day, and threats close in on all sides. Let us choose carefully. Let's not be blinded as Kota was by the dream of an easy victory. We learned the hard way that this will never be our lot."

Juno knew she was thinking of the Death Star, still lurking somewhere in an unknown state of readiness. They had come so close to the Emperor and failed to take him down. Had they only succeeded then, they would never have been having this conversation.

Juno forced herself to use the only name she could bear to think of *him* as, anymore.

"You wouldn't be saying that if Starkiller were here."

Mon Mothma's expression hardened. "He's not here, so the point is irrelevant."

"I think you've said enough, Captain Eclipse," interrupted Commodore Viedas with a pronounced Rodian lisp. "Leave us now, while we discuss what happens next."

"I'm prepared to resign my commission over this," Juno said, reaching up to tug off the four red pips of her captain's insignia. The very thought of it pained her, but to stand aside and do nothing, to wait while a golden opportunity slipped them by . . .

"Don't be so hasty," said the commodore. "We might well court-martial you first."

She dropped her hands to her sides, feeling nothing but defeat. Of course: That was what he had meant by *what happens next*. Adding impulsive defiance to her case wasn't going to help the matter of her disobedience with regard to orders.

"Yes, sir," she said, snapping off a quick salute. "I await your decision."

"Corporal Sparks will show you to the officers' mess."

The door opened behind her, and she exited quickly, without glancing at Mon Mothma or Leia. Garm Bel Iblis gave her an encouraging look, but he was as powerless as she was, outvoted by his co-leaders of the Alliance and hemmed in by logistical realities. Without ships, they couldn't fight; if they couldn't fight, they'd never get any more ships. At this rate, the Rebellion would either tear itself apart or die of attrition before another year was out.

She was shown to the mess by a bright-eyed young woman who looked barely old enough to be a private, let alone a corporal. Advancement came quickly in any movement afflicted by heavy losses. In the mess, Juno was offered refreshments and a chance to rest, but she declined everything. She simply stared out the viewport at the vistas of molten Nkllon and its fiery sun. She imagined that she could feel the heat even through half a meter of transparisteel, burning her defenses away.

Finally she felt a hand on her shoulder. She turned to find none other than Commodore Viedas standing behind her.

"I thought I'd better come myself to give you the news," he said. "I'm sorry, Captain, but we're standing you down from the *Salvation*. The demotion is only temporary, while Senator Mothma goes over the case again, and may not last longer than a day or two. Both of you just need an opportunity to cool down. I hope you understand."

She bit down on her disappointment and the urge to argue. Viedas was going out of his way to explain, something he was under no compunction to do. "Yes, sir. I understand."

"In the meantime, the Princess sent you this," he added, patting the head of a blue-and-white astromech droid she hadn't even noticed at his side. "She hopes that you will put it to good use."

"I'm sorry, sir?"

"She understands that you have a faulty droid in your possession. He's being brought from the *Salvation* as we speak. The corporal will show you to a maintenance suite that has been put at your disposal. You have the time to see to your droid now, and I suggest you don't waste it."

With that, he left her. Juno watched him go, frowning. What did he care about her droid? What did the Princess?

"Is it possible," she asked herself, "that I'm dreaming all this?"

The R2 unit burbled something electronic she couldn't understand. It didn't help.

"This way," said the perky corporal, reappearing at her side.

"After you," Juno told her. The R2 trundled patiently in their wake.

PROXY was already waiting for her when she arrived, stretched out on an examination table in a private workshop. His familiar, skeletal form was dented and scarred by countless rough patch jobs and the occasional field welding. His yellow eyes were extinguished now, as they had been for months. Just seeing him made her uncomfortable for reasons she found difficult to express, even to herself. Surely she should be over it all by now?

"Let's fire him up," she told the R2 unit when the corporal had gone, "and see what you can do."

She reached a hand into PROXY's innards to reactivate his power supply, but instead of moving to help her, the R2 unit rolled back a step and projected a hologram onto the floor between them.

"I apologize for the deception, Juno," a miniature version of Princess Leia told her. The recording had been taken not long ago: She was still wearing the clothes she had worn to Juno's interview; only the background had changed. "I hope you'll forgive me for not standing up for you before. I cannot speak freely, even when I know what my father would have me say. While he is in hiding, it's my job to keep the Alliance together, and I know you appreciate how hard a job that is. Mon Mothma is my friend and teacher; I would not defy her openly, when we all know that what she says is at least in part correct. We *must* proceed cautiously. But at the same time, we must act decisively. No agreement is possible—so it's better that she doesn't know what you are about to do."

Juno squatted down in front of the hologram, feeling a faint revival of hope within her.

"Artoo-Detoo here will do what he can for your droid," the Princess went on. "You'll need help convincing the Mon Calamari and the Quarren to join our cause, even with Ackbar on your side. I've arranged for one agent of the Organa household to meet you and PROXY at Dac's Moon and coordinate the rendezvous, but that's all the help I can spare you, I'm afraid. From here on, it's up to you." She smiled. "I'd wish you good luck, Juno, but I'm hoping you won't need it."

With that, the recording fizzled out, looped back to the beginning, and started to play itself again.

"That's enough," Juno told the R2 unit.

She settled back onto her haunches to think.

Leia wanted her to bring the Mon Calamari to the Alliance table without Mon Mothma learning of it. Did Garm Bel Iblis know? Probably not, since he was elsewhere in the galaxy and even private transmissions could be overheard. But Commodore Viedas had to be part of the scheme. It was he who decided how officers in his attack group were disciplined—in Juno's case by relieving her of her command—and he who had delivered the droid to her. He was definitely a conspirator in the plan to give Juno not just the means to complete this mission, but the opportunity.

Yet without the *Salvation* behind her, she wondered,

what could she possibly achieve in the fight against the Empire?

She snorted at her own cowardice. What *couldn't* she achieve, without that great lumbering mass of responsibility hanging over her head? Kota had been a master of this kind of work, employing small teams of handpicked militia in fast strikes to achieve well-defined outcomes. If he could do it, so could she.

"Hello, Juno," said a familiar voice from the table. "I can't tell you how relieved I am to see you again."

She braced herself to look at PROXY, but the sight still came as a shock.

Sitting on the table was a perfect replica of *him*. Of Starkiller. Of the man she had loved, who was now stone-dead—but re-created down to the last detail by the droid that had served him.

"Artoo-Detoo, was it?"

The droid beeped happily.

"See what you can do to fix his faulty holographic circuits," she ordered. "His primary programming is gone, too, but I can live with that if you can fix the other. It's been getting worse, ever since we found him on Corellia."

"Thank you," said the perfect image of Starkiller as the R2 unit moved in. He was wearing the same Jedi uniform the real one had worn during the attack on the Death Star. "I am aware that I cause you distress. It would please me to serve you again, as my master wished."

"Stop," she said, raising a hand and turning away. "Just stop."

"Yes, Captain Eclipse."

She held her breath until the little droid went to work, and the crackling of an electric arc banished all possibility of conversation.

CHAPTER 3

Present day . . .

CATO NEIMOIDIA'S ORBITAL LANES buzzed with nervous activity. A strong Imperial presence vied with a steady flow of freighters to and fro, many of them escorted by TIE fighter or mercenary squadrons. Even from orbit, Starkiller could see evidence of recent military activity, particularly a deep black scorch mark near one of the planet's famous hanging cities. Some kind of heavy munitions had been in play, although probably not nuclear. There was no sign of evacuation of the nearby populace.

Starkiller had never had cause to come to this world before, not during his brief period of recruitment for the nascent rebellion, nor during his first apprenticeship to Darth Vader, when his role had been as much assassin as apprentice. Indeed, surviving and defeating those who challenged his former Master had been as important a part of his former self's training as anything on the *Executor*. Those challengers had been his first real targets, apart from PROXY droids. Only when he had proven himself capable had the Dark Lord deemed him worthy of combat with him.

Starkiller orbited Cato Neimoidia once, safe in Darth Vader's TIE fighter, and simply stared. He had been down a pit on Kamino for thirteen days, and in Vader's clutches for what felt like a lifetime. He had forgotten what sunlight looked like. He had forgotten what it felt like to be a free agent. There was so much he had forgotten, and so much that was slowly coming back to him.

Juno.

She felt strangely close, even though he had no reason to suspect that she was nearby. In his mind, she was coming clearer with every hour. He couldn't believe that she had almost slipped away. Oh, he understood it well enough. He knew all about Darth Vader's mind games and the power of the dark side. He had lived with it, and prospered from that, too, in his original lifetime. He could exert his will over others in order to get what he wanted, but he didn't doubt that . . . didn't doubt that Vader had almost succeeded in driving every last memory of the woman Starkiller had loved from his mind.

Now she was back, and it seemed incomprehensible to him that she had ever gone away. Even when he had lost everything in his former life, when every last hope of victory had been taken from him, he had thought of her. His demise had meant nothing compared with the knowledge that she had escaped safely from the Emperor's deadly space station.

Then . . . death. And revival. And forgetting, powerlessness, and fear.

But now he was back. Nothing could stand between him and Juno. Not for long, anyway. With her ahead of him, leading him on, he felt stronger than ever.

From the depths of his memory, he heard the murdered Jedi Master Shaak Ti: *"You could be so much more."*

Then his own voice, speaking not to her, but to Juno, in another place, another time: *"The Force is stronger than anything we can imagine. We're the ones who limit it, not the other way around."*

Starkiller breathed deeply and closed his eyes. His mind was just one speck in the endlessly shifting sea that was the galaxy. He felt the eddies and currents of the combined life force of every living thing sway through him—and with only a small effort he detached himself from himself and joined that flow, seeking the one he needed.

The roar of a crowd filled his mind. Movement scattered his mental vision, made it hard to make out anything specific. Was that fluttering wings, or banners? He couldn't quite tell. Figures that might have been beings glowed blue all around him. Above him hung a giant eye, staring downward.

Are you still with me, Kota?

His vision shifted, became red-tinged—*deeply* red, as though someone had cut the throat of a giant beast and drained it onto the ground. Something snarled. Something roared. There was a flurry of limbs, a wild rush of violent intent.

"It's all in your mind, boy," said Kota from his memory. Green light flashed. More blood. Severed limbs fell

onto the dirt. The crowd roared.

General Rahm Kota, leaning back on his heels, breathing heavily, surrounded by a ring of corpses. How long had he been fighting now? Six days? Seven? Fatigue was taking its toll. With every wave he came closer to making a mistake—and when that happened, it would all finally be over.

Starkiller opened his eyes. His lips were pressed into a thin line.

"Hold on, old man," he whispered, and brought Darth Vader's TIE fighter smoothly out of orbit.

The Imperial forces on Cato Neimoidia were clustered around one particular bridge city suspended over a deep sinkhole that led an unfathomable distance into the planet's crust. Why? Perhaps the local dictator liked to throw his prisoners off the edge so they would serve as examples to their friends. Starkiller didn't care. He wasn't going over the edge. He was coming for just one thing: to rescue General Kota, or at the very least learn from him where Juno could be found. Nothing else mattered. Not even the endless vistas of space, or the light of an unfamiliar sun.

His ship had been noticed the very moment he had arrived. On descent, it was immediately joined by a full escort of TIE fighters, acting on the assumption that the being piloting it was Darth Vader, the Emperor's chief enforcer, as its transponder code suggested. Starkiller didn't disabuse them of this notion. Anything that eased the path ahead was fine by him. The TIEs broadcast warnings and cleared a landing bay ahead of him, and then peeled off to resume their regular duties. He brought his stolen starfighter safely to a halt on the swaying platform, conscious but not caring that there was nothing between him and the sinkhole below but several layers of metal. It might intimidate others, but it made no difference to him.

Several skiffs parked on the platform had scattered as he approached the waiting hangar. A squadron of stormtroopers stood to attention in two perfectly parallel lines, their weapons honorific, not threatening. If Vader had guessed that he was coming here, word had not yet reached the local potentate. That was good.

He landed, shut down the engines with smooth efficiency, and climbed out of the pilot's seat. The hatch opened with a hiss. His booted feet hit the hot metal of the landing deck with a ringing boom.

A new person had arrived, a balding man dressed in heavy robes with Imperial insignia mixed with Neimoidian trappings, standing at the head of the double line of troopers. He looked nervous, but that soon turned to puzzlement as Starkiller strode into view.

Starkiller realized only then how he must have looked. The flight suit he wore was torn and filthy, thanks to weeks in Vader's pit and ceaseless combat training. In the former Starkiller's life, he had had the art of stealth and invisibility drummed into him, but he was in too much of a hurry now to worry about that.

"I was expecting Lord Vader," said the robed man—the potentate himself, judging by the air of authority he thought he radiated.

Starkiller recognized his voice; he had heard it in a vision on Kamino, saying, *"Try the Corellian razor hounds."*

This was time for neither small talk nor mystical catch-ups.

"The Jedi," Starkiller said. "Where is he?"

"He's alive, for the moment."

"I asked *where* he is."

The robed man straightened, sensing a challenge. "What are the security codes for this sector?"

Starkiller ignored the question and kept walking between the double lines of stormtroopers.

"The security codes!"

With a rattle of plastoid, the stormtroopers shifted their weapons to point at him. The robed man drew a blaster and aimed with a steady hand.

The Imperials stood between Starkiller and Kota. With a tightening of his lips that might have been a smile, Starkiller ignited his lightsabers.

"Kill him!" ordered the potentate, snapping off two precise shots. Starkiller deflected both of them harmlessly into the floor. The troopers opened fire on both sides, and he turned to deflect the incoming blaster bolts. In the corner of his eye, he saw the potentate heading for the turbolift.

Not so fast, he thought, reaching out to pull the man back.

The lift doors opened, and a pair of heavily armed troopers emerged, already firing. Pressed on three sides, Starkiller forced himself to forget about the potentate and concentrate on the immediate threats. Blaster bolts ricocheted wildly around him, deflected by his double blades and hitting neck joints, visors, and breathing systems. Missiles from the newly arrived pair peppered him, filling the air with smoke. His Force shield kept the worst of their effects at bay, and he pressed forward, reaching out to telekinetically crush the missile launchers and trigger the remaining charges. With a bright flash and a deafening boom, the last of his obstacles disappeared.

A powerful excitement thrilled through him. For the first time, in the middle of combat, it came to him that he was truly alive. He wasn't a shadow lurking in a hole somewhere, dreaming of being. The Force was with him, and he was free. He was free, and he had a mission.

The potentate was long gone. Starkiller tore his way into the turbolift shaft, bypassing security codes by means of sheer power, and rode to the upper levels. The transparisteel walls revealed the hanging city in all its glory, curving away from him to his left and right, but he wasn't interested in taking in the sights. He studied the buildings looking only for tactical information. The vision of Kota had hinted at an open space and a large gathering of people. The scans he had taken from orbit hadn't showed anyplace like that. The largest structure in the city was the Imperial barracks, a circular building at its direct center.

When the turbolift reached the summit and the doors opened on the city, he was greeted by the distant roaring of a crowd.

He stepped out and listened closely. The roar was coming from the barracks.

He set off on foot, running swiftly through the streets. They were only sparsely populated, with the occasional green-skinned Neimoidian scuttling by, determinedly staying out of his way. He could hear no audible alarms, but had no doubt that they were ringing somewhere. That suspicion was confirmed at the sound of booted feet stamping along the streets behind him.

He shifted to an aerial route, climbing to the top of the nearest building and leaping from it to the next in line. That way he could avoid the roads entirely. He felt weightless as he swung from handhold to handhold with the Force thrilling through him like the purest oxygen. The city's lower levels clustered around the bases of several broad, circular towers, connected by looping tramlines, and it was a simple matter to travel from one to the other into the city's heart, as light as air itself.

When the Imperial security forces got wise to his plan and activated gun emplacements in the city's upper levels, things became considerably more interesting.

Dodging weapons fire from tram-track to building and back again, Starkiller felt a familiar calm creeping over him. It was a calm born not of peace or tranquillity, but of violence and anger. Countless hours of meditating on the dark side, fueling the negative energies that Darth Vader encouraged him to embrace, made this kind of combat trance almost second nature to him. Fighting people was harder than fighting PROXY droids, but there was a greater pleasure in it too, more of a challenge. A warrior who fought only rationally and without emotion fought exactly like a droid. People were stranger, more unpredictable, and therefore fundamentally more difficult to defeat. He swung his lightsabers as though in slow motion. He watched reflected energy bolts creep between him and his targets with a laziness that belied their deadly power.

Once, in his other life, he had been sent to Ragna III to quell an uprising of the hostile Yuzzem. Barely twelve years old, he had been betrayed by the weapons his own Master had given him. All had failed on landing, along with his starship, leaving him armed only with the Force and his wits. Singlehandedly, he had fought to the nearest Imperial installation and escaped off-world, expecting either rebuke for failing his mission or praise for having survived. He had received neither—and the memory of his puzzlement came to him now, as clear as the crystal in the heart of his first lightsaber. The lesson hadn't been to survive, he had eventually come to understand: it had been to come to terms with his own destructive power. In his wake, he had left dozens of Yuzzem injured or dead. Until it had been forced upon him, he had never known just what he was capable of—and just how little praise he needed to keep on doing it.

Later in that other life, Starkiller had raged against all the deaths he had caused in the service of his dark Master. Starkiller had been Darth Vader's weapon, aimed squarely at the Emperor's enemies, and nothing, he had sworn, would stand in his way. Only at the last minute had he swerved aside, deflected by Juno's love from his former purpose, to another he had been unable to complete. He was no one's weapon now but his own, but he still felt an echo of that remorse, that nagging feeling that killing wasn't the answer, despite the calm acceptance he felt while waging war on Kota's captives. Trained for violence, remade in violence, he struggled with the concept that anything other than violence might constitute a solution to any problem, but he was willing even in the heat of his familiar battle trance to entertain the possibility.

The crowd noise grew steadily louder as he approached the barracks—chanting, roaring, filled with mob fury. The weapons fire concentrated on him intensified, too. Jump troopers equipped with jetpacks were beginning to converge on his location. He angled toward a slender tower connected to the barracks by several high-rise accessways. When he was within leaping distance, he jumped for one of its transparisteel viewing platforms, lightsabers stabbing ahead of him. The window shattered.

He rolled across the platform and came up running for the stairs. Bystanders leapt out of his path, waving their upper limbs and screaming for help. They were extravagantly dressed, and few of them were Neimoidians. Humans vastly outnumbered aliens. They didn't look like Imperial officers, though.

Starkiller ground his teeth together as he entered what looked like nothing so much as a casino. That was why there were so many extra ships around the Imperial compound: the potentate was running a decidedly non-official credit-making venture on the side. He was no different from the many Starkiller had rooted out for Darth Vader while still in the service of the Empire. Venal, self-serving, and cruel, they squeezed their minions with an iron grip while at the same time currying favor from those like them higher up the chain.

The Empire's well-being was no longer his concern, but the galaxy as a whole would be better off if he took another corrupt Imperial down along the way.

He could feel the crowd's roar through the soles of his feet. He was close now, very close. The casino's defenses were tight but no match for him. What he couldn't fight through, he simply destroyed. At the final juncture, he guided a sky-tram off its tracks and into the side of the building, tearing a hole large enough for an army to burst through. He jumped into the maelstrom of sparks and molten metal and ran to where he could sense Kota, still fighting for his life in the potentate's theater of death.

One long, straight corridor led to a double door made of durasteel. It was guarded by six stormtroopers. Starkiller didn't bother stopping to fight them. With a gesture, he pushed them aside, then burst open the doors.

The full-throated roar of the crowd hit him hard, like a physical blow. He slowed to a walk as he passed through the door and found himself in a giant stone arena—a combat zone painted red with blood, exactly as he had seen in his vision. The steep sides were full of spectators, but only a handful were present in the flesh. The rest attended via hologram. Their blue, flickering fists, claws, or tentacles were upraised, chanting in numerous languages at once.

Starkiller didn't understand what they were saying, but he could work out the gist of it.

"Kill, kill, kill!"

In the center of the arena, surrounded by a legion of dead and wounded assailants, was Rahm Kota. One fist was wrapped tightly around the throat of a dying stormtrooper. His green lightsaber blazed as he raised it to deliver the killing blow. Starkiller felt the stirring of another memory: he had been in such positions before, tossed into arenas and forced to kill everyone who came against him. That was for training, though. He didn't think there was anything remotely educational about this spectacle.

"Kota!" he cried.

The aging general raised his head, searching for the source of the voice over the baying of the crowd. "It can't be . . ."

Starkiller ran out into the center of the arena. The crowd howled and hissed.

From far above came a booming command. "Send out the Gorog!"

Starkiller came to a halt in front of his second Master.

"By the Force," Kota whispered, staring at him with eyes that no longer worked—thanks to an injury Starkiller himself had delivered—but seemed to see regardless. His exhaustion radiated from his filthy skin like the heat of a sun. He was battered and weary and on the verge of collapse. He staggered back, looking almost drunk with fatigue. "I saw you die . . ."

"You saw me in your future, too."

"I did, but—"

A series of thudding clangs came from a vast gate on

the other side of the arena, and the huge metal doors began to open. From the darkness on the other side came a vicious snarl.

Starkiller turned to face the latest threat.

"Why don't you sit this one out, General?"

Kota gripped Starkiller's shoulder and bared his teeth. "Never. I've got a score to settle."

Something moved on the other side of the gates. Something heavy and bestial and very, very big.

Starkiller grinned back, although he didn't know what was funny. He wanted to ask about Juno, but just then wasn't the time. "You were never very good at taking orders."

Out of the darkness thundered a bull rancor, roaring and spraying drool. Starkiller came forward three paces, putting himself squarely between the beast and Kota, feeling nothing but confidence. On Felucia, his former self had defeated just such a beast. This one, he was sure, would prove to be as significant a foe. He raised his lightsaber to strike.

There was something wrong with the way it was running, though. Its eyes were wide and staring, but they weren't quite focusing on either Starkiller or Kota, and the light he saw in them wasn't fury. It was something else, something Starkiller didn't immediately comprehend.

"I don't care whether the restraints have been tested or not," boomed the voice a second time. "Open the Gorog gate now!"

Starkiller recognized the voice as belonging to the potentate who had "welcomed" him on the landing deck, and heard another loud clang. The bull rancor glanced over its shoulder, and Starkiller realized then that it wasn't running toward him, but away from something else.

The look in its eyes was *fear*.

Through the open gate behind the rancor came a giant hand, attached to an arm as thick as a small cruiser. Each clawed finger was as long as a starfighter. With surprising speed, it reached out and snatched the bull rancor off the floor of the arena, right in front of them, and pulled it screaming back into the darkness. Something crunched, and the screams were cut off. Bones cracked and splintered with a sickening sound. Sinewy tissue stretched and tore.

The crowd was utterly silent, now. Not a soul moved.

Starkiller backed up a step, staring up into the shadows in shock. What exactly had he just seen? Was it a hallucination?

An earsplitting roar came from the darkness, and he braced himself to find out.

CHAPTER 4

Two days earlier . . .

DAC'S MOON, Juno very quickly discovered, was as unexciting as its name suggested. It was a gray, airless rock tidally locked to the waterworld it orbited, so its back side pointed endlessly outward at the stars. Juno had spent several hours watching those stars—and the faint specks that indicated ships traveling to and from the Mon Calamari system—waiting for the Organa operative she was slowly beginning to believe wasn't coming at all.

"I have completed my scan of Dac's traffic control," PROXY told her. "There is no mention of a ship or ships intercepted on suspicion of anything related to the Rebel Alliance."

She irritably tapped the controls of the two-seater R-22 Spearhead interceptor she'd found waiting for her in the *Solidarity*'s hangar bay. How long did she have to wait before she gave the mission up as a waste of time? She had better places to stew over her lot than the back side of this sterile dustbowl.

At least, she told herself, PROXY was working properly now. The damage to his holographic camouflage systems that had frozen him in the image of his former Master had been successfully repaired by R2-D2. Only occasionally now did he adopt one of his many stored templates—including Juno's—but most of the time he was just his skinny metal self, with glowing yellow eyes and an unflinching desire to serve her. The latter was the one remaining fragment of his primary programming, given to him by his deceased Master. The rest had been burned out of him by the Core on Raxus Prime.

"Ten more minutes," she said, "and that's it, Princess or no Princess."

"Will we attempt this mission on our own, Captain Eclipse?"

She had been giving that a lot of thought. "Dac won't save itself."

But she wasn't Starkiller, and she didn't want to become him. All her life, she had been part of a system. It suited her, the hierarchy of command and her place in it. Yes, she argued sometimes, and she especially didn't like being reprimanded, but on the whole she preferred it to going alone. Nothing had made her happier than when the Rebel Alliance firmed up its command structure, with Bel Iblis providing strategic and tactical advice, Bail Organa or his daughter supplying access to crucial resources and intelligence, and Mon Mothma presenting the public face of the Alliance to those beings who required inspiration. The Alliance fleet didn't have a Supreme Commander per se—it didn't actually have much of a fleet to speak of yet, just a ragtag accumulation of ships—but the fact that a vacancy existed had reassured her. Someone would eventually step up to fill it, she had been certain.

And for a while, the system had worked. Orders filtered down from one commander or another, and the Alliance had held intact. Now, though, with Bail Organa absent and something of a schism developing between Mon Mothma and those of a more military bent, including Bel Iblis, nothing was certain anymore. Who exactly *did* tell Juno where her duties lay? Did the leaders have to take a vote now before making any kind of decision? If Leia Organa felt compelled not to take sides while her father was absent, what happened next time there was an emergency and the Alliance needed to act quickly?

These thoughts circled endlessly through Juno's mind as she waited.

It was an improvement, she supposed, over wishing Starkiller would come back to shake everyone back into line.

"I have detected an approaching vessel," said PROXY.

Juno was instantly alert. "Where?"

Information on the screens in front of them enabled her to locate the tiny dot in the endless starscape. It grew brighter by the second until the blocky outlines of a cargo shuttle became identifiable. Markings on its hull identified it as belonging to a small mining company on the inward face of the moon. It had no visible weapons, no shield, and offered no explanation for its presence. As it neared the surface of the moon, the cargo hatch on its port side opened wide, revealing nothing at all within.

Juno's hands rested on the R-22's controls, ready to
fire or flee as circumstances demanded.

Dust puffed as the cargo shuttle touched gently down.
From the brightly lit interior unfolded a reticulated
loading arm. It pointed once at her starfighter, then once
into the shuttle's hold. Juno examined the prospect with
a critical eye.

"We could shoot our way out of there if we had to,
right?" she asked PROXY.

"I foresee few difficulties on that score," said the droid.
"There appears to be no armor on the inside of the shuttle,
and its crew space is small."

"Lucky we didn't come in a Y-wing," she muttered as
she activated the starfighter's attitude controls, "or we'd
never have fit."

The arm folded back into its niche as the R-22
hovered gently across the rocky gray terrain. Juno took
it as a personal challenge not to ding either vessel as she
slid inside. Such maneuvers were unfamiliar to her after
years of fighting combat and recon missions—and, more
recently, simply telling the staff of her frigate where to
go. She was pleased to feel old reflexes stirring, guiding
her hand as much by instinct as by anything her head
could identify.

With a gentle thud, the metal surfaces of the two ships
met. The cargo shuttle's hatch slid closed. Juno took her
hands off the controls and waited.

When the space inside the shuttle had repressurized, a
small hatch opened and a tall human male stepped out
of the crew chambers. He wore a gray-green pressure

suit, minus its helmet, and could have been any one of a million unskilled cargo shufflers from anywhere across the galaxy.

Only he wasn't. Juno recognized him the moment the R-22's landing lights caught his features.

It was Bail Organa.

The starfighter's hatch swung open above her, and he helped her out of the pilot's seat.

"You're a little overqualified for this, aren't you?" she said.

His Serene Highness, Prince Bail Prestor Organa, First Chairman and Viceroy of Alderaan, patted down his oil-smudged outfit. "What, haulage, or convincing the Dac resistance to join the Alliance?"

"Maybe both."

"Well, I offered you a job once, and you said you'd think about it."

"You called me a pilot with a conscience," she said. "I'd never work for someone with such poor judgment of character."

They grinned and shook hands.

"Nice to see you, too, PROXY," he added as the droid unfolded from his own seat. "Come on through."

"So this is how you stay out of the Emperor's scopes," Juno said as he led them into the cramped, ozone-stinking cockpit. He was the shuttle's only occupant.

"Part of the time." He tapped the outdated instrument panel with some affection. "In this I can go practically anywhere, anytime, and no one gives me a second look. Same with this." He indicated the mirror-finished helmet hanging on a rack behind the pilot's chair. "Cheaper than a cloaking device, and no messing around with stygium crystals."

"Tell me about it."

"Oh, yes, you've had experience with them, on the *Rogue Shadow*." He sobered. "I heard about Kota. That's terrible news."

She took the copilot's seat. "It was bound to happen eventually. The man had crazy luck, but it couldn't last forever."

"He made his own luck. As we're about to."

He operated the controls with the ease of recent practice, lifting the cargo shuttle off the surface of the moon with the starfighter safely inside and sending it on a long arc around to the Dac-lit side. Juno noted with approval that he didn't fly *too* well: Anyone watching would see the occasional jerk and misdirection, as they would expect from a clumsy grunt.

"I presume Leia explained the situation," she said.

He nodded. "We're meeting Ackbar in an hour."

"What's the plan?"

"We don't have one yet."

"Where's the rendezvous point, then?"

"A mining colony called Sar Galva."

"Sar Galva is located on the Murul Trench," said PROXY. "We are not designed for aquatic environments."

"No, but the Quarren are, and we need them if we're ever going to get the Dac resistance movement into the Alliance."

Dac rose over the moon's forward horizon—a

crystalline blue world streaked with high-altitude clouds. The cargo shuttle glided slowly upward until it broke free of the moon's gentle gravitational pull and began powering for the planet. Its main drive was inefficient and noisy, making conversation difficult. Juno settled back into the seat, thinking over everything she'd learned about the world and its resistance movement before leaving the *Solidarity*.

Home to numerous sentient species, although predominantly the deep-ocean Quarren and the semi-aquatic Mon Calamari, Dac had a long history of conflict with the Empire. With the Declaration of a New Order and the beginning of the Imperial regime, their Senators had been arrested and a new, corrupt regime had been installed, helped by indigenous collaborators who had sabotaged Dac's planetary shield. The takeover of the shipyards and the subjugation of the native population hadn't broken the planet's spirit, however. A resistance movement had struggled on for many years, and then foundered when the Empire destroyed three of the planet's floating cities in reprisal. Since then, Quarren and Mon Calamari had squabbled more often than they had worked together, and the Empire's grip on their homeworld remained crushingly tight.

Ackbar had been one of the failed resistance movement's earliest and most promising leaders. So impressive had been his fight against the Imperial forces that the officer who had eventually captured him had presented him as a trophy to the Grand Moff in charge of the occupation, who had kept him as a slave for more than a decade. Rescued in one of the Rebel Alliance's earliest coordinated attacks against the Empire, Ackbar had returned to Dac to stir up revolt—and met surprising resistance. Discredited by historians, their shipyards nationalized, and their leaders enslaved, the population of Dac had very nearly lost their spirit. It would take a show of strength to whip them into the proper frame of mind to retake their world.

The shuttle rocked from side to side as it hit atmosphere. Organa pulled back on the throttle, allowing them to talk again.

"Dac has no aerial defenses to speak of," Organa said. "The planetary shields have never been repaired, and the remaining cities suffer constant bombardment. An entire fighter wing is stationed here, its mission to terrorize and to crush any signs of an air force forming. Ackbar has tried, but he can't get so much as a recon droid in the air without it being shot down and his equipment destroyed."

"So where do the Quarren fit into this? They live underwater, not in the air."

"The fighter wing only patrols the air, not the oceans, and particularly not the deep trenches. By following those trenches, the Quarren can go anywhere without being seen. They can construct supply lines, establish headquarters, even build submersible launch platforms that would be less vulnerable to attack than anything on the ground. With the Quarren on their side, the Mon Calamari would have a real chance."

"So what's the problem?"

"You'll see."

Ahead of them, the ocean was rising up rapidly to meet them. Organa did nothing to slow their descent. All he did was tip the shuttle in order to present the smallest possible cross section to the approaching wave tops. At the last instant he fired the forward thrusters on full, not to stop the shuttle but to turn the water ahead of them to steam, cushioning the impact.

Even so, Juno was thrown forward against her harness. A rushing, swirling sound enfolded them, and the deck rocked beneath their feet. The main drive cut out and repulsors kicked in. Instead of pushing up, they pressed the shuttle down against the resistance of the water.

Her ears popped as they dropped rapidly into the depths. Darkness fell outside. The shuttle's many joints and seams creaked under the rising pressure.

Juno felt queasy but refused to let it show.

"I'm guessing," she said, "that the plan is for the resistance to take out the fighter wing and thereby show the locals what they're capable of."

"Spot-on, Captain."

"What's the wing's designation? Would I have heard of them?"

"Quite possibly. It's the Hundred Eighty-first."

She shook her head. "Never come across them before. Just be glad it's not the Black Eight."

"Your old command?"

"I'm sure it's gone downhill since I left," she said, "but I doubt its methods have improved."

She thought of the forests of Callos melting into black sludge and tried not to imagine what Dac would look like after such an attack. Oceans were different from forests, but the principle was the same. Where life got in the way of the Emperor's plans, its very existence was forfeit.

The scopes showed the hard surface of the seabed approaching. Undulating hills punctuated by the occasional sharp spire stretched off into the murky distance, covered with fields of thick, waving weeds. Organa leveled off and headed north. They hadn't traveled far when an enormous chasm opened up before them. The Murul Trench, Juno presumed. Clinging to its side was an artificial structure that projected out over the depths. Several thick cables and pipes stretched vertically downward. What lay at the bottom, Juno couldn't tell. The scopes didn't even show a bottom.

"Welcome to Sar Galva," Organa said as he guided the shuttle to a halt near a docking tube. "This is nominally an Imperial station, but just in case . . ." He handed her a fake ID, which she affixed to her flight uniform. "If anyone asks, my name is Aman Raivans. You're Pyn Robahn."

When the docking tube was empty of water and full of breathable atmosphere, they headed back to the air lock and cycled through. Juno stepped warily into the station, testing the air and finding it more than a little fishy. Literally. Sar Galva stank like an aquarium that hadn't been cleaned for a decade.

Organa led the way. PROXY took up the rear. They passed a checkpoint without incident and headed deeper into the station through a maze of tubes and spherical-shaped compartments. Vast machines chugged and bubbled all around them. Juno didn't have the first idea what the station extracted from the depths; fearing that asking might expose her as an outsider, she stayed quiet.

They passed several bulging-eyed Mon Calamari, but by far the majority of workers here were Quarren, with their tentacled faces and clawed hands. Juno didn't suffer from speciesism as many of her old Imperial colleagues had, but she was still getting used to the variety of beings she encountered through the Alliance. Mon Calamari looked cheerfully guileless to her, while the Quarren were utterly unreadable. The language they used when talking to one another was unlike any other speech she had ever heard. She hoped the individuals she would be dealing with could at least understand Basic.

"Through here, I think," said Organa, waving her ahead of him into a cramped mess.

"You're not sure?"

"Let's just say that down here, everything's uncertain."

The room contained a long table and several individuals. Five orange-skinned Quarren huddled in a group at the far end. Closest to them was a slender Mon Calamari who looked up as they entered. Juno recognized him instantly from holos.

"Senator Organa," Ackbar said, reaching out with one long-fingered hand. "Thank you for coming. And you must be Captain Eclipse."

Juno returned the handshake. Ackbar's skin was damp and cool, and his grip surprisingly strong.

"Don't close the door," he said to PROXY, who had turned to do just that. "We're expecting someone else."

The five Quarren looked up, and he introduced them in turn as Siric, Nosaj, Rarl, Cuvran, and Feril. "Siric is an underwater explosives expert," Ackbar explained. "He lost his family during the destruction of the Three Cities. He and his assistants are keen to help in any way they can."

"We're grateful to you for meeting us here," said Organa, offering them a brisk bow. "I'm as keen to see your planet freed as you are."

The Quarren exchanged a handful of short words, none of them in Basic.

"Are they always this conversational?" asked Juno.

"Don't be discouraged," said Ackbar. "They're a brave and proud people, like my own, when roused."

A tenth person came into the room from behind them, and instantly the five Quarren were on their feet, bulbous eyes staring, tentacles waving and fingers pointing. They tongue-spat and snarled in their alien tongue, as much at Ackbar as to the new arrival, who was another Quarren, as impenetrable as the rest.

"This was a mistake," this one said in heavily accented Basic. "I knew I should not have come."

"Stay, Seggor, stay." Ackbar put a hand on the Quarren's arm and turned to the others. "He's here at my invitation," he told the others. "Don't you think I have as much to be angry about as you?"

An uneasy silence fell. Juno studied the dynamic closely as the newcomer eased farther into the room and Ackbar encouraged everyone to sit with him at the table. He introduced the people who didn't know one another in a matter-of-fact way, downplaying the dramatics with his brisk, no-nonsense tone. Juno felt some of the tension ebb, even though it was never remotely close to vanishing.

When it was Seggor Tels's turn to be introduced, he offered a brief explanation regarding his fellows' outrage.

"A young fool I once was," he said. "A fool who thought my enemy's enemy must be my friend. It was I who sabotaged our world's planetary shields, resulting in our home's occupation and my people's enslavement. In the many years since, I have learned to regret that action, and to understand that my kind is not alone in its persecution. We must put aside our differences and work together to reclaim our world. We must stand together."

He addressed them with a conviction that spoke more of necessity than real commitment, but Juno admired the attempt. In the face of years of animosity between his species and the Mon Calamari, plus the very personal antagonism displayed by Siric and the others, he was bravely standing his ground when it would have been much easier simply to go into hiding and never emerge.

"We're here to help you," she said. "If you'll let us."

Siric said something in the Quarren tongue, which Tels translated.

"He says you're only here to help yourselves. You care about starships, not the oceans or the people who live in them."

"The right of all beings to live freely and in peace," said Organa, "is what the Rebel Alliance cares about. Ships will help us, yes, but that's not our primary objective in coming here. We need leaders and soldiers; we need people who will spread the word; we need translators and medics and all manner of specialty. What we need most of all, though, is to know that the people we're fighting for are behind us. We're risking our lives—and the lives of our families—every time we so much as speak out against the Emperor. Forgive us if we ask for a little commitment in return."

Organa's expression was severe, and Juno could tell that he was thinking of more than himself. Now that the Emperor knew he was a traitor, Leia was in constant jeopardy. Only a constant pretense of innocence and compliance had saved her thus far—that and the fact that even the Emperor balked at murdering such a well-known and well-liked young woman.

Tels translated Senator Organa's words, and some of the aggression left the five. Siric looked down at his hands, which were splayed out in front of him. Juno noticed that two of his digits were missing from his right hand. *Explosives expert,* she remembered, and wondered what efforts he had already made to repel the Empire from his world.

"The Hundred Eighty-First fighter wing is based in Heurkea," Ackbar went on, producing a datapad and displaying images as he spoke. The first was a map of the southern territorial zone, with the floating city appropriately marked. "We can approach from the east, behind the cover of Mester Reef. The Hundred Eighty-First patrols every three standard hours, in groups of two, with a ten-minute overlap, but there's a period once every five days when all the pilots are recalled for debriefing.

That can last anything up to an hour. The next such briefing is in six hours."

Siric said something in his native tongue.

"I know we have no air force," Ackbar said. "Ask yourself what a frontal assault would achieve. Reinforcements would arrive within hours, and any advantage we gained would be quickly reversed. And more. The Empire does not take kindly to insurrection."

"As we know all too well," said Tels.

"You've got something else in mind," said Juno, relieved she wasn't going to be asked to mount a single-handed assault on the fighter wing, and thinking of Siric's missing fingers.

Ackbar outlined the essence of the plan in a few brief sentences, and Juno learned why his mind had been so highly prized by the Grand Moff who had made him a slave. The plan was within their means, yet certain to have a far-reaching effect on the Imperial forces in the region. If it succeeded, they were bound to galvanize the resistance into a single force. If it failed, no one would ever know.

"I like it," she said. "Count me in."

"And I," said Tels.

All eyes turned to Siric and his assistants, who conferred in a series of hurried whispers. Siric asked Tels a question, and he translated it for the benefit of Juno and Bail Organa.

"Siric wishes to know how he can be sure that he can trust you."

"He can't," said Ackbar. "He can only take as a form

of assurance the fact that I will be fighting alongside him."

"We all go down together, in other words," Juno said, "or we all give up and go home."

The Quarren conferred again, and this time they agreed. Five nods indicated their willingness to be part of the mission.

"Thank you," Ackbar said. "We will never forget your decision today."

"Neither will the Rebel Alliance," said Organa. He glanced at his chrono. "Six hours, you said, Ackbar? If we're going to make that window, we'd better get started."

"You're coming with us?" Juno asked him.

"Of course. I didn't come here just to make introductions and pretty speeches."

"But you're not trained for this kind of work. I wouldn't want to answer to your daughter if you were killed."

"Don't worry about that, Captain Eclipse," he said with an expression that was part smile, part grimace. "I think you'll find that I can handle myself."

Juno didn't press. Organa's experiences with the Emperor stretched farther back even than the formation of the Empire itself. No one lasted that long on luck alone, she supposed.

Ackbar stood and, with a powerful sense of gravitas, shook hands with Seggor Tels. Only then did the mission truly get under way.

CHAPTER 5

Present day . . .

STARKILLER STARED UP in awe at the massive beast that emerged from the shadows. All muscle and bone and teeth and claws, it walked with a hunched, thundering gait that made the stone beneath him shake. Its thick, powerful legs looked disproportionately small compared with the reach of its arms, but the strength they contained—capable of propping up a creature larger than most spacecraft and actually propelling it, too—was almost beyond comprehension. Were it to raise itself upright, its hands would brush the arena's distant ceiling.

Thick duranium shackles that pierced its dense flesh down its back prevented it from coming any farther than the center of the arena. It strained against the chains, roaring. One mighty fist lunged forward to take out its frustration on the tiny creatures standing before it, with their bright blades raised in futile defiance.

Starkiller went one way, Kota the other. The stone cracked beneath them. Dust and splinters of rock flew like shrapnel. Starkiller rolled on landing, then jumped again as the Gorog groped after him. It missed by barely a meter, amazingly fast for a creature so large. He slashed at it, but although his blades parted the red-black skin, he couldn't cut deep enough to do any real damage.

He was going to have to fight the Gorog some other way.

"You're a Jedi!" said Kota from his memory. *"Size means nothing to you!"*

The Gorog's heavy, domed head swung to its left, looking for the general. Starkiller drew its gaze back to him, pushing through the Force at its nearest foot. It barely moved, but the effort didn't go unnoticed. Keeping its center of gravity low and stable probably took much of the creature's resting energy, so the last thing it would want was to be nudged off balance in the middle of a fight. Whether it reasoned consciously or simply reacted by instinct, Starkiller didn't care. He definitely had its attention now.

Both fists came for him, converging with enough force to crack a moon in two. He stood his ground, adding his defiant shout to the creature's angry roaring. The fists came together, making Starkiller's world shake, but he went unharmed behind the strongest Force barrier he could muster. When the fists lifted, he found himself buried almost a meter deep in a gravel pit of shattered rock.

The Gorog stared down at him in slow-witted surprise. He took the opportunity to leap onto one of its arms and run along it all the way up to its mountainous right shoulder.

It swiveled from side to side, trying to track him, and

scratched blindly at its back. The heavy chains clanked and rattled. Starkiller leapt onto one of the anchors that bit deep into the creature's flesh and braced himself against the filth-stained metal. His arms could barely reach from one side to the other. Starkiller took a moment to concentrate, and then poured a powerful stream of lightning through the thick metal teeth, directly into the rippling muscle tissue.

The Gorog flailed and roared. It rose up and up until the surface Starkiller was clinging to became very nearly vertical. He ceased shocking it and climbed from anchor to anchor, heading for its head. Its hands groped blindly, swinging the chains from side to side. He dodged claws longer than his entire body and leapt, finally, onto the great bald skull. A metal plate sealed shut a massive rent in its skull, where some genetic defect or wound had left its brain exposed.

He didn't know if it could feel him yet, but he didn't doubt that it would soon. Raising both lightsabers blade-down, he stabbed deep into the metal plate and ran forward, melting a double line downward, toward its hideous face. At the same time, he shocked it with lightning, using the plate and his lightsabers to conduct the electricity directly to the creature's giant neurons.

The Gorog's fury doubled. The head whipped from side to side with a great grinding of vertebrae and sinew. Huge ropes of spittle splashed from its slavering mouth. The sound of its roars was deafening at such close range.

Starkiller leapt onto one of its thick, plated eyebrows and clung tight to a branch-like hair with one hand. The other pointed down into the creature's nearest eye, ready to send a shock along its optic nerve, right into its brain.

The eye rolled, fixed him in its black stare. The pupil tightened. It had seen him. Before Starkiller could move, one mighty hand came from behind him and, with the force of a mass-drive cannon, swept him from his precarious perch.

For a moment he was both weightless and stunned. The world turned around him, and he thought he heard Juno saying, *"Have you done this before?"* and himself responding, *"Trust me. I'm doing the right thing, for both of us."*

Then he hit the stadium, and only a Force-barrier reflex honed by thousands of hours of punishing training stopped him from breaking every bone in his body.

His senses only slowly returned. Holograms flickered and sparked around him as he climbed groggily to his feet.

He was halfway up the side of the arena, surrounded by spectators from afar, chanting for one side or the other. Starkiller wondered if it mattered to them exactly who was fighting, and why. The promise of violence was all they cared about.

Well, he could give them that.

The Gorog hadn't given up on him, either. It had broken half of its chains during its frenzied writhing, and it pulled free of the rest to follow him into the seating. The few spectators who hadn't already fled Starkiller's vicinity now did so, fearing what might come next. The stadium's walls shuddered as the huge creature applied its full weight to them.

Starkiller took a moment to look for Kota. The old man was neither lying squashed on the arena floor nor foolishly rushing in to help, and both relieved him. He needed Kota alive, if he was going to find Juno soon, and he didn't want to be distracted by keeping the old man that way. But he didn't want to lose him, either.

A quick search through the Force revealed him to be climbing upward through the stands, slashing at anyone who stood in his way. Settling that score he had mentioned, Starkiller assumed. Then there wasn't time to ponder the matter any further.

The Gorog approached, dark blood running down from the gash on its scalp and dripping into its gaping mouth. The taste seemed to enrage it.

One arm swept across the stands, destroying hologram generators and snapping pillars by the dozen. Starkiller ran in the opposite direction. Someone was shouting orders from the skybox above, but he didn't pay any notice.

The creature followed him around the stadium, making it shake and reel.

A huge slab of stone, dislodged by one of its wild grabs, came down just in front of him. Starkiller leapt higher, to the very top of the stands. There he found a ramp along which the very last of the spectators were fleeing. He followed it to the roof of the stadium, and waited to see if the Gorog was following.

It was, using its arms to drag itself higher and kicking out with its legs to gain extra thrust. Through deep rents in the stone floor of the stadium, Starkiller could see the open air below.

He ran from the ramp onto the roof. The Gorog followed without hesitation, shouldering through an opening barely wide enough for its arm, let alone the rest of its body. It blinked in the daylight. All the lights and buzz of the suspended city meant nothing to it when its quarry stood just out of reach, tantalizingly still.

It lunged, and missed. Lunged, and missed. It didn't care what damaged it caused. Metal supports bent. Guy wires snapped and whipped away. A handful of jetpack-equipped stormtroopers buzzed about its head, trying to bring it back under control, but it had eyes only for Starkiller.

He led it halfway around the arena before he felt the first lurching from below. A number of supports and stanchions were broken, ruining the integrity of the entire arena. The Gorog just kept on coming. Only when they had returned almost to their point of origin did it seem to notice the way the surface beneath it was sinking, beginning to drop.

The broad disk of the arena roof shuddered. Starkiller jumped to the only structure still attached to the city above: the skybox from which the potentate, he assumed, had enjoyed the best possible view. He landed on the roof just as the last support for the arena gave way and began the long tumble to the sinkhole below.

The Gorog howled as it, too, began to fall.

Starkiller cut a hole in the roof of the skybox and jumped nimbly inside.

There he found the potentate standing his ground in front of an ornate gold throne. A half circle of slain

Neimoidian aides lay at his feet. He held his blaster on Kota, who was approaching with lightsaber at the ready, unhindered at all by either fatigue or blindness.

Starkiller's arrival distracted the potentate, who snapped a quick shot at him, easily deflected.

Before Kota could strike—settling the score for a week of endless slaughter—the whole skybox lurched, sending all three of them flying. Metal squealed. Transparisteel shattered. The roar of the Gorog filled the air. Starkiller clutched a console as the skybox lurched again, tipping the floor steadily closer to vertical.

"You fool," cried the potentate, spread-eagle on the floor. "You've killed us all!"

Starkiller peered warily out the nearest window. It was immediately clear what had happened. The Gorog had arrested its fall by catching hold of the skybox with one hand, and now it was trying to climb to safety. In doing so, however, it was steadily destroying the skybox itself.

The gold throne broke free from its restraints and slid toward the shattered viewport. It scooped up the potentate as it went, dragging him down with its considerable mass. He clutched at the floor but could do nothing to arrest his fall. He screamed as he went out the window and fell straight into the Gorog's gaping mouth.

The tiny meal galvanized what was left of the Gorog's facility to reason. It looked up into the skybox, seeing it for the first time as a container, not simply something to hang on to. It saw the shining of the energy weapons that had stung it. With its free hand, it lunged for them, but succeeded only in bringing down still more of the structure. There was no way now to avoid falling. It knew that in the depths of its deranged mind. With the last of its strength it lunged again, and caught its enemy at last.

"Kota!" Starkiller shouted as the Gorog ripped the Jedi general from the skybox and dragged him down with it.

"*Turn away, boy,*" he heard Kota saying in his mind. "*Get on with your mission. There are some things you aren't ready to face.*"

He blinked. The words were another memory, not an instruction from the falling general. He wasn't going to take orders from the past—especially when he hadn't followed them the first time around.

There's nothing *I can't face,* Starkiller thought.

He let go of the console and took a running jump through the shattered window.

It was surprising just how far the Gorog had already fallen toward the gaping mouth of the sinkhole, but he refused to be discouraged. He dived in a straight line, using the Force to propel him through the whipping wind. He remembered with perfect clarity his former self's plummet to the surface of the incomplete Death Star, and hard on the heels of that memory came the sensation of Juno's lips against his. Longing for her filled him, driving him downward even faster.

The stench of the Gorog's fear and rage came heavily on the air as he approached it. The beast was tumbling. The fist containing Kota flashed once in front of him, then a second time. The general was slashing at the fingers holding him pinned, to little effect. Starkiller had to get him free before Kota's strength gave out and he was crushed to a pulp.

Selecting his point of landing with as much care as he was able, Starkiller came down on the creature's back, close enough to one of the duranium anchors to take hold of it. He braced himself with both feet against the spine, ignoring the way the world was spinning around him. The Gorog didn't know he was there. It wouldn't be expecting an attack from this side.

He took a deep breath, reaching deeper into the Force than he had before. He had never journeyed to the center of a planet, where the molten metal raged and burned under pressure hard enough to make diamond out of dust, but he imagined something much like that. This time, he wanted to do more than just enrage the Gorog. He could feel the web of veins thudding a panicky beat beneath the skin. He concentrated on that beat, on the rapid pulsing of life that would be extinguished when it reached the bottom of the sinkhole. Why wait that long, when Kota's life was at stake as well?

For a moment, he faltered. He had never killed anything this big before.

But it was just one life, and it stood between him and his goal. He had no choice.

Instead of a wild crackle of lightning, he discharged a single pure bolt into the metal anchor, stabbing deep through the creature's chest into its heart.

Its back arched. A strange, fluting cry emerged from its mouth. Starkiller rode out the spasm, maintaining the electric shock for as long as he was able. Muscular waves rolled back and forth, twisting him from side to side. It felt like a groundquake—a *fleshquake* on a planet-sized monster.

The pulsing coming through the soles of his boots ran wild, faltered, ceased.

He sagged as the mountain of flesh finally grew still. The fight was over, but darkness enfolded them as they entered the mouth of the sinkhole and went into free fall.

Starkiller used rough pits in the creature's skin to pull himself up to the shoulder, then down the limp arm that had held Kota captive. The general was clinging to the slackened thumb, head cocked as though he could see the sinkhole walls sliding by. He shouted a greeting over the sound of the rushing wind.

"I hope you've got a way out of this, boy."

Starkiller put an arm around Kota's shoulders. Together they leapt off the Gorog's hand. Starkiller could slow their fall somewhat, but he couldn't fly. The beast fell ahead of them. Maybe, he hoped against hope, it would go some way toward arresting their impact.

"If you're wearing a comlink," Kota said, "hand it over."

Starkiller did so, even though that was as faint a hope as his own. "The whole city's jammed."

Kota punched keys on the comlink. "Let's hope she can reach us in time."

Starkiller's heart quickened. *She?*

He glanced down into the shadow, wondering how deep the sinkhole could possibly be. Above, he saw only the shrinking circle of cityscape. He stared until it was occluded by something solid. He thought he recognized the silhouette. The roar of a starship's engines echoed down the sinkhole, as the familiar angles and planes of the *Rogue Shadow* dived down toward them, and then overtook them so it could intercept them from below.

Though Starkiller pushed down against the starship's hull with the Force to cushion their fall, they still hit the surface hard. Starkiller blinked away stars and groaned under the return of gravity. Kota was faring no better, clutching his shoulder and struggling to sit up. A hatch popped open nearby, and the old man waved the younger man ahead of him.

Starkiller was already moving. His entire being thrilled at the certainty that Juno was here at last. He could practically see her already, waiting at the controls for him to arrive, ready with some quip about being late to his own funeral.

He dropped down through the hatch and ran breathlessly to the cockpit.

"Juno!"

He stopped dead. The cockpit was empty. All he heard in reply was a ghost of her voice, speaking from the depths of his memory.

"Please don't make me leave another life behind."

CHAPTER 6

One day earlier . . .

JUNO TOOK ONE LAST look at the fluted domes of Heurkea a floating city, before diving under the waves. Its shell-like buildings gleamed red and gold by the light of Mon Calamari system's primary, looking more like something grown than built—much like the coral of Mester Reef beneath her. None of the reef protruded above the water, and she was submerged up to her waist, buffeted by the alien sea as she stared at the city. She wanted something beautiful to hold in her mind before entrusting her life to air that stank of rotten rubber.

Ackbar ducked under without hesitation, followed a second later by Bail Organa, who had donned an old clone subtrooper breathing apparatus like hers. In a wet suit and mismatching white helmet he looked about as ridiculous as Juno felt. For the first time she didn't worry that her weapons would be sealed in their packs until they emerged at the other end. If anyone saw them climbing out of the water at the far end, they would certainly not regard them as any kind of threat.

The Quarren were already underwater. Holding her breath instinctively, Juno took a single step forward, off the rough coral surface, and let herself sink into the water.

It was blue and clearer than she had expected. The cargo freighter was moored safely out of sight at the base of the reef, guided there by remote control once the ten conspirators had disembarked. She could see its featureless nose almost as though through air. She couldn't, however, see their destination. Trusting to the Quarren's sense of direction, she followed strongly kicking feet around the bulk of the reef and into the open ocean. PROXY took the shape of Seggor Tels, using repulsors to swim rather than sink straight to the bottom. Juno kept careful track of which Tels was which, just in case.

Strong currents favored them half the way, then shifted direction as the seabed grew nearer, making progress much more difficult. Heurkea was a true floating city, with no structural connections to the bedrock, but several chunky cables did run from its undulating base down into the sludge. Ferrying waste one way and geothermal power another, she guessed, but just then wasn't the time to wonder about the city's inner workings. As its underside came into view, she kept her eyes open for the vent Tels had described. PROXY had sliced into plans of the city and confirmed that it was still there. The vent had been sealed up early in the Imperial occupation of the city, but laser-cutting equipment designed for underwater use would make short work of that obstacle.

There: a dark patch against the city's white underbelly. She waved to catch the others' attention, and pointed.

She could have used the subtrooper gear's comlink, but they were maintaining strict radio silence.

White light flared as one of Siric's apprentices activated the cutting equipment. Bubbles of steam spread upward and flattened out against the city's hull, forming rippling streams and threads. Juno waited for lights to flash and alarms to sound, but nothing happened. The Imperials had clearly grown complacent about security, at least in this damp corner of the galaxy.

With one last flash, the white light died. The grille fell out in a single circular piece and dropped to the ocean floor far below. Tels went through first, staying carefully clear of the still-hot metal. His feet disappeared. A minute later his hand reappeared, giving a definite thumbs-up. One by one, the rest of the team followed him into the pipe.

Juno swam ten meters to a ladder that led up to a level deck. There the water was below knee height and the atmosphere was breathable. She gratefully dispensed with the breathing apparatus and took in a chest full of sweet, if slightly scum-tainted, natural air. The deck was illuminated by faint down-lights that flickered weakly with age. It didn't look as if anyone had visited that level in at least a decade. Still, she moved as quietly as she could to a higher section, where the way was completely dry.

There she slipped off the wet suit and straightened the flight uniform she'd been wearing beneath. PROXY flickered back to his usual form and followed her, yellow eyes flickering in the dim light.

"Are you feeling all right?" she asked the droid. Apart from an occasional flutter, his chameleon circuit remained stable, but he had hardly spoken since his awakening. "Is there something I should worry about?"

"Oh, no, Juno. I am simply processing my lack of a viable primary program."

"Does it seriously impair your function?" she asked, wondering if she had made a mistake involving PROXY in the mission.

"No," PROXY said, "but it does concern me. I have been deactivated twice since Raxus Prime, and each time it seems a miracle that I have returned. Who am I, if not my primary program? What am I, if I have no reason to function?"

That seemed a very human concern, and one that had no easy answer. "I guess you're just you," she said. "And you seem okay to me."

"Thank you, Captain Eclipse. That is of some small reassurance."

"Every being is the sum of its experiences and actions," put in Bail Organa, coming up alongside them and dropping his discarded wet suit next to Juno's. "Sometimes we don't know what our primary program is, or was, until we've lived long enough to look back at our lives."

"I'm afraid I do not understand how to function under such circumstances," the droid said. "Droids are not designed to program themselves."

"I'm sorry, PROXY," Juno said, with real feeling. "I didn't realize you felt so strongly about this. Do you wish I hadn't woken you up this time?"

"Not at all, Captain Eclipse. I am glad to be in the world again, and I remain optimistic that I will be assigned a new primary program one day. I cannot be the only example of my class in operation."

Juno wasn't so sure of that. She'd never seen a droid like him before, and assumed that he was something Darth Vader had commissioned years ago to act as plaything and tutor to his young apprentice.

The thought of Starkiller darkened her mood. Why was she thinking about him so much? Sometimes she wished *her* primary program could be changed as easily as a droid's. It would certainly save her a whole lot of grief.

When the Quarren were ready, they gathered at the top of the ramp, where a corridor led off into two opposite directions.

"This is where we split up," said Ackbar. "Siric, you know what to do?"

The bomb expert and his assistants patted their waterproof packs and nodded.

"All right, good luck. Make your move on Seggor's signal."

The five headed off into the gloomy distance, feet slapping softly against the floor. Ackbar guided Juno, Organa, PROXY, and Seggor Tels up the other way. They moved silently, conscious of the fact that the city was entirely in Imperial hands. They could trust no one, and carried blasters openly in case they happened across anyone so deep in the basements.

Around them, the city hummed and shifted on the

surface of the endless sea. There was no sense of motion, just a constant creaking and groaning of welds. Juno wondered if any of these floating cities ever sprang a leak, but didn't think right then the time to ask. That was the least of their problems.

Ackbar and Tels swapped positions when they reached the upper levels. The Quarren had the codes for the fighter wing's secure compound—obtained, he said, by bribing a maintenance team who had worked briefly for the city administration. Tels padded softly ahead of them, moving with stealthy confidence along the metallic corridors. If he was nervous, it didn't show.

They reached the checkpoint, one of seven scattered across the city. This was the least frequented but still under heavy guard. Seven stormtroopers patrolled the area, keeping a close eye on anyone who approached.

"Your turn to shine, PROXY," Juno said. "You've assimilated the Imperial files?"

The droid's holographic generators flickered and flashed, hiding his true appearance behind another—that of a rotund, balding white human male dressed in an Imperial uniform.

"Yes, Captain Eclipse." His voice changed, too, to match that of the fighter wing's commander. "If you will follow me . . ."

"Sorry about this," whispered Juno to Ackbar as she aimed her blaster at him. Organa did the same for Tels. "You know it's just for show."

"No hard feelings," said Ackbar, slipping his own blaster out of sight.

PROXY strode confidently into view, leading the two humans and their Dac native "captives" to the checkpoint. The guards looked up as they approached and stood to attention.

"Commander Derricote?"

"Indeed," said PROXY, not breaking step.

The trooper who had spoken raised a hand. "I'm sorry, sir. I just need to record your companions."

"Of course. Two informants and two members of the Dac resistance for urgent interrogation. I have reason to believe that an attack is imminent."

The troopers exchanged nervous glances.

"Security codes?" asked the squad leader.

Juno hid her anxiety. Why was a stormtrooper asking the flight wing commander for security codes? Something was going wrong. She tightened her grip on her blaster.

"Twenty, thirty-five, nineteen, sixty-seven," said PROXY without hesitation, quoting the information he had sliced from the Imperial network.

"Thank you, sir. Move along."

The troopers parted ranks, allowing the group of five an unobstructed path through the checkpoint. Juno held her breath as she passed between the troopers. All it would take now was for PROXY's holographic impersonation to flicker and the ruse would be exposed.

"Commander Derricote, hold a moment."

PROXY stopped in mid-stride but didn't turn. "What now? Can't you see I'm in a hurry?"

Juno didn't learn what had made the trooper suspicious. A bolt of blasterfire from Bail Organa caught him in the throat, throwing him backward. A second bolt took out the trooper closest to him, and a third spun the next one along in a circle. The speed and accuracy of the three shots was as impressive as they were unexpected. She took two shots of her own as the opposing groups scattered, leaving just four troopers to return fire.

Bolts of energy flashed back and forth. Small explosions threw fragments of plastoid from the walls and ceiling. Smoke thickened the air, made her eyes water.

It didn't last long. Ackbar and Tels took out three of the remaining troopers, and the last soon keeled face-forward across one of his compatriots, hit by Juno and Organa from two sides at once.

"Nice shooting," Juno told the Senator as she emerged from cover. The compliment was sincerely meant. Shot for shot, he was both faster and more accurate than she was.

"I'm a little out of practice," he said, checking up and down the corridor for signs the ruckus had been noticed. "You should've seen me during my Academy days . . ."

They dragged the bodies into a storage locker. With luck, no one would notice the breach in security before their mission was complete. PROXY maintained the illusion of Commander Derricote as they resumed their hasty march into the secure compound.

It was more crowded than the city proper had been. Droids and techs hurried through the corridors, but thankfully no more troopers. They received the odd askance look, and Juno wondered why. What about PROXY's impersonation didn't ring true?

When they reached the flight wings' empty barracks, she began to understand what PROXY had got wrong.

"It's filthy in here," she said, staring at the messily draped uniforms and unpolished boots. Weapons parts lay on bunks, next to scattered rations. Because grunts took their lead from their superior officer, she had no doubt that this reflected the real Derricote through and through. "Who are these guys?"

"I don't know," Organa said, "but we have to hurry. The briefing starts in ten minutes."

They found a passerby and grilled him on the whereabouts of the real commander.

"In the n-nursery," stammered the tech.

"They have *kids* here?" Juno's sense of outrage reached a new peak. She would never have allowed such laxity under her command.

"For his p-plants," the tech managed to get out. "The nursery's what he calls the g-greenhouse."

When he had provided directions, Organa knocked him out with a deft tap to the back of the skull.

"Tels and I will deal with the commander," he told Juno. "You and Ackbar go with PROXY to the briefing. Make it convincing."

"We'll do our best," Juno said, even as one growing doubt niggled at her. If Derricote was as slovenly as his pilots, that had to be what was giving them away.

They split up. Hurrying to the briefing room with Ackbar, she directed PROXY to look more like the real Derricote did. She hoped.

"Undo another button. Loosen the collar. Roll up the

sleeves, too, and mess the hair more."

"Are you sure this is an improvement, Captain Eclipse?" the droid asked her.

"As sure as I can be, PROXY. Let's keep our fingers crossed."

There was no guard at the briefing room entrance. Ackbar and Juno slipped to the back of the room as PROXY strode to the podium at the front. Pilots slouched in their seats and didn't rise to attention when their commander entered. Although she had left the Empire more than a year ago, Juno's blood still boiled. These guys were giving pilots everywhere a bad name.

No one looked twice at PROXY's modified disguise. His preamble was brief. "Forget the flight schedules you already have," he said. "I'm giving you a new assignment—practicing honor rolls over the city. All of you."

There were groans from pilots who had only just come off an active shift. "Is this something to do with the shuttle that arrived last night?" asked one.

"That is classified," said PROXY without missing a beat. "I want you in the air in five standard minutes. Dismissed."

The pilots complained and griped but slowly began to move. Some even managed a semblance of urgency. Five minutes would have been a very quick turnaround even for a well-practiced flight wing. Juno wouldn't have put a credit on this lot making ten, maybe not even fifteen.

Still, time was tight for the conspirators to get to where they needed to be next.

"Good work, PROXY," Ackbar told him when the room was clear. "Now back to the rendezvous point."

They retraced their steps through the secure compound, past the still-unnoticed checkpoint and into the city proper, where PROXY returned to his normal appearance. No alarms sounded; no shouts rang out. Everything appeared to be going according to plan, so far.

The five Quarren were waiting for them in the shadowy lower levels, rehydrating themselves in the rippling water. They communicated by hand signals that the charges were laid and the triggers set exactly as required.

So far, thought Juno, *so good.*

"Bail and Tels should've been here by now," she said, checking her chrono and counting off the minutes. The TIE fighters of the 181st would be in the air soon, even by her most conservative estimate. "Search for them in the city's security grid, PROXY. Maybe they've been picked up somewhere—"

"No need," called the Senator himself from the top of the ramp. He jogged down to meet them with Tels in his wake, pushing their prisoner ahead of them. "Sorry to hold you up. Our friend here moves more slowly than we planned for."

"What is the meaning of this?" blustered the real Evir Derricote, commander of the 181st fighter wing. He looked even scruffier than PROXY had portrayed him, although perhaps that was a result of his capture. "You'll never get away with it!"

"Take those binders off him," said Ackbar when the commander was before him. "We have a message for

the Emperor. Get off Dac, and stay away from the Mon
Calamari system, or—"

Something moved in the shadows. Ackbar reached
for his blaster, and so did Juno. The Quarren huddled in
closer to one another.

"Who's there?" called Organa. "Come out!"

"I think they've said enough," called a voice. "Take
them."

"It's a trap!" gasped Ackbar.

Two dozen stormtroopers stepped into the light,
weapons trained on the knot of conspirators they
encircled. At their head stood a tall, thin man in the
uniform of a senior officer in the Imperial administration.
So senior, in fact, that she had never seen the insignia in
person before. He had a nose like a knife-blade and eyes
to match, and his cruel mouth was practically lipless.

It was clear that Ackbar knew him. He instantly raised
his blaster to shoot at him, but a well-timed blaster-bolt
from one of the troopers knocked the weapon from his
hand.

"There's no point resisting, Ackbar," said the stern
figure in a chillingly polite voice, striding confidently
toward them with his hands behind his back. "You're
quite outnumbered. Please drop your weapons, or I will
have you executed right here. All except you, Ackbar.
I'm looking forward to having you back in my employ.
That'll remind my other slaves that escape is simply not
an option."

Ackbar's mottled skin had turned a sickly yellow. "I
will never be your slave again, Tarkin. *Never*."

Grand Moff Wilhuff Tarkin smiled coldly. "That choice is now well and truly out of your hands."

Derricote pulled free, rubbing his wrists. "Thank you, Grand Moff. Thank you for rescuing me."

"I won't say it was my priority, but I will accept your gratitude. Be careful it doesn't happen again." Tarkin turned to face Bail Organa. "Your weapon, Senator. I asked you to drop it."

Organa obeyed, and so did the others. All except Tels. His gun remained in his hand, and none of the Imperials moved to force the issue. Slowly, without saying a word, he walked to join their numbers.

"*Why?*" Ackbar asked him.

"Once a traitor, always a traitor," answered Tarkin for him, with a gloating tut-tut. "You Rebels should choose your friends more carefully. He contacted me a day ago, offering to return my slave in exchange for greater freedoms for his people and a place in the civil administration. He won't get either, of course. I'm not known for changing my mind, particularly when it comes to negotiating with aliens."

It was Tels's turn to go pale. "You mean—"

"Yes, put your blaster down and stand with the others while I decide if you're important enough for the Emperor to kill himself, or whether I should just dispose of you now. I'm leaning toward the latter, simply to spare the mess—"

At that moment, a series of explosions rocked the city. The floor moved beneath them.

"What's that?" asked Tarkin of his nearest trooper. "Find out!"

Another trio of blasts brought part of the ceiling down. Tels raised his blaster and fired at the lights, extinguishing them. Utter darkness instantly fell.

In the confusion, Juno dived for her blaster. She heard a stormtrooper say, "It's the Hundred Eighty-first, sir. They're firing on the city."

"Impossible!" blubbered Derricote. "I gave no such order!"

"To me!" Tarkin ordered his men from the ramp. "To me!"

Juno fired in the direction his voice had come from. Her shot went wide, revealing his high-cheeked visage in the flash. She rolled before the stormtroopers could return fire. Soon the space was a maelstrom of light and sound as more explosions rocked the city, one after the other, and the two sides exchanged blasterfire. She found Organa and stood with her back to him, admiring the elegant precision of his shots. When he fired, he nearly always hit, even in the dark.

The stormtroopers retreated up the ramp, following the voice of the Grand Moff. Juno and the others stayed exactly where they were, waiting for the echoes of the last explosion to fade away. When it did, there was blessed silence, apart from the tinkling of debris and the lapping of water.

A torch flared, held high in Ackbar's hand. "Are we all here?"

Juno took a quick head count. Everyone was accounted for except PROXY and one of Siric's assistants, who had been hit in the chest by a stray shot. Organa found

Derricote huddling in a ball in the corner of the room with his hands over his head. He didn't seem to notice that the firing had ceased until the Senator pulled him upright, blinking and fearful.

There was no sign of Tarkin.

"He must have slipped away in the skirmish," said Ackbar, looking disappointed.

"Never mind," said Organa, patting his shoulder. "That we *almost* got him sends the same message."

"And we still have this one," said Tels, squeezing Derricote's face between his long fingers and peering close. "For what he's worth."

"You mean you're not—" stammered the flight wing commander, looking from face to face in confusion. "And you are—"

"All on the same side, yes," the Quarren said. "Thanks for your help."

"But I didn't—"

Juno almost felt sorry for him. "Explosions, timed to coincide with the honor roll you didn't order. It won't fool anyone for long, but it had exactly the right effect in the moment, don't you think?"

Footsteps sounded on the ramp above. They looked up to see PROXY returning, the Tarkin disguise he had adopted during the battle slipping away with an electric crackle.

"I led the troopers, in the opposite direction from the real Grand Moff," the droid said. "They are currently on their way to the landing pads, with orders to arrest the pilots responsible."

"Good work, PROXY. It went almost perfectly."

Derricote stared at the droid in shock, clearly beginning to piece events together.

"What are you going to do with me?" he asked.

"Nothing," said Ackbar.

His eyes narrowed. "Nothing?"

"Tarkin will accept your explanation," Organa explained, "but I'd say your career is pretty much ruined here regardless. Grand Moffs don't like inferiors who draw attention to themselves. You might want to pull your head in for a while, if you still have one."

The Senator released him, and Derricote stepped slowly away, as though expecting to be shot at any moment.

"You're really letting me go?"

"Yes," said Ackbar. "You are a witness to what happens when one interferes with the Dac resistance."

The commander was too busy hurrying up the ramp to promise anything, but Juno didn't doubt that the message would get out. With one short action, the Empire had been humiliated and the local resistance strengthened. It was the very embodiment of Kota's methods.

Juno wondered if Mon Mothma would see it that way, when she found out.

When they were alone, Organa put one hand on Tels's shoulder, the other on Ackbar's. "I don't think I need to say anything," he said, echoing Garm Bel Iblis's philosophy: *Actions speak louder than words.*

"In this case, yes," said Tels, tentacles curling tightly in gratitude. "Thank you from the free people of our world for showing us that we can fight together—and must fight together in order to remove the Emperor's net from our world. We will join your Rebellion as one world, in the spirit you have shown us."

"Does he speak for you, too, Ackbar?"

"You know he does, my friend. And I thank you, too." Ackbar's large, golden eyes took in Juno and PROXY. "We owe your Rebel Alliance much already."

"It's not ours," said Organa, and for a moment Juno feared that he would declare it to be Starkiller's, as Kota had on Felucia, once. "The Rebellion can't belong to any one person, or it's no better than the Empire. It's yours. Everyone's. It belongs to all of us."

"Our dead, too," said Tels, acknowledging the body his fellows had lifted in preparation for leaving the city. "We have lost so many already."

They stood in silence for a moment, Juno thinking of Kota and Starkiller and wondering what they would make of this strange moment of communion among three species in a waterlogged basement.

There was no way of knowing, now. No way at all.

Part 2

REVELATION

CHAPTER 7

The same day.

"WHERE IS SHE?"

Kota stumbled into the cockpit behind him. He was covered in blood and dirt and looked on the verge of collapse.

Starkiller didn't care.

"Where is she?"

"I don't know."

"Why not? This is her ship."

"It was. It isn't now. She's moved on." Kota slumped into the nearest seat and put his scarred face in his hands. "The Rebel Alliance fleet is scattered across the Outer Rim, constantly on the run. She could be anywhere now."

Starkiller frowned. It just didn't make sense. "She wasn't with you when you came here?"

"She was, but I had my own squad on the ground." Kota's blind eyes came up. "All dead now, of course. I was the only one Baron Tarko 'spared' when he captured us. The ship went into hiding, awaiting my signal. Then you came. Thank you." The last was said with great gravity and sincerity. "I don't know how much longer I would've lasted."

Starkiller dismissed that with a wave of one hand and checked the controls. Now that his anticipation at seeing Juno had been punctured, more mundane concerns took priority—like making sure the ship wasn't being followed by any of the deceased Baron's underlings.

The *Rogue Shadow* had brought itself out of the sinkhole and was heading for orbit, where it would await further orders. He didn't know what those orders should be, now. And he wasn't ready to take the empty seat at the controls where Juno should have been sitting.

Should have been, in his previous life. But now Kota had his own squad and Juno had "moved on," whatever that meant. Things had changed in ways he had never considered.

"Tell me exactly what happened."

The general related the circumstances of his capture with his usual economy. An unofficial raid on a local despot had gone unexpectedly wrong, thanks to bad intel regarding the size and capabilities of the forces on Cato Neimoidia. Under other circumstances, that might not have been the complete disaster it had very nearly turned out to be, but with no backup to speak of, apart from a small frigate in orbit, there had been no second chance for Kota and his squad.

"She tried her best," Kota concluded, "and I don't blame her for leaving. She couldn't take on the entire Empire herself, although I'm sure she wanted to."

"She *was* here?"

Kota nodded. "She was the captain of the frigate. Mon Mothma recognizes talent, even if she won't always put it to good use." He leaned forward excitedly. "But now you're back, and she will *have* to see what an opportunity this represents. We must capitalize on it immediately—a major strike to take the fight back to the Empire—"

"Wait." The return of Kota's vigor took Starkiller by surprise. One moment he was half dead; the next he wanted to wage war on the entire galaxy with Starkiller leading the charge. Kota's faith in him was touching, but it needed to be tempered with a little reality. "Don't you want to know where I came from?"

"Why? You're back; that's all that counts."

"But I'm *not* back. I'm not *him*."

Kota shook his head emphatically. "I may be blind, but I'm still connected to the Force. I know what I'm sensing."

"I'm not Starkiller!" It was vitally important that Kota understand that much, at least. The general wasn't his Master, and couldn't be until he was certain who he was. They couldn't just pick up where they had left off. "Not the original Starkiller, anyway. I'm a clone, grown in a vat by Darth Vader to take the old Starkiller's place at his side. That should worry you, shouldn't it?"

Kota leaned forward and scratched at his filthy beard.

"I figure I already know the worst you can do," he said, tapping the corner of one dead eye, "but I've experienced the best, too, so I'm prepared to take my chances."

Starkiller backed down, wondering if Kota was referring to his blinding alone or to something much worse?

"You should know that Shaak Ti is dead," he heard Bail Organa say, out of the past. *"She was murdered by Vader or one of his assassins."*

"Probably the same one who did this to me," Kota had replied, making much the same gesture Kota had in the present.

The guess had been correct, but had Juno told him? Had he furthermore connected Shaak Ti's death to the disappearance of Kazdan Paratus, whom Starkiller had also murdered? Kota had forgiven Starkiller for blinding him, but the deaths of two Jedi—one of them a former Jedi Master on the High Council—were an entirely different magnitude of guilt. Could such a thing ever truly be forgiven?

"Light, dark," Shaak Ti had said. *"They are just directions. Do not be fooled that you stand on anything other than your own two feet."*

Even from the grave, she had something to teach him, as Kota had taught him in life. He was no longer a creature of the dark side, or the light side. The only direction he cared about was the one leading to Juno, where his emotions led him.

Kazdan Paratus, moldering on Raxus Prime in his junkyard version of a living death, was another educative example for him, courtesy of one of his victims: If he were to avoid living entirely in the past, he would have to focus on what really mattered.

"Help me find Juno. That's all I'm asking you to do."

Kota studied him with senses that had nothing to do with his eyes.

"Head for Athega system," the general finally said. "That was the last rendezvous point. When we get there, maybe we'll find some hint of where they've gone."

"They could still be there now, couldn't they?"

Kota shook his head. "If there was any chance I or one of my squad could have survived, the fleet would have had to move. Even Mon Mothma would see the sense in that."

That was the second time Kota had downplayed Mon Mothma's role in the Rebel Alliance. Starkiller filed it away for future consideration.

"I'm going to the 'fresher," Kota said as Starkiller turned to the controls and began plotting the jump. "And then I'm going to sleep. Wake me when we get there."

"All right."

Kota paused on the brink of leaving the bridge. "I'm glad you're back, boy."

Before Starkiller could say, *He's not,* the general turned and limped away.

THE *ROGUE SHADOW* had been modified since he had last flown it, and not entirely for the better. Its shielding was heavier, giving it a different feel when under thrust, and some of the compartments had been expanded to make room for Kota's squad. That left several critical components crushed uncomfortably together, at constant risk of overheating. Starkiller kept a constant eye on the instruments as the ship jumped through hyperspace, waiting for a warning light to flash.

Amazingly, none did. Whoever had rejigged the

systems had made absolutely sure to push the envelope, but never cross it. Someone with extensive battlefield engineering experience was responsible, he suspected. He also assumed they had died with Kota's squad on Cato Neimoidia, so he would never be able to ask how they had done it.

Ultimately, it didn't matter. They were under way, and that was the main thing.

He had time to think, too, although that wasn't necessarily something he welcomed.

His brief exchange with Kota had stirred up a whole raft of anxieties he hadn't even known he possessed. *"I've already seen the worst you can do . . . a major strike to take the fight back to the Empire . . . I'm glad you're back."* He hadn't considered what might happen after finding Juno. Did the rest of the Rebels know about Shaak Ti and Kazdan Paratus? Had they forgiven him for the trap he had unwittingly set on Corellia? Would the stain of Darth Vader's Mastery ever wash off him?

"He stinks of Sith, all right," Kazdan Paratus had said. *"You reek of that coward Vader,"* Shaak Ti had agreed. Only Kota had sensed the goodness within him. Did he really sense it now, or was that just blind hope speaking? Starkiller would have to wait until Kota woke up to ask him.

The issue of what came next connected inevitably to what he had been created *for*. Until Vader had pushed him too far, he had assumed that his purpose was to serve at his former Master's side, killing his enemies and possibly assisting him one day in making a grab for the Imperial throne. That was how he had been trained in his former life, after all, and it was easy to default to that status.

But now, with his memories gradually piecing back together, and more and more of the former Starkiller's life becoming clearer, he began to question that assumption. Darth Vader had plans within plans, making them hard to unravel.

Starkiller's first resurrection had been on the *Empirical,* after the Emperor had ordered Vader to kill his secret apprentice—the betrayal Starkiller had remembered on Kamino, when Vader had declared him a failure, fit for the same fate meted out to the others he had made. Starkiller remembered the almost-blackness of something much like death, and then awakening on an operating table to receive new instructions. Vader said that he had faked Starkiller's death in order to make him a free agent, free to target the Emperor more directly. That had seemed plausible, for that was what Sith did, according to Shaak Ti: betray each other as a matter of course.

But then, on Corellia, Vader had revealed that this had never been his plan, that his intention—the *Emperor's* intention—had been to use him to gather all the Empire's enemies into one spot, in order to destroy them once and for all. And then, Vader had hinted, it would be time to take on the Emperor, but not with Starkiller.

"I lied, as I have from the very beginning," Vader had said.

Vader *always* lied, Starkiller now realized, but somewhere underneath the lies there had to be a measure of truth. A cloned Starkiller must serve *some* purpose, otherwise why go to the trouble? Did he exist to continue one of Vader's previous plans, or an entirely new one? Was Vader still following the Emperor's orders? Or was the Emperor's enforcer making it up as he went along?

That didn't seem likely. One thing Starkiller *did* know was his former Master's nature. Darth Vader was meticulous and controlling. He would leave nothing to chance. His motives and intentions might be hidden for the moment, but they would have to become visible sometime. Perhaps, with enough thought, the clone of his former apprentice might be the one to work it out.

"Without me, you'll never be free," he had told Vader on Corellia. On the Death Star it had seemed that only death would release his Master from servitude, for the Emperor himself had so thoroughly steeped Vader's mind in the dark side—and there had been a moment when the Dark Lord's life had literally been in Starkiller's hands. He could have released his Master from a life of torment had he chosen vengeance over the lives of his friends among the Rebels. If he hadn't, he might not have died and been reborn as a clone. Or he might have died for good.

He wasn't sure which would have been better.

"Do not forget that you still serve me," Darth Vader had said.

In the back of his mind, ever present, was the fear that this would always be the case. That any semblance of freedom he might find would only be an illusion. That at any moment his Master would walk back into his life, as he had on Corellia, and destroy everything he had built.

He swore to himself that it would never happen. He hoped it was a promise he could keep.

And if only he *could* forget. His mind was full of so many things . . .

The controls beeped at him. Time had passed with uncanny speed while he sat in silent contemplation. The *Rogue Shadow* was due to arrive in Athega system at any moment. Starkiller thought about waking Kota, but decided to let him sleep. After fighting seven days straight, the old man deserved his rest.

The blue-white streaks of hyperspace vanished. Blinding yellow radiation took their place, making the ship shake. Starkiller's hands danced over the controls, raising shields and frantically scanning the environment. It felt as though he'd landed right in the middle of an explosion, but what could produce so much force without ebbing in intensity? This was no isolated blast. It was a sustained rage.

The answer was simple: a sun. The sun at the center of Athega system, to be precise. It was huge and highly active, throwing off corona loops longer than most ring systems and deeply pitted with sunspots. Hull temperature was rising fast. Even with the extra shielding, the *Rogue Shadow* wasn't going to last long.

Sensors indicated two rocky planets. A cluster of small dots sheltered behind one of them. He grinned and punched in the coordinates as fast as he was able, assuming that he had indeed found the Rebel fleet.

The relative calm of hyperspace enfolded him. His ears rang in the sudden silence. He took a moment to catch his breath while the ship ticked and pinged around him, slowly shedding its excess heat into the infinite vacuum of an empty universe. He eyed the countdown on the chrono, sure that conditions would be more temperate in the world's shadow. Why else would the Rebel fleet hide there?

The hop was a short one. Barely a minute passed before the ship emerged from hyperspace again, and this time the ride was considerably smoother. The ship's shields were more than adequate to keep the worst at bay. He scanned the ships around him, hoping to find the frigate Kota had mentioned. The *Salvation:* Juno's ship.

None of the transponders matched that name, however—and very quickly another hard fact became apparent. None of the ships belonged to the Rebel fleet. They broadcast the standard transponder signals of the Empire. The fighters swarming around him matched, too. TIE fighters, in their dozens.

He had landed in the middle of an Imperial fleet!

"Identify yourself, unknown vessel," snapped a voice from the comm. "Cease accelerating and prepare to be boarded."

Starkiller wasn't going to sit around and let his ship be taken over. He was already driving hard for the edge of the planet's shadow cone. *Rogue Shadow*'s engines roared as the TIE fighters came about in pursuit. He frantically piloted while at the same time calculating the next jump.

He hit the sun's blazing light the very instant the ship jumped.

Then it was quiet again.

"I told you," Kota said from behind him. "They always find us, no matter where we hide."

Starkiller turned to face him. "Spies?"

"Informers, traitors, lucky guesses—the Force, even, if Vader is looking." Kota fell into the copilot's seat with a weary sigh. His armor was marginally cleaner, but still dented and scratched beyond recognition. "Nowhere is safe."

The ship traveled smoothly to its next destination—the empty shadow behind the second moon. There Starkiller performed a more thorough sweep of the system. He found no signs of a prolonged space battle, which came as a relief. The Rebel fleet must have moved on before the Imperials arrived. But there was no sign, either, of where they might have gone next.

"The fleet doesn't leave coordinates behind," Kota said. "They could be decoded too easily. The only way to find the fleet again, once you've lost it, is to work back up through Rebel contacts."

"That'll take too long."

"What's your hurry? The Empire isn't going anywhere."

Starkiller didn't know how to explain. If Kota didn't already understand, maybe he never would.

Instead, he closed his eyes and reached out with the Force.

Juno.

He could see her in his mind's eye as clearly as if she were standing before him. Blond hair, blue eyes, strong jaw, proud nose—he would carry her face with him for the rest of his life, now that he had escaped Darth Vader's dire influence. When they were together again, they would never be separated. It was just a matter of closing the gap between them—and what was distance but an illusion of the mind? To the Force, all things were one.

Faintly, he heard the *Rogue Shadow* creaking and swaying, but he didn't let himself be distracted. He was out among the stars, seeking, searching. There were quadrillions of minds in the galaxy, and he was looking for just one of them. He sensed fear and great tragedy, cruelty and petty hate. He saw death everywhere, and life, too, ebbing and flowing in that eternal tide. The Force surged within him, primal, powerful, potent—like a beast one never entirely tamed. He felt Kota next to him, full of anger and impatience. He sensed—

A hint of Juno flashed through his mind.

"I don't trust that kind of power. A lesson learned the hard way is hard—perhaps impossible—to unlearn."

They weren't her words, and it wasn't her voice, but she was near their source, which was itself a tantalizingly familiar presence.

Water.

Kota's urgency flared, pulling Starkiller out of his meditation. A dozen floating objects fell to the floor with a loud clatter.

"What is it?" He checked the scopes for any sign of the Imperials, but they were empty. "What's wrong?"

"I didn't say anything," said the general. "Or do anything. I'm just sitting here, waiting."

There was no denying what he had felt. Kota was

impatient, and that impatience was throwing Starkiller off. "You think I'm wasting my time. You don't think I can do it."

"You're right on one point, boy. The galaxy is a big place, and the whole point of the Rebel Alliance is to stay hidden—but I'd never try to guess what you're capable of or not."

"So you think I'm wasting my time."

"I think your priorities are wrong."

"Like Mon Mothma's."

"Yes, exactly so. You're letting your own fears cloud your judgment."

Starkiller turned to face Kota. "What do you think I'm afraid of?"

"Being yourself. Being Starkiller. Being Ga—"

"Don't say that name. I'm not him. I'm a clone, a copy—and a bad one at that."

"Is that what Vader told you?"

"Yes."

"I don't believe it." Kota spoke with surety and great force. "No one can clone Jedi. It's never been done."

"That you know of."

Kota grabbed Starkiller by the shoulders. "I can sense how powerful you are—and here you are wasting it—"

"By rescuing you? By looking for Juno?"

Kota stalked to the far side of the cockpit and rubbed at his forehead with his right hand. "Listen. The Alliance leadership is deadlocked. It can't agree on our next move. We don't have the firepower to take out a meaningful Imperial target, but nobody wants to risk lives making small hit-and-run attacks, either. We need to do *something*, anything. We need somewhere to start."

He stopped and turned his blind gaze back onto Starkiller.

"With your power we can—"

"No."

"Why not?"

"Juno is more important."

"Why is she more important?"

"Because . . ." Starkiller swallowed. He had never admitted this to anyone, not even Juno. "Because . . ."

Kota waved the question away. "It doesn't matter. We both know the answer—and still I have to ask you what difference that makes. She's one person. We're fighting an entire galaxy."

"The Emperor is just one person."

"And so is Darth Vader, and so are all their minions. They add up, boy."

"But we have to defeat them one at a time."

Kota made a dismissive noise and resumed pacing. "Don't try to trap me in riddles. You're no philosopher. You're a fighter like me, and you hold the fate of the Rebel Alliance in your hands."

"*Nobody fights the Empire and wins.* You told me that once. Do you remember, Kota?"

"Yes, I remember." Kota dismissed that, too. "I was a different person back then. You brought me back to myself, back to the Force. You showed me what was possible."

"Maybe I'm really showing you now," Starkiller said. There was a very large, very complicated thought in his mind that he struggled to put into words. "Maybe— maybe where we begin is as important as what we do."

"You sound like a teacher I once had, and you make about as much sense as he did. Do you think *she* cares one bit about that?"

Starkiller hadn't considered that point. He had no idea what Juno was thinking. He couldn't even find her.

So much time had passed. He felt disconnected from everyone he had known best: Juno, Kota, even himself. He felt the world around him slipping away, as though he were becoming a ghost, insubstantial and irrelevant.

"I just want . . ." *Juno*. There was no point saying that again. "Kota, listen to me. I rescued you so you could help me, but you're not helping at all. I need a place to think this through on my own. To meditate without you distracting me."

Kota stared at him, a disbelieving expression on his face. "We're at war, and you want a quiet place to *think*?"

"It's important to me to find her. I won't stop until I do."

"And meanwhile the Alliance will be destroyed. Is *that* what you want?"

Starkiller stood, tired of being loomed over and yelled, "You talking like this is why I have to go!"

"Fine, then. Go to the forests of Kashyyyk or the caves of Dagobah, or wherever you think you'll find what you need and let the galaxy die."

"What are you talking about? I'm not going to let the galaxy die. I want what she wants—what you want, too, just in a different order."

Kota faced him, standing straight and tall. "Is that true?"

"Yes."

"Can I believe you?"

Starkiller hesitated. His feelings were muddied on everything beyond finding Juno. But he meant Kota no harm, and he was certainly no ally of Darth Vader and the Emperor.

"Yes," he said. "Yes, you can. I'm not a coward, Kota, and I will *come* back."

Kota shook his head and seemed to deflate. He looked old and tired, and for a moment Starkiller wished he could take back everything he had said and give Kota, his mentor and friend, everything he wanted. But there was no doing that now, and it would have been a lie. Juno came first. Then the Rebellion. That was how it had to be.

"All right." Kota headed toward the exit of the cockpit. "Go wherever you want. Take the ship: It's always been yours anyway. Just drop me at the nearest spaceport before you get lost in the stars, so I can find someone who will *fight*."

Starkiller swiveled the pilot's chair toward the console and stared, without really seeing anything, until he was sure Kota had gone. Then he lowered his head onto the blinking instruments and closed his eyes. The face of the empty moon rotated far below, unnoticed, irrelevant.

He was doing the right thing. He was sure of it.

The only question remaining was: where to start?

Water.

He looked up and began calculating a course for the first waterworld he thought of—Dac, the home of the Mon Calamari.

CHAPTER 8

THE CARGO FREIGHTER TOUCHED DOWN on Dac's moon with a dust-softened thump. Bail Organa, back in his grunt pilot's pressure suit, released the controls and set the instruments to standby. No one had followed them on the short journey, and no one would look twice at an authorized vessel in such an utterly uninteresting place. For as much time as they could spare, they would be unobserved and unsuspected of anything at all.

"Nice spot for a summer palace," Juno said as PROXY went aft to warm up the R-22. "You should think about moving here."

"The quiet is tempting." Organa's wry tone perfectly matched hers. "But I don't think I'll be settling anywhere soon. The Emperor will get tired of looking for me eventually, and that's the time to reappear. There's a lot of work to be done out there."

On that last point Juno heartily agreed. They had discussed the Senator's plans on the way from the surface. He believed that he was too well known to be assassinated in public. Robbed of the hope of quiet, out-of-sight murder, the Emperor, Organa said, would stick to the philosophy of keeping his enemies close and rely on other methods to deal with the growing Rebellion.

Juno supposed that he knew the Emperor better than anyone alive, except Darth Vader, but she wondered if he was secretly as worried as she would have been. Painting a target on one's head and sticking it out into the firing line had never struck her as being particularly life affirming. For oneself or one's family.

"Any idea," she asked, "what this work you're planning to do might actually be?"

"I know what you're really asking. You want to know which way I'll side with respect to Mon Mothma and Garm Bel Iblis."

"Spot-on, Senator."

"Well, it's a tricky question at the moment. With the Dac resistance movement on our side, we'll soon have more ships, but that doesn't mean we can afford to be complacent. One shipyard doesn't make us the equal of the Empire. And for that I'm glad. I don't trust that kind of power. A lesson learned the hard way is hard—perhaps impossible—to unlearn."

"Assuming we don't all get killed along the way."

"Assuming that, yes." He looked at her with one hand cupping his cheek. "Where do *you* sit on this, Juno? You're not afraid of action, but I don't see you running off to start your own revolution."

She didn't dodge the question. "I think we need to act decisively, but smartly, too. What we did here, for instance—it made a difference. And if we'd taken Tarkin hostage, it might have made a *big* difference."

"Do you think the Emperor would have cared if we'd threatened to shoot Tarkin? I don't."

"No, but those around him might have. When the ruler of the galaxy doesn't lift a finger to save a Grand Moff, what kind of message does that send?"

"True." He nodded. "For what it's worth, I agree with you. There are tipping points and levers we can use to apply force all through the Imperial administration, and the sooner we start applying them, the sooner the Emperor will start to feel the pressure. But the importance of a symbolic victory should never be downplayed, and neither should the risks. Too many choices, too much at stake, as ever. The future will judge us, not each other."

"If we *have* a future."

"Oh, there's no doubt about that, Captain Eclipse. The question is: What sort?"

Juno smiled, noting how cleverly he had avoided giving a direct answer to her original question. But she didn't pursue it. It had been good seeing him, and she didn't want to spoil the moment with politics.

"Pleasure serving with you again, Senator Organa," she said, extending her hand.

He gripped and shook it. "The feeling is mutual, Captain Eclipse. I hope this won't be the last time I hear from you."

"And vice versa."

"That job's still going, remember."

She rolled her eyes. "The best you could offer at the

moment would be low-pay haulage. I did enough of that when I was with the Empire."

He laughed and saluted as she retreated to the cargo bay. PROXY had the R-22's landing lights on and the repulsors thrumming. She climbed up into the cockpit and slid easily into the pilot's seat next to him. When the hatch was sealed, Organa opened the bay doors and she guided the fighter outside, into the gray, lunar light. Juno lifted a hand in farewell, knowing that Organa would be watching through the forward observation ports. The cargo freighter lifted off, hatch slowly sealing shut on its empty hold.

"All systems are fully operational," PROXY advised her. "We are ready to return to the fleet and report."

She wasn't looking forward to that. The question of what she should tell who remained very much open. Should she debrief with Leia or report on developments with the Rebel Alliance leadership?

"First we have to find out where the fleet is, exactly," she said. "Plot a course for Malastare. That's the best place to start looking."

"Yes, Captain Eclipse."

Juno tapped her index fingers on the instrument panel while PROXY performed the hyperspace calculations. The mission on Dac had been an unqualified success, but it had left her with a faintly empty feeling, as though opportunities had been missed and the obvious overlooked. She didn't know where that feeling came from, exactly. Perhaps no more than because every time she worked with Bail Organa one-on-one it reminded her of Starkiller.

On Felucia they had discussed the mystery surrounding his past and whether she trusted him. On Corellia they had been looking for PROXY, lest information the droid contained fell into the enemy's hands. This time, there had been no mention of Starkiller, but thoughts of him had been unavoidable. If he hadn't died, Kota wouldn't have died; if Kota hadn't died, they wouldn't have been on Dac in the first place. The shadow he cast still stretched long over the Rebellion, a year after his death.

She physically shook herself. How much longer would it take before she got over him? Hadn't she grieved enough?

"Coordinates prepared," said PROXY. "Are you well, Captain Eclipse?"

"Yes," she said, rubbing her eyes and telling herself to get a grip. "I'm all right. Give me the controls. I'll take us there."

"Yes, Captain."

The R-22 hummed under her hands, ready for dust-off. She took a deep breath. This was what life was about, she reminded herself: the roar of engines; the flow of data; the magical yet utterly mechanical routine of traveling from A to B through hyperspace. She had missed being directly behind the controls of a ship. That was the one thing she regretted about accepting the commission to command the *Salvation*.

She wondered briefly how Nitram and *her crew* were faring without her. They felt unimaginably distant, like a dream she had once had.

Like the past she couldn't call back.

"Enough," she told herself, and hit the repulsors with a firmness that surprised her.

SHE SLEPT BRIEFLY during the hyperspace jump, in several short bursts. It was a long journey, from the Outer Rim on one side of the galaxy to the Mid Rim on the other. First they followed the Overic Griplink to Quermia, where they joined the busy Perlemian Trade Route. The risk of discovery was greater where traffic flowed most readily, so at Antemeridias they took a side route, following the Triellus Trade Route around Hutt space all the way along the galactic arms to the Corellian Run. There they took a series of complicated legs incorporating parts of the Llanic Spice Run, the Five Veils route, and the Sanrafsix Corridor to an uninhabited world called Dagobah on the Rimma Trade Route. They followed that particular route to the Hydian Way, and thus came to Malastare from the opposite direction to the one she had originally set out on.

Juno stretched as far as she could in the cramped cockpit when the high-gravity world hove into view. Orbit was a mess of ships displaying Imperial and independent transponders. The world's last Chief Magistrate had been transferred thanks to his habit of shooting the locals for sport, and the Empire's rule had been contested ever since. High-gravity AT-AT walkers hunted for Rebel outposts in deserts while insurgency groups picked off Imperial officials in the city. Both indigenous Dugs and settled Gran fought fiercely alongside each other to maintain their independence. Juno hoped the citizens of

Dac would look to Malastare as an example of how to proceed in the coming months.

Even here, she realized with a sinking heart, was a reminder of times past. The former Chief Magistrate had been Ozzik Sturn, who had moved from Malastare to Kashyyyk, where he had come last in an encounter with Starkiller.

Ripples in a pond, she thought, as she had over Cato Neimoidia. Starkiller had been a particularly large pebble . . .

She took the controls and descended on course for Port Pixelito, the world's capital city and largest spaceport. A trio of TIE fighters buzzed her, but she easily outflew them. Unlike Dac and Cato Neimoidia, Malastare had little the Empire actually wanted; otherwise there would have been Star Destroyers descending en masse to remind the world of where its loyalties should lie. The low-level campaign against its citizens was just enough to remind them that they shouldn't get too comfortable. Their time would come.

Port Pixelito was a tangled sprawl of low, squat buildings, as befit the higher gravity. Air traffic was lighter and less regulated than elsewhere, and Juno guided her straining R-22 to an empty berth without needing to register with the local authorities. Malastare was, effectively, a free port for non-Imperials, making it a perfect place for the Rebel Alliance to reallocate goods and staff. She had visited several times prior to gaining command of the *Salvation,* and made several important contacts, as well. The man she was coming to see was just one of them.

The repairman.

When the starfighter was in its berth, she shut down the engines and popped the hatch. City smells rushed in, prompting her to pull a face. A crumbling civil administration had disadvantages, too.

"Stay with the ship," she told PROXY. "If anyone comes near it, do your best Wookiee impersonation and scare them away. I won't be long."

"Yes, Captain Eclipse. I will inform you of any unexpected developments."

She checked the charge on her blaster and hurried off, scowling at a number of unsavory characters checking out the R-22's well-maintained lines. Poor security was another problem Malastare suffered from, thanks to the ongoing urban conflict. Starfighters were valuable machines that could be easily adapted to other purposes. Left unguarded, the R-22 wouldn't last an hour.

Juno emerged from the spaceport and checked her bearings. The streetscape had changed somewhat since her last visit. At least one of the major landmarks was gone, probably demolished during a strike from either side. People brushed by her, grunting impatiently. She spotted a dozen different species in the first ten seconds.

There. She found the sign she was looking for and cut a path through the crowd toward it. In blinking yellow and green pixels, it promised repairs—no questions asked and hung above the entrance to a green, two-story building that might once have been a small theater. Graffiti advertising the latest Podrace covered the walls almost entirely from ground to roofline. She had watched one of the planet's high-speed extravaganzas the last time she had visited; it had made even her pulse race.

Juno walked through the door, brushing past an elderly insectoid Riorian clutching a dented gyrostabilizer to his chest. He chattered something to her in a dialect she didn't understand then hurried away.

"Another satisfied customer," said the Gran behind the shop counter, smiling hopefully. Its three stalked eyes blinked at her in the low light. Two Kowakian monkey-lizards, possibly a rare breeding pair, chased each other across the tops of shelves stuffed with dusty machine parts. Their squawking voices were loud in the claustrophobic space.

"I'm looking for your boss," she told the Gran. "The repairman."

"Lots of people looking for him. Who says he's here?"

"He never goes anywhere. Tell him it's Juno."

The Gran hesitated, and then lowered its snout to speak into a comlink fixed to the counter. Its native tongue was another Juno couldn't interpret, but she heard her name mentioned at least twice.

A voice answered in the same dialect, and the Gran nodded and pointed at the shelves.

"You know the way?"

"Unless you've changed it, sure."

The Gran pushed a concealed button, and a section of the wall slid aside. Juno went through it and waited for the panel to close behind her. There was a moment of absolute darkness and silence, and then the inner panel clicked. She slid it aside and walked into the workshop.

It was a mess of starship components, droid limbs, photoreceptors, sensors, wires, core processors, field generators, environmental units, and more. Stacks of parts stretched high up to the distant ceiling, while some hung suspended in nets cast from corner to corner. Several ramps led up and down to farther layers, and Juno knew that the deepest levels contained the components required to make weapons and targeting computers. Many of the broken machines that came through the store contained information relating to the Empire's activities in the system and beyond, and the Rebel Alliance had gained valuable data by tapping into this inadvertent leak, as well as sourcing much of its military matériel from reclaimed or completely rebuilt items.

She looked around, standing on the tips of her toes to see over the piles.

"Over here, Juno," called a familiar voice. "Come on through."

A mop of blond hair was just visible on the far side of the room. She wound her way through the close spaces of the workshop to where its owner was working. The main workbench had moved, but it looked about as messy as it had the last time she'd been here. Myriad fragments of a multitude of machines covered its surface, mixed with all the delicate tools of the trade, material, sonic, and laser. As she approached, the owner of the tools put down the blue-spitting lance he had been working with and flipped back his visor.

"Well, well. It *is* you! Pull up a seat and tell me where you've been. You don't write, you don't call—I was beginning to get worried."

She dragged a stool over to the bench and gratefully perched herself on it. Her calves were killing her in the high g. The so-called and literal repairman, Berkelium Shyre, was a human technician who had been living on Malastare for more then a decade, and—after an initial hitch or two—had successfully ridden out the transition from Imperial to independent rule. He was broad-shouldered and very strong, thanks to the local conditions, and his loyalty to the Rebellion was matched only by his skill with machines. Juno couldn't tell how old he was, for the freshness of his features and skin were matched by stress and worry lines, the origins of which she had never asked about. They had become friends over the months she'd helped the Rebellion strengthen its hold on the planet. She'd lost count of the number of late nights they'd spent discussing tactics and drinking cheap Corellian whiskey. He'd sent her the occasional cheerful message since, letting her know that all was well on her old patch. She'd always been too busy to respond.

"I'm looking for the fleet," she said. "Do you know where it's moved to?"

"Hey, not so fast," he said with a grin. "I mean it. Tell me what you've been up to. I won't let you go without having at least a halfhearted conversation."

She caught a faint edge to his tone and wondered if he suspected she might have turned traitor. That was a reasonable concern, and a reassuring one. He shouldn't hand out the fleet's location without proper cause, even to someone he thought he knew.

"Well, you know I was promoted," she said.

"You told me that when you were last here. We've missed you in the sector. How's it going?"

She didn't want to tell him about her contretemps with Mon Mothma, but she found herself doing it anyway. It felt good getting it off her chest. Shyre had always been easy to talk to. There was something so direct and open about him. She saw no judgment at all in his cheerful blue eyes.

"Suspended, eh?" He pushed a couple of fuses around his workbench with the tip of magnetic screwdriver. "That must be hard."

"Well, I've been keeping busy."

"I bet. You couldn't help yourself. That droid of yours still playing up?"

"Actually, he's on the mend now. No more visual glitches, mostly. He worries sometimes about his lack of a primary program, though. I don't suppose you could help me with that?"

He shook his head. "Afraid not. Specialized units like PROXY, you probably need to replace the whole core."

"That's what I figured, and they're thin on the ground. Thanks regardless."

"Anytime, Juno."

There was a small but awkward silence.

"So," she pressed him, "the fleet . . ."

"It's not far from here," he said, not taking his eyes

off her. "In the Inner Rim, just off the Hydian Way. Ever heard of a place called Nordra?"

"No," she said, "but I'll find it."

"Stick around the area and they'll find you."

"Thanks, Shyre."

She hopped carefully down from the stool, mindful of twisting an ankle.

"Wait," he said, taking her arm. "Do you really have to go so soon?"

"Places to be, Emperors to overthrow," she quipped.

"But you've only just got here. You haven't told me about what you're feeling these days, where your head is."

She didn't remember ever talking much about that kind of stuff, with anyone, and it was her turn to wonder what was going on. Could he have notified Imperial agents who might already be converging on her location?

She tried to pull away, but his grip was too strong. She did throw him off balance, though, and the gyros of his stool whined in complaint. From the waist down, he was entirely machine. His legs had been lost in the early days of Malastare's independence, when a thermal detonator had gone off in the middle of a squad of saboteurs he had been helping, leaving him crippled. He had built the prosthetic himself and traded active combat for offering support behind the scenes, professing perfect satisfaction with his lot. But there were those worry lines . . .

Was that what this was about, she wondered—turning on those he felt were responsible for ruining his life?

"Let go of me, Shyre."

He did so immediately. "Sorry, Juno. I don't mean to be pushy. I just wish you'd stay."

"I'll be back. Don't worry about that."

"No, I mean *stay*. Here. With me."

Understanding suddenly dawned, and she felt like an utter fool for misreading the cues so badly. *Betraying* her was the last thing on his mind.

"Don't," she said, backing away.

"Hear me out," he said. "I have to say this now. You left too quickly before, and you never responded to my messages."

"I don't want to hear it. I can't hear it."

"But maybe you *need* to hear it," he said with much more than simple entreaty in his voice. "You've been in a funk ever since that friend of yours was killed. I don't know who he was or what happened to him, but I can tell what he meant to you. I can read you, and I know you needed to grieve for him, for what you lost; believe me, I understand that all too well." He rapped the knuckles of his left hand against the metal of his mechanical stool. "But it's been over a year now. Don't you think it's time to move on?"

She turned away to hide the pricking of tears in her eyes. Was it time? Yes, probably. Was she able to? No, it didn't seem that way. Starkiller came so readily to mind. It was like he was still with her, even in death. She couldn't move on until he was gone.

But when would that be? Maybe never, and she didn't want to give Shyre false hope. He was a good man—handsome, smart, loyal, brave, and good-humored. He deserved better than her. She couldn't even speak to him now, let alone give him what he wanted.

"I'm sorry," she said. "I think it might be better if you stopped worrying about me, and moved on yourself."

He was silent for a long time. When he finally spoke, his tone was subdued, but not resentful.

"All right," he said. "I hope you don't think less of me for trying."

"No," she said, turning back to face him. "And I hope you don't think less of me for saying no."

"That wouldn't be possible," he said with a brave smile.

She squeezed his broad shoulder, marveled briefly at the rock-hard muscles, and then hurried away.

AFTER THE CLOSE DIMNESS of the workshop, the light outside seemed very bright and the noise was deafening. Instead of going straight back to the landing bay, she scoured the streets until she found a food seller she remembered from her previous visits, a wise old Cantrosian who made the best pashi noodles she'd ever tasted. The hit of familiar and very powerful spices cleared her head almost immediately. She was able to push the stricken look in Shyre's eyes out of her mind for long enough to start thinking about the safest route to the Inner Rim. There were so many interdictors stationed on the Hydian Way, pirates and Imperials alike. It wouldn't do to get caught by one of them.

"It's been over a year now. Don't you think it's time to move on?"

As she threaded through the crowd back to the landing bay, she thought she glimpsed Kota's silver topknot standing high above the heads, in a crowd of haggling mercenaries. That was impossible, of course. He had fallen on Cato Neimoidia over a week earlier.

Shaking her head and walking on, she admonished herself severely. When she started hallucinating dead friends, she knew she really *was* stuck in the past.

CHAPTER 9

DAGOBAH WAS A SMALL green-brown world with no moons. It seemed utterly uninhabited, and further examination didn't prove that impression wrong. Starkiller checked the rest of the system, wondering if he'd come to the wrong planet, but there was no doubt. Its sibling worlds were boiling, airless, frozen, or gaseous. There was nowhere else to go but here, assuming he wanted to survive longer than a minute outside.

For the hundredth time, he asked himself what he was doing.

There was no ready answer.

Mon Calamari had been an utter dead end. With an Imperial administration boiling over from recent resistance activity, he had only barely managed to slice into records deeply enough to find out that no one called Juno Eclipse had ever officially come to the planet, let alone in the last week. With no other way to search for her open to him, he had been forced to retreat and think of something else. Unfortunately, another search through the Force had been fruitless. She was either dead, in hyperspace, or hiding somehow. The second was the most likely, of course, but a long wait and then another search had still given him nothing. If she was going somewhere, it was taking her a long time to get there.

Studying a map of the galaxy in frustration, he had stumbled across a name that Kota had used. *Dagobah*. Starkiller had never heard of it before, and the ship's records had nothing to add, beyond its location. All he had to go on was Kota's brief mention of it.

"Go to the forests of Kashyyyk or the caves of Dagobah or wherever you think you'll find what you need, and let the galaxy die."

The forests of Kashyyyk brought back memories of wood smoke and the face of a man who must have been his father. The *original* Starkiller's father. He had found his birth name there, but that wasn't where his quest was leading him now. He was going forward, not backward. His gut told him that there was nothing on Kashyyyk for him now.

What *Kota's* gut was telling him was the issue. Had he mentioned Dagobah for a reason or entirely at random? Was the Force moving him in ways even he didn't understand?

Either way, Starkiller had no other leads to follow. Kota had jumped ship to Commenor long ago, so Starkiller plotted a course to the Sluis sector and raced to the distant world as fast as the *Rogue Shadow* was able.

Now that he was here, he didn't know if he'd found something or gotten more lost than ever.

Skimming over the planet's atmosphere, carefully cloaked in case there was someone watching, he detected no hint of Juno, but he could feel a pervasive aura radiating from the planet. Like Felucia, where the original Starkiller had fought Shaak Ti and her young Zabrak apprentice, this world was rich with the Force. A multitude of life-forms thrived in its rich biosphere, which only made it stranger to him that no one had settled there.

Life was in principle a good thing, he reasoned, but living things weren't always good to one another. Perhaps Dagobah was infested with giant predators, or its vegetable life ate anything that moved, or something he hadn't come close to imagining.

He would have to be careful if he were to land there.

Was he going to do that?

He weighed up the pros and cons as thoroughly as he could. On the one hand, he had no reason to think that anything useful to his quest lay on the planet below. On the other hand, Kota was no fool, and he had deep connections to the Force of his own, connections that might become apparent if explored more deeply.

It was his own original instinct that convinced him. His first thought on leaving Vader had been to seek out Kota. On finding Kota, he had been disappointed that he couldn't tell him anything about Juno's whereabouts, but maybe *this* was why Kota had been important. Turning away now might leave him more lost than ever, even if he couldn't see where this path might lead him. At the very least, he might find a place to meditate, as he had told Kota he was going in search of.

Operating the *Rogue Shadow*'s controls by feel, he followed his instincts down into the atmosphere and sought a safe landing spot.

It wasn't easy. The tree canopy was dense and hid marshy, treacherous soil. Thick clouds clung to promontories and low mountain ranges, making them visible only to radar. He imagined a thousand hungry eyes peering up at him as he circled. Eventually he decided on a narrow strip of isolated land, just visible through a gap in the clouds. The *Rogue Shadow* swooped down with repulsors whining and settled onto the green-furred soil. Nothing lumbered out of the undergrowth to taste it. No huge vegetable jaws closed shut around it. Nothing happened at all, which only made him more nervous.

At least the ground was stable. He shut down the engines and waited as the ship grew quiet around him. A patter of rain rippled across the hull, sounding like asteroid fragments against shields. Streamers of mist blew through the trees.

When he got up and opened the hatch, a powerful smell hit his nostrils. The mixture of pollen, pheromones, and decay originated from all around him, from every living thing on the tiny world. He had never encountered anything like it before. Felucia was more cloying, with a thick fungal edge; Raxus Prime was just rot, all the way through; Kashyyyk's distinctive odor came from wood and its by-products. Dagobah was something else entirely.

Maybe, he thought, that stink was why no one had settled here.

He jumped lightly from the ramp onto the mossy

ground. Water dripped from trees and leaves all around him, maintaining a steady patter. There was no wind to raise a sudden tattoo. The air was thick and motionless, as though it never moved, ever.

Juno wasn't there. He was sure of that. But what *was* there? Where were the caves of Dagobah?

He closed his eyes and let the Force tell him what it could.

Life roiled around him, tugging his mind in a dozen directions at once. He let himself be buffeted, tilting his head from one side to the other, testing the flows. There was a hint of something unusual to the east, a knot in the Force unlike any he had felt before. It drew him and repelled him at the same time. The longer he studied it, the more he felt as though it was studying him right back.

He opened his eyes. A large reptilian bird was staring at him from the trees. Its black eyes blinked, but otherwise it didn't move. With a flutter of leathery wings, another of its kind swooped in to join it.

Starkiller reached behind him to seal the *Rogue Shadow*'s hatch. Then he ignited one lightsaber as a precautionary measure. Still the reptavians didn't move.

With every sense alert for danger, he loped off into the swampy forest.

THE GIANT SLUG had twenty-four legs and a mouth full of teeth. Eight meters from snout to tail, it loomed over him, roaring. Its breath was vile.

Starkiller hacked a double line down its belly with both his lightsabers and jumped to avoid the rush of foulness that released. Among the body parts expelled from the creature's stomach was the head of one of the giant reptiles he had encountered farther back. The slug writhed and whined in pain. He left it to die on its own time. His destination was close.

He forced his way through a tangle of long, leg-like roots, scattering a clutch of big, white spiders as he went. The knot he had felt lay dead ahead, at the base of the largest tree he had seen so far. Despite its size, the tree looked sick with a malevolence that surprised him. If Dagobah as a whole was alive with the Force, then this tree had been poisoned by the dark side.

His searching gaze found a deep hole choked with roots and vines at its base. This was undoubtedly the source of the poison that had ruined the tree. A lingering evil lurked here, wedded to the place as firmly as the tree itself. Its roots dug deep and stretched far.

He approached more cautiously, no longer worrying about the planet's more obvious predators. Was this the cave Kota had alluded to? Part of him hoped it wasn't, even as he yearned for this particular part of his mission to be over. Juno wasn't here, and he didn't want to be, either, any longer than he had to.

There was a clearing in front of the cave. He ran to it, and braced himself to enter the cave. His head was thick with foreboding. He felt as though black tendrils were reaching into his mind, stirring up memories that had been mercifully dormant until now. The voices of Darth Vader and Jedi Master Shaak Ti warred within his mind as though fighting over who controlled him.

"The dark side is always with you."

"You are Vader's slave—"

"Your hatred gives you strength—"

"You could be so much more."

"You are at last a master of the dark side."

"Are you prepared to meet your fate?"

A gentle tapping brought him out of his mental deadlock.

He spun around with both lightsabers upraised. Something was watching him—a tiny green creature dressed in swamp-colored rags with green skin, long, pointed ears, and a heavily lined face. It stood on a log with the help of a short cane that it held in both hands, and it was this that made the tapping noise.

The creature didn't flinch at the sight of the lightsabers. Its brown eyes were alive with amusement, if anything. It nodded once at him—in acknowledgment or recognition, Starkiller couldn't tell—and the cane ceased its gentle *tap-tap.*

He lowered his blades and, after a moment, deactivated them as well. He sensed no threat from this unexpected being. Quite the opposite, in fact. The yawning void of the cave seemed to retreat for a moment, clearing his mind of confusion. The being before him might be small in stature, but he was much greater than he looked.

"You guard this place?" Starkiller asked him, gesturing at the cave with the hilt of one of his lightsabers.

The creature chuckled as though pleased by the question. "Oh ho. Only a watcher am I now."

"Then you'll let me pass?"

That earned him a shrug. "Brought you here, the galaxy has. Your path, clearly this is."

Starkiller turned and looked behind him, into the cave mouth. The swamp jungle had fallen utterly silent around them. The air was as thick as glass.

"You know what I'm looking for?"

Something poked the back of his knee. He jumped. The little creature had hopped off the log and approached close enough to test him with his cane—so lightly and silently that Starkiller hadn't noticed.

"Hey!"

The creature persisted, poking his flight suit and lightsabers and gloves, and dissecting him with intense eyes.

"Something lost," he said. "A part of yourself, perhaps?"

Starkiller brushed him away, profoundly unnerved by the accurate and unasked-for reading of his situation.

"Maybe."

"Whatever you seek, only inside you will find."

The creature settled back with his hands on his cane, staring up at Starkiller with so powerful a gaze that for a moment he felt as though he were being looked at from a great height. All trace of humor was gone.

"Inside?" he repeated.

The tip of the cane lifted, pointed at the cave.

Starkiller hesitated. The insidious pressure of the hole in the tree roots grew stronger, and his mind clouded again.

"*Be careful, boy,*" said Kota from the past. "*I hear the long shadow of the dark side reaching out to you.*"

Like a diver preparing for a long descent, he took a deep breath and entered the cave.

IT WAS DARK INSIDE, of course, but somehow it managed to be even darker than he had expected. He struggled through thick curtains of roots and vines, resisting the urge to slash at them with his lightsabers. He kept his weapons carefully inactive, intuitively understanding that any aggressive move that he took might be reflected back at him a hundredfold. Intuition was all he had to guide him now.

His groping fingers encountered a wall of stone ahead of him. Instead of a dead end, however, he found that the cave bent sharply to his right. He pressed on, feeling the dark side throbbing in his ears and beating against his useless eyes. The air seemed to vibrate. Every breath made him want to scream—but in dismay or delight, he couldn't tell.

Another wall ahead of him. This time the tunnel turned to his left. His grasping hands were wet with moisture. He could see them now, somehow, reaching ahead of him as he felt his way into the far reaches of the cave. Gradually the vines fell away, leaving just the roots to obstruct him.

Through a dream-like fog, he stumbled into a larger chamber, the outer limits of which were obscured. He looked down at his feet but couldn't see them, either. The ground was hidden by a crawling gray mist.

He realized with a shock that his flight suit was gone. He was now, somehow, wearing the traditional robes of a Jedi Knight. A flash of memory came to him then, of seeing himself exactly like this on Kashyyyk, wielding his father's blade.

He heard himself asking Darth Vader.

"Your spies have located a Jedi?"

"Yes. General Rahm Kota. You will destroy him and bring me his lightsaber."

The voices from his memory seemed to echo through the room, whispering, tugging him on.

". . . at once, Master . . ."

". . . one more test . . ."

". . . as you wish, my Master . . ."

". . . one step closer to your destiny . . ."

". . . will not fail you, Lord . . ."

". . . do not disappoint me . . ."

He emerged into a much larger cave. The fog cleared, revealing muddy walls overgrown with roots. The floor was treacherous underfoot. He walked carefully forward, seeking the source of the whispers, but stopped dead on realizing that the tangled roots ahead of him were moving.

It was too dark to see properly. The time had come to shed some light on his unusual situation. Igniting both his blades, he held them up above his head, crossed in an X.

The light they cast was blue, not red. That was the first unnerving detail. By their cool light, he made out something hidden by the roots—and it was this that was moving, struggling against the winding net. He stepped warily closer, peering into the shadows. Was that an arm he saw, with a hand clutching vainly at freedom? Was this a hallucination, a vision, or something that was really happening?

A face shoved forward through the muddy roots. Starkiller gasped and stepped back, bringing his lightsabers down between him and the figure caught in the roots. He recognized those features. They were his own: lean and desperate and full of hunger.

Movement came from his right. Another body struggled against the grasping vegetation. Another version of him. And another. They were all around him, dozens of them, writhing, twisting, straining, whispering in agony.

"Yes, my Master."

"I am strong, my Master, and I am getting stronger."

"When will my training be complete, Master?"

They wore the black uniforms of Kamino. They were clones like him.

"What will you do with me?"

Starkiller shuddered and moaned. He looked about for an exit from the chamber, and saw a narrow crack in the stone. He lunged for it, but not so quickly that he avoided the hands that clutched at him. They gripped his flight uniform with his own strength, trying to hold him back, entrap him with them, where he belonged. He cried out and pulled free, falling back into the chamber. He raised his lightsabers automatically, thinking to hack his way free.

"Kill me and you destroy yourself."

He heard the voice clearly, as he had on Kashyyyk. That time, he had not hesitated to strike down the doppelgänger he had seen in his mind. This time he listened to himself, and once more extinguished his blades. The decision renewed his strength, gave him the courage to continue.

In the near darkness he faced the clutching hands of his other selves, and pushed firmly through them. Their slippery fingers skidded off his flight uniform and fell away. Behind him their whispers became moans and then faded to silence. All he could hear now was his breathing—fast and heavy, as though he had been running. He had been underground for hours, or so it felt. How much farther until he reached the end of the cave and found what he was looking for—or what was looking for him?

Another chamber, this one swirling with shadows. He kept walking, and the shadows rose up around him, forming short-lived figures that loomed and retreated, blocking his path. He tried to force his way past them, as he had with the visions of his other selves, but found himself confused and disoriented. His head spun. Twice he found himself facing the way he had come. He put out both hands to stop the world turning. There had to be a way out somewhere, if only the cave would let him find it.

He could hear rain in the distance, and he stumbled toward it.

Thunder boomed—

—and suddenly he was standing in the cloning facility on Kamino, near the hole he had ripped in the wall during his escape. Visible through the hole, the sky hung wild and low, racked by a fierce electrical storm. Spray-slicked metal gleamed even in the gray light. The howl of wind was relentless and eerie.

A figure walked closer to the hole in order to inspect

the torn metal. Armored from head to foot in gray and green, with an unfamiliar T-shaped visor and some kind of jetpack affixed to his back, his voice had the inflectionless grate of a vocoder. It was clear, though, that he wasn't a droid. Perhaps his vocal chords had been damaged.

"He has a healthy head start."

Starkiller moved closer. Only when he moved did he recognize the closeness of armor, the heaviness of limb, the sensation of being trapped. He had experienced all these sensations before.

He said in leaden tones, "The Empire will provide whatever you require, bounty hunter."

Starkiller strained to move his former Master's limbs, but he was powerless to do anything other than ride out the vision. He could only see through Darth Vader's eyes and wait for it to end.

"I'll need backup," said the green-armored figure.

Starkiller's black-gloved left hand gestured out the hole, toward the landing pad. There a long line of troopers was marching into two Lambda-class shuttles, followed by a type of droid he had never seen before. It was huge, with long legs, powerful armament, and heavy shielding. It was so big, the full extent of it was hidden behind the buildings near the landing bay.

The bounty hunter turned to Starkiller and said in a satisfied tone, "They'll do."

A flurry of rain obscured the view and—

—he was back in his body, and the shadows were retreating, forming a dense knot in front of him. He reeled away from it, holding his hands in front of him. They

were flesh and blood, with no sign of prosthetics. He was himself, wholly and only himself, which came as a great relief even as the knowledge that his former Master was hunting him sank in. That was what the vision had been telling him, beyond all doubt. He thought himself free, but Darth Vader thought otherwise.

The shadows swirled and burst apart, and came rushing at him, filling his head—

—*with an image of PROXY, which surely couldn't be possible, since he had been destroyed by Darth Vader on Corellia. This had to be something from the past, Starkiller decided. But when, and where, and who was he now?*

There was none of the heaviness of Vader, and no sign of an Imperial presence at all. He was on a ship of some kind, a large one, bigger than the Rogue Shadow. *Crew members rushed around him, briskly but without urgency. They wore uniforms identical to the ones he had trained against on Kamino.*

Soldiers of the Rebel Alliance.

A canine-faced officer turned to face him.

"I'm having trouble with the forward sensor array, Captain."

Starkiller looked through the observation canopy, out at the space ahead. A small cluster of ships dotted the view, accompanied by an escort of Y-wings. In the backdrop hung a dense and beautiful nebula, all curls and swirls, glowing every color of the spectrum.

A familiar voice asked, "Interference from the nebula?"

PROXY turned from an instrument he was studying.

"Perhaps. I'll try to pin it down."

"Let's not take any chances."

Starkiller barely heard the words. He was stunned by the knowledge that it was Juno speaking. He was experiencing what she was experiencing. Whatever had happened to her would happen to him now.

He punched a button on the console with her hand, not his.

"This is Captain Eclipse." Her voice echoed through the ship. *"Set defensive protocols throughout all ships. Prime your shields and check your scanners for anything that's not one of ours."*

The canine-faced officer nodded and checked the screens in front of him. *"All clear, Captain."*

"Keep looking, Nitram. We can't be too careful."

"Of course, sir."

Starkiller watched the screens with her, searching for any sign of disturbance. His senses prickled. Something was coming. She could feel it, and therefore he could, too.

A voice crackled over the comm. *"Captain Eclipse— we're picking up five, no six small warships, coming in fa—"*

Explosions puffed alongside a ship ahead. Starkiller didn't see where the attacking vessels had come from, but he could see what they were doing. Four precisely aimed missiles cracked the ship in two, sending crew and air gushing into the void. With one ship down, the focus of the attack turned to the center of the group: the ship containing Juno.

"Shields to full," she called over the intercom. "Open fire, all batteries!"

An impact rocked the deck beneath her. The bridge swayed.

"We've been breached," said her second in command. "Troopers boarding!"

"Send a security detail to the main reactor. Seal off life support."

Another explosion, closer than before. Rebel crew went flying, but Juno held on to her post.

"Get those deflector shields up!"

PROXY leaned into view. "Internal security beacons are going crazy. Captain Eclipse, I think we should—"

The bridge doors blew in. Smoke and burning debris filled the air. Through the cloud stalked two heavily armed troopers, already firing. Juno ducked down, blaster pistol in hand. One precise shot to the throat seal put one of the troopers down. Another barely missed the second.

Four more troopers rushed into the bridge. The maze of blasterfire intensified. Starkiller felt his heart racing as he edged to a better vantage point, picking off troopers as best he could. His crew died around him. First PROXY, blown backward in a shower of sparks, then the dog-faced second in command. Rage rose up in him, pure and clean. He stood up in order to see more clearly through the thickening smoke.

A blaster bolt took him in the shoulder, sending him spinning sideways, falling—

—and when he hit the ground in the cave he realized that, although it had been Juno's heart pounding all along, his still kept perfect time with hers. He was covered in sweat, and the stink of the smoke was thick in his nostrils. The pain of the bolt to Juno's arm hurt all the more for knowing that he hadn't been there to stop it.

The timing of the vision tormented him. Juno hadn't been captain of anything larger than the *Rogue Shadow* while PROXY had lived—or while the original Starkiller had lived, for that matter. She hadn't been shot, either. Was it conceivable that PROXY had been brought back to life—or simply replaced? He had seen other droids of his make on Kamino, so that wasn't impossible. That placed the vision sometime after the events of the Death Star. But when? Had they already happened, or were they still to come? *Could he prevent them from happening?*

He struggled to his hands and knees. The shadows crowded him, made it hard to move. His lightsaber hilts had fallen from his hands and rolled out of sight. He scrabbled about for them in the gloom, but they were nowhere to be found.

"Give them back," he told the shadows. "Give them back!"

All they gave him was another vision.

He was crouched on a metal surface, holding Juno in his arms. Rain pounded them. Her eyes were closed. She was covered in blood. He was covered in blood. She wasn't breathing. He tipped his head back and howled back at the storm.

The image of Juno faded into nothing and he fell face-forward onto the muddy ground of the cave, as though gravity had multiplied a thousand times. In that vision, he had definitely been himself. It was either the future or a past he could no longer remember. Or the work of another clone. Or some equally bizarre possibility he could not for the moment fathom.

"We form a strong team," said her voice out of the past. *"It's unfortunate we can't keep on as we are."*

The memory gave him strength to resist the terrible weight of the shadows. Juno had said that on their return to the *Empirical,* at which time he had expected to help Darth Vader overthrow the Emperor and she, he had assumed, would have been allocated to other duties. She had been wrong then, and this vision might be wrong now. Past, present, future—if anyone could change it, it would be him.

Juno could not die.

The pressure fell away. He leapt to his feet. His lightsabers flew out of the shadows and landed in his hands, and were lit an instant later. They were red once more, as red as the blood in his final vision. The shadows fled.

By the crimson light he could see that there was nowhere else to go. He had reached the end of the caves. The only direction he had left to go was back.

He steeled himself for a repeat of his clawing other selves, just in case the cave wasn't finished with him yet, and pressed on his way.

EVEN THE MURKY SWAMP LIGHT seemed bright and green to his eyes when he finally staggered out of the cave. The air smelled sweet and fresh. He clung to a fall of tangled vines and gave himself a moment to recover. He felt utterly drained by what lay behind him, and utterly daunted by what lay ahead.

Juno could not die.

That was the only thing keeping him going.

The click of a tiny wooden cane brought him out of his thoughts. His head came up. His searching gaze found the little creature sitting on a rock, calmly watching him.

How he stayed so close to the cave was beyond Starkiller. He could feel the dark side rolling in waves at him. The undertow was powerful. He had only just escaped. To be constantly within range of such an assault, and to remain sane—or what passed for it on this sodden, forgotten world—was utterly inconceivable to him . . .

The little creature possessed a power out of all proportion to his appearance.

"Whatever you have seen," he said, pointing the tip of his cane at Starkiller's heaving chest, "follow it, you must."

Starkiller nodded. If that was wisdom, then he shared it. "To the ends of the galaxy if I have to."

The creature returned his nod and lowered the cane. His eyes closed, and Starkiller knew that his audience, if such it was, had ended.

Leaping out of the clearing, propelled by a sense of urgency that transcended time and space, he ran as fast as he could for the *Rogue Shadow*.

CHAPTER 10

NORDRA WAS ANOTHER HIGH-GRAVITY WORLD, but one that was extremely tectonically active, with numerous precipitous mountain ranges crisscrossed by deadly blue glaciers. From orbit Juno spied several low-altitude lakes of bubbling lava, alongside which the inhabitants had built several heat-devouring cities. She tapped into their local version of the Holonet News, NordFeed, and found a hardy if not particularly lofty race that had learned to live with constant physical threat and danger. Some of the reports were openly critical of the Emperor's policies. Only their isolation saved them, Juno suspected. Although technically on the Hydian Way, the well-traveled hyperroute detoured around a nearby nebula, bypassing Nordra and several other nearby worlds.

Juno bided her time waiting for the Rebel Alliance to pick up her transponder by half watching NordFeed, half staring blankly out her viewport at the vast and beautiful nebula ahead, all the while trying very hard not to think about Berkelium Shyre. She hadn't intended to hurt him.

She had thought they were only friends. She had valued his friendship, and was guilty only of wanting everything to stay the same between them, even though she knew now that it could never be . . .

They couldn't go back, but they couldn't go forward, either. She wasn't ready for anything like that, and she didn't *want* to be ready, ever. It seemed stupid even to think it, but if she couldn't have Starkiller then she wouldn't have anyone. His death had left such a huge empty space in her life that no one seemed likely to fill it.

"We have you on our scopes, R-Two-Two," came a voice over the comm. "Identify."

She scanned her own screens but couldn't pin down the source of the transmission. There were five ships in orbit around Nordra, any one of which could belong to the Rebel Alliance. Possibly all of them did.

"Juno Eclipse," she broadcast. "Authorization Onda Cuvran Twenty-three Seventeen Ninety-one. Is the *Solidarity* here?"

"The *Salvation*, too, Captain. Here are the coordinates."

She fed the data into the navicomp, thinking: *Still Captain.* That was a welcome sign.

"These coordinates are on the other side of the nebula," PROXY warned her.

"Ion drive only, I presume?" she checked with the Rebel contact.

"You presume correctly. Itani Nebula is diffuse, for the most part, but it casts a big enough mass shadow to ruin your day."

"Understood. Thanks."

She fired up the ion drives and pulled the starfighter out of orbit. Ion drive would take longer, but it was worth it to ensure that the Alliance fleet couldn't be surprised by ships appearing out of hyperspace right on top of them. Thus far Commodore Viedas had managed to keep one step ahead of the Empire's spies, but it was only a matter of time before something critical leaked.

And that, she told herself, was of much greater concern than a broken heart.

JUNO DOCKED WITH THE *SOLIDARITY* and turned the R-22 back over to the hangar crew. She half expected to find Leia or her droid waiting for her, but the welcoming committee awaiting her consisted solely of an aide asking her to meet the commodore in his quarters, immediately. She said she would. No off-the-record chats in the officers' mess this time, she thought. That could be a good or a bad thing.

"You should consider yourself fortunate, PROXY," she said as they wound their way through the ship's corridors. "Not having a primary program means you don't have to worry about losing it."

"I do not feel fortunate, Captain Eclipse," he said in a mournful tone. "It makes me wonder if droids have a layer of programming even more fundamental than the one I am missing—a layer that makes us feel incomplete without instructions. We are built not just to serve, but to crave to serve. I cannot decide if this is slavery or a form of liberation."

"From choice, you mean?"

"From doubt."

Juno wished she could alleviate her own doubts by undergoing a quick memory wipe and restoring her factory presets.

She saluted the sentry outside Viedas's door and was waved through. The Rodian commodore was sitting behind a desk, studying charts. He half stood when she entered and waved her to a seat, then he sat back down again. PROXY stayed by the door, yellow eyes watching unblinkingly.

"Congratulations, Captain Eclipse," was Viedas's opening remark. "The inquiry found you not guilty of putting Alliance resources and staff in undue peril."

"Thank you, sir," she said, feeling an immediate lightness in her chest.

"As of now you are reinstated to full rank, privileges, and security clearance. But of course you have a whole new hurdle to leap over."

"Sir?"

"There's a meeting of Alliance leadership in half an hour to discuss the situation on Dac. You've been asked to attend."

"By whom?"

"By Mon Mothma."

Juno nodded. "I don't suppose I could get back in my starfighter and circle the nebula until it's over?"

"Not a chance. And we'll know if you send that droid of yours in your place." Viedas's antenna twitched in something that might have been amusement. "Go freshen up. I'll have someone call your droid when we're ready."

"Thank you, sir."

"Oh, and you might be interested to know, Captain, that your mission to Cato Neimoidia is now being considered a success."

Juno frowned, thinking of Kota. "How is that possible, sir?"

"Baron Tarko was killed during insurgent action shortly after you left. Clearly you started something that someone else chose to finish. That's all."

She returned his salute and left the room, still puzzling over this latest development. There was very little to think of it, though, except to feel fortunate that someone had done her that favor. If she ever found out who it was, she would be sure to express her heartfelt thanks. With Cato Neimoidia now seen in a more positive light, it would be easier to talk about Dac, surely.

The sentry gave her directions to the nearest common area, where she did her best to look as though she had only just stepped off her bridge. She couldn't wait to get back to the *Salvation* and see what kind of mess Nitram had made of her duty rosters.

She studied her face in the mirror for a long time, wondering despite herself what Shyre saw in her. Couldn't he see how wrecked she looked? Was he oblivious to the bags under her eyes and her flight-helmet-hair? Would he still like her if he saw her as she really was, psychological scars and all?

Not for the first time she wished there were someone among the Rebels she could talk to about things other than tactics and starship specifications. If her mother were still alive . . .

A hand touched her shoulder. "Excuse me, Captain Eclipse. The commodore has asked for you."

She tore her eyes away from her face—and saw another version of her standing behind her.

"Thanks, PROXY. You know you're doing it again? Only this time you look like me."

The droid's holographic image shimmered and vanished with a flash. "I'm sorry, Captain Eclipse. I don't know what compels me." He put a hand to his metal forehead. "Perhaps another overhaul is in order."

"Next time we see that handy little droid, I'll put in a request." She took a second to make sure her uniform wasn't out of order. "Come on, or we'll be late."

The meeting was in the same place as before. This time, she and the commodore were the only flesh-and-blood participants. Mon Mothma and Garm Bel Iblis attended via hologram. Their gray-blue forms flickered and crackled, thanks to interference from the looming nebula. Leia Organa was conspicuous by her absence.

"Difficulties arranging transmission," Viedas explained when he saw her glance at the empty projector. "I suggest we begin regardless."

"We've received an overture from the Dac resistance," said Mon Mothma without preamble. "Ackbar has successfully united the Quarren and the Mon Calamari and convinced them to openly stand against the Empire. He promises ships, if we help him liberate the shipyards."

"That's excellent news," said Bel Iblis. "And excellent timing, given our recent conversation on this matter."

"The very thing that makes me suspicious," Mon

Mothma said. "Where were you these last two days, Captain Eclipse?"

"I was relieved of command," Juno said, "so I took the opportunity to tie up some loose ends."

"On Dac, perchance?"

"I'm flattered, Senator, if you think I could pull off something like this on my own—"

A third holographic figure flickered into being next to the others. Instead of Leia, though, it was Bail Organa, looking scruffy and cramped in his miner's disguise.

"Sorry to hold you up," he said. "I had to move to Mon Eron to obtain a secure line. It's a mess here at the moment. You might have heard."

"We were just talking about it," said Mon Mothma, looking unsurprised at his appearance, rather than his daughter's. "Captain Eclipse here denies any involvement."

"Actually," Juno put in, "what I said was that I couldn't have done it alone."

"Indeed." Mon Mothma raised an eyebrow. "I suppose, Bail, your daughter would say the same."

"I don't know what Leia would say," said Organa, "and I'm not sure why you're asking me. Why don't you ask her directly instead of hauling me in out of the cold?"

Mon Mothma's disapproval was a formidable thing, even over a hologram. "She might deny it, but I know that Leia orchestrated this unsanctioned operation, with Captain Eclipse and Ackbar as her conspirators, using confidential, *privileged* information. She acted precipitously and without consideration for the decisions we had made regarding the future direction of the

Alliance. She abused her position as your representative and betrayed our trust in the process."

"Perhaps she did, but what do you expect me to do about it? I can't suspend her like you suspended Captain Eclipse."

"I believe it's time for you to come out of hiding and resume your position on this council, before she comes up with yet another wild scheme."

"I thought it was rather a good scheme, myself. That was why I was part of it." He threw Juno a self-deprecatory salute. "If you're going to censure Leia, you'd better censure me, too."

Mon Mothma's lips tightened. She looked around the gathering, taking the measure of everyone present.

"Did you know about this, Garm?"

Bel Iblis looked warily amused. "Not the slightest thing—but I can't say I disapprove. This is everything Kota believed in: small, strategic strikes employed to great effect. This little action might change the course of the battle, if we follow it up quickly."

"But the *risk*," she said. "We might have lost Ackbar *and* Bail."

"There's no such thing as a risk-free war," Bel Iblis said. "And you can't force people not to fight, if they want to. Isn't that a kind of tyranny, in its own way?"

Mon Mothma stiffened as though physically threatened. Then she sagged. "Yes, I suppose you're right—and even if you're not, it's clear I'm in a minority. So what now? Do you propose we hand control over to an eighteen-year-old girl and let her decide our course?"

"Hardly," said Bail, "but you can listen to her and act on what she says. She speaks with my voice. Trust her judgment, as I do. If her plan on Dac had failed, I might well have died—but it didn't. She's an Organa, remember. We bring more than just our money to the cause."

"Very well," said Mon Mothma. "I shall do as you say. But that doesn't change the situation right now. The Mon Calamari star cruisers are promised but not delivered. Ackbar is in no position to replace Kota, dealing as he is with his own planet's problems. Our resources are precious, and stretched very thin."

"The Rebellion isn't something you can put on hold," said Organa. "It's a living thing. It needs to be *doing* something, not just being."

"A symbolic strike," said Juno, remembering what Organa had told her on Dac's Moon. "That's what we need. Something that will show our own people we still mean business, as well as the Emperor."

"Agreed," said Bel Iblis. "All this skulking around, effective or not, doesn't do much to bring in new recruits."

"All right," said Mon Mothma. "All right. A symbolic strike it is—but against what? There are thousands of potential targets, each as dangerous as the next. What are our criteria? What's our time frame? Who leads the operation?"

"These are important questions," said Organa. "I leave them in your capable hands, Senators. For now, I'd better sign off. The Empire is closely watching every signal that leaves the system. I don't want a squadron of TIEs landing on top of me, just as things are starting to get interesting."

"We understand," said Bel Iblis. "When we've reached a decision, we'll let you know."

"Thank you, Bail," said Mon Mothma. "Be safe."

The third hologram flickered out.

"Leadership is hard," said Bel Iblis to Mon Mothma, not unsympathetically, "when there are three of us trying to lead at once."

"If it were easy," she said, "we would have finished this long ago."

The two remaining Senators signed off, leaving Commodore Viedas, Juno, and PROXY alone.

"I think we just witnessed some progress," said the commodore, standing. "Of a sort."

Juno understood what he meant. Mon Mothma had given ground, but the leadership might still argue for weeks before settling on an appropriate target. And this time, something low-key simply wouldn't do. It would have to be extremely visible to have the effect required.

"I guess being seen to do something is better than doing nothing at all," she said, "even if it's hard to tell the difference sometimes."

"Careful, Captain Eclipse. You're becoming a cynic."

"Politics will do that to you."

"There are few immune to it, unfortunately."

Starkiller would have been, she wanted to say as the door closed between them, but she kept that thought to herself.

ON THE BRIEF SHUTTLE RIDE to the *Salvation,* PROXY changed shape without warning.

Juno looked up from the controls.

"Is that really you, Princess, or is PROXY playing up again?"

"Call me Leia," came the instantaneous reply. Wherever she was transmitting from, the signal was good. "Congratulations on the success of your mission, Captain. How did the meeting go?"

"Well enough, I think," Juno said, glad the shuttle was empty apart from her and PROXY. "I'm relieved your father was part of it."

"Yes. He can handle the others better than I."

"I wouldn't say that," Juno said. "You have the advantage of being young. I think it puts Mon Mothma off her game."

"It doesn't feel like an advantage when you're arguing with some of the old fools I have to deal with here at home. Alderaanian politics makes the Empire look like child's play."

"Still, you got what you wanted. Don't discount that."

"All right. Maybe I softened them up, but Father sealed the deal. And we couldn't have done it without you, of course."

"Happy to serve," Juno said, "although that might be a little more difficult now that I've got my command back—thank goodness."

"There was never any doubt of that. You'll be exactly where we can use you best—in the middle, not too far away from the action that you forget what's at stake, and not so close that you can't see the big picture. And you have a frigate at your disposal, which is nothing to be sniffed at when it comes to winning arguments."

Juno smiled. It didn't sound so bad, the way Leia put it.

"The important thing," Leia went on, "is that we keep fighting on all fronts at once. Big stuff, small stuff, everything in between. The Empire isn't just the Emperor: it's all the people beneath him who serve him willingly. We have to take the fight to them, too."

"Sounds exhausting."

"I get tired just thinking about it."

They laughed together, more out of companionship than at anything particularly funny. Juno couldn't remember the last time she'd had anything at all to laugh about.

"What are your plans now?" she asked.

"Well, the Death Star is still out there," said the Princess. "The Emperor has it well hidden from us, but it's too big a project to keep out of sight forever. We'll find it, one way or another, and we'll do our best to disrupt its construction. That's our number one priority, because if it's ever operational, the entire galaxy will suffer." She shrugged. "Apart from that, life goes on. University, training, all that ridiculous Old House palaver. If my aunts had their way, I'd be paired off to some brainless boy before the year is out—and there'd go any chance I had of doing something *real* ever again."

Juno was forcefully reminded then of how young Leia was. Boy troubles, parental expectations, frustrated ambition—for teenagers some things were universal, even in the middle of a galactic revolution. Leia reminded Juno of herself, not so very long ago.

"My father tried to set me up with the son of a friend

once," she told the Princess. "A horrible boy, not much more than a recruit. Thought he was going to be the next High Commander but could barely button up his uniform right. Somehow just being from the right side of the planet mattered more than anything about who he was."

"What did you do?"

"Learned to be the best pilot in my sector and got myself transferred. The kid stayed behind—never made it above corporal, for all his talk. My father probably still thinks I missed my chance."

"Parents have no idea."

They laughed again, even as Juno wondered what was going on. Did the Princess have so little contact with the people around her that she, too, had no one to talk to? That didn't seem possible: She had mentioned the university, after all, where there would be lots of people her age, and Juno was sure Bail Organa wouldn't let his daughter grow up isolated and socially inept.

At least Leia still knew her father, Juno thought. Her own father was so distant and alienated that she didn't even know if he was alive.

"Do you have a boyfriend at the moment?" Juno asked her, testing the moment to see where it led.

To her credit, Leia didn't blush. "No one my aunts would approve of."

"Ah, it's like that. Watch out for the bad ones, Leia. They're the ones who really mess you up."

"Everyone says that."

"Because it's true. Don't learn it the hard way, like I did."

Instead of lumping Juno in with "everyone" and dismissing the advice, Leia nodded soberly. "I guess you did."

Juno sobered, too. She hadn't even been thinking of Starkiller, but now she was. The pain was sharp and piercing, causing her to lower her eyes from the Princess's searching gaze.

And suddenly it was clear just how Leia saw her. Not as a friend or confidante, although she might claim either if directly asked. What else could a Princess of the Royal House of Alderaan with rebellious aspirations see in an independent-minded officer who always seemed to be in the thick of things but a role model?

Now, *that* was a daunting responsibility.

"I'm sorry," said Leia. "I can't imagine what it must feel like to miss someone so badly."

"I hope you'll never know." Juno collected herself and forced a smile. Time to change the subject. "It makes fighting the Emperor and our friends the Senators look easy in comparison. At least they're fights we can win."

Like a good diplomat-in-training, Leia picked up on her signals. "Well, I'm sure we'll find ways to keep you busy. Thanks for your support, Juno. I'll be in touch again soon."

"We won't be sitting on our hands out here, that's for sure. The moment we have a target, the fleet will be ready to move."

Leia smiled and raised her hand as though to hit a switch at her end.

"Oh, before I go," she said, "if your droid is playing up again, have you considered that it might not be a random malfunction? There could be a reason for it, beyond a simple glitch."

"Like deliberate sabotage, you mean?"

"Maybe. Or a message. Or something else entirely." Leia shrugged. "I don't know. It's worth thinking about, though."

Juno nodded. "I will. Thank you."

Leia fizzled out, and suddenly Juno was sitting face-to-face with the droid himself.

"What do you think, PROXY? Are you trying to tell me something?"

"I can't imagine what, Captain Eclipse. When I have something to communicate with you, I use the verbal interface my makers gave me."

"You're all talk, in other words."

"Correct."

"My thoughts exactly." That left sabotage or a message from someone else. But who would go to so much trouble just to send her images of Starkiller and herself? It didn't make sense.

"We have you on approach, Captain Eclipse," said a familiar voice over the comm. "Welcome back."

"Thanks, Nitram," she said, quickly taking stock of the shuttle's location. It was decelerating smoothly on autopilot for the *Salvation*'s mid-spine docking tube. Taking the controls, she adjusted its trim and gave the thrusters an extra nudge. Just seeing the frigate raised her spirits. "Break out the Old Janx Spirit. It's good to be home."

"Uh, seriously, sir?"

Juno smiled at her second in command's tone.

Sometimes the Bothan was too easy to tease. "Of course not. We have work to do. The bottle stays in my safe until the Emperor is dead."

"Yes, sir. Understood."

The *Salvation* loomed ahead. Juno put all other thoughts from her mind as she jockeyed the shuttle in to dock.

CHAPTER 11

FROM DAGOBAH TO MALASTARE was a relatively short journey, but it seemed to take forever. With nothing to do but think and worry while the *Rogue Shadow* was in hyperspace, Starkiller paced relentlessly from one end of the ship to the other, turning over everything he had seen and felt on the swampy world receding behind him.

"He has a healthy head start."

"We've been breached. Troopers boarding!"

Juno lying dead in his arms.

"Whatever you have seen, follow it you must."

He had gone to Dagobah hoping for clarity, and all he had received were visions and cryptic advice. Was he closer to Juno or getting farther away? Would he be able to save her, or was she already dead?

The Force reflected his inner turmoil, sending occasional shudders and shakes through the ship. He tried his best to calm down. If his mood disrupted life support or the hyperdrive, he might not make it to Malastare at all.

Finally the navicomp chimed, warning him that his destination was approaching. Leaving the meditation chamber, he hurried to the pilot's seat and took the controls. The moment the stars of realspace ceased streaking, he had the ship under power and accelerating toward the high-gravity world.

Starkiller had visited Port Pixelito just once, while in the service of Darth Vader. A treacherous Imperial aide who had run up gambling debts from podracing had been his target, and one soon dealt with, even in the early days of his apprenticeship. In disguise and with PROXY's help, he had infiltrated the security installation without being detected, then sliced into the mainframe to find his target. From there, he had crawled through ventilation ducts until he was above the target's private chambers, then Force-choked him while he worked at his desk. Escaping had been just as simple. To date, he was sure no one knew what had really happened that night.

Seeing the world brought back memories of his first pilot, a dour old sergeant who rarely spoke and who flew the *Rogue Shadow* like it was an ore barge. Like the murdered aide, he hadn't lasted long. Tardiness wasn't tolerated in Darth Vader's employ.

That mission had been five years ago, but the Starkiller in his mind seemed barely a child to him now. So much had changed since then. He had died at least once, for starters . . .

The crowd on the ground cleared his head of any kind of nostalgia. Spaceports were typically chaotic, but this one broke all the records. Since the collapse of Imperial control, all manner of beings roamed the streets, free to pursue whatever dreams or fancies took them. Starkiller kept his guard up, and his senses tuned for Kota. The old man had said that he was heading here after Commenor, and he had definitely arrived. Starkiller recognized that mix of anger and self-control anywhere.

The trail led him to a market, and from there to a machine repair shop. A cover, he assumed. Kota was very close now.

He went inside. It looked perfectly innocent, from the mess of spare parts to the three-eyed Gran behind the counter. Behind the façade, though, Starkiller could sense something very different.

"The Jedi," he said, exactly as he had on Cato Neimoidia. "Where is he?"

"No Jedi here," said the Gran, blinking its eyes one at a time from right to left. "Got something to fix?"

"I'm not a customer." He raised and passed his hand in front of the Gran's face. "You'll show me the way."

The Gran couldn't resist the Force. Starkiller's suggestion was as implacable as gravity, made all the more irresistible by his urgent need. The Gran pointed hesitantly at the shelves. There was no door visible. Starkiller didn't have the patience for guesswork, not when Juno's life might be at stake.

He faced the wall and Force-pushed, gently at first but with growing insistence. Machine parts rattled and shook. Glass smashed. With a groan and squeak of tortured metal, a section of the wall began to swing back.

There was movement on the far side. Someone fired

at him. He deflected the bolt effortlessly into the ground and leapt through the gap, sending what seemed like a mountain of spare parts flying ahead of him.

A green lightsaber flashed toward him. He blocked it with both of his. By the mixed light of their blades, he recognized Kota's face, and Kota recognized his in return.

The general performed a startled double take.

"What's with you, boy?" he asked, deactivating his weapon and stepping away. "You could've knocked."

"I'm in a hurry." Starkiller kept one lightsaber at the ready. The space was large and cluttered—not helped by the mess he had made on the way in—and he hadn't yet pinned down the location of the person who had fired the blaster at him. "I need to find the Alliance fleet."

"You've had a change of heart, then."

"I wouldn't say that. The fleet's about to be attacked. I need to stop that from happening at all cost."

"Lots of people looking for the fleet at the moment," said a voice out of the shadows. "Not all of them friendly."

Starkiller turned. Into the light stepped a broad-shouldered man holding an energy weapon trained at his head. His walked with an unusual gait and a strange whining noise. As he approached, Starkiller realized why.

His legs were gone. In their place were three multi-jointed prosthetics tipped with rubber "feet." They moved with a complicated grace that had nothing to do with the way ordinary humans walked.

"Who are you?"

"I'm the repairman," he said. "The name's Shyre. What's yours?"

"I don't have one anymore. Is that a problem?"

"That depends. Do you vouch for him, General?"

"I do."

"He part of your new squad? A spy, perhaps?"

"Not exactly."

"So how does he know the fleet's about to be attacked?"

"It's a long story," Starkiller said.

"I'm all ears."

"I had a vision," he said, directing his words to Kota. It didn't matter what Shyre thought. "The fleet was near a nebula, one I've never seen before. It was taken by surprise. Several fighters got through the defenses. Juno's ship was hit. She was hurt. Then I saw her die."

"Juno?" asked Shyre, lowering his weapon.

Starkiller glanced at him. "I don't know whether I was seeing something that happened in the past or the future, but every second you hold me up makes it more likely I won't be able to fix it."

"She was here yesterday," Shyre said. "I told her where to find the fleet. It's stationed just off Itani Nebula."

"Thank you," Starkiller said, deactivating his lightsaber. "That's all I need to know."

He turned to leave, but Kota stood in his way. The general's armor was still battered and bloodstained, but he had regained his strength and confidence.

"Just slow down, boy. How do you know this isn't a trap?"

"It might well be," he said. "Vader is hunting me. I saw that, too."

"What if the vision was a fake? You should at least

think it through before charging off on your own."

Starkiller saw the sense in that. There were inconsistencies in what he had seen that had bothered him ever since Dagobah. Painful though the events of the vision were, he forced himself to remember them, searching for incriminating details. If it *was* a fake, then maybe the other visions were, too.

"She was the captain of a frigate," he said, "but you told me that. I only got a glimpse of the instruments. It looked like a Nebulon-B. It was called the *Salvation*."

Kota nodded. "That's her ship, all right."

"Her second in command was an alien of some kind."

"Bothan."

"But I saw PROXY," he said, "and that can't be correct, can it?"

"She and Bail Organa found your droid on Corellia. She must have gotten him working again."

Kota and Shyre exchanged glances.

"Sounds real to me," said Shyre. "So what are we going to do about it?"

"You're not doing anything," Starkiller said. "I'll handle this."

"You won't get within a parsec of the fleet without me," said Kota. "You don't have the authorization codes."

"So give them to me."

"Are you ready to expose yourself like this? Have you thought through what'll happen when you turn up in the middle of the fleet as though you've never been away?"

Starkiller hadn't, but he was beginning to now. If the Rebellion was as riven by arguments as Kota had said—and if Kota had told anyone else about the Jedi Starkiller had murdered—then his arrival would be like an anti-matter bomb going off among them. It might take months for the pieces to come back together, if they ever did. Rushing in might end up placing Juno in more peril, in the long run.

"All right," he said. "You're coming with me."

"And if I'm coming, so's my squad. I'll call them and they'll be ready to lift off within the hour."

"I don't know—"

"How many ships did you see in your vision?"

"Seven, maybe eight."

"Let my crew handle them while you look after Juno. Besides, they need to bond. Fighting Imperials is just the thing for that."

Kota held out his hand, and Starkiller, resigned to the sense the general was making, shook it.

"You move fast, old man."

"Stand still too long and you're dead."

Kota left the workshop to call his squad, leaving Starkiller momentarily alone with the repairman.

Shyre was staring at him with an odd expression on his face.

"You're *him,*" he said.

A crawling sensation went up Starkiller's spine. "Him who?"

"Juno told me about you. You flew together. She told me she—" A pained expression flashed across Shyre's face. "She told me you died."

Starkiller didn't hesitate. He didn't need people talking

about him behind his back, not when Darth Vader was sending bounty hunters across the galaxy in search of him. The wrong word in the wrong ear could bring about a much greater disaster than the one he was trying to prevent.

He took three steps closer to Shyre and raised his left hand.

"You don't know me," he said.

The repairman stiffened and his voice took on a distant tone. "I don't know you."

"I was never here."

"You were never here."

"Neither were Kota and Juno."

"Neither was Kota."

"Or Juno."

Shyre's jaw muscles worked. "Or Juno."

"Good. You've got a lot to clean up and you'd better get on with it."

"Okay, well, I've got a huge mess to clean up here. Guess I'd better get on with it."

Starkiller released his hold over him. Shyre turned and went looking for a broom. Starkiller left him to it.

KOTA'S SQUAD HAD A SHIP, a modified Ghtroc 630 freighter that had seen extensive action, judging by the carbon scoring on the hull and the slightly cockeyed look to its drives. Kota arranged for them to assemble at the ship, a dozen berths up from the *Rogue Shadow*. Starkiller didn't want to meet them, but Kota insisted.

"The medic, at least. There's something you need to hear."

Starkiller grudgingly consented to listen. They found a quiet corner in a smoky cantina where the three of them could talk in private.

"Ni-Ke-Vanz." The medic was a fast-talking Cerean with a high domed skull and amazingly elaborate eyebrows. They rose up and down rapidly as he talked, providing a visual counterpoint to his words. "Kota tells me you want to make a clone."

That was news to him, but he could guess where it was going. "Do you know how it's done?"

"I ought to. For five years I worked with a Khommite. They're the galaxy's experts at this kind of thing."

"Where was this?"

"On Kessel."

"I didn't know they had cloning facilities there."

"They didn't," said Ni-Ke-Vanz. "We were slaves."

Of course. Starkiller indicated that he should continue.

"The Khommites have been cloning themselves for a thousand years and they've got it down to a fine art. It defines their entire culture. They have certain lines they reproduce over and over again—lines that are good at teaching, good at art, good at politics, and so on. Each line is basically the same person made multiple times over. On the whole planet, there might be only a few dozen true individuals. The rest are just repeats, passed on down the generations."

"That's not the kind of thing I'm after," said Starkiller.

"I know, I know. You're after immortality. Everyone is when it comes to clones. Either that or an army, and even the Emperor's worked out that this doesn't work in the long run. It's too expensive and dangerous. An army made up of the same soldier is either one hundred percent loyal or one hundred percent against you. When your enemy has to convince only one mind to turn, you're walking on thin ice."

"I don't want an army," Starkiller assured him. "Tell me what I need to know."

"You need to know that cloning won't make you immortal, either."

"Why not?"

"They've never managed to fix the memory problem. Not even the Khommites. Each clone they make is a new person—one based to a very large degree on the original, but still one that has its own identity, its own memories, its own weird quirks. They don't think they're the same people, just different versions of the same template. And that's not immortality. Sorry."

"I've often wondered," said Kota, leaning into the conversation, "why the Jedi didn't just clone ourselves after Order Sixty-six. I mean, there weren't many of us left. Why not take the ones we *did* have and create some more? It wouldn't matter if we didn't think we were the same person. We wouldn't have to, as long as we could fight."

"Ah, well now, that's an entirely different problem." Ni-Ke-Vanz leaned forward, too. His eyebrows attained a whole new level of animation. "You see, the other thing no one has ever managed to copy is Force sensitivity. Worse than that, it actually gets in the way of the cloning process. We don't know how. It just does. The Khommites are aware of the problem and they do everything they can to stamp it out."

Starkiller's surprise must have shown on his face, for the medic nodded emphatically at him.

"That's right: They *weed out* Force sensitivity. Can you imagine? That's how big a problem it is."

"What would happen if you tried to clone someone Force-sensitive anyway?"

Ni-Ke-Vanz sank back into his seat with a dire look on his long face. "Terrible things. Insanity. Psychosis. Suicidal tendencies. Who wants a crazy Force-sensitive running amok in your lab? No one."

"No one," agreed Starkiller, thinking of Kamino and the damage he'd left in his wake.

"Sorry," said Ni-Ke-Vanz, misreading his grim mood for disappointment. "Looks like you're going to have to ride out the war with the rest of us."

"That's not—" he started to object. Then thought better of it. "Right. No pain, no gain. Guess I'd better get used to it."

THEY LEFT THE CANTINA and headed back to the ships. Starkiller left Kota to organize his squad, not particularly caring about the band of mercenaries and wannabe heroes he'd assembled in little more than a day. They would perhaps be useful in preventing any kind of harm coming to Juno—and Starkiller was more than happy to employ them in that regard—but he doubted their involvement together would extend far beyond the end of the mission, whichever way it went.

Juno's voice spoke to him from his memory.

"*We can help each other.*"

"*Nobody can help me.*"

"*I don't think you really mean that. I just think you're afraid to let me try.*"

"*Is that really what you think?*" he had asked. "*I'm afraid of you?*"

The very suggestion had seemed preposterous then, but it didn't anymore. Just the thought of Juno had a profound effect on him. He would slash his way through a hundred Emperors to save her, if he had to. There was nothing he wouldn't sacrifice. Not even the very Rebellion that the original Starkiller had created.

That truly *was* a frightening thought, one he kept carefully hidden from Kota.

The engines were warm and ready by the time the general walked up the ramp and into the bridge.

"You don't look terribly reassured," Kota said, taking the copilot's seat.

"Should I be?"

The *Rogue Shadow* lifted off with a louder roar than usual as the repulsors fought the intense gravity of the world. Turning the ship nose-upward, Starkiller aimed for the sky. Over the screaming of the drives, conversation was temporarily impossible.

Blue turned to black, and the first stars appeared. Dodging heavy orbital traffic, Starkiller didn't wait for the squad's disreputable freighter. He would meet them at the other end.

Space stretched and tore. The *Rogue Shadow* leapt

into hyperspace and began the flight for the Itani Nebula.

"Of course you should feel reassured," said Kota, with a persistence that shouldn't have surprised him. For more than fifteen years the Emperor and all his minions had been hunting the Jedi. It took a mammoth kind of stubbornness to have survived so long against such odds. "You're on your way to see Juno. You've got reinforcements. And best of all you know you can't be a clone."

"So why haven't you told anyone I'm back?"

"How do you know that?"

"Because the repairman didn't know. And the way he was talking, Juno didn't know, either."

"Well, I figure that's your business, who you tell and who you don't."

"Back in Athega system, you said it was entirely the Alliance's business."

"Maybe you convinced me to stay out of it until you're ready. There are already too many confused people running this Rebellion. Are you saying you're ready now?"

He searched his feelings. "No. Not until Juno is safe."

"And she'll probably need to see you with her own eyes, otherwise she won't believe that you're really back."

"I keep telling you: I'm not him."

The general's blind stare was full of disbelief. "Even now you think that, after everything Ni-Ke-Vanz said?"

"He didn't really tell us anything."

"Only that cloned Jedi can't exist."

"Have never existed in the past. That's an entirely different thing."

"The Khommites have been grappling with the problem for a thousand years! Do you think Vader solved it overnight?"

"With the help of the Kaminoans, maybe. Or they didn't solve it and I am as crazy as I feel sometimes."

"You act no crazier than you originally did." Kota wasn't joking. "A bit more obsessive, perhaps, but who can blame you? You love her. It's only natural to want to save her."

You love her.

Starkiller could say nothing to that for a moment. Those three words hit him harder than he could have anticipated. Not just because it was Kota saying them— Kota, the gruff career soldier who had never displayed the slightest amount of emotional awareness in Starkiller's presence. Because it was the present tense, not the past, and because it was about him.

There was a world of difference between Juno, the woman he loved, and Juno, the woman Starkiller *had* loved.

Perversely, that only deepened the blackness of his mood. Did he have the right to love anyone, if he was only a clone? She had loved the original, not him. What if she rejected him? What if she had put the original behind her and had no room in her life for him now? She was a captain in the Rebel Alliance; she had duties, responsibilities, staff, timetables. She couldn't drop everything and run off with him—and there was no guarantee that the rest of the Rebellion would accept him if he wanted to stay.

"Who wants a crazy Force-sensitive running amok in your lab?"

Acknowledging that he was a psychotic clone who would never be worthy of either Juno or the Rebellion was somehow more acceptable than believing that he was the real Starkiller, who, beyond all kinds of understanding, had managed to return from the dead.

To kill again.

Kota got out of his seat and opened a small wall compartment. He rummaged inside for a moment, then his right fist emerged, tightly holding something in its grip. He returned to Starkiller's side and opened his hand to reveal what he had found. There lay two bright crystals, as blue as Juno's eyes.

"Where did you get these?" Starkiller asked.

"Relics of the Clone War. It doesn't matter. The point is, they're yours if you want them."

Kota pushed his hand toward Starkiller, who made no move to take them.

"Does this mean you believe I'm not a clone?" he asked.

The general exhaled heavily. "Honestly? I don't know. But I'm beginning to think it doesn't matter."

Again the blind eyes pinned him, but for once they revealed more about Kota than the person he was looking at. Starkiller could feel the hatred churning inside the general as powerfully as it ever had. It was part of him that he had learned to live with, like his blindness. Sometimes it gave him strength; sometimes it worked against him. Starkiller couldn't imagine what it must have been like after Order 66, balancing the need to survive against the absolute requirement of all true Jedi Knights—that they never succumb to the dark side.

Kota's hatred was directed at the Emperor, but its focus was Darth Vader. Starkiller didn't know why; there were probably a thousand reasons, reasons Kota himself would never reveal or dwell upon, most likely. The general wasn't one for living in the past, or for worrying about the means as long as the end was in sight. To him, the return of Starkiller was an opportunity to strike at Darth Vader, just as, to Starkiller, Kota was a means of finding and saving Juno.

You love her.

Some obsessions were worth it. Starkiller took the crystals and made his way back to the meditation chamber, seeking a peace he suspected the general would never find.

THEY WERE MET AT NORDRA by outliers of the fleet and given the coordinates they needed. Kota quizzed them about recent traffic. There had been some, but nothing suspicious. Juno herself had come through less than a day earlier.

Starkiller felt all his hopes and fears magnify at that simple confirmation of fact. She was close, so very close. Soon he would be with her. What happened after that, only time and fate would tell.

The squad's freighter wasn't far behind the *Rogue Shadow*. For all its lopsided engines, it could clearly hold its own. The convoy of two headed off toward the nebula, scanners peeled for anything out of the ordinary. Slowly, slowly, the kaleidoscopic view shifted ahead of them.

"This is taking too long," Starkiller said through grinding teeth. "I'm using the hyperdrive."

"The mass shadow of the nebula—"

"I don't care." His hands flew across the controls. "The others can come the long way if you want."

"They'd better. None of them is as good a pilot as you."

Starkiller acknowledged the compliment with a brisk nod. When the navicomp was ready, he sat for a moment with his hands on the controls.

"I've been thinking," he said slowly, "about the Alliance."

"About your place in it?"

He shook his head. "About what it should do next. If I give you the nav coordinates and schematics for a secret cloning facility on Kamino—everything needed to launch a successful assault—will that go some way toward helping them believe in me again?"

Kota chewed this over. "The facility where Vader claims you were made?"

"If his claims are true, then Kamino is much more of a threat than any ordinary stormtrooper factory."

"Maybe. But the Alliance couldn't pull off an attack like this without your help."

"They'll have to," he said. He activated the drives. Realspace smeared and stretched, vanished into the paradoxical light of hyperspace. "They wouldn't trust me to lead anything yet, anyway."

"I would."

"The Alliance is more than just you and your militia, Kota."

Instead of being offended, the general grinned. "If what you saw comes to pass, you'll be glad you picked us up."

Starkiller acknowledged that, but his mind was unchanged. Judging by everything he'd learned from Kota, the Alliance didn't need someone to lead them into battle. It needed to find strong leadership among the leaders it already had.

The ship shook, disturbed by the widely distributed mass of the nebula. He gripped the console, urging it to fly straight by the force of his will. This had to work. He had to arrive on time. There was simply no other option.

The *Rogue Shadow* exploded out of hyperspace, tumbling wildly. He corrected its trim automatically, firing retros even as he searched the scopes for the fleet. The sky was a mess of glowing gas and light. The scanners picked up two minor asteroid fields, a distant protostar with a single gas giant, and, finally, a small scattering of starships.

He brought the ship about, ion engines blazing.

"No sign of attack," he said.

"Stay on guard," said Kota. "A powerful glimpse of the future like you experienced is rarely wrong."

The fleet grew larger and more detailed through the cockpit viewport. Starkiller searched the ships for the one he was after. He recognized the *Salvation* more by instinct than knowledge. Like all Nebulon-B frigates, it was heavy at fore and aft, with a relatively thin spine connecting each end. Engines and reactor were confined to the rear; command and crew quarters were up front, near primary communications and sensor arrays. This example looked old but well maintained, a reliable worker that had found a good home with the Rebel Alliance.

The *Salvation* wasn't the biggest or the newest ship in the fleet. But Juno was inside it. He was sure of it. Finally he had found her.

"*Rogue Shadow*," came a voice over the comm, "please transmit landing codes."

Starkiller froze at the sight of something on the side of the approaching frigate.

"What is it, boy?"

He could only point at the crest adorning the *Salvation*—adorning every ship in the fleet, he saw as they grew nearer. He remembered seeing it only once before, on Kashyyyk, but he knew what it was. It had been an integral part of the life Darth Vader had stolen from him, when he was a child.

"My family's crest," he said. "It's . . . everywhere."

"Yes," said Kota, tapping the chest plate of his armor—where, Starkiller belatedly realized, the same symbol lay buried under a thick layer of muck. "I suppose I should've told you about that."

"What does it mean?"

"That you're part of the Rebel Alliance whether you want to be or not."

"*Rogue Shadow*," came the voice from the fleet a second time, "landing codes immediately."

Four Y-wings were nosing in their direction—to either escort or intercept, Starkiller thought through the fog of surprise.

Kota leaned over and punched the comlink.

"This is General Rahm Kota," he said, "requesting permission to board the *Salvation*. Authorization Talus Haroon Ten Eleven Thirty-eight."

The voice didn't respond immediately. When it did, there was no mistaking the surprise. "Code checks out. Good to have you back, General. You're cleared for docking."

The Y-wings peeled away.

"If you give me the data on Kamino," said Kota, "I'll do what needs to be done."

Starkiller leaned forward and peered through the canopy at the *Salvation*. The crest painted on the hull loomed over him like a shadow.

His father's voice came to him from the deepest refuges of his memory.

"I never wanted this for you."

He sensed the final pieces falling into place, the last of the gaps closing up. He was here, on the brink of seeing Juno again, and his mind was whole. Whoever he was, wherever he had come from, he was complete.

He only hoped, against hope, that he would be enough.

CHAPTER 12

Juno stood on the bridge of the *Salvation,* feeling the smooth operation of the ship and crew around her as though they were parts of her physical body. With a change of uniform and a decent meal in the recent past, she felt entirely transformed. Being restored to command had felt like being returned to life. There was indeed something in what Leia had said about having a frigate at her disposal: It was truly nothing to be sniffed at.

At the back of her mind, though, was something her flight instructor had drummed into her all the way through her training. Getting too comfortable was just asking for the universe to provide a kick in the pants. She went through everything that had happened in recent days, searching for the one thing that had gone wrong, for the boot that might already be on its way to shake her out of her complacency.

"Uh, Captain," said Nitram with surprising hesitancy, "we have the *Rogue Shadow* in view."

"Impossible," Juno said automatically, assuming

someone had made a mistake. "It was destroyed on Cato Neimoidia."

But even as she said the words, she saw it in the scopes, accelerating smoothly toward her.

"It can't be him," she said to herself through a stab of surprise and guilt in equal measures.

Then a more likely possibility occurred to her: "The Imperials must have captured it and are using it as a disguise. Target it—all weapons!"

The bridge crew jumped into life around her. Alert sirens wailed.

Then Kota's voice boomed out of the comm.

"This is General Rahm Kota, requesting permission to board the Salvation."

"He can't be," she repeated, barely hearing the authorization code he gave. "It *can't* be him."

"Captain?"

She blinked. "If it's a trick, there's only one way to find out. Let him board. We'll greet him with every soldier available."

"Yes, sir."

She stood straighter and kept her hands behind her back. They were clenched into fists.

You abandoned him, she told herself. *You gave up on him. You left him behind.*

Any relief she felt at the possibility of his survival was buried under the crushing weight of remorse.

"Blackguard to Blackout," came Kota's voice over the comm.

"I'll take it," she said, reaching for her comlink.

Nitram patched the transmission directly through to her.

"This is Blackout," she said, taking a deep breath. "What's your status, Blackguard?"

"Back in the game," he said with obvious relish. "I have intel on a major target that I can't take out on my own. Do you think the Alliance will be interested?"

The meeting with Mon Mothma, Garm Bel Iblis, and Bail Organa was still fresh in her mind. "I think they'll be very interested, Kota."

"Good. Here it comes."

A second later the intel arrived on the bridge. She picked up a datapad and scrolled through the files, seeing floor plans, security systems, troop deployments—everything the fleet needed to ensure a victory over what appeared at first to be some kind of Imperial medical base. No, she realized: a *cloning* operation. It was way past the Outer Rim, too far for reinforcements to come in time, but obviously important, or else it wouldn't be hidden so far off the usual hyperroutes. One of many such super-secret facilities supplying stormtroopers for the Emperor's ever-expanding army, she assumed.

"Looks good," she said, hiding a rising excitement. There was only one problem: Without knowing the provenance of the data, she couldn't be entirely sure it wasn't misinformation, even a trap. "Where did you get this intel, Kota?"

There was a pause. She thought she heard movement on the other end of the open line.

"It's best you see for yourself," he finally said. "We'll

be aboard in a few minutes. Meet us then."

"Will you also tell me how you killed Baron Tarko and got off Cato Neimoidia?"

There was another pause, shorter than the last.

"You did the right thing, Juno. I would've done the same."

The line disconnected with a *click*.

She looked down at the comlink in her hand, feeling simultaneously drained and buoyed. Kota's return, with or without the data, was a momentous turnaround for the Alliance. The mission to Cato Neimoidia really could be considered a success now. They had lost nothing and succeeded on every front. Mon Mothma would find it much harder to argue against such missions in the future.

If Kota was the boot, it was suspiciously wrapped in velvet.

Nitram was staring at her with an expression that mirrored her own feelings—and she understood, suddenly, that he was the one who had informed the Alliance leadership of her activities with Kota. He, her loyal second in command, was also a loyal Alliance soldier, wanting to do the right thing for the cause. It was only natural that he would experience the same internal conflict she had over helping Kota in his unsanctioned activities: he wasn't an automaton, after all.

Instead of feeling betrayed, Juno felt nothing but sympathy. How long had he agonized over what to do? Why hadn't he come to talk to her first? What was he feeling now that the right thing he *thought* he had done turned out to be utterly baseless?

He opened his mouth as though to say something, but an alarm cut him off. He turned and checked the console in front of him.

"I'm having trouble with the forward sensor array, Captain."

She studied the display screens around her.

"Interference from the nebula?" They had been having the occasional blackout ever since the fleet took up its current station, the result of nothing more sinister than natural forces.

PROXY was examining the problem, too. He looked up with bright yellow eyes. "Perhaps. I'll try to pin it down."

She considered numerous factors at once: the arrival of Kota, the promise of a target, this strange glitch in the sensor array . . .

It added up to something, but she didn't know what it was.

"Let's not take any chances," she said, punching the all-stations button on the console in front of her.

"This is Captain Eclipse," she said. Her voice echoed back at her from throughout the frigate. "Set defensive protocols throughout all ships. Prime your shields and check your scanners for anything that's not one of ours."

Nitram nodded, still checking the screens. "All clear, Captain."

"Keep looking, Nitram. We can't be too careful."

"Of course, sir."

In a secondary screen, she saw the blip representing the *Rogue Shadow* coming in to dock. She watched it, wondering what its arrival foretold. Something nagged at her, an instinct that had for the moment no precise focus. The ground was shifting under her, but the landscape hadn't changed yet. At any moment, she expected her whole world to be overturned.

A light flashed on the display in front of her, signaling a private call from Viedas. He probably wanted to ask about her alert—not that there was anything wrong with reminding the crews of the various ships that they should be on constant guard against discovery and attack. Complacency had killed more soldiers than the craziest battle-lust.

She reached for the comlink to answer the call.

A voice crackling over the comm beat her to it.

"Captain Eclipse—we're picking up five, no, six small warships, coming in fa—"

There it is, she thought, turning her attention to the screens. The *Lexi Dio,* an assault bomber, was under attack. Bright explosions pockmarked its hull. The missiles came from two of seven small vessels darting and weaving across the sky. Whoever was piloting them was good: The next four missiles split the *Lexi Dio* from nose to stern, resulting in the decompression and death of everyone aboard.

Horrified, she gripped the console with both hands. Where had the ships come from? They hadn't come out of hyperspace or the fleet would have noticed them. The same with the nearby asteroid fields—unless they had cloaking systems as sophisticated as the *Rogue Shadow*'s, which meant they weren't standard Imperial manufacture.

Where they came from took second place as all seven vessels turned their attention to the *Salvation* and began attacking.

"Shields to full," she called over the intercom. "Open fire, all batteries."

A coded signal came from Commodore Viedas. Around her, the fleet began to break apart—standard protocol in the event of discovery. A new rendezvous point lay in a code cylinder carried by every ship's commander. The surviving ships would regroup in that location, and the fleet would count its losses. Juno vowed not to be like the poor *Lexi Dio*.

A missile got past the shields and exploded in the engineering section, making the deck shift beneath her. Red lights began to flash, signaling vents and structural damage near the hyperdrive. Four of the seven ships were targeting the main spine but found stiff opposition from the frigate's Y-wing escort. As she watched, one of the remaining three hostiles rammed the *Salvation,* just aft of the surgery suite. The ship didn't explode. Lodged nose-first in the hull of the larger vessel, its engines flickered and shut down.

"We've been breached," barked her second in command. "Troopers boarding!"

"Send a security detail to the main reactor. Seal off life support."

A much more powerful impact sent crew flying. Juno gripped the console for dear life. Diagnostic systems showed red in the forward sensor unit.

"Get those deflector shields up!" she shouted into the

intercom. Another hit like that and the frigate would be effectively blind.

She checked internal cameras. They were flickering, full of static. Through thickening smoke she glimpsed her crew fighting both fires and invading troops. The latter flickered and shimmered as though they had cloaking systems of their own. She had never heard of such things. Luckily they were struggling in a complex, ship-bound environment. Only against relatively still backgrounds did they have a clear advantage, and there weren't many of those on the *Salvation* at that moment.

The ship couldn't risk jumping until the hyperdrive was looked at. Their only option now was to fight.

A metal hand took her shoulder. PROXY's yellow eyes filled her vision. "Security beacons are going crazy. Captain Eclipse, I think we should—"

Before he could finish the sentence, the bridge doors blew inward. She raised a hand to protect her face. Burning shards peppered Juno's skin, followed by a wave of intense heat. She ducked instinctively, along with everyone else on the bridge. Blaster bolts speared out of the cloud, fired by two stormtroopers wielding high-powered rifles. Juno's right hand found the blaster at her side. She had never fired it on the frigate before. When she'd strapped it on an hour ago she'd had no conception that she would be doing so now.

The universe's boot was firmly in play now.

She came out from behind the main display console and released two bolts twice, fast, then ducked back down again before she drew return fire. The first shot took out one of the troopers. She heard his respirator wheezing as he went down, showering sparks. The second missed by a margin small enough to spook. She braced herself to fire at him a second time, but the arrival of four more troopers put paid to that plan.

She wasn't the only one defending the ship. Nitram was crouched behind a display like her, peppering the troopers whenever they crossed his line of fire. PROXY had taken the blaster from a fallen navigator and was using it to harass the invaders, his image displaying a flickering form of camouflage of his own. Juno saw her own features come and go, with hints of Mon Mothma and Leia, too. There didn't seem any rhyme or reason to it, but she didn't have the time to think it through just then.

The sound of fighting echoed all through the ship, not just in the bridge. Reports came from soldiers in a steady stream, but went unheard. Two more troopers went down near the entrance, taken out by concentrated fire from three sides. Juno rolled to a new position, covered by Nitram. He may have ratted on her to Mon Mothma, but against the Imperials she could trust him implicitly.

Her goal was to stop the troopers reaching the main console, even if it killed her. That was the symbol of her command. They weren't going to get their hands on it.

Even as she blasted another trooper to oblivion, the smoke swirled oddly between the walls where the bridge doors used to be. The small hairs on her arms stood on end. Ships with cloaking systems, troopers with camouflage— how was she supposed to fight an invisible enemy?

She targeted the swirls, to some effect. One lucky hit killed the camouflage of one of the troopers, and she finished him off with a second shot. But she had no idea how many had arrived with him, how many were left to fight. There could be no others at all, or dozens already in the bridge. Perhaps if she killed the lights, they would all be at a disadvantage . . .

Even as she thought that, PROXY was hit in the chest. He went over backward, showering sparks, innards screeching. She couldn't tell where the shot had come from. Nitram was next, shot from behind by someone he couldn't even see.

The muscles in her jaw were like rock. The unfairness of the fight appalled her. Scrabbling for PROXY's fallen blaster, she stood up tall and began firing at random with both hands, screaming her rage and frustration.

From the corner of the bridge, where the smoke was thinnest, came the shot that put her out of action. The trooper might have been standing there for minutes, unseen, awaiting each opportunity as it came. She had given him one, and he took it.

The shot hit her in the shoulder, almost knocking her down. Her right arm went limp and the blaster she held in that hand went flying. The pain was unbelievable. She fell to one knee, then ground her teeth even tighter and raised her left hand to fire at the trooper who had shot her. Her aim was good. He flickered back into visibility and crumpled forward.

Her satisfaction was short-lived. A bolt of energy flashed past her, and the pistol exploded from her hand.

She stared at the hand, momentarily surprised to see that she still had fingers. Some type of stun weapon, obviously. A trooper stepped toward her through the smoke, holding his weapon at the ready, just in case she had another blaster secreted on her somewhere.

She didn't. Neither did anyone on the bridge. They were all dead. The pain in her shoulder peaked, making the world seem gray and distant.

The figure came closer. He seemed enormous. He wasn't a trooper at all, she distantly realized. His armor was green.

"Who—?"

He didn't let her finish the question. His blaster flared again, as bright as a sun, and the world vanished.

CHAPTER 13

STARKILLER HAD JUST SECURED the *Rogue Shadow* when the first of the proximity alarms went off. He watched the initial attack unfold from the bridge, with Kota leaning close over his shoulder. What Kota "saw," exactly, through his heightened senses, Starkiller didn't know. But he was keeping up: that was the important thing.

"The asteroids," Starkiller said, hastily scanning the surrounding space. "That's where they were hiding."

"They must have been lying dormant ever since the fleet arrived." Kota's right hand rested on the grip of his lightsaber. "What brought them out of hiding now?"

There was only one possible answer. "Me," Starkiller said. "It's one of Vader's bounty hunters. He found out where the fleet was due to gather next and, instead of turning it in to the Imperial Navy, waited here until I showed up. Now he's springing his trap."

"We should leave," said Kota. "Give him the slip."

Starkiller shook his head as, on the screen in front of

him, a small assault bomber was ripped apart. "I have to get to Juno before she's hurt."

"Even if it means putting yourself at risk?"

"Our bounty hunter friend will find it works the other way around."

Starkiller checked the disposition of the attacking ships. They were homing in on the *Salvation*, exactly as expected now that the *Rogue Shadow* was docked alongside it. One of the larger ships was heaving around to ram. If the move was successful, that would give the hostiles easy access to the frigate.

Around them, the fleet was dispersing, protecting the ships that could be saved before a much larger Imperial presence arrived. Only he and Kota knew that there were no other ships coming.

"Your new squad shouldn't be far away," he told Kota. "Call them by comlink when they're in range. They can keep the fight going outside while we get to Juno. Come on."

He hurried from the bridge and through the air lock. Even as he went, the frigate shook from a massive impact, presumably the ship ramming into its hull. He braced himself to ride out the impact, estimating that it came from the forward half of the ship. If the boarding maneuver had been successful, that meant there would be hostiles between them and the *Salvation*'s bridge.

For a split instant he felt a crippling sense of guilt. He and Kota had had the chance to warn Juno that something was going to happen, while they were approaching her ship, but they hadn't taken it. By not doing so, they might inadvertently have helped the vision he received come true.

The feeling didn't last. The future was always in motion. If willpower alone couldn't change it, then brute force would have to do.

The deck steadied underfoot. He lit both his lightsabers, now brilliant, fiery blue, as they had been on Dagobah, and leapt through the docking tube into the *Salvation*. The lights were flickering relentlessly from on to off, red to black, creating a surreal landscape full of smoke and sparks. Figures moved ahead of them, but it was impossible for the moment to tell who was on what side.

Kota rushed forward, sensing directly through the Force and therefore unimpaired by lack of light or visual distractions.

Starkiller watched his back, happy for him to take the lead. His concentration was taking a hit from more than just the lack of light. Being so close to Juno and yet still separated from her was a constant distraction. Until they were in the same room together—better yet, in each other's arms—he would remain on edge.

The figures he had seen at the end of the corridor were Alliance soldiers, firing around a corner at a trio of Imperial stormtroopers who had formed a barricade across a major intersection. Wind whistled around them: Clearly shields and self-repair facilities hadn't quite sealed off the breach formed by the ramming ship. Flecks of ash and soot swirled in short-lived eddies as Kota ran boldly toward the barricade, deflecting every shot that came at him back to the person who fired it. White-armored limbs flailed as the troopers went down. Starkiller waved for the Alliance soldiers to secure the position while he and the general carried on toward the bridge.

They passed the surgery suite, where medics were patching up crew members hit during the early strikes. The suite itself had been hit, creating a chaotic, body-strewn battle hospital where a sterile environment should have been. Starkiller didn't doubt the surgery had been deliberately targeted. The ship had a complement of more than a thousand; the more crew members the attackers could put permanently out of action, the better for the invaders.

Explosions boomed in the major access tubes leading toward the forward compartments. Starkiller and Kota headed straight for them, ignoring the trams that occasionally whizzed overhead. They were too vulnerable to sabotage and ambush. Better to run, Starkiller thought. What he lost in speed he more than gained in the surety of getting where he needed to go. Nothing would stop him getting to the bridge, to Juno.

They reached the impact site of the ramming ship. No one guarded it. Clearly the stormtroopers had another way off the ship, or they expected to take control and fly the frigate itself. Either way, a blackened trail led forward from the site, cutting through walls and blast doors, heading in a perfectly straight line through the ship. Dead Rebels lay everywhere, sprawled or slouched where they had fallen. There were a lot of them. Too many.

"Juno trained this crew?" Starkiller asked Kota.

"Yes."

"They know how to fight, then—which means they're not fighting ordinary troopers."

Starkiller stooped over a fallen sergeant who clung barely to life.

"Who attacked you? Or what?"

"Out of nowhere," the sergeant breathed. "Invisible."

"Stormtroopers?"

But the Rebel had said his last. His head lolled back to the deck, and Starkiller closed his dead eyes for him.

"Camouflage systems—something new," Kota said. "Keep all your senses alert."

Starkiller nodded, acknowledging another situation in which Kota's odd substitute for sight gave him a unique advantage.

They hurried through the ship with their lightsabers at the ready. Starkiller remembered one of his training sessions, when Darth Vader had placed a blast helmet over his young apprentice's eyes and locked him in a cage with a trio of starved howling rasps. The hunger-maddened birds had pecked and bitten at him until, by sheer necessity, he had learned to listen to what his instincts, not his covered eyes, were telling him. Not one of the birds had survived.

Apart from soldiers clearing away rubble and healing the injured, the way ahead *seemed* clear, but it paid to be too careful.

More explosions came from the decks ahead and below. Their direction of travel became less horizontal, more vertical, as they reached the steeply pitched nose of the ship. He and Kota forwent lifts and descended the dark, booming shafts by their own means. Severed cables snaked around them as they jumped from level to level. The bridge grew rapidly closer.

Blasterfire strobed at them out of a gaping doorway. The lift doors had been blown away and a pair of stormtroopers waited there to make sure no one followed by that means. Starkiller and Kota made short work of them, downing one with his own fire, slashing the other in two once they were in range. Immediately fire came from the next floor down. This time their adversaries weren't visible.

Kota stood over the fallen troopers and pointed down into the shadows. Starkiller could see nothing with his eyes, but he drew the full power of the Force into his hands and blasted the empty air. Blue lightning made short work of the camouflage system of the trooper hiding there. He writhed and sparked until Starkiller released him, letting him drop heavily to the depths below.

They moved more cautiously from then on. The sound of blasterfire echoed around them, but none was aimed at them. The lower decks were where most of the fighting was taking place. Starkiller longed to know what was happening outside, but didn't dare break his concentration to check.

Three invisible troopers guarded the entrance to the bridge level. He blasted his way through them, not giving them the slightest chance to fight back. Four more stood outside the bridge itself. Emergency lighting and smoke made details hard to discern, but it looked like the doors behind them had been blown in.

Starkiller rushed forward. If he was too late—if they had—

Kota cut in front of him, holding him back with one hand on his chest.

"What are you doing?" Starkiller growled as he tried to find a clear line of approach.

"Cool down, boy," said the general. "Fight without hatred, or you'll lose the war."

Starkiller took the advice to heart. He recognized the feelings rising inside him, and he reminded himself where they could lead. He wasn't Darth Vader's servant anymore. He was no instrument of the dark side. He didn't want to find Juno only to have her reject him for being a monster. He needed to be calm, to find himself, to proceed with surety in any direction but toward his doom.

Doing so slowed him down by less than a second. The four troopers fell, sparking and whining, and he was through the shattered doors, into the bridge.

Thick smoke hid the carnage, but he could smell it in the air. A fire was burning and no one was putting it out. He extinguished the flames with one sweep of the Force and sucked the acrid black smoke into the corridor outside. The unnatural wind howled, echoing the tension in his heart.

Bodies everywhere, most in Rebel uniforms. He stepped across them, searching their faces, turning them over when they lay facedown. There—the dog-faced officer he'd seen killed in the vision. No sign of PROXY. Lying in a pool of deep red blood—

Juno.

He ran to her side, stifling a scream growing in his chest. Too late! He had arrived too late! The attack had happened exactly as he had seen it, and now the third of the visions was about to come true. He would hold Juno's body in his arms and—

"Boy," Kota cautioned him. The ship was shaking, echoing his distress. Starkiller tried to rein in his feelings, but they were too overwhelming. If she died, what reason did he have to live?

Juno's eyes opened.

He fell backward in surprise. She stared up at him and tried to lift her head. Only then did he notice that there wasn't a scratch on her, or her uniform. The blood she was been lying in had belonged to someone else.

"Master?"

Sparks flashed through a rent in her skin, and suddenly the illusion failed.

"PROXY!"

"Yes, Master. I—" The droid held his head as though in pain. One of his eyes had shorted, and there was a broad hole in his chest. His left arm was missing from the elbow down. "I was informed that you were dead. So was Captain Eclipse. I believe she will be most surprised to see you."

"She's alive?" Starkiller gripped PROXY by his narrow metal shoulders. "Where? Tell me where!"

The droid's innards ground together, like the workings of a sand-filled machine. His image flickered and changed again, becoming an image of a green-armored man with a T-shaped visor. PROXY's right arm lifted to point at the bridge entrance.

"The Imperials took her toward deck seven," he said, returning to his true form. His arm fell to the deck with a clank. "She is injured."

Starkiller stared at the droid in confusion and alarm. The green armor matched the vision of the bounty hunter he had seen talking to Darth Vader on Kamino, accepting instructions to recapture the missing clone. But what was he playing at? Why invade a ship, effectively destroy its command structure, and not take it over? Why was Juno in particular, the ship's captain, still alive?

Because she was more than just a captain.

She was *bait*.

He stood up, full of a dark and terrible determination.

"Order the attack on Kamino, General," he said, moving for the exit.

Kota looked around him in momentary confusion. "But the crew—"

"Your squad can fly this thing. Inform the rest of the fleet. We need to send Darth Vader the message that we mean business."

"All right, but what about—?"

"Deck seven is the cargo bay. If I hurry, I can cut them off."

Starkiller ignited both his lightsabers and ran out into the smoke.

CHAPTER 14

JUNO STRUGGLED BACK TO CONSCIOUSNESS through thick and suffocating fog. She had been dreaming of the *Empirical,* of being confined to shackles and strung up for weeks on end, with her wrists bleeding and her shoulders aching. The pain seemed utterly immediate and unceasing now, particularly in her left hand and right shoulder. It shouted at her with a voice that was almost audible.

"Wake up, Captain Eclipse. You have to walk now. My troopers are needed elsewhere."

Lights flashed in her eyes. She felt a sharp jab in her neck. Something jetted into her bloodstream with an audible hiss.

Bright alertness rushed through her, accompanied by a sharp taste of metal. She was being held upright by two armored storm- troopers with her head dangling forward and her feet brushing the ground. Her muscles jerked. Pain flared.

Suddenly fully awake, she struggled against the hands

holding her, and tried to pull away from the armored figure standing in front of her. His green-gray duraplast visor came closer, filling her vision.

"You are expendable, Captain Eclipse," said the man within. "I warn you against inconveniencing me too much."

The coldness of his tone convinced her more than his words. She stopped pulling against the stormtroopers who held her and stood as straight as she was able. A third trooper affixed binders around her wrists so her hands were held securely in front of her. The movement pulled at her injured shoulder and prompted another flare-up of pain. She remembered being hit by blasterfire and nothing after that. Someone had applied a field bandage to the wound, which was something, but it meant she couldn't tell how severe it was. The fingers of her left hand were burned and red, otherwise undamaged.

"Why haven't you killed me already?" she asked the man in green. He didn't lack the capacity to do so, judging by the impressive array of blades, dart launchers, and flame projectors strategically placed about his person, not to mention the BlasTech EE-3 carbine rifle he carried in one hand. "While I live, I'll do everything in my power to regain control of the ship."

"It's not your ship I'm after." He waved one gloved hand and the troopers fell away. With the other hand he clipped a chain to her binders. "When my employer is done with you, you can have it back for all I care."

"Your employer—?"

He turned and tugged firmly on the chain. The wrench to her shoulder blotted out all other thoughts but to follow him. Sparks danced in her vision for a moment, and when they cleared the troopers had fallen behind. Her captor was leading her through a broad corridor literally blasted through the ship, one of several, if she remembered the data PROXY had shown her right before the bridge was invaded. It was hard to match its trajectory to the ship's original designs, but she thought they might be headed toward the base of the primary communications array.

"If you have an employer, that makes you a bounty hunter," she said, fishing for information. "At least, you don't look like any kind of Imperial I've ever seen. But you use Imperial troops, so you know people in high places. Is Grand Moff Tarkin still ticked off about what we did on Dac? Is that what this is about?"

The bounty hunter said nothing. They turned a corner and arrived at a vertical shaft.

"You've got a jetpack, but I haven't," she said. "Unless you want me to climb tied up like this . . . ?"

He whistled and from above descended a cable and harness, which he wrapped around her, pinning her arms to her body.

She braced herself for the ascent, but even so, when the cable started moving, she almost blacked out. The pain was incredible. Whoever had put the bandage on had cared less about her comfort than merely stopping the blood flow from the wound.

The roar of the bounty hunter's thrusters ruled out any further conversation. She concentrated instead on trying to find a way out of her predicament. The binders were very tight, so tight her hands were already going numb. No chance of wriggling out of them, then. Her blaster was probably still back on the bridge, and she had no way of calling for help, except by shouting. Thus far she had seen no sign of her crew, anywhere along the route. Chances were they were busy elsewhere, with a diversion staged by the bounty hunter's troopers.

Her best chance of escape, then, lay at the other end of their journey, when the binders came off and her hands were free—and even then she had to hope for a distraction to give her an advantage. There was no way she, injured, could take on an exceedingly well-armed bounty hunter in a fair fight and expect to prevail.

The cable jerked to a halt next to a hole carved in the wall of an empty mess. The bounty hunter came up beside her and landed safely on the deck. His thrusters cut out with a hiss. He reached out and bodily hauled her onto the solid deck. Juno didn't struggle. One wrong step when the cable came off and she'd fall to her death below.

From around her came the sounds of fighting: blasterfire, explosions, screams and shouts, feet running in all directions. The air was laced with a thick, dangerous tang, as though the ship itself were wounded. She hoped the guards she'd stationed at its critical points had managed to repel at least some of the boarders. If she were to die, she didn't want her last recorded act in the Alliance to be the destruction of her ship.

"Whatever your employer is paying you," she said, "the Alliance will double it."

He said nothing, pulling her after him along the charred makeshift corridor.

"You're a man of principle, then?"

"It's about repeat business, and your Alliance most likely won't exist long enough to pay my first fee."

"You're overconfident, like the Emperor."

"I have reason to be. His credit's good."

"Is *he* your employer?"

He said nothing.

"It *must* be Tarkin, then," she said, thinking: *Try to get him talking. Sooner or later he's bound to let something slip*. "He's the only one I can think of with a motive for capturing me. He wants me to be his new slave, right?"

He ignored her.

"Who, then? Who would go to so much trouble?"

"It's not about you."

"But you need me. Why?" An idea struck her. "This is all about Kota, for what he and I did on Cato Neimoidia. It must be—but I didn't think Baron Tarko was so well connected—"

"Quiet."

The bounty hunter had slowed as though sensing danger ahead. She listened but could hear only the sounds of distant demolition, communicated through the floors and walls around her. It sounded like a wrecking droid was coming through the ship toward her.

"At least tell me how you found the fleet," she said. "Who did you torture to get that information?"

He didn't answer.

Behind them, metal tore and glass shattered. The

bounty hunter turned and raised his rifle. Someone or something was coming up through the floor, ten meters away.

Juno stared in shock as a figure dressed entirely in black leapt out of the new hole in the floor, swinging two bright blue blades through the air. The bounty hunter fired at the figure, three precise shots in quick succession. The energy bolts were deflected into the walls, where they discharged with bright flashes. By their light, Juno saw the face of the man running toward her.

It was *him*.

Time stopped. The universe shattered around her. Natural laws unraveled and everything she thought she knew dissolved to nothing.

It was him, but it couldn't be. It couldn't be, but it was. Her heart leapt even as all the pieces fell into place, forming a terrible new pattern. She knew now who the bounty hunter was really seeking, and who was behind the plan. The pattern made sense in an instant, even as everything else seemed to fall apart. Starkiller was heading into a trap, and she was the lure.

Her mind teetered on the brink of hysteria. First Kota and now him. *Doesn't anyone stay dead anymore?*

More questions flooded in.

He's back—but how? And how did the bounty hunter know about him before I did?

The seconds ticked again. Her heart restarted. There was suddenly no more time to think. The man she had loved began to run toward them, his face a mask of fierce determination, and she knew that he had seen her, too.

She opened her mouth to shout a warning, but the bounty hunter shoved her through a doorway, out of view. She jerked to a halt at the end of the chain and went down to her knees, fighting waves of agony. Behind her, she heard Starkiller call her name, but his voice was drowned out on the second syllable by a massive explosion.

Smoke and debris rushed out of the corridor and filled the room. Even out of the blast's direct line she was still stung by the shrapnel. She covered her mouth and closed her eyes an instant too late. Blinking, coughing, deafened, she fought waves of unconsciousness as the bounty hunter dragged her back to her feet and pulled her into the corridor.

Through streaming eyes she saw a huge hole where Starkiller had been standing. Drips of molten metal rained down on the cavernous space below.

"If you killed him—" she started to say.

"You're as foolish as he is," the bounty hunter said with a sneer in his voice. He hurried along the corridor, pulling her after him. The tugs on the chain were sharp and insistent. Between the pain and trying to maintain her footing on the uneven floor, she had no inclination to talk anymore. Wherever he was taking her, he was in a much greater hurry than he had been before.

They left the burned corridor and entered an area that was relatively undamaged. Juno thought she recognized the location, and that was confirmed when she and her captor reached a large double door, lying open in their path. The cargo bay. It was empty apart from a dozen crates and two dead Rebel crew members. Dim red light flickered and played across the vast space. Again she worried about the reactor's functionality.

The bounty hunter tugged her inside and closed the doors behind them. As they slid shut, she caught something moving in the shadows above, but couldn't make out what it was. Not the cargo arm, that was for sure. It was much too big.

Behind them came the sound of destruction once again. The bounty hunter hurried to the matching double door on the far side of the bay, dragging her behind him like a recalcitrant child.

"You have no idea who you're dealing with," she said, and received only silence in reply.

The doors began to open ahead of them, revealing the orange-yellow vista of the Itani Nebula. The fight continued for control of space around the *Salvation*. Energy weapons flashed and flared. Starlight gleamed off wreckage and combative starships alike.

On the other side of the force field preventing them from being sucked into space was a transport the likes of which Juno had never seen before. Too compact to be a freighter but too stocky to be a starfighter, it was much taller than it was either wide or deep, giving it a slightly long-trunked appearance. It had the same functional and highly customized look as the bounty hunter beside her, and Juno had no doubt at all that it belonged to him.

"Shame it's the other side of the force field," she said. "Now what are you going to do?"

As the sound of rending metal behind them grew louder, the bounty hunter punched another button on his right gauntlet and turned to face the opening.

Figuring that he was never going to be this distracted again, Juno grabbed the chain with both hands and pulled it out of his grasp. Simultaneously, she rocked back on one leg and kicked him in the back with all her strength, propelling him toward the force field. While he was off balance, she ran for the other doors, hoping to get her hand on the activation switch before he recovered.

What came next happened almost too quickly for her to take in.

First, the doors ahead of her burst open, punched by unimaginable force from the far side.

Then the force field collapsed, sending everything in the room rushing toward the endless vacuum of space— including her and the dark figure standing where the inner doors had once been.

She lost her footing and jarred her shoulder. Dazed by pain, she would have tumbled helplessly out of the cargo bay but for a cable that whipped about her waist and dragged her back toward the bounty hunter.

At the same time, a stubby missile protruding from the top of his jetpack launched itself out into the void. Halfway between the cargo bay and the hanging ship outside, its tip unfolded into a grappling hook that an instant later found solid purchase on the side of the ship.

The cable binding Juno brought her within arm's reach of the bounty hunter. Unaffected by the rapidly thinning atmosphere, he slapped a breather across her face and bodily threw himself out of the cargo bay, taking her with him.

She kicked and struggled but his grip and the cable combined were impossible to resist. Her cry of anger and frustration fogged up the mask of the breather, so for a moment she couldn't tell what was happening behind her. They jerked to a halt, and she assumed at first that it was because they had reached the bounty hunter's ship, but a rapid volley of blasterfire back the way they had come, followed by the straining sound of the grapnel retractor, revealed that something very different was happening.

She held her breath, cursing the foggy visor and willing it to clear more quickly. By the fiery light of the nebula she glimpsed the *Salvation* looming ahead of her, sparkling jets indicating where breaches were venting air into the vacuum. Flames burned on the other side of several transparisteel windows. Bodies tumbled like dead stars, too many to count.

Clinging to the edge of the cargo bay door, withstanding the emptiness of space, the doors that were trying to close on him, and the shots fired his way by the bounty hunter, was Starkiller. One hand reached for her, fingers straining as though clutching at something invisible. Through the Force, he was trying to bring her back.

The whining of the grapnel reached a higher pitch. It was only a matter of time before something snapped— either the cable or the motor trying to reel it in. Juno had no doubt of that. Starkiller had shifted whole Star Destroyers. It would be nothing for him to overpower a single motor.

The bounty hunter reached around her to push yet another button on his gauntlet. For a second it had no obvious effect. Then, in the cargo bay behind Starkiller, something vast and angular moved.

Sparks flared. Starkiller turned with lightsabers swinging. The force pulling her back to safety faltered—and then died entirely as the cargo bay doors slammed shut between her and him.

Juno could hold her breath no longer. She raged against her captor, calling him things she hadn't called anyone since her earliest days in the Academy. She kicked and flailed against his chest, not caring how much it hurt her shoulder. The pain she felt ran deeper than flesh. Her entire being was in agony.

He was alive. She had seen him. A thousand questions barraged her—questions she didn't want to ask, but would have to address later, because they weren't ever going to go away.

How did he survive?

Where had he been for the last year?

Why had he stayed away when the Rebel Alliance had needed him so badly?

Why didn't he tell her?

For now it was terrible enough that she was being taken from him, and there was nothing she or anyone could do to stop it.

CHAPTER 15

JUNO.

Her proximity filled his mind, making it hard to deal with anything or anyone else around him. After leaving Kota, his comlink had squawked and blared about distant events and conflicts, so he had switched it off in irritation. He didn't care what happened outside the ship, only what happened to Juno inside it. When stormtroopers had crossed his path, he had blasted them out of the way with disinterested ferocity. Nothing could slow him. Nothing would stop him. The only thing keeping him and Juno apart was distance, and that could easily be overcome.

"Whatever you have seen, follow it you must."

"To the ends of the galaxy if I have to."

But the man in his vision was wilier than Starkiller had anticipated. The trail he had been following led nowhere, and was seeded with numerous traps and troopers designed to slow him down. If Juno *was* being taken to the cargo bay on level seven, then she was going by a very different route.

He forced himself to concentrate, seeking her through the many walls and decks of the *Salvation,* and finally sensed her presence two decks up. They were connected through the Force, by invisible lines that might fade but would never entirely break. Now he saw them clearly, it was just a matter of following them. Forgoing stairwells or lifts, he simply blasted his way through the ship's infrastructure. Metal and plastoid could be repaired. Wires and hydraulics could be rerouted. Human life—*Juno's* life—could not be replaced.

And he had seen her, briefly, face white and spattered with her own blood, eyes wide and staring at him in utter disbelief. What was going through her mind he could not begin to guess. Joy? Confusion? Relief? Doubt? They had only locked stares for a moment before the man who had taken her captive pushed her out of sight. Then he had fired a missile at Starkiller's feet that had blown a massive hole in the frigate. Starkiller had thrown up a Force shield at the last instant, but had still found himself four decks away when the blast dissipated. By the time he had retraced his steps, Juno was gone.

She was nearby, though, and it had taken him less than a minute to catch up, thinking hard all the way. If Juno was bait, why hadn't the trap been sprung? Starkiller was still alive and unfettered, and so, presumably, was Juno. Where did this particular gambit end?

"I do not expect you to survive," the voice of his former Master said in his mind. *"But should you succeed, you will be one step closer to your destiny."*

Starkiller could clearly remember the moment those

words had been spoken. It seemed an eternity ago, while receiving orders to kill the mad Jedi droid maker, Kazdan Paratus. He had succeeded in that mission, but his destiny remained as elusive as ever.

What did Darth Vader *want*?

Sometimes it seemed that only Darth Vader could answer that question.

Starkiller reached the cargo bay doors. They were locked, but that didn't slow him for longer than a second. Inert matter was no match for the Force, and therefore no obstacle to him. Had Juno not been on the other side, he would have vaporized it in an instant, sending scalding metal shrapnel flying all through the cargo bay.

She was facing him, being dragged backward by a loop of cable wrapped around her waist. The armored man blew out the cargo bay's external force field, and the vacuum pulled them with the rushing atmosphere outward into space. Starkiller grabbed hold of the nearest solid object in order to stop himself from sliding out after them. There was a stocky ship hanging just outside the air lock, obviously waiting to scoop them up and take them elsewhere. Juno's captor fired a grappling hook toward it and began to reel him and his struggling prisoner aboard.

Starkiller braved the hurricane pouring past him and skidded to the very edge of the air lock. There he found purchase against the bulkhead and stretched one hand out toward them. Again, he could have wrenched them back into the frigate without great difficulty, were it not for fear of hurting Juno in the process. If he pulled too hard, she might be crushed. Also, the man holding her was armed and unafraid to use his weapon. If he turned the weapon on her, she might be killed before Starkiller could prevent it.

Still he tried, straining against the cable winch and, when that proved too difficult, actually dragging the ship in toward the frigate. Why fight the winch when he could just as easily move the anchor it was attached to? The stocky ship rocked and swayed and began to creep toward him, Juno and her captor with it . . .

Then a shadow fell across him from behind. His concentration wavered. Something was moving toward him. Not a stormtrooper, visible or otherwise. It came from above, and got bigger the more it came into view.

Dying wasn't going to help Juno. He turned, lightsabers upraised to strike whatever it was. A droid of some kind, with multiple glowing photoreceptors and a vast, armored body that towered over him, balanced on eight thick legs.

He had seen it before, in his vision of Kamino. That knowledge didn't help, however, as it raised its forelegs and tried to spear him with four powerful lasers. He jumped, and the orange beams followed him, leaving glowing lines in their wake. It was big but fast, and he barely stayed ahead of its deadly attack. Behind him, the cargo bay doors slammed shut and life support began pumping in air. It smelled scorched and acrid under the giant droid's relentless assault.

Running wasn't helping, either. It was only wasting time. Starkiller took stock and decided to try another tactic.

He leapt into a corner and faced the droid with his

lightsabers crossed. The convergent beams hit both blades and were reflected back at their source. The droid's mirror finish bounced them right back at him, doubling the number of attacks he had to deal with. Instead of retreating, he changed the angle of his blades. The four laser beams reflected by him sliced down toward the ground, slicing arcs in the durasteel floor. Metallic smoke rose up around the droid in thick streamers. By the time it realized his intentions, it was too late.

Already straining under the droid's weight, the floor sagged and gave way. The droid's lasers switched off, entirely too late. The sharp tips of its eight legs scrabbled for purchase, leaving deep scratches in the floor, which only gave way further.

With a grinding of metal, the droid dropped out of sight and crashed through the levels below, one after the other.

Almost before it had vanished from sight, Starkiller was moving. The external door was shut, but he forced it open and braved the renewed storm of air to see outside. Juno and her captor were no longer visible. The stocky ship's trio of engines was firing, pulling it away from the frigate. Starkiller reached out to catch it, too late. The craft barely wobbled as it receded into the distance, and vanished into hyperspace.

"No!"

His cry disappeared into the vacuum. He had lost her again, and for all his frustration and fury, there was nothing he could do about it now. The Force couldn't accomplish miracles, even in his hands.

It could, however, help him get revenge.

The dark side rose up in him, seductively powerful. Darth Vader had sent the bounty hunter to capture Juno, knowing that Starkiller would try to save her from him. There was only one place, then, that she could be headed: back to where it had all started. *Kamino*. He *would* go there, but he would not succumb to the trap Darth Vader had undoubtedly prepared. His wrath would know no bounds. All who stood in his way would suffer.

A new vision came to him, rushing out of the void to fill his mind.

Lightning. The Dark Lord on one knee before him, helmet slick and shining in the rain, disarmed. Starkiller's lightsabers formed an X between them, and Vader's neck lay just millimeters from their intersection. With a flick of his wrists, Starkiller could behead the galaxy's greatest monster, and gain revenge for everything he had done.

But what would revenge get him? It couldn't turn back time. It couldn't tell him who the real Starkiller was. It couldn't bring Juno back.

None of those things, he decided, but better than nothing.

His face formed a determined expression. He tensed to execute the man who had made him into what he was: a killing machine, with no hope for anything better.

Before he could complete the move, a red blade erupted from his chest, exactly as it had in a former life, on the Empirical. Only this time his former Master couldn't have wielded it. He still knelt before him, awaiting the death blow.

The pain and shock were too great. Starkiller arched backward, lightsabers falling from his hands. With an agonized cry, he crumpled to the ground, and stared up at the man who had killed him.

It was himself.

Darth Vader rose to his feet. Blasterfire erupted around them. Starkiller heard screams and cries and the sound of people falling. The battle was intense but short-lived, and he had eyes only for the pair in black looming over him.

"I lied when I told you that the cloning process had not been perfected."

His former Master's words fell like blows upon his stricken form. The version of himself sanding at the Dark Lord's side was upright and whole in every way. The Sith training uniform he wore was immaculate and lethally adorned. The two red lightsabers held crossed over his chest didn't waver a millimeter as their eyes locked.

Starkiller's breath was growing shallow. The fire that had burned in him was dying, as it always died in the end. The dark side consumed everything. Hatred was never a substitute for love, and the price of pursuing it was life itself.

In the corner of his view, lying drenched in the rain, lay a limp, shattered form. He could not bear to look at it. Instead he clutched the burning hole in his chest and watched the Dark Lord give his new apprentice his first orders.

"You have faced your final test."

The reborn Starkiller knelt at the Dark Lord's feet. "What is thy bidding, my Master?"

"Take the Rogue Shadow. *Scour the far reaches of the galaxy. Find the last of the Rebels and destroy them."*

"As you wish."

"Then, and only then, will you achieve your destiny."

The new apprentice rose and walked away, stepping over Juno's body as he went. Kota's body lay nearby, and PROXY's, sliced neatly in two. Darth Vader looked down at Starkiller's body and, with a contemptuous flick of his wrist, sent it skidding over the edge of the platform and into the sea.

The last thing Starkiller saw was storm clouds and lightning far above, as he had on the first day of his freedom, just days ago.

Thunder boomed, and Starkiller came back to himself with a gasp. The sound echoed around him, disorienting him. It couldn't be real. He had been seeing the future, not something happening in the present.

The deck beneath him shook. The sound came again. Not thunder, he realized, but the giant droid fighting its way back up to him, intending to finish their battle.

He felt weary, then. Weary of hatred and pain and loss and despair. He would fight on, but not by giving in to the dark side. He would find his own way, even as he ran headlong into a trap and put everything at risk.

He reactivated the cargo bay's force fields, and air rushed back in once more. Staring out at the nebula, he pulled the comlink from his belt and switched it on.

"Kota? Come in, Kota."

"I'm here, boy."

"Where's *here*, exactly?"

"On the bridge. We've regained control of the *Salvation* and repaired the hyperdrive. The hostile ships are retreating. What's your status?"

"That doesn't matter. Juno has been captured, and I know exactly where she's going. It has to be Kamino, where it all started. Which means that Darth Vader is there, too. I think he's set another trap."

"For you or the rest of us?"

"Just me, I think."

"Then he won't be ready for the entire Rebel fleet when it arrives on his doorstep. I told the Alliance about this chance to strike. The fleet is converging exactly as you wanted it to."

"Good," said Starkiller with a faint smile, "because if you hadn't sent the order I was going to go without you."

"Prepare for lightspeed, boy," said Kota from the bridge. "Let's hope you know what you're doing."

The booming from below grew louder. Behind it came a new scuttling sound that Starkiller hadn't heard before, as of giant metal insects crawling across a hollow deck.

Outside, the stars stretched and snapped. The angular impossibility of hyperspace filled the cargo bay doors.

Starkiller activated his lightsabers and stood facing the hole in the floor. The dark vision he had just received ate at his confidence. Thus far, three of his visions had come true: The bounty hunter had been sent after him, resulting in Juno being injured and deprived of her command, and his lightsabers had turned blue. That left two visions, the grimmest of them all. Was there any way he could avoid both their deaths? Was the other Starkiller, perfect and deadly in every way, something that already existed, or could he be a mere possibility, or even nothing more than a manifestation of his deepest fears?

"*What happens if you do clone someone Force-sensitive?*"

"*Terrible things. Insanity. Psychosis. Suicidal tendencies.*"

The list of symptoms Ni-Ke-Vanz had rattled off was frighteningly close to what Starkiller himself was experiencing—but he had begun, perversely, to take hope from that. Perhaps Kota was right, and he had always been this way, even in his first life. Maybe learning to hate the way one felt was part of growing up. Maybe—

The rattling of tiny feet reached a crescendo. Five miniature versions of the huge droid rushed out of the hole on four sharp-tipped feet. He snapped out of his thoughts and ran forward to meet them, wearily grateful for the opportunity to act rather than think. The first two leapt at him, and he sliced them in pieces right out of the air. The other two split up and came for him from opposite sides. He met both advances with a lightsaber outstretched in each hand, using the Force to guide his blows. The droids shot piercing darts of energy in streams at him, trying to get through his guard. They, too, were immune to their own reflected fire, so instead of pursuing that tactic he danced closer to one and sliced its domed midsection in two, then brought his free hand around to blast the other with lightning. The miniature droid went wild, spinning in circles and sending energy darts about the cargo bay. Its green eyes glowed blue, then purple, and then its head exploded. Tiny bits of metal rained all over the hold with an almost musical sound.

More rattling came from the hole. Starkiller approached the lip and peered cautiously over the edge.

No less than a dozen droids were climbing toward him, hopping from deck to deck through the gaps the larger version had created. He reached out for the crates remaining in the cargo hold and sent them tumbling down on the droid's heads. They fell with legs spinning and were crushed far below.

Barely had they been dealt with than more appeared, leaping upward to attack him.

He pulled out his comlink again. "Kota, we have a problem."

"You might be right," came the gruff reply. "PROXY's picking up red lights all through the lower decks. Something you did?"

"We have a droid loose. I think it's headed for the secondary reactor."

"If it takes that out, we could lose the navicomp—and we don't want that to happen out here."

Starkiller glanced at the swirling madness of hyperspace. "Send as many troops as you can spare to defend it."

"That won't be many. The ship took heavy losses, so we're on a skeleton crew."

"All right, all right. I'll be there in a minute."

Starkiller ended the call and leapt feetfirst into the shaft. He lashed out with his lightsabers as he fell, taking out all of the miniature droids, one at a time. When he landed lightly at the bottom, a rain of droid parts fell around him, red-limned and bleeding sparks.

More were waiting for him in the path of the larger version. He glimpsed it far ahead, cutting through bulkheads and beams that lay in its path. The smaller droids seemed to be dropping from its underbelly, unfolding with a snap and hurrying back to confront him. The "parent" droid was definitely heading for the secondary reactor—but why now? The question occupied his mind as he fought his way past the smaller droids. Why not earlier, before the ship entered hyperspace?

The answer lay in the very question, he decided. Losing navicomp midjump would be disastrous. They might be blown to atoms, or never return to realspace. Should the droid even get close to damaging the reactor, then, they would have no choice but to drop out of hyperspace rather than take the risk.

It was a delaying tactic. Just like everything else had been, ever since Starkiller had engaged with the Imperials. Their leader, the bounty hunter, had wanted to grab Juno only in order to lure him elsewhere. He had never intended to engage directly with Starkiller. And that was a good call, for Starkiller would have blown *him* to atoms had he stood between him and her. Instead, the bounty hunter was forcing him to come face-to-face with the only man in the galaxy who had ever killed him.

Starkiller would face his creator and make the choice: live as a monster or die as himself, whoever that was.

Starkiller thought it unlikely that Darth Vader saw the irony in the situation. It was doubtful he saw anything in his plan other than objective methodology. Like Starkiller,

Vader had been trained in the art of betrayal by a Sith who somehow expected nothing but absolute servitude in return. The finer points of existence—not just irony, but humor, sarcasm, regret, and many more—were completely lost on him. Darth Vader was, for all intents and purposes, the machine he looked like.

He fought like a machine, too, with relentless blows and single-minded aggression. The first time they had dueled, in Starkiller's first life, Vader had displayed no anger at all—just determination, not to kill his apprentice, but to wear him into submission. The fight had raged across the training deck of the *Executor* for hours, with Starkiller never landing a single blow, no matter how he tried. He had gone from excitement at thinking that he had graduated to a new level of mastery to realizing just how much he had left to learn. More fuel had been added to the hatred he had felt for his Master and tormentor, along with a twisted kind of love for the man who made him stronger by showing him how weak he was. The fight had only stopped when Starkiller collapsed unconscious from exhaustion and was dragged by PROXY to his meditation chamber.

And maybe there, Starkiller thought, in that single-mindedness and determination that Darth Vader had handed down to his apprentice, lay his own weakness. Machines were exemplary at certain things. They were monomaniacal and focused, as PROXY had been in Starkiller's early life, when his mission had been to protect his charge—while at the same time training him by trying to kill him. Contradictions existed in their worlds, but they caused no conflict. They were simply assimilated and worked around, like the droids Starkiller had fought during his training on Kamino.

The galaxy wasn't a machine, and neither was the Rebellion. It would confound Darth Vader, perhaps even surprise him.

"You can teach me nothing," Darth Vader had told him on the Death Star.

Starkiller vowed to prove him very wrong on that score.

Part 3
RETRIBUTION

CHAPTER 16

JUNO WOKE WITH A START. She was lying on her side in complete darkness. Her hands were unbound, and her right shoulder was numb all the way down to her elbow. There was a sickening throb between her eyes that spoke of another stunning at the hands of her captor. The last thing she remembered was being dragged into his ship and the air lock sliding closed behind them. The *Salvation* had loomed over her like a mountain, glowing red and yellow by the light of the nearby nebula. The remaining TIE fighters had broken off their attack and were retreating back into the asteroid clouds. A smattering of turbolaser fire chased them as they went.

Then, nothing. And now, blackness, with nothing connecting the two periods. Juno wondered when, if ever, she would see her ship again.

That day wouldn't come any sooner by just lying there, she told herself. Reaching out with her left hand, she felt around her and slowly sat up. There was nothing above her head she might bang into, and nothing but empty flatness on the floor in any direction. The surface she had been lying on felt like unadorned plastoid, but there was a distinct smell of duralloy in the air, and a complex whine in the background that spoke of a ship under power. They were under way, wherever they were going. It was probably for the best, she told herself, that they hadn't yet arrived.

The shoulder of her uniform had been cut away and new bandages placed over her blaster wound. It seemed to her questing fingers like a capable job. She supposed bounty hunters would have to learn at least basic medical skills, if they were to keep their prisoners alive long enough to earn a reward. For that she was grateful, if nothing else.

She rose up onto her hands and knees and explored the space around her more thoroughly. She soon learned that it was a cage approximately two meters high, wide, and deep, with horizontal metal bars along two walls and plastoid elsewhere. She searched for a hinge or a lock but found nothing: The bars most likely recessed into the walls and would only retract on the ship's owner's command. With no tools and no light, she could see no way of getting out of the cage, let alone taking control of the ship and turning it around.

She put her head in her hands. That she had to go back was something she didn't doubt, at first. Starkiller had returned. What else was there to worry about? But the unremitting darkness began to get to her, the questions she had asked herself while being dragged from the *Salvation* returned.

Starkiller was undeniably back. How? Why? How long? And where was he now? Could he possibly be dead again?

Time wore on and she began to doubt the evidence of her eyes. She had only glimpsed him on the *Salvation*. It was conceivable that she had mistaken someone else for him—but was it conceivable that there was anyone else in the galaxy with the ability to do what he did?

It had to be him. But the rest of her doubts weren't so easily dismissed. Starkiller *was* alive, and while the part of her that had mourned him rejoiced, the simple fact of his existence wasn't enough to reassure her completely. The ramifications of his return weren't going to go away simply by assuming that he would eventually come for her, or hoping that she could escape, in order that they would be together again.

How *had* he come back? She had seen him consumed in a massive explosion while rescuing the Rebel leaders from the Death Star—an explosion that Kota had assured her had definitely killed him. She had felt as though part of her had died, and she had moved forward in complete faith that what she had seen was real, that Kota had neither lied nor been mistaken. Starkiller *had* died. But now he was back. The explanation for this apparently simple fact had to lie far beyond what she regarded as normal, perhaps even *possible,* and the source of that explanation worried her.

Had he been alive all this time, or had he only recently returned from the dead? That was another question with powerful undercurrents. If he had been alive the last year, why hadn't he contacted her? What had he been doing?

When had Kota learned about it? It was clear to her now that Starkiller had been aboard the *Rogue Shadow* when it docked, and that he was most likely the source of the tactical information Kota had given her. How long had they been in league to keep this knowledge from her? How far, in that light, should she trust the information?

On the latter point, she had no choice. Sealed up in the belly of a bounty hunter's prison ship, she might as well have been in another universe as far as the Rebel Alliance was concerned. They might even think her dead, if the battle went badly and the *Salvation* was destroyed. She might never get the chance to share her concerns, or to ask Kota why he had deceived her.

The painkiller was wearing off. A long, throbbing ache spread outward from her shoulder, down her arm and spine and up into her skull. She embraced the pain at the same time as she hated it. It cleared her thoughts.

She remembered the *Empirical,* the last time she had been a prisoner. Then she had thought Starkiller dead, killed by his Master under the orders of the Emperor. Then, as now, he had returned from the grave. Darth Vader had told him that he had been rescued before his life signs had faded away completely, but that could have been a lie. Had whatever process brought him back then been used now, too? How many times could a man die and be reborn and still remain the same man?

Escape had seemed impossible from the *Empirical.* It was Starkiller himself who had rescued her. His appearance in her cell had seemed a miracle, or a pain-induced fantasy designed to ease her own passage from life. She had put out of her mind what the guards had called him then, but those words came back to her now. They had called him "experiment" and "lab rat." They had feared him long before he had attacked them, for reasons she had never wondered about before.

"I saw you die," she had told him. *"But you've come back."*

All he had said in reply was, *"I have some unfinished business."*

As though that explained everything. She wondered now if he could have used a Jedi mind trick on her in that moment, to assuage her concerns. He had been mostly Vader's tool at that point, so she could readily understand why he might have done so. But those concerns about his survival returned a hundredfold, as though they had compounded at the back of her mind in the time since.

What would she say to him now, if he appeared in the cell with her?

Would he tell her what his unfinished business was, this time?

Did it matter?

If it was *her*, perhaps it made all the difference in the universe.

She got up and paced as best she could. The diagonal across a two meter-square cell was less than three meters, but it gave her something to do. She didn't know how soon they would arrive at their destination, wherever that was. It could be hours, yet. She needed a distraction from her thoughts, because they were leading her down a very dark path.

If Starkiller was back because he loved her, why hadn't he revealed himself before now?

If love had nothing to do with his return, what reason did she have to be glad of it?

She thought of PROXY mourning the loss of his primary programming and desperately seeking a new one. For the first time, she truly understood his pain. How simple it would be, if such a thing existed for humans, to plug a module into her head and have all these thoughts erased. To forget Starkiller and all he had meant to her. To finally get on with her life at last. What unimaginable freedom!

But it would be a lie, she knew. She wouldn't be who she was anymore. Starkiller had given her a new and better life. To turn her back on him would be to turn her back on the Alliance as well as everything she had become. That was a betrayal she could never contemplate.

As the ship rushed on through hyperspace, Juno remembered a moment on Felucia when she had been sure Starkiller was about to kiss her. She remembered making that thought come true above the Death Star, and the way her heart had pounded from fear and excitement at once. And she remembered Kota telling her about what he had seen in Starkiller's mind: *"Among all the dark thoughts in his head I glimpsed one bright spot, one beautiful thing that gave me hope—and that he held on to, even at the end."*

She had asked what that was, and Kota hadn't told her, but she had known—and she still knew now. They had been each other's salvation in very dark times. They would be so again.

Come rescue me, she said in her mind, knowing the words would be lost in hyperspace forever but hoping that he would hear her anyway. *Rescue me, Starkiller, so I can return the favor.*

CHAPTER 17

STARKILLER FACED THE GIANT DROID and stared hard into its two remaining eyes. It had lost four of its legs and numerous gaping rents had been carved all across its underbelly and back, but it remained a formidable opponent. It had killed every soldier Kota had thrown at it, leaving only Starkiller between it and the secondary reactor. He could feel the damage already done to the frigate as a deep, irregular vibration that rose and fell in the normally semi-audible rumble of the hyperdrive. There was no doubt in his mind that any more fluctuations in power would result in a catastrophe.

He feinted to his left. The droid shifted right to block him. He feinted in the opposite direction. It shifted again. Internal mechanisms thudded and groaned behind its durasteel shell. It crouched low, preparing to spring, and issued a noise like an antique boiler hissing its last.

Mentally, Starkiller triple-checked the layout of the secondary reactor against the rest of the frigate. He and the droid had been sparring vigorously for what felt like hours, and he was afraid of getting everything back to front. Without a clear landmark, that would have been very easy. Two decks, uncountable rooms and corridors, and one water tank had been completely destroyed during their fight, leaving an immense tangle of wreckage in their wake.

He hoped Juno would forgive him for the damage when he finally found her. It was still her ship, after all, and she might not take kindly to his giving it such a battering.

Still, he thought, shifting a couple of meters to his right, it wasn't as if he had much choice . . .

The droid tracked his movement, and pounced.

He ducked as he had many times before, and gave the droid a solid shove as it went over his head. Its lasers flashed around him, cutting yet another hieroglyphic pattern deep into the metal deck. Its innards whined as it spun to reorient itself, intending to arrest its trajectory against the wall ahead with three feet, and then leap back at him, stabbing with the fourth limb, hoping to impale him on its deadly, sharp tip.

He stayed still just long enough to give the machine the impression that this time, unlike all the other times, its plan might work.

The droid hit the bulkhead with a mighty thud, and kicked its three legs as hard as it could. The bulkhead, strained and scarred by many such impacts, gave way with a shriek. The noise was instantly joined by another, much louder sound—that of atmosphere rushing out into the void.

This was no ordinary bulkhead. It was the outer

hull of the frigate, and it had been pushed far beyond its tolerance. The droid, realizing its error, scrambled to withdraw the legs that now stuck through the hull, outside the ship, but Starkiller wasn't having any of that. He braced himself firmly against the interior bulkhead behind him and pushed. The droid sank a meter deeper into the metal, which tore and stretched further in response. Through the rents he glimpsed the abstract angularity of hyperspace rushing by, and he felt the droid's desperation increase. Starkiller didn't know what happened to ordinary matter when it was separated from the hyperdrive that lay at the heart of a starship and left to founder in the unreal spaces beyond. He suspected the droid didn't, either. It was about to find out.

One last flurry of laserfire slashed and burned at him. He ducked but held his ground, not caring if the droid scored a few light hits at this terminal stage. There was only one possible outcome now.

He pushed again, and the hull bent outward. The droid gave up all attempts to fight back and concentrated solely on survival. Its legs left deep scratches in the metal as they fought to maintain their purchase. But Starkiller's strength was too great, when combined with the strange effects of hyperspace outside. One claw slipped, then another, and then, with a final shriek of metal, it vanished, swept away by forces neither of them could understand.

Starkiller staggered backward, weakened by the effort and feeling giddy from the sudden drop in pressure. He hurried to a hatch leading down to the secondary reactor that had been the cause of all the fuss. It was sealed tight against the vacuum, but with the last of his strength he forced it open and fell through. He landed heavily on his back and stared up at the ceiling. The hatch slammed shut behind him. Deeply, gratefully, he filled his lungs.

Gradually he became aware of alarms and his comlink squawking. He reached down and brought it up to his mouth.

"What is it, Kota?"

"I've been trying to ask you the same question," the general shot back. "The hull breach on deck three—your doing?"

"The reactor's out of danger now," he said. "How's the rest of the ship?"

"Holding together."

"ETA?"

"You might want to get moving if you intend being on the bridge when we arrive."

Starkiller groaned and sat up. Two nervous reactor technicians he hadn't noticed before backed deeper into the corner they occupied.

"It's okay," he said. "I'm one of the good guys."

They didn't look terribly reassured, and he couldn't blame them. His black flight uniform was torn and charred; laser-cauterized wounds covered almost every square centimeter of his exposed skin; his face was smudged and bruised. Favoring his right leg very slightly, he left the technicians to tend the machine in their care, and began the complicated ascent back to the bridge, through damaged decks and past mounds of wreckage and bodies everywhere.

One of the good guys. The technicians hadn't known who he was, and that was undoubtedly for the best. Maybe they had heard of a young man who had played a role in the formation of the Alliance; they might even have heard rumors of his death on the Death Star; they were very unlikely to connect him to that person, and even if they did, who would believe them? People didn't come back from the dead. It just wasn't possible, even for Jedi.

Starkiller wondered if Darth Vader thought *himself* one of the good guys. He wondered if any servant of the Empire did, for long. Juno had been having doubts long before she'd met him. Vader had guided her toward evil the same way he guided everyone he encountered. Anyone who fought back, or tried to, was killed.

He wondered, not for the first time, who the Dark Lord had been before being subsumed by the Emperor's plan for galactic domination. Could he have been a Jedi Knight, perhaps one of the many whose bodies had never been found after the execution of Order 66? Several times Starkiller had strained to detect a hint of Jedi training in his former Master's own teaching techniques— but there was little evidence to pore over from a man who let actions speak louder than words, and whose philosophies concerned only power and domination. The only subtlety Starkiller could discern was that, although the lessons were brutal and the cost of failure high, there was no malicious cruelty. Once the equation was laid down—obey and succeed versus fail and die—the rest was entirely up to him.

The world was black and white through Darth Vader's mask, Starkiller thought. There were no grays. He imposed this view on everyone around him, and people either fell in line or fell by the wayside.

That didn't stop Darth Vader from emulating his own Master, though. He plotted treachery and had schemes that might take years to unfold. He was smart, and had learned the hard way to be cunning—probably thanks to the long years of his own tutelage under the galaxy's ruling Sith Lord.

But Vader preferred the direct approach, whenever possible. He fought the way he thought. It was easier to lure Starkiller back to him by using Juno as a hostage than any other method, so that was what he did. Instead of negotiating with Starkiller, he would simply kill him. Black, white—open, shut. Vader's mind was a puzzle box from which he let little escape, but the shape of the box said much about him.

I will surprise you, Starkiller promised his former Master, *if it's the last thing I do.*

In this life, he added, *or any other.*

The bridge was scarred with the signs of battle—blood, blaster scoring, burned consoles—but amazingly functional nonetheless. Like any band of mercenaries, Kota's squad had plenty of experience with operating in less-than-perfect conditions. They patched sensors out of spilled components; they rewired control systems by hand. The medic, Ni-Ke-Vanz, was nowhere to be seen. Starkiller assumed he was in the surgery suite, doing what he could to patch the crew back together.

PROXY was helping, too, stabbing at buttons on two consoles at once. After a hasty repair job on his chest and eye, he seemed to be back to his old self, more or less. A flicker of Kota swept across the droid's metal body, and Starkiller wondered why.

"Forget about the cargo bays," Kota shouted into a comlink. "If engine six fails in the next five minutes, we won't care about what stores we've lost."

He glanced up as Starkiller walked to stand next to him. Kota looked as battered as he had on Cato Neimoidia. Clearing out the last of the camouflaged stormtroopers had taken its toll, it seemed.

Kota acknowledged Starkiller with a nod. "We're running slow. The fleet will get there ahead of us at the rate we're moving, but we *will* get there in the end. That I guarantee you."

Starkiller was somewhat reassured, but the anxiety he felt for Juno was unabated. If the fleet had arrived at Kamino, that meant the bounty hunter had arrived, too. She was almost certainly in the hands of Darth Vader right now, suffering in a thousand unknown ways.

To distract himself, he checked on the *Rogue Shadow*. It was still docked along the frigate's spine, seeming undamaged. Its shields had protected it during the dogfight, and it hadn't been boarded. That was something. Just having a solid link to the past nearby helped him settle his thoughts.

Get to Kamino, he told himself. *Find Juno. Free her. Easy.*

"I'm sorry, General Kota," PROXY was saying, "but I

have been unable to restore the targeting computer to its
full capacity."

"So we'll be firing by hand," Kota said, "which will
drain some crew-power. Fighter complement is down to
fifteen. Make sure they're ready to launch the moment
we come out of hyperspace," he called to one of his
squad members.

"How long now?"

"Two minutes." Kota studied Starkiller's face. "Don't
worry. We'll find her."

Starkiller acknowledged the general's attempt at
reassurance with little more than a grunt. He knew what
Kota wanted. He wanted Starkiller back in the fight.
Kamino was just a means to that end. Once Juno was
free, presumably, Kota hoped to announce Starkiller's
return, reunite the Alliance behind him, and storm the
Emperor's stronghold on Coruscant.

Perhaps, Starkiller thought, he was being unfair
to Kota, but he saw little compassion in the general's
blind eyes. Just determination to win—at all costs. If
the operation at Kamino was a success, there would be
another one, and another one, and another. It would
never end, until the Empire itself was ended.

Starkiller didn't know how to tell Kota that what
came after finding Juno was a mystery he himself hadn't
unraveled yet. He could barely think farther ahead than
the next few minutes.

Get to Kamino. Find Juno. Free her.

Everything else could wait. Whether it was his faulty
clone brain talking or a clear-eyed certainty that Juno

mattered more than anyone else, he was sure of that much. The near future, as glimpsed in his visions, needed to be changed before he would think about what would happen afterward.

A long, slow shudder rolled through the ship in response to a random power fluctuation from the main reactor. Starkiller took hold of a nearby console and rode it out. There was nothing else he could do. This wasn't an enemy he could fight with force. He could only trust the people around him and the machines they maintained to bring him safely to where he needed to be.

When it passed, Kota addressed the makeshift crew.

"We're nearing Kamino. All power to forward deflector shields."

"Yes, General," replied PROXY.

The ship shuddered again, this time in reaction to the drain caused by the shields. Starkiller held his breath, hoping the hyperdrive wouldn't fail just moments before reaching its destination. Or that it would bring them to a point light-years from where they needed to be. There was no guarantee they could get the drives working again, once they were shut down.

Ahead, the tortured topology of hyperspace began to transform into the familiar streaked stars of realspace. The ship was spinning around its long axis, making the view even more disorienting than normal. Metal creaked and decks swayed. Pressure alarms went off in a dozen quarters.

Again, Starkiller wondered what Juno would think of the condition of her ship when she got it back. Again, he relegated that concern to join the others he would worry about later. *After*.

The *Salvation* slammed back into reality with a bone-shaking thud, and suddenly it was in the middle of a war.

Kamino hung dead ahead, its white-streaked blue face looking deceptively placid against the unfamiliar constellations of Wild Space. Starkiller counted a dozen Rebel starships facing off against no less than five Imperial Star Destroyers. Clouds of TIE fighters, Y-wings, and Z-95 Headhunters engaged in dogfights across the hulls of the larger vessels. Bombers stitched bright trails in their wakes. Energy weapons and shield flashes painted the sky in every wild color imaginable.

Just seconds after it exited hyperspace, the *Salvation* was hit by a blast from one of the Star Destroyers.

"Cannons on those warships!" Kota ordered. "Scramble fighters!"

Starkiller went to leave the bridge, intending to take the *Rogue Shadow* into battle, but Kota took his arm.

"Not you. I want you on the primary forward turbolaser. Whoever's firing down there couldn't hit a planet from low orbit. Operate the controls by remote." He indicated an empty console. "When the planetary shield is down, we'll take the *Rogue Shadow* to the surface together."

Starkiller didn't argue, although he yearned to be out in the thick of it. Being a gunner wasn't the same thing as cutting and weaving through the mess of ships and energy outside, but he could still do good from where he was. A frigate's primary turbolaser wasn't a weapon to be dismissed easily.

He called up the remote controls and settled into a seat. The interface was one he hadn't used before, but it was easily navigated. *Gas charges. Galven coils. Cooling. Tracking.* He smiled. *Trigger.* That was what he wanted.

A holographic display of the battlefield hung in front of him. He swung the targeting reticle from Star Destroyer to Star Destroyer, seeking a weak spot. The weapon was more sluggish than the *Rogue Shadow*'s armaments, but that was only to be expected. He took opportunistic shots at TIE fighters that darted nearby, guided by the steady hand of the Force, and soon made a significant dent in the Imperial numbers.

Targeting ion cannon and bridge towers to great effect, Starkiller brought the *Salvation* to the attention of the Star Destroyers' gunners. The frigate's shields groaned and complained while the Rebel starfighters did their best to retaliate.

With half an ear, Starkiller listened to panicky comm chatter from the pilots.

"We're getting ripped apart up here!" one cried as a concentrated blast of turbolaser fire tore his squadron apart. "Order the retreat!"

Kota's response was immediate. "Hold your position, Antilles." He changed frequencies to broadcast to all ships. "Keep pressing the attack! We won't get another chance to take this target!"

A flickering hologram appeared in front of him. It showed a stocky Rodian in what looked like a commodore's uniform.

"The planetary shield around Kamino is proving

stronger than we thought," he said. Static ate up a couple of words. "—ground assault is impossible until they're down."

Kota looked desperate. Starkiller knew what he was feeling. This was the Rebel Alliance's first and best chance to strike the Empire hard. If it failed, the symbolic defeat could be much worse than a mere military setback.

"PROXY," Kota said, "can you slice into the defenses and bring them down from out here?"

"I have been trying, General, but it will take too long. The *Salvation* is suffering heavy damage. We've already lost decks eight through twelve, and can't hold out much longer."

"There has to be a way." Kota gripped the edge of the main display so tightly, his knuckles were pure white. Tiny images of starships danced and whirled in front of him. The commodore waited, image dissolving and firming every second or so. "But what can we do? The ship is falling apart around us. The fleet is being pounded. And we're no closer to the target than we were when we arrived."

Starkiller restored control of the turbolaser to the crew and went to join Kota. An idea was forming in his mind—an idea that ought to be crazy but might, he thought, barely be crazy enough to work.

"Where are the planetary shield generators?" he asked.

PROXY leaned over the main display and pointed out the location on a map of Kamino. Among the domes and towers of the facility, he instantly recognized the familiar lines of the main stormtrooper breeding facilities and, nestled among them, the secret spaces in which Darth Vader had conducted his experiments.

"Here, Master. Both generator and reactor are in the same location, making it exceptionally vulnerable. The shield it creates, however, is strong enough to prevent any form of attack, so we are unable to take advantage of that fact."

Starkiller nodded. Crazy indeed, he told himself, and Juno was certain not to approve, but it was the one plan he could think of that had the slightest chance.

"Head to the *Rogue Shadow*," Starkiller told Kota. "I'm pretty sure those shields can't take a direct hit from a frigate."

Kota's blind eyes stared at Starkiller for a full second. His chin came up as he fully grasped the details of the plan. "You sure about this?"

"It's the only way. Just be ready to clean up."

"All right." Kota's fist slammed into a button on the console. "Abandon ship! Abandon ship!" His gruff voice echoed through the frigate. "All crew, abandon ship!"

He took his hand off the button and reached for Starkiller. They shook hands firmly, without saying anything. Then the general turned and swept with his squad from the bridge.

"You too, PROXY."

"Yes, Master." A re-creation of Starkiller's own face flickered across the droid's features. "Even without primary programming, I remain committed to the principle of self-preservation."

For some time after PROXY was gone, and even as

he threw himself into the complicated issue of slaving the ship to his commands, Starkiller wondered at the droid's parting words. They had been stated with great significance, but he didn't think they were intended as an attack on his own motives. PROXY wasn't trying to imply that he was suicidal—he hoped. And he hoped his motives weren't remotely bent that way. The plan wasn't half as crazy as others he had been party to. It was just the voice of Ni-Ke-Vanz again, adding to his uncertainty.

Insanity. Psychosis. Suicidal tendencies.

But for that, he told himself, crashing a frigate from orbit into a planetary shield generator might seem a perfectly sane thing to do.

The image of the Rodian commodore had long flickered out for good. Starkiller assumed Kota had passed on the decision, and the disposition of the fleet bore that out. Starfighters converged on the *Salvation*, offering covering fire while he was distracted with realigning the ion engines and turbolasers. The frigate's shields bore the brunt of everything coming his way, and that situation was certain to worsen when the Star Destroyers' commanders realized what his intentions were.

Slowly, the damaged frigate came about. All seven ion engines flared to full thrust. Every forward turbolaser and cannon fired continuously at the planetary shield below. Starkiller adjusted the *Salvation*'s trim so it was aimed directly at the shield generator. A chron began to count down in the main display, estimating how much time remained before impact.

There would actually be two impacts, Starkiller

reflected as the frigate picked up speed. First, against the shield; second, against the surface of the planet itself. There was no way to tell how far apart they would be spaced. It would depend on how successfully the shield managed to keep the *Salvation* at bay. Not long, he estimated, but even a second could significantly reduce its momentum, to the point, perhaps, where the frigate didn't so much ram the generator as simply fall on it.

That would still be enough. He was sure of that much. Nothing was designed to withstand an impact like that.

Not even him.

The planet grew large ahead of him. The Imperials gradually figured out what the frigate accelerating toward them was intending to do. Energy weapons and TIE fighters came in wave after wave, attempting to destroy the *Salvation* before it got anywhere near impacting the shield. The Rebels literally threw themselves between him and the Imperials, taking hits for him in an attempt to ensure the success of his last-ditch gambit. A Star Destroyer rumbled by, too slowly to physically intercept the falling frigate. He wondered who had issued the order to attempt a ram—Darth Vader or the ship's commander. Probably the former. If anyone could guess who was at the controls of the *Salvation*, it would be him.

And Darth Vader, of all people, would know what Starkiller was capable of. On Raxus Prime, he had changed the course of a Star Destroyer using nothing but the Force.

"What is mass?" Kota had asked him. *"Concentrate on what's important."*

Kamino loomed large ahead. Already he felt the faint fringes of atmosphere.

Starkiller clung tightly to the edge of the main display and held an image of Juno's face steady in his mind.

CHAPTER 18

JUNO FELT THE PITCH of the prison ship's engines change beneath her, and she was on her feet in an instant. The hyperdrives had cut out. A second later, ion engines kicked in—three of them, mounted at the base of the craft. That was an unusual configuration, one that would make it easier to identify the ship later. There were no portholes to peer through, and no visits from her captor, either, so she had no way of knowing what, exactly, was happening outside. But she could guess. They had reached their destination and were accelerating into an equatorial insertion trajectory, preparatory to landing.

That guess was confirmed when she heard repulsors kick in. The ship rocked a couple of times and shook from nose to stern. Wherever they were, it was bumpy.

She stayed where she was, riding out the short trip to the surface with an uneasy sensation in her stomach that wasn't motion sickness. She hadn't been face-to-face with Darth Vader since her arrest, the first time Starkiller had "died." His opinion of her was unlikely to have improved since then.

The ship's flight steadied. She imagined it hovering over a pad, preparatory to landing. Gravity shifted minutely as the ship's artificial field gave over to local ambient levels. She lightly jumped twice into the air. There wasn't much change, which didn't help her refine the possibilities at all.

The ship settled with hardly a bump as it touched solid ground. The repulsors eased off, and all the other noises of flight gradually ceased. The hull allowed very little sound from outside into her tiny cell. She heard a faint hiss that wasn't life support, and an incessant, threading whine that might have been wind.

A door she hadn't noticed before slid open to her right, allowing a shaft of natural light into the caged areas. She blinked and raised a hand to shield her eyes. Through the unaccustomed glare she saw straight into the cockpit and out the visor on the far side. The skies were heavily overcast. As she watched, a ribbon of lightning ran from left to right. Thunder followed, muffled to the point of inaudibility.

The ship's pilot—and only crew member, she could now confirm—walked through the hatch and approached her cage. His rifle was slung over his shoulder. She didn't doubt he could have it trained on her in a microsecond.

"Hands," the bounty hunter said, demonstrating with his own how he wanted her to stand.

She slipped her forearms through the bars so he could reach her wrists. He clamped binders around her, not so tightly that it hurt, but leaving no possibility of slipping free. When she was secure, he hit a stud on the wall and the bars retracted.

She didn't run or attack him. There was no point. Better, she had decided long ago, to save her energies for when they were needed. The only thing resistance now could get her was another injury, or worse.

The bounty hunter pressed a second stud, opening the inner door of a small air lock, probably the one through which they had entered the craft. It was just large enough for two.

"Where are we?" she asked.

"Kamino," he said, waving her ahead of him.

That rang a bell. "Imperial cloning facility?"

He shrugged and closed the inner lock behind them. An instant later the outer lock opened and rain poured in.

He took her arm and roughly pulled her from the ship. She understood instantly that this was part of the act. The customer had to see that they were getting their money's worth.

The odd-looking prison ship sat on a landing platform belonging to a high-tech facility mounted on long columns directly over an ocean—an ocean that stretched as far as her eyes could see. A broad walkway connected the platform to a series of tall habitats constructed in a distinctly Imperial style. She must have seen hundreds like them, all across the occupied worlds. At the nearest end of the ramp was a welcoming committee of ten stormtroopers, their white armor slick with rain. The building behind them showed signs of recent construction, or possibly repairs. A tall door opened in its side, and through it stepped Darth Vader.

She tensed without wanting to, and the bounty hunter felt it. Perhaps fearing that she might make a break for the edge of the platform, there to hurl herself into the sea, he tightened his grip and pulled her forward.

"You returned sooner than I expected, bounty hunter," said Vader when they were within earshot.

"I work faster than most." The bounty hunter pushed her forward. "She's all yours."

"And Starkiller?"

"He's your problem, Lord Vader. I know my limitations."

"Our arrangement is not complete until he is in the Kamino system."

"I don't think you'll be waiting long."

Juno swallowed her fear as Vader's attention turned to her.

"Captain Eclipse, you and your fellow subversives in the Rebel Alliance have caused me considerable inconvenience. I should execute you now as the traitor you are, but there is one last service that I would have you perform."

"I will never willingly serve you."

"Your compliance is not required." Vader raised his right hand, but stopped at the sound of footsteps. A signals officer had emerged from the doorway and was proceeding in haste along the ramp, slipping occasionally in the rain.

"Lord Vader," he said. "We are detecting the signatures of several large vessels entering the Kamino system. They lack Imperial transponders and will not reply to our hails."

Vader's hand clenched into a fist. "Excellent. Notify Fleet Commander Touler that it is time." He turned to the man next to her. "You have done well. You will be rewarded handsomely once this matter is concluded."

"But you said—"

"Bring her." Vader stalked off, not waiting around to hear the bounty hunter's objections. Stormtroopers shoved him aside and closed in on Juno.

Gloved hands took her shoulders and elbows. Armored figures blocked her front and back. She could barely see the top of the bounty hunter's broadband antenna as he turned away and trudged back to his ship.

VADER WAS MOVING FAST. The stormtroopers hustled her to keep up, occasionally making her stumble. She hadn't gotten a good look at the facility before they entered it, but it seemed enormous, the furthermost tip of a city-sized structure that covered a significant amount of ocean. They passed long-necked aliens who shied away from Vader with either respect or fear, or both. Native Kaminoans, she assumed: The geneticists responsible for the army of clones that had given the Emperor an unbeatable advantage in his overthrow of the Republic.

She didn't like how fast they were moving. Vader had something in mind. The more she could do to distract him from it, the better.

"He's coming, you know," she called after Vader's back. "Doesn't that worry you?"

He walked on, unchecked.

"I mean, he's beaten you once before. You know it as well as I do. A lesser man would have killed you there and then. Do you really want to give him the chance to change his mind?"

Nothing. Just the grating draw and release of his respirator, as implacable as his heavy footfalls.

"And when you're gone, what chance do you think the Emperor has? *You're* the one everyone's afraid of. Or don't you care about the Empire? You just want to protect your tiny piece of it—the piece your Master lets fall from the table, to keep you compliant."

Still nothing. Grudgingly, she decided that taunting him was probably not going to work, in terms of him letting something slip. But that wasn't the only reason why she kept at it.

"To be honest," she said, "I'm a bit disappointed. Using me as bait shows real desperation. How do you know it'll work? What makes you think he cares a bit what happens to me? He's more likely to come here for you, because you're the one he wants."

She waited a moment, and then added, "Which is odd, when you think about it. The harder you drive him away, the harder he comes back. No matter how you punish him, no matter how many times you betray him, he keeps returning for more. I'm beginning to wonder if he's been on your side the whole time, and just doesn't know it."

They entered a new section of the facility, one containing vast cloning spires studded with growing bodies destined one day to become stormtroopers in the Emperor's army. That prompted her to change tack.

"You probably want me to think that you brought him back," she said. "Well, I don't. You know what I believe? I believe he brought himself back, and you found him while he was weak, convinced him that he owed his life to you, and thought that this way you'd have power over him. Like you didn't learn the first time that no one has power over him. Not you, not me, not the Emperor himself. You're wasting your time trying to control him—but hey, if that's how you want to end it all, don't let me stand in your way."

Without turning, Vader raised a hand and cocked two fingers to the lead stormtrooper. Their little troupe came to a halt. Juno backed away, expecting to be stunned again. She hated that.

Instead, the stormtrooper produced an armor sealant patch from his thigh pocket and placed it firmly over her mouth.

Fair enough, she thought. Her failure to get a rise out of the Dark Lord was beginning to wear her down, too. But at least now she knew one thing for sure.

He definitely wanted her alive.

Her mouth sealed shut, the long walk resumed. At the base of one of the cloning spires they stopped to wait for a turbolift. Four of the stormtroopers entered with Vader, including the one who had gagged her. The rest stayed behind, improving her odds but not by much.

They went upward, fast. Her ears popped. The only sound was the harsh in–out of Vader's respirator. Not for the first time she wondered what lay inside the black, expressionless helmet. She hoped she would never know.

The lift slowed and she was escorted out again. They were perhaps halfway up the cloning spire, in a section heavily guarded by stormtroopers. The tubes around her were different—larger, darker, connected to more wires and tubes than those below. The figures within were shrouded in shadow.

One moved as she was led to a second turbolift, farther around the tower. Its leg kicked out, blindly. One hand batted against the curved glass. Then it stilled and went back to growing.

They reached the base of the second lift, where they waited for the cab to descend. She had time to study the nearest tube in more detail. The clone within was taller than the average stormtrooper, and leaner. It, too, twitched, as though it could sense her watching it. It rolled over, like a child turning in its womb.

Its face approached the curved glass, and she flinched on seeing its features. They were younger, slighter, not entirely whole, but they definitely belong to just one man.

Starkiller.

She gasped and recoiled from the tank, resisting the explanation even though she admitted to herself, was *forced* to admit, that no other made sense. The only alternative was the one she had offered Vader—that Starkiller was so strong in the Force that he could stave off death itself—and at accepting that she had to balk. As Bail Organa had said, such power was too great to be trusted, in anyone. And if the Emperor ever got his hands on it, there would go all hope for the galaxy.

But cloning was dangerous and unreliable. It was

impossible to imagine what was going through the mind of the Starkiller she had seen. Clones had gone mad from identity crises many times in the past. Why would he be any different?

Her shoulders slumped as a new thought sunk in. The clone in the tank before must have come from the real Starkiller's cells—from his corpse's cells—and she didn't want to think about that at all.

But what difference did it make, really? Clone or otherwise, Starkiller was back. He had come to find her. He was following her now. What right did she have to say that his feelings were counterfeit? Who was her captor to suggest that she never give him a chance to at least put them into action?

Behind the gag, Juno's jaw worked. She noticed Vader watching her reaction closely and pulled herself together.

She had to believe Starkiller was himself until proven otherwise. It didn't matter where he came from if he was the same at the end of it. And she would know *that* the moment she saw him, the very second they were standing face-to-face.

You can clone his body, she wanted to tell the Dark Lord, *you can torture him any way you want, but you'll never turn him into a monster.*

The second turbolift led to a section far above the clone tubes and the second Starkiller she had seen. A series of irregular terraces rose upward to the very top of the spire. Water dripped in a steady cascade from the uppermost platform, and she wondered if the building was entirely finished. That would make sense, she supposed, if Vader's cloning experiments were relatively new. For all she knew, Starkiller was merely the test subject. Vader's long-term plans might be to create an army based on himself.

She shuddered at the thought. One of him was bad enough—and he was *damaged*. A copy of Darth Vader, perfect in every way, would be an unstoppable force for evil. Beyond evil, perhaps. Not even the Emperor could withstand him.

They ascended on foot from the last turbolift, right up to the exposed platform. The facility dome was open, allowing in the rain. Juno, the only one not wearing armor and a helmet, felt the full effect of the storm. In a way, she welcomed it. The chill precipitation and swirling wind provided something new to think about, apart from her predicament.

"Bind her," said Vader, pointing to a restraint harness erected on one side the platform.

The stormtroopers did as they were told, attaching her legs first, then undoing her binders and placing her arms in shackles. When they were finished, she could hardly move.

Vader was standing on the far lip of the platform, staring up at the clotted sky as though waiting for something to happen.

Juno followed his gaze and imagined she saw faint streaks and flashes of light through the clouds, as though something momentous in scale were taking place on the far side, something much brighter than lightning.

A space battle.

Abruptly, Vader turned and stalked back to her, his

cloak heavy and wet from the rain. He raised a gloved hand as though to strike her, and she didn't pull away. She couldn't fight him; she knew that very well. But she wouldn't cringe before him, either.

"I sense your fear," he said. With a single, surprisingly swift motion, he ripped the patch from her mouth. "Your doubt, too, is clear to me."

The rain was cooling against her red-raw lips. "What doubt?" she asked, attempting to brazen out his uncanny insight into her mind.

He took one step to his right, and turned to face the way he had been before. Ahead of them, in the clouds, was a patch of yellow light. Not the sun, or even a bright moon. This was shifting slightly and growing brighter by the second. A meteor, she thought, coming right at her.

"Is that . . . ?"

Vader put his hands on his hips and nodded in satisfaction.

"He is almost here."

CHAPTER 19

BARELY A MINUTE into the dive, Starkiller knew he had to move. Nebulon-B frigates weren't designed for rapid reentry. Anything over eight hundred kilometers an hour risked tearing off control vanes and external sensors—and the *Salvation* was already doing far in excess of that.

The ship shook and thundered. Strange screeching noises ran from nose to tail, as though it might tear apart at any moment. It would physically hold together long enough—he was sure of that, but the controls in the bridge were already approaching useless. The main display was full of static. He could barely make out the planet, let alone the location he was aiming for.

He needed a better vantage point if he was going to pull this off.

That he was effectively riding in a giant metal coffin was an additional thought he tried to suppress.

The ship could fly itself for a short time. He had patched the navicomp into what remained of targeting computers, leaving him reasonably certain that it could point and thrust effectively while his hands were off the controls. He didn't want to leave it long, though, so he ran for the exit and headed upward as fast as he could, taking turbolift shafts and passages cut by the bounty hunter wherever he could. He ignored bodies, personal effects, fires—everything. Where doors or bulkheads lay in his path, he telekinetically ripped them aside and kept running.

The ship lurched beneath him as he entered the upper decks. That, he presumed, was the result of the primary forward laser cannon being ripped away by the rising atmospheric friction. Its center of gravity perturbed, the ship began to sway from side to side. He tried not to imagine superheated air boiling up through the infrastructure from the hole left behind. He would be exposed to the same soon enough.

He reached the freshwater tanks and began moving horizontally, toward the rear rather than forward. When he reached the surgery suite—even more of a bloody mess than it had been before—he headed upward again, to where the short-range communications array protruded from a bulge on the frigate's upper fore section.

He could hear the air rushing past as he approached the outer hull. It sounded like a mad giant screaming.

The ship lurched again, but less noisily this time. The rupture was more distant—probably the static discharge vanes on the aft section, he decided. That would rob the ship of even more stability.

Even as he thought that, the *Salvation* began slewing from side to side.

"Hang in there," he told the ship. "I'm coming."

He found a maintenance ladder leading to an air lock and leapt up it in two bounds, blowing the inner hatch as he came. He could feel a wild drumming from the far side of the outer door. The ship was moving so fast now that unexposed flesh wouldn't last a microsecond. He would have to rely on a Force shield to keep him safe. A single lapse in concentration would be the end of him.

He took a second to compose himself.

For Juno.

Then he raised a hand and telekinetically burst through the outer hatch.

Instantly the world was fire. The air around the ship consisted of a blinding plasma, hotter than any ordinary flame. He forced his way into it, bracing himself against metal rungs that had turned instantly red on exposure to the outside. His eyes narrowed to slits in order to make out even the nearest outline. He could barely see the fingers in front of his face.

He didn't need to see. The Force guided him, move by move, out onto the hull, where he braced himself with his back to the short-range array and turned to face forward. Like Kota, he would see without eyes.

A trembling shape up and to his left chose that moment to give way, showering molten fragments all along the spine of the ship. The primary array was no great loss: he couldn't have heard anyone anyway over the racket in his ears. But the forward turbolasers and primary sensor unit, the next two chunks to go, were more of a concern. The ship was seriously unbalanced now. It shuddered underfoot, pulling wildly in different directions. If he was going to prevent it slipping into an uncontrollable tumble or tearing apart, he had to act quickly and decisively.

This was where it got difficult. He needed to maintain the Force shield against the sort of heat he might find in the outer layers of a star. He also had to keep in mind the target ahead—a target he couldn't see through the plasma, but had to hit square-on or else the planetary shield generators wouldn't fail. No matter what happened, he had to fly straight.

Starkiller took a deep breath. The cool trapped air behind the shield would last long enough, he hoped. He had been too worried about frying to consider suffocating to death.

He raised his hands and spread his fingers wide. His eyes closed tightly against the fiery brightness of the plasma. With each bucking and shaking of the ship beneath him, he encouraged himself to ride with it instead of fighting it. He was part of the ship, not a passenger. He *was* the ship, not a reckless pilot guiding it to destruction.

In the same way that he could feel his fingers and toes, his mind seeped outward into the metal and plastoid of the frigate, until every joint and weld, every porthole and deck became part of his sense of being. There was no line anymore between Starkiller and the *Salvation*. They were one and the same being, from the perspective of the Force.

He raised his right arm, and the ship followed the movement, listing slowly and heavily to starboard. Some of the headlong shuddering faded, as though it were grateful to have someone at the helm again. Even the wind's shrieking seemed to ebb.

Something tore away at aft of the ship, and he bent his knees slightly to absorb the shock.

The *Salvation* steadied, found a new center of gravity, and roared on.

Confident that his vast metal charge was now under control, he cast his mind outward. He was shocked by how far he had fallen. The *Salvation* must have punctured the planetory shield itself some time ago, and he simply hadn't noticed in all the turbulence. Now the cloud cover was less than a hundred meters below and coming up quickly. Behind the *Salvation*, a long fiery wake stretched across the sky, trailed by starfighters, and, farther back, capital ships on both sides, coming through the hole in the shield. The generators below would soon repair the hole, if he didn't guide his hurtling missile correctly, leaving the Rebel ships on the inside trapped, with him.

Assuming he survived . . .

For Juno.

The frigate slammed into the clouds with a tearing sound. At that speed, individual droplets of water hit like thermal detonators. The *Salvation*'s own shields were holding, barely, but even so it lost still more of its mass to the ongoing battering. Several lower decks peeled back and were swept away, including the bridge. Most of the short-range array was gone, leaving him with just the base to hold him steady. He clenched his hands into fists and *willed* the ship to keep going.

Something succumbed to the plasma with a flash.

A bright spark tumbled in his wake—the secondary reactor he had spent so much energy saving from the giant droid. He ignored it. The bottom of the cloud layer was approaching, and with it would come his first clear glimpse of the shield generators.

The air became still and relatively quiet when the *Salvation* punched through the clouds. The extra friction had slowed the frigate somewhat, making it a more manageable beast. Starkiller opened his eyes and discovered that he could see over the bulge of the forward decks to his destination. Perhaps some of the hull had been ripped away there, too.

The cloning facility lay spread out ahead of him. Had he wanted to, he could have hit it dead-center and wiped it off the face of Kamino. And had Juno not been inside, he would have been tempted. He felt no sentimental attachment to the place of his rebirth, and if there was any chance of taking out Darth Vader with it, all the better.

His sole target, however, was the shield generator buildings, and at last he saw them, as clear as they had seemed from the bridge, directly ahead.

Carefully, wary of putting too much strain on an already overtaxed chassis, he nudged the *Salvation*'s nose down. If he came in low and hit the ocean first, he could concentrate the damage to one location. If he over-reached by so much as a degree, he might miss the ocean completely and scrape a long, fiery line right through the heart of the facility.

The *Salvation* resisted. He pushed harder. The nose

descended and held there for ten seconds, strain echoing all through the ship. It wasn't made for anything like this. Nothing larger than a starfighter was. Neither was he.

With a bone-jarring crack, the spine connecting fore and aft sections of the frigate snapped clean through. Starkiller reached out with the Force, trying desperately to keep the two pieces together, but nothing could be done. They were already moving on slightly different trajectories. Air and debris sprayed from the great wound that separated them, providing entirely unpredictable thrust.

Groaning, juddering, the fore section began to lift again. Starkiller didn't fight it. With so much mass already stripped from it, the damage it would do when it hit was negligible. The rear was the priority. The heavy engines and main reactor continued powering forward on the trajectory it had originally been following. Was that the right trajectory or not? Starkiller anxiously studied its fall, projecting it forward to the best of his senses.

It looked good. He felt positive about it. Keeping an eye on the stubby rear section as it passed under him, he braced himself for impact. Barely a minute remained now. If he survived the crash, he would soon know whether he was right or not.

Ahead, a series of cloning towers loomed, standing as upright and tall as wroshyr trees on Kashyyyk. The fore section he stood upon was going to come down among them, doing a considerable amount of damage in the process. Starkiller didn't mind. Until their memories were activated, clones weren't truly alive; they were little more than meat in suspended animation. And the technicians attending them were servants of the Empire, and therefore viable targets. Some of them, perhaps, were responsible for his birth, if clone he truly was, and for their complicity in Vader's twisted plans. He smiled as his fiery steed descended toward them, imagining them fleeing in the face of the meteor as it grew large in the sky.

He could actually see tiny long-necked figures running through the complex, white-armored stormtroopers resolutely standing at their stations, and a black-robed figure looming high above them all, watching him approach.

Vader.

Below and slightly ahead, the engines struck the surface of the sea, sending a wave of superheated steam radiating outward along the wave tops.

Starkiller couldn't take his eyes off his former Master. He was right in his path, and not even moving! For a moment Starkiller couldn't understand why—until, next to Vader, bound in shackles and so small he had barely noticed her, he saw—

Juno.

A huge eruption heralded the impact of the engines into the side of the shield generators. The sky and sea convulsed. A shock wave spread through the facility, making the cloning towers sway. The fore section of the *Salvation* rolled to starboard, but not by enough to miss the cloning towers. Its terminus was fixed.

Just seconds remained before the *Salvation*'s fore section hit Kamino. The facility was in close focus ahead of him, and he imagined he could see Juno's eyes widening on seeing him, haloed with his Force shield on top of her precious ship. Did she know it was him, or did she wonder at this strange apparition? Did she imagine that he was her death coming at last, from the skies instead of Darth Vader's hand?

Starkiller closed his eyes. He didn't have time to wonder what was going through her mind. He had to think of something fast, or Juno was going to die.

There was only one thing he could do, and although he knew he wasn't likely to survive, he didn't hesitate. What was death when the love of his former life was at stake? Besides, anything was possible. Dying, as he had thought once before, always seemed to bring out the best in him.

With his mind and all the power of the Force, Starkiller embraced what remained of the frigate beneath him— and blew it into a billion pieces.

CHAPTER 20

JUNO WAS HYPNOTIZED by the fiery blaze in the sky. Ever since it had broached the cloud cover, two things had become clear. It was a ship, a big ship, and it was going to hit the facility. The roar it made vied with thunder for loudest sound in the sky. Lightning scattered from the disturbed clouds in its wake.

Then the falling ship had split in two, with one half powering down at a steeper angle, and the other continuing onward. Only then had she realized that the second one was coming right for her.

"Was this part of your plan?" she asked Vader, who still stood, unmoving, beside her.

He didn't respond. Neither did he make any move toward the ramp that might take him to safety. Maybe, she thought, he had other means of protecting himself, means that neither she nor the stormtroopers possessed. She could see that they were getting nervous, too. The fiery balls grew brighter and brighter until they were almost too painful to look at. She refused to avert her eyes.

The first came down hard and fast, striking a well-defended portion of the facility outside the dome immediately surrounding her. There was a bright flash of light. The boom followed later, along with a rising sensation that she assumed was the shock wave rolling through the flexible foundations of the ocean-bound facility. She could *see* the cloning towers swaying from side to side. A vast column of flash-boiled steam and wreckage rose up into the sky. Hot, damp air rushed outward in its wake.

Still the other fragment of the ship came toward her. Seconds remained before it hit—not long enough to think anything coherent, barely time even to observe what was happening. The stricken ship was glowing red, with the last shreds of plasma still clinging to it like flames. Its class was almost unrecognizable, but she made out stumps that might once have been a communications array on the upper port side. That made it a Nebulon-B frigate, one of many EF76s in the service of either the Empire or the Rebel Alliance. It could have been any one of them.

So why, then, did she feel a cold stab of certainty in her gut that this was none other than the *Salvation*?

Her own ship was going to kill her.

The irony wasn't lost on her.

At the last instant she made out a tiny human figure standing on the upper hull. The flames and rushing wind swept past him, as though he were impervious to their touch. His arms were upraised in defiance and his head was tipped back so she couldn't see his face. But she knew. Just as she knew that it was the *Salvation,* she knew it was him.

He *would* come for her in flames and smoke, wreaking destruction all around.

Despite the apparent certainty of her death, she smiled. Either he would save her—in which case there was nothing to worry about—or he wouldn't, and she didn't want to live anyway.

The ship was almost upon them when the figure brought his hands down in a fierce, pounding motion, and the last solid fragment of the *Salvation* exploded into fiery pieces.

She had to close her eyes. The conflagration was too intense, and the sound was that of worlds ending. The cloning tower kicked beneath her. She was momentarily afraid that she might be falling with it into the sea. But then she was rising again, and she understood that the structure had survived, somehow, and so had she.

Her eyelids flickered, braving the brightness that only slowly faded around her. A cloud of hot metallic fragments was spreading across the city. Dense splinters rained from it, hissing where they landed. Heavier fragments struck with more substantial thuds, near and far. None struck her. The rain ceased for a moment, and then returned, settling the cloud of dust still further. Of the *Salvation*, nothing at all remained.

Darth Vader lowered the hand he had risen to shield his helmet and took stock around him. Juno did the same. Fires blazed in the wreckage where the rear half of the *Salvation* had come down. Alarms sounded through the facility, loud enough even for Juno's blast-numbed ears to hear them. Ash was settling on every horizontal surface and forming a thick, gray sludge.

Above, the clouds, already disturbed by the *Salvation*'s fiery passage, were being torn apart by a new outrage. Starfighters and capital ships powered down from orbit in large numbers, dodging and firing at one another as they went. Juno recognized more frigates, and dozens of Headhunter, Y-wing, and TIE fighters. There were bombers, cruisers, even Star Destroyers bringing up the rear. An all-out war was taking place above Kamino, between Imperial and Alliance forces, and it, too, was growing ever nearer.

"I ask again, is this part of the plan?"

Instead of answering, Vader stalked off, waving for the stormtroopers to remain where they were. When he was gone, they stationed themselves several paces away from her and carefully watched the perimeter around them. High above their heads, the secure facility's dome began to close.

Juno coughed and wished she could wipe her eyes clear of ash. Her ship had blown itself practically to atoms; she had seen it happen, right in front of her. There was no chance at all that Starkiller could have survived. He had been riding right on top of it.

But she knew as well as they did that this wasn't the end. He had come back from the dead sufficient times now to make anything possible. Anything at all.

CHAPTER 21

THE GIANT REPTILIAN *biped loomed over him, roaring in its own language. He didn't understand what it was saying. Fear made it almost impossible to think. All Starkiller wanted to do was run.*

A bright yellow blade slashed across his vision, and the lizard fell backward, dead. The woman who had wielded the blade rushed to him and enfolded him in her cloak. He tried not to cry, but the fear was too great.

"Take him, Mallie—take him somewhere safe!" His father's voice cut through the screams and shouts that filled the village. "I'll hold them off."

"Don't be a fool, Kento. You can't do it alone."

"I can slow them down while you get into the forest. Go!"

"No." Mallie stood up and faced her husband. "You know Kkowir better than I do."

"All you have to do is get to the Kerritamba, or if they're under attack, try the Myyydril caverns as a last resort—"

"But there's the Sayormi to think about, and the dead

area. You're the expert, Kento. If anyone goes, it should be you."

The boy looked up at his parents in anxious confusion, unable to understand what the argument was about. Weren't they both coming? Wasn't it time to run now?

Explosions sent trees tumbling nearby. One of them crushed the hut he had known all his conscious life. There his mother had told him stories of the great Wookiee warriors and showed him how to braid his own friendship band. There his father had thrown him up to the ceiling and held him floating aloft, spinning as though sitting on air. The crushing of the walls sent splinters flying, and he screamed at the thought of everything he loved disappearing in an instant.

More of the big lizards came running out of the trees, firing at the villagers and setting their hair on fire.

His father went to run forward, his blue lightsaber raised, but his mother caught his arm.

"Kento," she said in a soft but firm voice, "you know I'm right."

His anguish was plain to see, even for a very young child. When he sagged, something broke inside him.

"You always are, my love."

They embraced, quickly, and then she ran toward the lizards, shouting a battle cry. Her son cried out, too, wondering where she was going, but his father scooped him up and began running for the trees.

"Don't worry, son," he said as they escaped. "I'll keep you safe. And when she comes back, we'll make a new home. Somewhere safe and special, I promise you."

Behind them, the lizards cried out in surprise and pain. He tried to look, but his father held on too tightly. And when the trees enfolded them, the sound of his mother fighting became muffled and indistinct. Slowly, over the course of many years, it faded into silence.

STARKILLER'S EYES JERKED OPEN. Where was he? All was dark around him. He smelled smoke and his body felt as though it had been hit by an asteroid. The last thing he remembered was tightening the Force shield around him and destroying the *Salvation* so it wouldn't kill Juno. He was somewhere on Kamino, then. But his mind remained full of strange images and feelings that he had never experienced before.

Kashyyyk. Trandoshan slavers. His parents . . . ?

He tried to shrug them off. They had been dead for a long time, and the living mattered more. But he was struck by this brief glimpse of the woman who had given birth to him. Tall, with short brown hair and a physique honed by years of training, she, too, had been a Jedi Knight, like her husband. She had been a warrior, and yet she had loved her son as well. She had loved him and most likely died defending him and the Wookiees they had befriended. And until this moment, he had never known she existed or that his father had made a promise he couldn't keep.

Where had the memory come from?

It didn't matter. *She* didn't matter. Starkiller had to get moving, or the promise he had made to himself would also go unfulfilled.

For Juno.

He reached for his comlink, but it was gone. Lost during the fall, presumably. He sat up and felt around him, seeking the dimensions of the space he found himself in. It was a deep, stone pit—and for a terrible moment he feared that he was back in the training rooms Vader had confined him to ever since his reawakening. But then he found a doorway, not far from the pile of rubble he had brought down with him. Somewhere far above, he was sure, was the hole he had made when he had hit the facility. There was no way of telling now just how far he had tumbled, burning and smoking like a meteor.

He wrenched the door off its hinges. Outside was marginally lighter. A corridor led off into the distance. He loped along it, concentrating on faint sounds of fighting in the distance. Numerous varieties of weapons were in play, and several starfighters screamed overhead. That meant the shields were safely down, and the Rebel forces were making their way into the facility. He allowed himself a small feeling of satisfaction, even though he knew the battle was far from won. The Imperials were well entrenched on Kamino. They wouldn't go down without a fight.

The corridor led to a darkened command room. He flicked a switch and its blast shields opened, letting in the cool gray light of the outside world. Details assaulted him, too many at once. The first thing he needed to do was work out where he was. To his right were the cloning spires where he had seen Juno, now protected behind a clear, curved dome. They were too smoke-blackened to make out if she was still there. A thick column of steam rose up from the shield generators, forming a spreading mushroom cloud high above the facility. Fighters on both sides dodged and weaved around the cloud, while higher up capital ships vied for ascendancy.

Closer at hand, he made out flashpoints of engagement where Rebel forces were trying to penetrate the high-security dome around Darth Vader's restricted area. They were coming under heavy fire from all directions. Troop carriers descended under close escort to provide reinforcements, but for every one that landed two were diverted or destroyed. Bombing runs softened up the Imperial defenses, which had both the advantage and disadvantage of being relatively fixed. TIE bombers returned the favor, attempting to blow the Rebels to pieces whenever they stopped moving too long. Cannon emplacements strafed any Rebel ships that came too close in their attempt to penetrate the dome, while AT-STs patrolled the perimeter, constantly vigilant.

Starkiller needed to get through the same defenses as the Rebels in order to save Juno. He scanned the controls in front of him, looking for maps or hidden routes that he could access. There were maintenance hatches spaced irregularly around the base of the dome, but he didn't have the codes required to open them.

He didn't let that bother him. There were alternatives to codes.

Picking the closest hangar hatch, he memorized the way there, activated his lightsabers, and left the control room.

* * *

THE MEMORY OF KASHYYYK stayed with him as he fought his way through the Imperials, occasionally dodging the odd Rebel who thought he was on the Imperials' side. He didn't know the location of his birthplace, and knowing now that both his parents were Jedi made it even more difficult to guess. Their relationship would have been forbidden by the Jedi Council, and then endangered even further by Order 66 and the subsequent slaughter of all their kind. How they had stayed hidden was unknown. Somehow they had ended up on Kashyyyk, where an attack by Trandoshan slavers had forced the two of them to come out of hiding. It was this, probably, that had brought Darth Vader to the planet, in search of Starkiller's surviving father.

The death of his mother was now his earliest memory. And was it really his? That, too, he had no way of knowing. If Vader was telling the truth, his true birthplace lay ahead, under the high security dome, and the memory of Kashyyyk belonged to another man.

He reached the maintenance hatch and cut his way through it. A stormtrooper armed with a flamethrower tried to roast him once he was inside, but a solid Force push threw him back into his squadmates, where his fuel tank exploded. Starkiller took a moment to bring down the ceiling over the hatch, so no one could follow him, then crawled on hands and knees into the secure facility.

He kicked out the vent on the far end of the tunnel and dropped onto a walkway that followed the base of the dome. Inside the dome, the battle was even more difficult for the Rebels. They had no air support and only a handful of limited access points. Several TIE fighters patrolled from above, ready to rain fire on anyone unauthorized. The Rebels desperately needed a way to get their own fighters into play.

Starkiller ducked as shots from a weapon lanced out at him from the far side of the dome. Snipers. He ran along the walkway to his right in order to present a moving target, speeding up and slowing down to make getting a bead even more difficult. There was no sign of Darth Vader, and Starkiller was too far away to see if Juno was on top of the cloning spires.

Down among the Rebel fighters, though, he spotted a familiar white topknot. Kota was fighting his way toward a command center, accompanied by the members of his squad, but sniper fire was making their progress slow. Starkiller looked up and waited for the muzzle flashes. The snipers harrying Kota were situated in a tower not far away, within reach of the walkway he was following.

He ran faster and leapt when he was at the closest point to the tower. For a moment he was in free fall, and then he hit the side of the tower with lightsabers pointing forward. They arrested his downward slide just above an observation window, which he shattered with a quick Force push. Swinging himself down and through the window, he made his way to the nearest stairwell before any of the snipers could turn their high-powered weapons inward.

He burst in the door on the uppermost level and found himself at the center of a web of concentrated blasterfire. Each of the snipers was armed with at least one nonspecialist weapon, and they had all abandoned their harrowing of Kota in order to deal with him. His lightsabers swung like propellers, reflecting every shot back to their source. The air filled with smoke and cries, until finally the last sniper fell, slumped over his weapon.

Just in case another team of Imperials came to reactivate the emplacement, Starkiller ran his blades through each of the sniper weapons, rendering them useless. Then he left the room and went up onto the roof. A passing TIE took a potshot at him, but he jumped before the bolts could hit him. The top of the tower exploded into flame as he dropped in a carefully controlled fall to where Kota and his squad stood below.

They were hunkered down at the entrance to the command center. Kota had his blade deep in the armored door while one of his militia tried to slice through its lock. Both succeeded at the same time, and the squad burst inside with Starkiller hot on their heels. They made short work of the Imperial officers within and immediately took control of the consoles they found.

"Get those hangar doors open," Kota ordered. "Quickly!" He turned to Starkiller. "Vader's TIE fighters are going to keep us pinned down here until we get air support."

"Good to see you too, General."

"I knew you'd be back." His attention was directed through the curved window and the facility outside, as though he could see without the slightest impediment. "I'm just surprised it took you so long to catch up."

"I need to get to the cloning towers."

"Well, be quick. They'll be coming down around your ears once we get through the dome."

A close strike from one of the TIE bombers made the command center shake.

"Time's running out," Kota growled at one of the Rebels, furiously tapping at his console.

"I almost have control of the hangar doors," was the response. "Just give me—"

A second blast tore one corner of the roof away, taking the Rebel technician with it. Kota cursed and led the dash forward, out of the center and back onto the walkways.

"I'll deal with the hangar doors," Starkiller told him as they dodged fire from snipers and cannon emplacements on all sides. "You just give me time to get Juno before you take everything out."

Kota didn't argue. "Good, good. We'll find the security hub and try to prevent any more lockdowns."

They split up at the next intersection, and Starkiller leapt from ledge to ledge toward another command center near the base of the dome. Behind it was the nearest hangar entrance, and its thick durasteel doors were tightly sealed against the Rebels outside. The Imperials inside the command center saw him coming and took steps to prepare: by the time he had burned his way in, the controls were locked, and when he tried to interfere with them they self-destructed.

There went that plan. But it wasn't the only one he had. Leaving the ruined command center behind, he leapt to the base of the hangar door and, facing it, spread his arms wide, palms forward.

For Juno, he thought, and pushed.

The hangar doors shook in their tracks, but didn't give.

He stepped back, changed his stance, and tried pulling instead.

Again, nothing.

A sniper had taken a bead on him. He took a moment to deflect a shot very precisely back to the other side of the dome. The resulting explosion seemed tiny from such a great distance, but had the desired effect. No more shots came his way.

Starkiller turned back to the doors and extended his widespread fingers to the stubborn metal.

Waves of intense electricity surged into the doors, shorting out systems both physical and electromagnetic. He gave them a good twenty seconds before stepping back and trying to pull again.

This time the doors responded as they were supposed to. With a shriek of complaint, the metal buckled and curved inward, allowing access to the outside. When the doors were protruding vertically from the wall, he pushed each side back so it was flush. Barely had he finished when the first Rebel Y-wing swept by, saw the opening, then came around to rush through.

It roared past him, a wave of exhaust hot in its wake. The pilot took in the situation and began firing at the TIE fighters pestering Kota, turning the fight a little more in the Rebels' favor.

Starkiller felt that he had discharged his responsibility to Kota. It was time now to go for Juno. But the spires were on the other side of the dome, and the lower levels were crawling with AT-STs and stormtroopers.

Seeking the best shortcut available, he climbed to the top of the ruined hangar door and waited for the next starfighter to come through.

Two TIE fighters followed the Y-wing, then a Headhunter. He let them go unmolested: There were insufficient handholds on the top of either model's canopy. The fifth was a Y-wing—exactly what he was after.

As it rushed through the open hangar entrance, he jumped onto it and caught the R2 unit protruding from its exposed chassis tightly about the domed head.

The impact nearly tore his arms off at the shoulders, and the Y-wing dipped sharply under the unexpected weight. The droid squawked in alarm, prompting a barrel roll from the starfighter's pilot. Starkiller hung on tightly as the world turned around him.

"Tell the pilot I'm on your side!" he shouted over the roaring of the Y-wing's twin ion jet engines.

The starfighter banked to avoid the fire-blackened tower where Starkiller had dealt with the snipers, then it leveled out.

"You're not doing any damage back there," crackled a voice from the R2's vocoder, "so I guess you really aren't an Imp. But what *are* you doing? Do you have a death wish or something?"

I hope not, Starkiller thought. "I need a ride. See those spires over to starboard? That's where I have to go."

"Where the firepower's heaviest?"

"If you're not up to it, I'll find myself another ride . . ."

The pilot laughed. "No one's ever called Wedge Antilles

a coward. Hold tight and we'll see what this wishbone can do."

The Y-wing began to curve around the inside of the dome, dodging fire from turbolasers and TIE fighters. Starkiller braced himself with both feet and one hand gripping a manipulator extended by the R2 unit. With his free arm, he supplemented the starfighter's energy shields with one lightsaber, bouncing laser blasts up into the dome and Force-pushing ion torpedoes away.

At first it looked as though getting to the spires would be easy, but the more the number of ships under the dome increased, the harder it became to fly in a straight line.

After a tense dogfight with two TIEs flying in tandem—which ended with them colliding thanks to some deft flying from Antilles—the Y-wing rushed the spires head-on, but was driven back by fire too concentrated to fly through.

"Okay, now what?" asked Antilles as he swept them smoothly out of range.

Starkiller thought for a second. "That depends on what kind of odds you like."

"I make my own odds."

"Good. Go down."

"What? We can't go down. There's—"

"There's an opportunity. The facility sits on platforms over the ocean. Find a gap in the platform and you can get under it. Then it's just a matter of finding a way back up near the spires. See?"

"All I can see is my life flashing before my eyes." The pilot laughed again. "But that's okay: I always skip the boring bits. Get ready—here we go!"

The Y-wing's nose suddenly dropped. The R2 unit wailed. Starkiller held on with both hands as the rooftops of the facility rushed up at him. The terrified exhilaration he felt was more intense than when he had surfed the *Salvation* down onto Kamino. He was a passenger now, trusting entirely in the flying abilities of a pilot he'd never met. The chances were he'd misjudge the insertion into the infrastructure and kill both of them. But it was too late to bail now. They were committed.

The Y-wing sped down a gap between two buildings, dodging bridges and walkways. At first Starkiller saw no gap through the rapidly approaching lower levels, but then he caught a gleam of light on wave tops through a square hole. Antilles must have spied it by radar from above. It looked very small, barely enough room to fit the widely spaced twin ion engines, even on the diagonal.

"Keep an eye on that eyeball for me, will you?"

Starkiller looked behind him. A TIE fighter had their tail and fired twice, just missing their port engine. Starkiller didn't know what Antilles expected him to do about it. He couldn't let go, not with a sudden course change just seconds ahead. All he could do was hope the rear deflector shields would last long enough.

The hole rushed for them. The pilot jockeyed the Y-wing from side to side, adjusting its trim by minute degrees. Then suddenly they were through, and Starkiller was wrenched to his right by the violent delta-vee. His legs were swept out from under him, leaving him hanging by his fingertips from the R2 unit. The ion rockets roared. A mist of flash-boiled seawater sprayed him. He swung back and forth violently before the Y-wing found horizontal again and sped off, ducking and weaving around the facility's many deep-sea supports.

Behind them, the TIE fighter clipped the edge of the hole and exploded with a flash of yellow light against the surface of the sea.

Starkiller's knees touched the back of the Y-wing and gratefully took some of the pressure off his hands. It was dark under the facility, apart from the odd shaft shining down through the lower levels and a distant glimmer shining past its outer edges.

"Good flying," he said breathlessly.

"You're still there? That's a relief. Deesix has gone quiet. I think he's in shock."

The R2 unit made a mournful sound.

"Just hold on a minute longer," Antilles told it, "then we'll get back to shooting bucketheads." The Y-wing curved gracefully around a trio of heavyset columns supporting something weighty above them. "If my guess is right, and it always is, we're coming up on the spires now. All we need is a way in . . ."

"No need to be subtle about it," Starkiller told him, shifting position to see more clearly over the canopy. "What about up there, near that access ladder?"

"Set. Get ready for some more g's, whoever you are!"

The Y-wing surged forward, laser cannon firing in a steady stream. Hot gas and molten metal exploded from the impact site. A new shaft of light beamed through the hole Antilles had made in the lower levels. He hit the retros and swung his starfighter in a complicated maneuver that left it tail-down and nose-up, directly under the hole. Both ion engines roared and they shot upward through what might have been a garbage chute, back into the secure facility.

They emerged in the midst of the cloning spires. Turbolaser emplacements instantly spotted them and began firing. Multiple flashes indicated hits to the Y-wing's shields. Almost immediately, Antilles grew concerned.

"I can take this heat, but not for long. Where do you want me to put you down?"

Starkiller tried to get his bearings, but he had lost them under the facility. His instincts told him that Juno was ahead, and he hoped they spoke truly.

"Keep on as you are. No need to slow down."

"You're not going to jump again, are y—?"

Wedge Antilles's voice was swept away as Starkiller launched himself off the back of the Y-wing and into space. The side of the nearest spire rushed toward him, and he lit his lightsabers an instant before striking the glass wall. He landed in a shower of glass shards, rolled, and stood unscathed.

The Y-wing swooped back to check he was okay, and Starkiller waved his lightsaber blade in thanks. The stubby craft acknowledged him by dipping its nose, then roared away.

HE WAS ALONE. Splinters of glass crunched softly underfoot as he jogged to the end of the corridor in which he had landed. Alarms vied with the sound of explosions and starfighter engines for dominance, creating a dissonant racket all around him. He heard no footsteps or voices. If there had ever been Kaminoan technicians in this area of the spire, they had almost certainly been evacuated now.

He passed through an open doorway and passed into the heart of the spire itself. He stood in the entrance for a moment, eyes tracking upward along a seemingly endless series of cloning tanks, affixed to platforms barely wide enough for droids and technicians to gain access. Stormtroopers patrolled the tanks, but Starkiller didn't think they were specifically stationed to watch for him. More likely they were guarding the beings who would one day swell their own ranks—for these were ordinary stormtrooper clones, nothing experimental or sinister. And as such they were a valid target for an attack by the Rebel Alliance.

Starkiller had his sights set much higher. He was sure now that he had the right spire. He could sense both Juno and Darth Vader in the cavernous spaces above him. It was just a matter of getting to them.

But if he could sense Vader, then the Dark Lord could sense him in return, and that made the game that much more complicated.

The stormtroopers in the cloning tower were too dispersed to take on all at once. Instead, and in order to confuse the trail he would inevitably leave in his wake, he chose a very different strategy.

Once, he had been paralyzed and abandoned in a trench full of bloodwolves, with no way to reach safety except by using the power of his own mind. It was a lesson Darth Vader had made sure his apprentice learned before even beginning combat training. Killing enemies wasn't the same thing as controlling them. Each method had its uses, but they weren't interchangeable.

Running lightly around the base of the tower, he approached the first clutch of sentries from behind. A judicious use of telekinesis triggered a life-support alarm a dozen clone tubes along, prompting a quick inspection by the stormtroopers. While they were distracted, he ran up the stairs they had been guarding, to the next platform.

There he put the thought into the mind of another trooper that he had heard a disturbance some distance away. The moment he and his fellows were busy, Starkiller crept past them, too. The Force absorbed all sound of his movement and shrouded his form in shadow. He didn't just fade into the background: he *became* the background.

Before long, though, the guards became suspicious. They were of course in constant contact via their helmet comlinks, and a plethora of false alarms was itself unlikely to be innocent. So Starkiller turned the screws a little tighter, creating half-seen phantoms in the minds of the troopers that literally ran circles around them. Pressure hoses exploded with the force of grenades when Starkiller blocked them from afar. Clone tubes opened unexpectedly, spilling disoriented, half-minded bodies across the decks.

By the time he had reached the summit of that tower, the stormtroopers were in utter disarray, and he hadn't used his lightsabers once.

Satisfied, he entered a narrow junction between that

cloning tower and the one above it. There he met his first real opposition. Camouflaged troopers guarded a bottleneck between the towers. On seeing him, they opened fire immediately. He shocked their armor back into opacity and quickly dealt with them, but the damage had been done. Troopers above and below the junction knew he was there, and they converged on his location en masse.

He fought his way into the second tower against a steady rain of blasterfire, while at the same time defending his back. He buckled lofty platforms, tipping stormtroopers to their deaths far below. He used cloning tubes as flying bombs, turning the floor underfoot slick with spilled amniotic fluids. He peeled plates from the walls and sent them flying into clutches of stormtroopers too time-consuming to confront head-on. Ruination surrounded him.

More death, he thought. Even when he tried, the curse of Darth Vader's training lay heavily upon him. Was this the way it would always be? Would he never shake off that fatal legacy—or was there another way to resist that he hadn't found yet?

Great mastery of the Force *had* to lead to more than just the increased capacity for violence—or else every Jedi would be a Sith, and the galactic civil war would never have happened.

Again he thought of the first time the original Starkiller had faced his Master in a duel. If Vader *had* been a Jedi, what kind of Jedi had he been? A hero or a failure? Starkiller had a hard time believing that such great evil could have come out of indifference or inability—but at the same time he could barely credit that someone with such natural talent could have gone unnoticed, as his own had not. Perhaps the young Darth Vader had been kept secret, too. Perhaps the mask was a matter of habit rather than necessity.

Starkiller reached the top of the second tower unscathed. An open turbolift awaited him there. He faced it for a moment, not knowing where it would take him but sensing it was somewhere he had to go. Whatever awaited him at the other end, he needed to face it.

He supposed his mother had felt this way on Kashyyyk, while fending off the Trandoshan slavers who threatened her family. She, too, had had no choice, but still she had fought—for something greater than her own survival, for love. Her legacy was a powerful one, and Darth Vader had never entirely managed to expunge it from the boy who would be his apprentice. Or even a clone of that boy.

He stepped into the turbolift. The doors closed, and he was taken upward. He readied himself for what was to come both physically, with lightsabers raised and ready, and emotionally, inasmuch as that was possible.

The cab slowed, stopped, and the doors slid open.

The space beyond was gloomy and vast. Starkiller emerged slowly from the lift, keeping all his senses peeled. Darth Vader was close, very close. In the shadows above he made out the faint outlines of platforms much like the ones in the cloning towers below. Beyond them, faint light gleamed on curved glass tubes, but he could not make out what lay within.

The skin of his arms prickled. Something was very close, very close indeed.

"Whatever you seek, only inside you will find."

The words of the wise little creature he had met on Dagobah reassured him, oddly.

"A part of yourself, perhaps?"

The sound of another lightsaber echoed off the metal and glass surfaces around him.

"You have returned."

Starkiller looked around. He couldn't pinpoint the origin of his former Master's voice.

"As you see," he said, moving slowly forward in a confident but wary stance.

"It was only a matter of time."

"Where is Juno?" he asked. The last he had seen of her, she had been on the roof of the spire. She could have been moved anywhere since then.

A dark figure lunged at him from the shadows. Starkiller blocked a powerful slash to his head, and retaliated with a double sweep to Darth Vader's legs. The Dark Lord leapt upward, out of reach of his weapons, and Starkiller followed.

When he landed on the first platform, Darth Vader was nowhere to be seen.

Something moved to his right. He spun to face it, lightsabers upraised.

A slender form stepped out of the shadows.

"I knew you'd come," said Juno, smiling. "At last, we are together again."

Almost, he lowered his weapons. It was *her*. She held

out her arms to embrace him. He longed to run to her. But an instinct told him something was wrong.

A flash of memory—a memory of a vision—came to him. He had seen a vision of Juno on the bridge of the *Salvation,* when the bounty hunter had captured her. Everything about that vision had come true, right down to the last detail. PROXY had been taken out, along with her canid second in command. She herself had been shot in the shoulder.

This Juno was uninjured.

"Stay back," he said, tightening his defenses.

Juno's smile faded. Her arms came down. When she moved, she did so with a speed that wasn't human, reaching behind her back with both hands to produce two Q2 hold-out blasters. With blank-faced, depersonalized lethality, she came for him, firing both blasters at once.

Starkiller deflected the shots right back at her, and she staggered backward with a cry. Then he was on her, bisecting her abdomen with his left lightsaber and taking her head off at the neck with his right.

As the body fell in pieces to the metal floor, showering sparks, Starkiller stood over her, breathing heavily.

The illusion died, revealing the wreckage of a PROXY droid at his feet.

"It's a lot easier to fight the Empire when it's faceless," he heard her say from the past, *"when the people whose lives are ending are hidden behind stormtrooper helmets or durasteel hulls. But when they're people we knew, people like we used to be . . ."*

He spun, catching the faintest echo of an in-drawn,

artificial breath from behind him, and caught Darth Vader's lightsaber on the downstroke. They stood that way, locked blade-to-blade, for a moment, and then Starkiller pushed the Dark Lord back. He swept one lightsaber on a rising arc that would have taken off Darth Vader's left arm while the other he flicked sideways, hoping to catch his opponent in the chest unit.

Vader blocked both blows, then leapt a second time, the next platform up.

"How much harder is it going to get?"

Starkiller scowled.

"Are you having second thoughts?" he had asked Juno that same day—the day after he had seen the vision of his father on Kashyyyk. Her answer had been immediate: *No.* But he had sensed an uneasiness within her, just as his former Master had sensed uneasiness within him shortly afterward. Their loyalties were being tested. Principles, too. Such testing was never easy.

Darth Vader was playing a very obvious game now. Starkiller could see it, and he would not be deflected from his course.

He jumped to the second level, and there came face-to-face with Bail Organa, then Kota, then Mon Mothma, then Garm Bel Iblis. When all the leaders of the Rebel Alliance lay dead at his feet, their droid bodies exposed beneath treacherous holograms, Darth Vader attacked again. His blows were swift and economical, and the threat no less than it had ever been, but Starkiller sensed more was to come. Darth Vader would kill him, yes, without hesitation, but he would rather turn him first.

On the fourth level, he came face-to-face with his own father, and struck him down without hesitation. Dreams and memories had no power over him anymore.

He spun to face the attack he had come to expect from the real Darth Vader, full of confidence and surety. The Dark Lord fell back under his blows, and this time, when he leapt for safety, Starkiller telekinetically pulled him back down. His former Master sprawled before him, lightsaber raised defensively. He slashed the hand holding it away, and then plunged his second lightsaber deep into his chest.

With a gasping, wheezing moan, Darth Vader fell back and dissolved into another PROXY droid.

Unsurprised, Starkiller stepped back and looked around for the real Darth Vader. He could see or hear nothing, but his senses tingled with an acute and insistent message.

Above him.

He somersaulted upward and landed in a crouch, ready for anything.

"You are confident," said Darth Vader. "That will be your downfall."

The Dark Lord was standing out of Starkiller's reach. Instead of attacking, he gestured at the rows of cloning tanks beside him. Lights flickered on inside them, revealing row after row of identical forms. Clad in stripped-down version of his former training suit and attached via tubes to complex feeders and breathers, they hung weightlessly in transparent fluid, twitching occasionally in their sleep.

Starkiller felt a shock of recognition jolt through him. These weren't stormtroopers. They were *him*. Incomplete, and oddly warped from true, but definitely him.

Vader gestured again, and the clones' eyes opened.

In them Starkiller saw nothing but hatred, anger, confusion, betrayal, madness, and loss.

Their glass cages shattered. Amniotic fluid boiled away. They pulled free from their cables and tubes and, with motions faltering at first but quickly growing stronger, climbed free from the wreckage.

Starkiller stood his ground as a circle of failed clones formed around him.

Behind them Darth Vader nodded once.

The clones came forward in one overwhelming rush.

CHAPTER 22

JUNO HUNG PAINFULLY in her shackles, doing her best to follow the fight unfolding around her although she could see little of it directly. Sometimes she closed her eyes to let her ears do the work. There was a music to the explosions and weapons fire that played out in waves and bursts all around her. Thus far none of it had impacted directly upon her, but she could feel it coming steadily closer.

After the crash and disintegration of the *Salvation,* a dome had closed above her, sealing this section of the facility behind a secure bubble. Outside, Rebel and Imperial forces had raged hard. Dogfights and furious standoffs between capital vessels lit up the cloudy skies of Kamino, with the occasional capitulation shining like a sun over the battlefield, albeit briefly. It was hard to determine who was winning, partly because of the clouds. She didn't know how many ships were engaging in orbit, or how many the Emperor and Alliance commanders were holding in reserve. What she saw could be the entirety of the conflict, or the merest hint of it.

At one point, through the dome, she thought she saw the unique outline of the *Rogue Shadow* behind the cloak protecting it from enemy gunners' eyes. Her heart leapt. If it was here, then Kota was here, too. Then it disappeared behind a building, just outside the bubble protecting her from the rain. Moments later, she heard the sounds of a concentrated assault on the bubble's walls. Not long after that, gunfire came from below, within the bubble itself, and she knew the fight was definitely coming her way.

She strained against the shackles, wishing she had some way, any way at all, to join the battle. Her four guards were growing restless, probably feeling the same.

TIE fighters circled the interior of the bubble with engines screaming. The fight had stalled while Kota's ground forces faced off against the aerial defenses, but before long the balance shifted again. Someone got a hangar door open, allowing Rebel forces access at last. Dogfights played out around her, and for the first time it occurred to her that, if the facility as a whole was the target, then she herself might not be safe.

That was a sobering thought. What if her presence was unknown—or worse, completely irrelevant—to the attacking forces? She would be collateral damage if the cloning towers fell, and there was nothing she could do about it.

Starkiller was her only hope. If anyone could get to her in time, it would be him.

Rebel starfighters buzzed the towers, but none of them attacked, yet. They were busy with the TIEs and the cannon emplacements. A series of large explosions suggested that Kota's new squad was attacking the dome itself, hoping to expose the facility to the superior firepower outside. When they managed that, she supposed, that would spell the end for her. Not even Starkiller could fend off a concentrated assault from above.

"I don't know about you," she told her guards, "but I feel like a sitting mynock out here."

They didn't respond, but again she could tell they sympathized.

When warning klaxons began to sound in the spire below her, their uneasiness redoubled.

"There goes your exit strategy," she said. "Bet you wish you'd slept in this morning."

Faintly through their helmets she heard the sound of the stormtroopers talking to one another, over their comlinks. Maybe discussing the value in shooting her and making a run for it, although she doubted any of them would risk incurring Vader's wrath. Even with such Rebel firepower arrayed against them, they would regard the Dark Lord as the greatest threat. She remembered feeling that way, once.

Something exploded in the spire, making it sway underfoot.

Juno felt breathless, as though the air were growing thinner.

It was *him*. She was certain of it. The stormtroopers knew it, too. They tightened around her, drawing a false sense of security from closer proximity to one another. They looked at her and glanced quickly away, looking more nervous than ever, and she realized only then that she was smiling.

He was so *close* to her.

The spire shook again, more violently than before. She wondered where Darth Vader was and what he was doing. Surely he wouldn't have brought her to Kamino only to leave her dangling in the trap—unless it had sprung already, and she was no longer needed. But in that case, why didn't the troopers just shoot her and be done with it? She didn't understand the finer details of Vader's plan. That was her only uncertainty.

Seven powerful explosions filled the interior of the dome. With a piercing splitting sound, the dome itself began to shatter. Cracks spread across the transparisteel, fissures dozens of meters long that joined one another and branched to create entirely new ones. They reached up from its base and converged on the center, high above. Where they met, gently, in slow motion, the first pieces began to fall. Each was larger than a starfighter, and easily as heavy. They turned as they fell, tumbling with ponderous grace.

When the first piece hit the buildings below, it shattered into a million pieces.

And from the interior of the spire came a terrible scream, as of a hundred voices at once, crying out in despair.

CHAPTER 23

STARKILLER FOUGHT AS he had never fought before. Clones—*his* clones, nightmarishly imperfect but powerful all the same—pressed in on all sides. Darth Vader's vile conditioning had a profound hold on their immature psychologies. The desire to kill consumed their thoughts. It was all they radiated. Together they could easily have turned on their creator and overpowered him. Instead they were driven to destroy their own.

Not their own. Just him. Whether he was the original Starkiller, as Kota believed, or simply the best copy to date didn't matter. He was their target, and they used every power they possessed to bring him down.

On Kashyyyk he had fought a vision of himself, and won.

On Dagobah, he had seen other versions of him, and spared them.

On Kamino, the choice was taken from him. He had to fight if he was to live, and he had to live in order to save Juno. Thought didn't enter into it. The Force rushed through him, and his lightsabers moved as though of their own accord.

His clones screamed as he cut them down.

It quickly became apparent that the first to rush in were the wildest and weakest both. In their eagerness to do battle, they didn't stop to plan their strategies. What they possessed in speed, they lacked in forethought. He was armed and they were not, so for being headstrong beyond all reason these brutish beings paid the ultimate price.

The next wave either learned from the fate of the first or had enough innate caution to stand back a moment and observe the way he fought. They came at him from all sides, using telekinesis to try to knock him off balance on the blood-slicked floor. He was too fast for them, leaping over their heads and attacking from behind, slashing at their overdeveloped shoulders and hunched backs without remorse.

Moving out of the center of the ring of converging clones brought him into contact with the third wave, the most cunning he had encountered so far. Long-armed and long-fingered, with blackened, blistering skin, these employed lightning when attacking him, and then by devious means. They would wait until he was distracted and attack him from behind, or come at him from three directions at once, or even use one of their fellow clones as an impromptu conductor. Deadly currents crackled and sparkled around him, kept barely at bay by the judicious application of a Force shield. Sometimes a lucky strike caused him pain, but he fought through it, found the source, and put the attack quickly to an end.

From above came the sound of lightsabers activating, and he braced himself for another, more dangerous onslaught. These, the most normal looking of all the clones, spun, slashed, hacked, and stabbed at him from all sides, one-handed, two-handed, with all possible variations of lightsaber combat styles. Red-eyed and hate-filled, they fought each other, too, and the ones who had come before. There were no allies, just a sea of individuals.

And yet . . . Confidence, determination, intelligence, and cunning—combined with physical strength and agility—the clones possessed every attribute he did, in greater or lesser degrees. He saw in their faces the same confusion he felt. They were all clones, so who was he to stand out from among them? What special qualities set him apart?

Who *was* Starkiller, in this mass of faces and bodies?

A desperate rage built up inside him. What if what he felt was nothing but a lingering imprint left behind by the first Starkiller? Did he cling to his feelings with all the more desperation because deep down he knew they were counterfeit? *"The memories of a dead man,"* Vader had called them, blaming them for the torment and confusion he had felt. *"They will fade,"* Vader had promised, but they had not. Did the other clones experience the same hopes and fears? Were their experiences any less worthy than his?

"Destroy what he created . . . hate what he loved . . . be strong . . ." That was the command Vader had given him, on threat of death. But who was the

deliverer of that death? Wasn't he the one delivering to the clones the very fate that he had feared? Had they all been given the same ultimatum?

"You will receive the same treatment as the others."

Death by lightsaber, at his own hand. Perhaps this macabre free-for-all was Vader's way of weeding out the imperfect stock. The last one left standing would be considered the perfect Starkiller, the one who would take his place at Vader's side. Perhaps *that* was his plan.

"You have faced your final test," Vader had told a victorious version of himself in the vision he had received on the *Salvation*. Maybe the vision he had received on Dagobah had warned him of a very real trial, not the metaphorical one he had imagined it to be.

The dark side awaited his call. But if this *was* his final test, then he would not fail. There was too much riding on it. If he gave in to temptation and became Darth Vader's apprentice once more, then it was clear from the vision that Juno would die. She was the whole reason he had escaped, and then returned. He would not turn his back on that, even to survive.

He sought strength from within himself, and pushed outward with all his might. Clones went flying. The empty tubes from which they had emerged shattered into millions of pieces. Platforms buckled and fell with reverberant crashes. The interior of the cloning tower rang as though struck with a giant hammer. Every muscle in his body shook with the effort of it.

The echoes faded, and he felt a peculiar kind of quiet descend. The air was misted red, and every surface was slick with blood. He tasted it on his tongue and smelled it in his nose. *His* blood. A veritable ocean of it.

He maintained a defensive pose, breathing rhythmically and deeply, regaining his strength. The tips of his lightsabers shook. He had never felt so exhausted, at every level of his being. He felt simultaneously cleansed and poisoned.

Nothing moved. Slowly, incredulously, he began to believe that it was over.

They were all dead. He had destroyed every last one of them. He was the only one left—of the many Darth Vader had created to do his bidding.

"Why me?" he asked the silent cloning tower.

"Search your feelings," Vader said, stepping into view at the very top of the tower, lightsaber held tightly in his right hand. "The answer lies within you."

Starkiller stared up at his former Master. What did he have that none of the other clones did?

He remembered:

"How long this time?"

"Thirteen days. Impressive."

And he remembered:

"The Force gives me all I need."

"The Force?"

"The dark side, I mean."

Slowly a dark understanding began to form. All the duels, all the tests, all the torturous mind games, had been to ensure his survival against every opponent—bar one. His Master. In a sense, they were still playing out the first time they had faced each other in combat.

He didn't remember the early days of his apprenticeship, when the memories of his parents had been strong and the young boy he had once been resisted Vader's absolute authority, but he was sure the battle had been even then, psychological. The battle would never cease until one of them won.

Was this what it was like to be a Sith? Forever at war with one's own Master?

"Your training made me strong enough to escape you," he said, "not obey you."

"Yet here you are." Darth Vader's words fell on him like heavy weights. "My most deadly creation."

"You lie!" Starkiller jumped up to the next platform, passion stirring him to action. "You never wanted this. You can't have. Once Juno has been rescued, your facility will be destroyed. You with it, if there's any justice."

"There is no justice," said Darth Vader, watching him ascend. "Only power."

Vader made no move to defend himself when Starkiller reached the very top of the cloning tower. Determined to prove him wrong, Starkiller didn't waste time announcing his intentions. He just lunged. Only at the very last moment did Vader raise his blade to block the blow, and even then the move seemed almost casual, disinterested. Starkiller struck again, with both lightsabers. Vader blocked one blade and used telekinesis to throw the other off target. The platform buckled and twisted, sending Starkiller flying.

He rolled and leapt, and came up swinging. Covered in blood—the blood of his fellow clones—and knowing

Juno was close, he fought his former Master with single-minded focus. Vader was still testing him; he sensed that more and more keenly, with every passing moment, but to what purpose he still couldn't tell. Vader himself fought more cautiously than he had on the Death Star, the last time they had dueled in earnest. His armor seemed to have improved, too; it was less vulnerable to lightning than it had been just days before.

Vader threw wrecked platforms and cloning tubes at him, while he scored three slashes to the Dark Lord's cape in return. They circled the top of the cloning tower, striking and assessing, then striking again.

Starkiller swore that he would not give in to anger or frustration. If that was what Darth Vader wanted, he wasn't going to get it. The only emotion he would give in to was love.

Finally, Starkiller saw an opportunity. They were exchanging rapid blows along the edge of the buckled platform, blades swinging so fast they were visible only as blurs. Vader's defenses were impenetrable; his lightsaber seemed to arrive a split second before Starkiller's, every time. He may have defeated Vader before, but Vader had learned from that mistake. He knew the measure of his former apprentice now.

But the same was true in reverse. And when Vader forced Starkiller onto his back foot and raised his lightsaber to strike him down, Starkiller fired a lightning blast into the side of Vader's armor that was so concentrated, even the new insulation couldn't absorb it.

The Dark Lord stiffened, betrayed by his extensive

prosthetics. The distraction lasted only a moment, but it was enough. Starkiller knocked his blade out of the way and moved in to strike.

Juno lying limp in his arms.

The vision struck him as powerfully as a physical blow. When he tried to push it aside, it returned with even more power.

Juno—dead.

He reeled in shock. Was this what would happen if he killed Vader? He had no choice but to believe so. But if he didn't kill Vader, how would he ever get to her?

The Dark Lord took advantage of his momentary confusion. He delivered a telekinetic shove that threw Starkiller backward off the platform and down to the lower levels of the ruined cloning tower. The blow and the fall had the welcome effect of clearing his mind. He turned in midair and landed on his feet. An instant later he was leaping upward again, his face a mask of determination.

Whatever happened to Juno, he saw no choice but to confront Darth Vader. The Dark Lord had killed his father, betrayed him at least once, and would kill Juno the very second she was of no more use to him. Their time of reckoning was long overdue.

The attainment of his true mastery of the Force—the destiny Darth Vader so often threatened him with—could only come one way. He saw that now. His final test was to kill Vader himself.

When he reached the top level, Vader was disappearing behind the doors of another turbolift. Starkiller ripped them open, but the cab had already begun to ascend. He had no intention of waiting for it to return. He braced himself on the inside of the shaft, and jumped.

One powerful leap saw him rising almost as fast as the cab. He reached telekinetically for its underside, and caught it. When the cab started to slow, he approached close enough to physically hold on to the underside, and raised one lightsaber to cut his way through.

The cab jerked to a halt. Vader was already gone by the time Starkiller emerged through a circular hole in the floor. Outside the cab wasn't another cloning tower. A short ramp led up to the roof of the spire itself, currently out of sight. Starkiller emerged from the cab, a tightness in his chest telling him that Juno was very close now. Very close indeed. She was exactly where he had last seen her.

It was raining.

The dome had been breached. All around him, the fight between the Rebels and Imperials waged on. Wrecked starfighters tumbled from the sky in flames. Debris gushed out of wounded frigates. A listing Star Destroyer vented air and bodies in huge quantities. Across the facility, dozens of dark columns of smoke formed a thick veil of carbonized ash, choking the air. A constant high-frequency pulsation of energy weapons came from all around him, punctuated by the occasional bass explosion. It was impossible to tell who was winning.

Wary of an ambush, Starkiller walked up the ramp. As he did so, Darth Vader came into view. The Dark Lord stood with his lightsaber extinguished in the center of the roof. Behind him, partially obscured by their lord, were four stormtroopers with weapons held at the ready.

"Get out of my way," he said.

"Your memories betray you," Darth Vader said.

"They make me who I am."

"You must turn your back on them in order to become who you will be."

Starkiller stopped in his tracks. Was *that* why Darth Vader burdened him with everything the original Starkiller had been—to demonstrate his strength and commitment by dismissing it, his former self with it? Or was there still some other motive that he couldn't discern?

Of only one thing was he certain. He wouldn't turn his back on Juno for any incentive.

"Never," he said.

"Then she will die."

Darth Vader stepped aside, revealing Juno in shackles. He gestured, and the four stormtroopers surrounding her raised their weapons and fired as one.

CHAPTER 24

WHEN DARTH VADER WALKED onto the roof, the stormtroopers stood to immediate attention. Juno straightened, too, but not out of respect. She didn't know what was coming, but she swore she would be ready for it. The strange sounds coming from below—the screams and clash of lightsabers—had encouraged her to hope that it would be Starkiller who came to her first, but that was dashed now. If he was dead, then Vader would surely have no reason to keep her alive.

Her guards' comlinks chattered too faintly for her to make out the words. Orders, she assumed, from the Dark Lord. They nodded and took new positions, two on either side of her. Then they all turned to face their Master, and he turned his back on them.

For a second, the world paused. The fighting around the spires seemed to lessen. Even the conflict in the sky grew still. She felt as though everyone in Kamino was looking in her direction—although surely, she knew, they didn't even see her. It was all about Vader and

Starkiller—if the man she had loved was still alive.

Footsteps came up the ramp. She strained against her bonds, but Vader was directly in her line of sight. She couldn't see past him.

She could hear, though, and she would recognize his voice under any conditions, just like the *Rogue Shadow*.

"Get out of my way," he said to Vader.

"Your memories betray you."

"They make me who I am."

"You must turn your back on them in order to become who you will be."

"Never," he said.

Vader stepped to one side, and past the swirling of his cloak, Juno saw him—Starkiller—and for an instant she didn't see the blood all over him or the tattered state of his flight uniform. All she saw was his eyes. And they in turn saw nothing but her.

"Then she will die," Vader said, raising one hand in a signal to her guards.

They raised their weapons, took aim, and fired.

It happened so fast she barely had time to flinch. Vader had been keeping her alive for so long now that it didn't seem entirely real that he would dispose of her so suddenly. She jerked forward as far as the shackles allowed her, straining to get away. Every muscle in her body tensed in readiness.

The weapons' muzzles flashed—

—and at that very instant a massive force struck her and the guards, flinging her backward so hard she thought her chains might break her wrists. The stormtroopers effectively disappeared, swept off the top of the spire in an instant. The shots they had fired all missed, deflected by the powerful force, although one burned her right cheek as it went by. The four energy bursts followed wild trajectories, outward across the crowded sky.

"Juno!"

Her shackles fell to the ground with a heavy clatter.

Alive but winded, she couldn't reply. She could barely even believe she was alive. She had caught just the fringe of the push that had killed the guards, and she knew that even so she had almost been killed herself.

A different force gripped her, one no less powerful than the first, but aimed at her, not at anything else. It gripped her cruelly about the throat and lifted her so her feet barely touched the ground.

"Bow before me," said Vader to the man she loved.

Starkiller took a step forward. The force gripped her even more tightly, closing her windpipe. She choked, kicking out and finding no ground at all beneath her now. Her hands pulled at her throat, but there was nothing there to grip, and no way to fight it.

"Juno!"

She heard the furious despair in Starkiller's voice, and understood that he was fighting for her, and losing.

"Bow before me," Vader repeated, "or she dies."

Don't, she wanted to say. *Don't do it. You've been down that path before. You know where it leads you.* But she couldn't speak. She could barely even see him. Black dots were crowding out her vision as her oxygen-starved optic nerve began to fail. *Don't let him trick you again.*

He couldn't possibly hear her, but she suspected it wouldn't make any difference. In his shoes, she would be tempted to give in, too. After all they had been through, after all they might have been but had been denied, they at last had a second chance. Arguably that was worth more than any political movement or philosophy. So long as they survived, their love would survive. Nothing else mattered.

She understood, but she felt no relief as Darth Vader's terrible grip loosened and she fell painfully to the ground. Cool air rushed into her lungs. She coughed as though retching, feeling pain all along her windpipe.

Over the sound of her hacking and wheezing, she heard two metallic clinks and looked up to see what had happened.

Starkiller had deactivated his lightsabers and thrown them at Vader's feet. They rolled across the rooftop, their residual heat making the raindrops steam.

Her vocal cords were red raw. Juno could only shake her head as Starkiller took three steps forward, and went down on one knee at Darth Vader's feet.

"I'll do your bidding," he said. "Just promise me you'll never hurt her again."

"That," said Vader, "depends entirely on you."

Starkiller bowed his head, and Juno fought the urge to weep. She understood the dark place from which his capitulation had come, but submission to Darth Vader was not the way to save her. That way lay nothing but more separation and death. And betrayal. And murder.

She had to find the strength somehow to free Starkiller—

just as he, clone or original, had somehow fought his way back from the dead in order to find her again.

Her desperate gaze caught sight of one of Starkiller's lightsabers. It had rolled in her direction and lay just out of her reach. If she was quiet, she might just be able to reach it.

The equation was very simple, really. Once before, she had abandoned her entire life for Starkiller. She could easily abandon this one too if it meant saving him from the horrible fate he had just accepted, thinking that it would save *her*.

Vader's back was to her, and Starkiller's head was still bowed.

She raised herself to hands and knees and reached out for the lightsaber.

"You will find and kill General Kota," Vader said. "If you refuse, the woman dies."

Starkiller said nothing. Maybe he nodded, but Juno couldn't see him. Vader had placed himself firmly between them once again, symbolically as well as physically.

"You will return to me and give yourself to the dark side," Vader went on. "If you resist, she dies."

The warm metal hilt slid into Juno's hand. She lifted it gently, afraid of making any noise at all, and raised herself to her knees. This was the first time she had held a lightsaber. She knew all too well that it was probably going to be her last.

"And when your training is complete," Vader said, "you will hunt down and execute the Rebel leaders."

Still winded and aching from head to foot, Juno rose

unsteadily to her feet, feeling for the lightsaber's activation switch and hardly daring to take her eyes off Vader's back as she did so. They were less than two paces apart.

"If you fail, she dies."

She pressed the activation switch at the same instant she lunged. The bright blue blade sprang to life with a startling hiss, but she didn't let herself be distracted. She had used vibroblades in her training days; she knew how to wield a sword. It was even simpler than the point-and-shoot quip about blasters.

She stabbed at Vader's back, taking the one chance she had left to reclaim her life with Starkiller.

For an instant, she thought it might actually work. Vader's attention was firmly on Starkiller, and the sounds of battle provided effective cover. What was one more energy weapon over the hundreds in play in the facility?

At the last instant, however, some arcane instinct must have warned him. He turned with inhuman speed. She could barely credit her eyes—black holes didn't spin so fast. The tip of Starkiller's lightsaber grazed the front of his chest panel, producing a shower of sparks. She felt no resistance.

Then he pushed her in exactly the same way Starkiller had pushed the stormtroopers. She felt as though the world moved out from under her, sucking all the air away with it. The lightsaber fell from her hand, and suddenly she was flying. Her head snapped forward, and the rain boiled around her. The air itself seemed to hurt, she was moving so fast. Vader receded into the distance with uncanny speed.

How far he pushed her, she couldn't tell. It seemed to last forever, but she knew she had to hit the ground sometime. She hoped it wouldn't be soon. Landing was going to hurt.

Something slammed into her from behind.

It *did* hurt.

The last thing she felt was rain falling into her open eyes. The last thing she saw were three lightsaber blades painting red and blue shapes against the encroaching black.

CHAPTER 25

STARKILLER RAN PAST DARTH VADER to where Juno lay broken on the edge of the cloning spire's roof. Horror and self-reproach filled his mind. He hadn't seen her crawling for the lightsaber; he hadn't sensed her desperate plan until the very last moment—and it was *his* alarm that had alerted Vader, he was sure of it. He and his former Master had reacted at the same time. If Starkiller had moved an instant faster, had a fraction more of a second to think the problem through, he would have pushed Vader just as Vader had pushed Juno, impaling him on the blade before it was whisked away. Instead, he had thought only of saving Juno—a plan, he feared, that might always have been doomed to failure.

He stopped her before she flew off the edge of the roof, at least, but the grisly crunch of bones when she landed was unmistakable. Her head was bent at an impossible angle, and her eyes didn't track him as he ran toward her.

"Juno!"

A black-gloved hand grabbed his shoulder. He pulled away, howling with rage. His fallen lightsabers snapped into his hands and came instantly to life. With both blades moving in tandem, he struck out at his former Master using all his strength, all his rage, all his grief. Darth Vader blocked the blow, but only just. Starkiller pushed, and the Dark Lord stumbled backward.

Instead of pursuing the attack, Starkiller went to go to Juno, but once again Darth Vader stood in his path.

"Get out of my way."

"Your feelings for her are not real," Vader said, not moving.

"They are real to me."

Starkiller attacked the Dark Lord again, but this time he was the one driven back.

With a sense of piercing despair, he saw exactly how the fight would go. He and his former Master would dance like marionettes while Juno lay dying—if she wasn't already dead—and the war raged around them, unchecked by this minor tragedy. In the context of the galaxy's suffering, Juno was just one freedom fighter who had died that day—one among many on Kamino alone. Only she hadn't given her life in combat or to save someone less fortunate than herself. She had been snuffed out thanks to the manipulations of one single tortured man, a man whose stubbornness would never allow him to give up, admit fault, or compromise.

Starkiller knew nothing about the Dark Lord's origins, but he knew what he had become. More monolith than man, his shadow bestrode the Empire, casting darkness wherever it fell. But what was the source of that scourge? What twisted psychology had brought him to where he stood now—risking his life to prevent the clone of his failed apprentice from coming near the body of the woman he had loved?

Sudden understanding burst in Starkiller's mind. This was what Darth Vader had wanted all along. He had been right to fear that Juno was in danger, but not just from clones like him—from Vader, who would use her death to destabilize Starkiller and lead him headlong back to the dark side via anger and despair. Where Starkiller had seen hope, where Starkiller had been willing to sacrifice his own destiny to give the woman he had loved a chance to live, his former Master had seen only opportunity for betrayal—for without Juno, what did Starkiller have left to live and fight for? He had no family, friends, or allies. Juno was always intended to be the catalyst for his downfall. Her precipitous attack had merely brought the critical moment forward.

Starkiller saw things very differently. It wasn't *Juno* who had to die to complete Starkiller's training. It was Darth Vader himself, and he had brought this moment upon himself. Had he been content to let Starkiller go, none of this would have happened. Were he dead or freely searching for Juno, either way, he would never have willingly come back to Kamino. He would have gone anywhere else, and never returned.

Darth Vader simply wouldn't let go. The massive cloning exercise itself was proof of that. He had raised Starkiller to be a monster, and he would let nothing get in the way of achieving that outcome. Not even Starkiller's own death. Even if it took a thousand reincarnations and the death of trillions of innocent people, Darth Vader would not give up. His persistence, his unwillingness to accept defeat, was both his greatest strength and his greatest weakness.

All the clones were destroyed. As far as Starkiller knew, he was the last one left—so that was one vision averted, at least. No matter what happened, no version of him would fall foul of Darth Vader's vile plan now.

They fought like the Sith Lords of old, raging back and forth across the roof of the spire, uncaring what happened around them. Starkiller maintained his efforts to get to Juno, and Darth Vader did everything in his power to stop him. Neither would capitulate. Neither would be the first to break. Their wills were locked.

They broke apart, lightsabers hissing in the ceaseless rain. Lightning split the sky into a thousand jagged shapes. Thunder rolled. Neither had noticed the battle fading around them.

"Let me go," Starkiller said, sounding much calmer than he felt. His heart was pounding, and his lungs burned. "You've taken everything from me. You must see that I will never serve you now."

"You are wrong. I have given you everything."

"This?" He gestured at Juno's inert form. He couldn't tell if she was breathing, but he still held out a distant hope. "You have done nothing for me."

"It is our destiny to destroy the Emperor. You and me, together."

There it was, Starkiller thought. That promise again. Surely Darth Vader could see that it meant nothing now, after so many times offered in the past, and none of them fulfilled?

Unless . . . A deeper layer of understanding presented itself. Unless Darth Vader felt exactly the same as he did.

What lengths had the Emperor, Darth Vader's Master, gone to in order to create *him*? And how far would Darth Vader go to get revenge? To attain his own destiny as a Sith?

"The Rebels want to destroy the Emperor," Starkiller said. "Why not work with them rather th—?"

Vader attacked before he could finish the sentence, a blistering combination of blows that left Starkiller on his back foot. Clearly he had hit a very deep nerve. For a fleeting moment, the plan had seemed almost inspired. With Darth Vader on Kota's side, what couldn't the Alliance accomplish?

But it was a dream. The Rebels would never trust the Emperor's apprentice, and Vader was making it very clear that he wanted no part of it either. The vehemence of his response left no doubt about that.

Starkiller found himself backed up almost to the edge of the cloning spire's roof. One more step, and he would fall, and to fall would give Vader the high ground. That might not result in his death, but it would certainly end the fight.

It needed to end now, or else it might *never* end.

Blow after blow rained on him, forcing him back. There had to be a way to free himself and avenge

Juno at the same time . . . but a stalemate seemed unavoidable. Any move he made was sure to lead him to an indefensible position.

Then it occurred to him. An indefensible position was exactly what he needed.

He lunged. Darth Vader saw him coming and swiped with unbeatable strength, sending Starkiller's left lightsaber flying in pieces. Starkiller lunged again, and his right lightsaber joined his left. He fell back, beaten, and stared up at his former Master.

"This is your last chance," Vader said, standing over him with the unwavering tip of his lightsaber pointed directly at Starkiller's chest.

Starkiller stared up at the black mask, sure of two things. Vader didn't want to kill him, but not out of mercy or sympathy for his lot. The Dark Lord had invested far too much time and energy in re-creating his former apprentice, and he wouldn't want to throw all that away. Not when he seemed on the verge of victory.

Juno was dead or dying. Starkiller was disarmed and helpless.

Any rational being would at least consider Vader's offer.

The second thing Starkiller knew was: *The best way to beat Darth Vader is to let him think he's won.*

Thinking of Wedge Antilles, he said, "I make my own chances."

With both hands he sent a wave of lightning into the sparking gash Juno had made in Vader's chest plate.

The Dark Lord staggered backward, transfixed by the

unexpected retaliation. Starkiller leapt to his feet and followed him, keeping up the lightning attack and using telekinesis to rip Vader's lightsaber from his temporarily weakened fingers. Sheets of energy spread out across the wet rooftop. Smoke and steam rose up in a tortured spiral. The grating whine of Vader's respirator took on a desperate edge.

He went down on one knee. Starkiller stood over him. Vader's lightsaber swept into his former apprentice's hand. The blade came to rest at his throat.

Starkiller stared into the black mask, breathing heavily. One twitch of the blade and Vader would be dead at last.

"Wait," said a voice from behind him.

Starkiller froze, remembering his vision of being stabbed in the back. But the other clones were dead. And like the owner of this unexpected voice, he didn't need to look to see what was in fact occurring.

Booted feet splashed in the water as Kota and members of his squad ran up the ramp and surrounded him, training their guns on Vader. Starkiller didn't move. He kept the lightsaber at Vader's neck, ready to finish what Vader himself had started.

"Why wait?" he asked. "You want him dead as much as I do."

"Yes, of course." There was no hiding the venom in the general's voice. "But not yet. Not until he's told us the Empire's secrets."

"You want to take him *prisoner*?"

"To a hidden Rebel base where we can interrogate him, put him on trial for crimes against the true Republic."

Starkiller felt Kota's hand on his shoulder. "And *then* we'll execute him, to show the galaxy that we don't need to fear him any longer."

For several seconds the only sounds came from Vader's wheezing respirator and the storm around them. Water ran down Starkiller's face in rippling streams. Kota's hand gripped him tightly, and it wasn't entirely a gesture of reassurance. There was warning in it, too.

Kota didn't understand. Starkiller was under no threat of the dark side. He wouldn't turn evil just by killing Vader.

"If I let him live," Starkiller said, "he'll haunt me forever."

The general came in closer and spoke in a whisper only Starkiller could hear. "Remember this: Vader is the only one who knows if and how you survived. He can't tell you if you are the original you if he is dead."

Starkiller looked at Kota. The general's face showed no sign of dissemblance. He meant everything he said, even though it pained him. Under any other circumstances, Kota would have relished killing Vader himself, but here he was arguing against it, with one hand on his lightsaber hilt to show that he meant business.

Starkiller looked at Vader, kneeling in the rain with his own lightsaber at his throat, waiting for Starkiller to complete his training and do what Vader had never been able to do himself: kill his own Master.

Either way, Starkiller thought, *I've beaten him.*

That was the only thing left that mattered.

He deactivated the lightsaber and turned away. Kota

instantly took his place, holding his blade at Vader's chest while the Rebel soldiers moved in.

"Get something to hold him," Kota ordered, "quickly!"

"Yes, General."

Starkiller didn't stay to watch. PROXY was kneeling next to Juno's body, checking for signs of vitality. Starkiller ran to them and dropped on his knees at Juno's side. Her eyes had closed. Wet hair lay flat across her forehead, limp and colorless.

"Is she—?"

"I'm sorry, Master," the droid said. "I can't revive her."

Juno's features flickered across PROXY's metal face, and then vanished.

"I have failed you again."

Barely hearing PROXY's words, Starkiller gathered her up into his arms and held her tightly to his chest. She was still warm, despite the rain.

"It's not your fault, PROXY. It's mine."

"Yours, Master? Is your primary program malfunctioning, too?"

All Starkiller could see was smoke and storm clouds and the ruination of war.

"I should never have left here, Juno," he said to her, although she was beyond all words. "I should never have come back . . ."

CHAPTER 26

AT THE SOUND of an unfamiliar energy weapon activating nearby, Juno looked up from her work and reached for the blaster pistol at her side. Putting down her welder, she disengaged the safety on her pistol and inched out from under the ship.

Two men armed with lightsabers leapt and tumbled with inhuman agility across the hangar. When they gestured, metal walls buckled and engine parts flew like bullets. One of the combatants rammed his crimson lightsaber through the chest of his opponent, and things took a decidedly strange turn. The arms, legs, torso, and face of the stricken man flickered and dissolved, revealing the bipedal form of a droid, which fell forward with a clatter of metal on metal.

"Ah, Master. Another excellent duel."

The droid struggled to stand and remain upright.

"Easy, PROXY. You're malfunctioning."

"It's my fault, Master. I had hoped that using an older training module would catch you off guard and allow me to finally kill you. I'm sorry I failed you again."

"I'm sure you'll keep trying."

"Of course, Master. It is my primary programming."

Droid and Master began moving through the maze of debris across the hangar.

"PROXY, who is that?"

"Ah, yes. Your new pilot has finally arrived, Master."

"You know why you're here?" Starkiller asked her.

"Lord Vader gave me my orders himself," she said. "I am to keep your ship running and fly you wherever your missions require."

Starkiller seemed neither pleased nor displeased. "Did Lord Vader tell you that he killed our last pilot?"

"No. But I can only assume he gave Lord Vader good cause to do so. I will not."

"We'll see. I'm sick of training new pilots."

FOR EVERY ENDING there was a beginning. And for every beginning, a middle.

In the cells of the Empirical, she stared in amazement not just at Starkiller, but at the slaughter he had meted out to her stormtrooper guards as well.

"Juno . . ."

Words didn't come easily. The last time she had seen him, he had been floating through space, to all appearances dead. "It's—really you!"

PROXY cut across their reunion.

"Master, hurry! She is part of your past life now. Leave her behind, as Lord Vader commanded!"

"I can't."

Starkiller destroyed the magna locks holding her captive. Weakened by months of confinement, she fell to the ground and had to be helped to her feet.

"I saw you die," she said, staring at him in disbelief. A thousand confused thoughts formed a pileup in her mind. "But you've come back."

"I have some unfinished business."

"Vader?"

"Don't worry about him," he told her.

Easier said than done, she thought, although the reality of her rescue was slowly sinking in.

"I've been branded a traitor to the Empire," she said. "I can't go anywhere, do anything—"

"I don't care about any of that. I'm leaving the Empire behind." He offered her an expression that might have been a smile. "And I need a pilot."

"I hope you have a plan."

He nodded. "There are two things I want, and I can't get them on my own. The first is revenge. To get that we need to rally the Emperor's enemies behind us."

"Go on."

"The second thing I want is to learn all the things that Vader couldn't—or wouldn't—teach me about the Force."

"If we're not careful," she had said, "we might end up in our old job again—hunting Jedi."

It had been a joke.

* * *

AFTER *EMPIRICAL* HAD COME KASHYYYK, and after Kashyyyk had come Felucia.

"Juno, wait, this isn't what—"

"Of course it is," she snapped, pulling away from him. "You're still loyal to Vader. After all he did to us— branding me a traitor and trying to kill you—you're still his . . . his . . ."

"His slave."

"Yes. But if that's so . . . why? Why did you defy your Master to rescue me?"

"My being here has never been about my piloting."

He neither denied nor admitted the truth of her accusation. She went to leave, but on the threshold she stopped.

"I don't know who—or what—you really are. Maybe I'll never know. But sometime soon, you will decide the fate of the Rebellion, not your Master. That's something he can't take away from you. And when you're faced with that moment, remember that I, too, was forced to leave everything I've ever known."

AFTER FELUCIA, Raxus Prime and Corellia.

Juno could see Starkiller's grief visibly turning to anger as he realized exactly how far he had been played for a fool by his Master.

"Yes, you did do what he wanted. There's no point hiding from it—and now the fate of the Alliance rests on your shoulders. The question is, what are you going to do about it?"

He wrestled with his emotions and thoughts. When he raised his head, he was resolved.

"We're going after Vader. And the Rebels."

"Where?"

"I don't know," he admitted. "Not yet."

"Do you know how this is going to end?"

He hesitated, and then shook his head. "No."

BUT THERE HAD TO BE AN ENDING. The only question was: When?

"Juno—"

"Don't say it. Don't say a word." She glanced at him. "Just tell me you're still sure. This is what we have to do, right?"

"It is."

"All right."

The air outside was cold but breathable. As the ramp opened, it rushed in around them, making her shiver.

The view down to the surface of the Death Star was giddying, but she was unable to look away.

"I have a really bad feeling about this."

"Then we must be doing the right thing."

She looked up at him. "Am I going to see you again?"

"Probably not, no."

"Then I guess I'll never need to live this down."

She pulled him closer to her and kissed him hard on the lips.

* * *

THAT LOOKED LIKE AN ENDING. It certainly felt like an
ending.

"He's at one with the Force NOW," Kota said.

AND WHEN THINGS ENDED, they stayed ended.

"We need a symbol to rally behind," Leia said.
   "Agreed," said Garm Bel Iblis.
   *The Princess wiped dust from the table, revealing
Starkiller's family crest etched into the wood. "A symbol
of hope."*

THEY WERE SUPPOSED TO, anyway.

Juno watched the Rogue Shadow *leave Corellia with a
sinking heart, although she knew it would be perfectly safe
in Kota and Bail Organa's hands. There were just so many
memories attached to it. Letting it go was like losing a part
of herself. Unfortunately, she wasn't losing the part of her
that still ached for* him. *That remained exactly where it was,
in the center of her chest, pounding like a funeral drum . . .*

"I hardly ever see you smile," said Shyre, tapping her
dangling boot with one of his metal legs. *"You wisecrack
and take shots at everyone, but you don't laugh. Is there
a reason for that?"*
   *Juno wished she hadn't had that last eyeblaster. It was
making her head ache but doing nothing at all to help
her forget.*

"It's old news," she said, wondering if maybe the problem wasn't having one too many, but not having had enough.

She was beginning to wonder if there would ever be enough.

"Congratulations, Captain," said Commodore Viedas on the bridge of her first command. "The Salvation is a fine ship. It will serve you well, and I know you will return the compliment."

"Thank you, sir." She tried not to stare around the bridge in wonder. The truth was that she felt proud and daunted at the same time. She had come a long way from TIE fighter squadrons and secret missions for Darth Vader.

Her expression fell, as it always did when he came to mind.

"Don't worry," said the commodore, coming closer to whisper a brisk reassurance. "We all feel nervous the first time out."

He had misunderstood her mood, but she didn't correct him. Better to let him believe what he wanted to believe, and to keep her scars hidden.

"Let's not be blinded as Kota was," said Mon Mothma, "by the dream of an easy victory. We learned the hard way that will never be our lot."

"You wouldn't be saying that if Starkiller were here."

Mon Mothmas looked at her sternly. "He's not here, so the point is irrelevant."

* * *

Juno stared, blinking, as a figure dressed entirely in black leapt out of a hole in the floor. The bounty hunter fired three shots in quick succession. The energy bolts were deflected by a pair of spinning lightsabers into the walls, where they discharged brightly. By their light, Juno saw the face of the man running toward her.

Juno stared at the clone in the tube, her jaw working. Through her distress and confusion, one core certainty remained. It didn't matter where Starkiller came from or what he was, just so long as he was the same man she had loved. She would know who he was the moment she saw him. Nothing in the universe could keep that truth from her.

Vader stepped aside. Juno saw Starkiller, and he saw Juno. In that moment she knew.

She knew that she was right and Darth Vader was wrong. Shyre was wrong. Mon Mothma was wrong.

EVERYONE WHO INSISTED STARKILLER'S story had ended was wrong.

"Your feelings for her are not real," Vader insisted.
"They are real to me."

NOT EVEN DEATH could stop her from hearing him call her name.

* * *

"*Juno . . . come back . . .*"

CHAPTER 27

JUNO'S FACE WAS WET. From tears or the rain, she couldn't tell. Her entire being felt relieved of a mighty weight—as though an incredible pain had just been taken from her, leaving her not quite of the world.

Kamino.

Memories rushed back in.

Vader.

An echo of that terrible pain swept through her, and then disappeared forever.

Starkiller.

He was holding her. She could smell him. When she opened her eyes, she could see him *right there,* so close to her, that he almost seemed part of her. His forehead pressed firmly against hers. His eyes were closed and his face was wet, too, although perhaps not from only the rain.

She reached up and touched his cheek, felt him start and almost pull away.

Their eyes met.

Weightless, impossible, miraculous—there were no words for how she felt. Time had rolled back, and so many wrongs had been righted, just by being here, now, with him.

She pulled herself up and kissed him properly, without fear, without regret, and without the smallest doubt that it was the most perfect thing to do in that moment.

He held her as though he planned never to let go.

"We're alive," she whispered into his ear. "We are both of us so very alive."

EPILOGUE: Kamino

SOMETIMES, ON EXCEEDINGLY rare occasions, it stopped raining on Kamino. On this occasion, Starkiller thought, there might be a very good, meteorological reason for the relatively fair turn in the weather. Numerous fires burned in the doomed facility, sending hot air rising into the cloud layer, while the upper atmosphere still boiled from the battle that had only recently finished. He wasn't, therefore, entirely surprised by the sudden sunlight that shone weakly down onto the restless ocean. He just knew it wouldn't last.

"The *Rogue Shadow*'s on its way," said Kota. "As far as containment and concealment go, that remains our best bet."

"Agreed," said Juno, all business. She stayed at Starkiller's side, tightly holding his hand, having made it clear several times that she was unwilling to be parted from him. He wasn't remotely inclined to force the point. It still seemed a miracle that they were together again, after all the obstacles the universe had placed in their path.

"And you," said Kota to him in a sharper tone. "Where do you stand now? Are you with us or going off on your own, now that you have what you want?"

Juno glanced anxiously at him. There hadn't been time to talk about how this changed things. He didn't know when they would find time to.

"I'm with you," he said, sure that Juno would have it no other way. Wherever his destiny lay, it would be with her and the Rebellion she served, if they would have him. "One hundred percent."

Kota nodded, although his relief was clouded. They had scored a significant victory against the Empire, but so much more needed to be done. If Kota still wanted him to be a rallying point, then so be it. As long as it got the job done.

In that sense, he supposed, it didn't matter if he was a clone or not. The ends justified the means. And the ultimate end was to defeat the Emperor. He was sure no one would quibble about his pedigree when that day arrived.

Still, the clones he had murdered on Kamino would haunt him forever, he knew. What gave them any less right to live than him? If he was one of them, the stain of fratricide—or suicide—would always be on his hands.

Unless, he suddenly thought to himself, the Starkiller who had died on the Death Star had been a clone, and he *was* the original after all. Maybe then, if that were the case, his doubts would be settled.

Only one person knew the truth. And he wasn't talking. Juno squeezed his hand, as though sensing his inner conflict and seeking to reassure him. He squeezed back, wishing they had time to be alone. They had so much to talk about, so many events to catch up on. Now that they had both returned from death, it was finally time to start living.

Someone shouted on the other side of the spire roof. Starkiller anxiously glanced in that direction, right hand reaching for the lightsaber hilt at his belt.

It was nothing. Just a slight disagreement over the proper fastening of the harness. Still, his attention was diverted.

"Go help," said Juno. "I've got a meeting to attend, anyway." She kissed him briefly on the lips. "Just don't go too far away."

Starkiller understood that sentiment completely. The power of love had brought her back to him—he could see no other explanation for it. It hadn't been the Force, and it hadn't been medical science, unless there was more happening on Kamino than simple cloning. However it had happened, he couldn't assume that just because it had happened once, it would ever happen again.

Only with great reluctance did he allow his hand to leave hers, telling himself that surely a few meters wouldn't hurt.

Leaving Kota and Juno to discuss Alliance business, he strode over to where the members of Kota's new squad were dealing with the weighty matter of the prisoner.

JUNO WATCHED HIM go and was unable to hold in a smile. She still couldn't believe it had worked out this way. Kota was alive, Vader captured, Starkiller back at her side, and the operation on Kamino a success. She was certain now that the Alliance would see the sense in Kota's approach and ultimately succeed in all its aims.

Feeling Kota's blind-eyed attention on her, she shifted the direction of her own stare. Above them, numerous capital ships orbited, including the gutted remains of the three Star Destroyers stationed in the system to defend the facility. She counted several Alliance cruisers and frigates, among them one whose configuration she didn't recognize.

"Where'd that come from?" she asked, pointing.

"The MC-Eighty?" Kota said. "A friend of yours on Dac heard you were in trouble and sent it to help. Tipped the balance in our favor."

Her smile broadened. *Ackbar.* Things were coming together with incredible speed. Whatever Starkiller had done to bring her back, he seemed to have made everything else right as well.

PROXY came to join them. "I am expecting the transmission at any moment," he said. "There have been some difficulties establishing completely secure protocols but I believe—"

The droid stopped in midsentence. His holoprojectors sparkled and shimmered. With a crackling noise, his appearance and posture changed, and Juno found herself staring at the youthful face of Bail Organa's daughter.

"I received your message, General," Leia said, "but as you're supposed to be dead, I'm not sure how much credence to give it."

"It's true, Your Highness," he told her. "We have him."

"Vader himself?"

"He's being prepared for transport as we speak."

Leia looked as though she still couldn't believe what she was hearing. "This changes everything! When the Emperor hears we've got his prize thug on a leash . . ." She visibly snapped herself out of her thoughts. "That's not for me to decide. Captain Eclipse, I'm relieved to see you in one piece, too."

"Thank you," she said.

"I hope you're not seriously injured."

Juno raised her left forearm, which was encapsulated by a field brace. Her shoulder still bothered her, but she didn't notice the pain anymore. "I'll live." She would indeed.

"My commiserations regarding the *Salvation*. I understand it was lost during the assault on Kamino."

"A small price to pay," she said, although she reminded herself to take Starkiller to task for that, later. If he made a habit of destroying her commands, she would never get anywhere in the Alliance hierarchy. "We'll use the *Rogue Shadow* to ferry Vader to Dantooine."

Kota added, "At the same time, we'll send a dozen freighters in a dozen different directions. Even if someone finds out we have him, they won't know which ship to follow."

"Excellent," said Leia. "And the security detail?"

Juno and Kota exchanged glances.

"We have it covered," she said.

"It's not just the Imperials we have to worry about,"

Leia said, her face very serious. "As I'm sure you're very aware, General, there are plenty of people on our own side who would like to see Vader dead. The mission to overthrow the Emperor is more important than any personal vendetta."

Kota cleared his throat. It sounded like the growl of a large and dangerous animal.

"Rest assured, Your Highness," he said, "that if Vader dies in custody, it won't be by my hand. And anyone who tries will feel the hot edge of my blade."

Leia nodded. "Thank you, General Kota. I know I can trust you."

Kota nodded stiffly, as he always did when offered a compliment. Leia smiled reassuringly, and Juno was impressed by the deftness with which she handled him. She combined the military understanding of Garm Bel Iblis and the diplomacy of Mon Mothma. Perhaps, Juno thought, *she* might turn out to be the one to marry both means and end and thereby unite the Alliance, not her father or Kota or even Juno. If she only had time to grow up . . .

"I'd like to debrief with you personally, Captain Eclipse," Leia said. "Do you think we'll have the opportunity on Dantooine?"

"I hope so, Princess," Juno said, surprised but pleased that Leia had made the overture.

Kota said, "We'll contact you again once we have Vader safely locked away."

"Good." Leia's expression was cautiously optimistic. After the bickering and confusion of recent weeks, it looked good on her. "This is a turning point for the

Alliance. You should both be very proud. May the Force be with you."

Juno saluted and Kota bowed. PROXY's holographic form dissolved, and Leia was gone.

"Keeping him a secret is going to be difficult," said Kota.

"Which 'him'?"

The general inclined his head to where Starkiller was assisting the imprisonment team. "My squad will never tell anyone. You can be sure of that. But they're not the only ones who've seen him. A pilot is asking about someone who hitched a ride on his Y-wing. Some of the survivors of the *Salvation* have been talking, too. I think we can trust Berkelium Shyre, but—"

"Starkiller was on Malastare?"

"Yes, two days ago. Why?"

She shook her head. It didn't matter. They would have plenty of time later to chart their near misses. Hopefully the repairman didn't say anything untoward.

"I thought you wanted him to lead the charge."

Kota sighed. "I do, yes, but our illustrious leaders need to sort themselves out first. He can't keep swooping in and fixing things for them. And the questions—people will insist on asking . . ."

"Is that why you didn't tell me about him?"

He nodded, jaw set like stone, and Juno could tell what was going through his mind. It had been going through hers, in the bounty hunter's prison ship. Until they knew for certain where Starkiller had come from, would the Rebel Alliance ever really believe in him? Would have

Juno herself, had she not seen him with her own eyes?

Bail Organa's words came back to her. *"I don't trust that kind of power."* He, at least, would be especially difficult to convince.

Juno felt a faint pang of regret at that. Of the few people she could have talked to about how she was feeling, Leia was the only one she trusted to be completely honest and objective. But her loyalty to the Alliance and her father was fierce, too. This was a bomb Juno couldn't afford to drop in her lap without being sure it wasn't about to go off.

War got in the way of friendship, just as it got in the way of love. The list of casualties wasn't confined just to people. She knew with a sinking feeling that the debriefing session on Dantooine, if it happened at all, would have to be all business, for both of their good.

So much for being a role model, she thought . . .

"I'll encourage him to keep a low profile," she said, confident that Vader and Kota himself would give the Alliance leadership plenty to argue about for now. "What about Kamino? I hope you're not thinking of leaving all this behind for the Emperor to start up again."

"We'll search the databases for any information on the space station the Emperor's building. I'm sure it's all been erased, but it's still worth looking. Then we'll ditch the Star Destroyers into the ocean and wreck the facilities with the resulting tsunami. In an hour or two, there'll be nothing left."

"Good," she said, thinking of Vader's sinister efforts to re-create the perfect—and perfectly evil—apprentice.

The sooner they were at the bottom of the ocean, the better.

She thought of Dac, and smiled again. If forest worlds were bad for her, then ocean worlds were the opposite. The sea air suited her, clearly.

A familiar shape swooped overhead. The *Rogue Shadow* had scored some new dents and scratches during the action, but looked unharmed in any significant way. Rebel soldiers had cleared a space for it on the rooftop, and Kota loped off to supervise the next stage in the operation. Juno watched the ship descend lightly on its repulsors, and found herself looking forward to getting behind the controls again.

Just like old times, she thought. With the Empire on their heels, an uncertain future ahead, and fragile hope in their hearts.

"Excuse me, Captain Eclipse."

Juno forced herself to tear her gaze from the ship. "Yes, PROXY, what is it?"

"While ascending through the cloning spire, I couldn't help noticing the remains of several droids of my class. I wonder if, with your permission, I could attempt to salvage some of the components I require to restore my primary programming."

The droid blinked anxiously at her, and Juno could see no reason to refuse. "All right, but don't take too long. Imperial reinforcements will be here soon, and you don't want to be left behind."

"No, I do not. Thank you, Captain Eclipse." PROXY hurried off, dodging and weaving around soldiers and technicians making ready the harness that would keep the *Rogue Shadow*'s new passenger secure.

Juno's mood darkened at that thought. Hardly like old times at all, with *him* aboard. Still, it wouldn't be for long, and if all went well, he'd soon be out of the picture entirely, and she, along with the rest of the galaxy, would breathe a heartfelt sigh of relief.

THE HARNESS SEEMED large enough to hold a rancor, and still the soldiers were nervous. Starkiller stayed nearby, in case of slip-ups or the slightest hint of an escape attempt. Except for one moment, when the harness swung a little too far to the right and threatened to hit the *Rogue Shadow*'s air lock frame, he let the soldiers do their work unimpeded. A slight nudge through the Force put the harness on course again, and no one was the wiser.

Kota followed the harness inside to check that it was firmly secured to the deck and ceiling. Starkiller didn't go with him. He still wasn't certain he had done the right thing.

Twice now, he'd had Vader at his mercy. Twice, Kota had talked him out of it. He wasn't sure if that was wisdom of the highest order, or madness utterly beyond his understanding. If Vader broke free, he knew he'd never get a third chance.

He had to make this one count.

Kota emerged, looking satisfied.

"Did he say anything to you?" Starkiller asked.

"Not a word."

"He never told me anything worth hearing in my

entire life. What makes you think he'll talk to anyone on Dantooine?"

"Everyone has their breaking point," said the general. "Even him."

"I think he passed his years ago."

Kota's blind eyes searched Starkiller's face, but he said nothing.

Starkiller told himself to be happy. He had everything he had set out from Kamino to find, and more. The only thing he had forgotten to think about was what happened next.

"Brought you here, the galaxy has," the strange creature on Dagobah had told him. *"Your path clearly this is."*

Maybe this *was* his path, then. But if so, he remained utterly in the dark as to what lay at the end of it.

PROXY hurried past them and up the ramp into the ship, clutching a tangled mess of droid parts to his chest. He looked like a droid on a mission, and Starkiller took that as his cue to enter the ship, too. He couldn't avoid going up the ramp forever. That was a journey whose end he *was* completely sure about.

He found the droid in the crew quarters, taking out bits and pieces of his own circuitry and plugging new modules in their place, prompting strange responses as he did so. His photoreceptors went from yellow to green and back again. Holographic limbs came and went. Weird buzzes and squeaks issued from his vocabulator.

"What are you doing, PROXY?" asked Starkiller, alarmed.

The droid looked up at him, and didn't seem to recognize him for a moment. He took a half-melted circuit block out of the back of his skull and inserted the original back in place.

"My primary program is still missing, Master," he said. "I am trying to replace it."

"Are these from the droids I killed?" Starkiller asked, stirring the parts with a finger.

"Yes, Master. It is clear now that my line did not end with my manufacture."

PROXY took out another block from his head and replaced it with one from the pile. Instantly his holoprojectors went crazy, shooting electrical arcs around the room. His arms and legs flailed, and Starkiller quickly reached over to remove the offending component.

"I think you should be careful," he said as PROXY settled back down. Thin streamers of smoke rose up from the droid's joints. "Better to have no primary program than no existence at all."

The droid looked disconsolate. "That is what Captain Eclipse says, but I do not understand why. My malfunctions upset her. I fear she may have me melted down if they continue."

"She would never do that," said Starkiller, hoping it wasn't true. "Describe these malfunctions to me. Maybe I can help."

PROXY did so, quickly and clinically, even though it clearly caused him discomfort to admit to his faults.

"Most disturbing," he concluded, "was the period when I looked like you, Master. For some reason I could not return to my normal form. That was when Captain Eclipse shut me down, for her good as well as mine."

"I understand," Starkiller said. He could imagine what Juno had felt with an identical copy of him hanging around, talking like PROXY talked, when he had been supposedly dead and gone. He hated the thought of it as well.

He understood on a deeper level, too.

"Something lost." The voice of the wise little creature on Dagobah returned to him again. *"A part of yourself, perhaps?"*

"I think you're trying to replace the wrong thing," he said, indicating the chips and circuits from the dead droids. "Look at the people you're imitating and ask yourself—do they have something in common? Maybe they possess something you're missing."

PROXY gravely considered the possibility. "Perhaps, but apart from all being human and known to me, I can't see how you, Captain Eclipse, General Kota, Mon Mothma, and Princess Leia are similar at all."

"Well, give it some more thought. That's an order."

"Yes, Master. I will do my best." PROXY began fishing around in the pile of spare parts again, clearly not intending to abandon that pursuit as well.

"Just remember that I need you in one piece, no matter what kind of primary programming you have."

"Yes, Master."

Starkiller stood. He and PROXY were still alone on the ship, apart from the prisoner, but that would soon change. It was time to get it over with.

Leaving PROXY to piece himself together, Starkiller walked through the ship to the entrance of the meditation chamber. There he took a deep breath and checked that Vader's lightsaber was safely at his side.

The door slid open at his touch. Two small overhead lights illuminated the entrance. More flickered on as he walked into the circular space. He didn't hesitate; his step never faltered. Inside, though, he felt only conflict and confusion.

He stopped in front of the harness. The last of the lights flickered on, revealing the harness and the prisoner contained within. Darth Vader's arms were hidden from the elbows down by thick, durasteel cuffs; his legs below the knees, likewise. Thick magna locks encased his waist, chest, and throat. A cage surrounded his helmet, leaving only the "face" exposed. A faint hum of energy fields pervaded the air. One more step closer, Starkiller knew, and he risked disintegration.

His former Master had no choice but to look down at him. Even Vader, with his prodigious strength and willpower, could barely turn his head. The only sound was the relentless in–out of his respirator.

Starkiller returned the stare, acutely aware that he had initiated this confrontation and that, even in the harness, his Master seemed more imposing and threatening than ever.

He didn't know what he had come to say, exactly, but he could feel his determination fading fast.

"I let you live," he said before he could think about it too much.

He meant it as a provocation, but it emerged more like a question, an expression of disbelief, as though he himself still didn't quite believe what he had done. If he *had* truly cast aside the Sith's notion of destiny—to kill his own Master—what did that leave him now? Did he even *have* a destiny, in this life?

Vader said nothing.

"You tell me I'm a clone—a *failed* clone. But I chose to spare you. Does this prove you right or wrong?"

Still Vader said nothing.

"Maybe Kota is right," he said more softly. "Maybe everything you told me was a trick. Maybe you were trying to get me so confused I'd forget who I really am and become your slave again."

His eyes narrowed as they took in the restraints keeping his former Master utterly helpless.

"Either way, I've finally broken your hold over me."

Vader stared at him, unable to convey anything by expression or body language. It was like talking to a statue.

With a small, disgusted sound, Starkiller turned to leave.

"As long as she lives," Darth Vader said, "I will always control you."

Starkiller stopped and almost turned. What was this? Another empty threat? A last desperate mind game? The truth . . . ?

It didn't deserve a reply. He wouldn't give Vader the satisfaction of seeing his face, and the uncertainty he was sure it displayed.

When he left the room, the lights flickered out and the door slid securely closed behind him.

THERE WERE SURVIVORS of the *Salvation* among the troops on the ground. Juno had no intentions of going anywhere until they were accounted for and provided with berths on Alliance ships. Several Imperial vessels had been commandeered from the landing bays on Kamino; she felt it her duty to ensure at least a couple of them went to "her" crew. She didn't know how long it was going to be before she would be in such a position again. Perhaps when more of the Mon Calamari cruisers came into service . . .

Juno thought of Nitram and how he had betrayed her to Mon Mothma. She couldn't begrudge him that, although it had caused her inconvenience at the time; just like her, he had only been trying to do the right thing. It didn't seem fair that he was dead, while she lived on. Had she been standing where he was on the bridge of the *Salvation*, she would be in his place. Had he had someone like Starkiller to champion him, he might still be alive.

One of the downsides of command, she told herself, was losing good crew to the vagaries of fate. Best she got used to it—just as Vader's bounty hunter would have to get used to the idea that he wouldn't be paid for this particular job, now that his employer was locked up for good . . .

Finally everything was ready for departure. The decoy freighters were loaded with fake cargoes and crewed by people either utterly loyal or, if there was a chance of a traitor among them, at least aware that they were part of a much larger deception. Only a handful of critical personnel knew precisely who was going where. The betrayal of the fleet's location by the Itani Nebula was still fresh in everyone's minds.

"Word will get to the Emperor eventually," she said to Kota as they took their leave of each other on top of the cloning tower. The whining of engines was rising all around them. "We can't avoid it."

"So we get our demands in earlier," the general said, "or we allow him to sweat for a bit. That's Mon Mothma's decision. Just get Vader to Dantooine in one piece and leave the rest to me."

"Of course." She saluted.

He returned the salute. "We'll be waiting for you."

"Not if I get there first."

Kota jumped into a waiting shuttle and ascended immediately in the direction of the new frigate. Juno took one last look around the surface of Kamino, and shivered. The clouds had closed over again. A new storm was brewing on the western horizon.

She was the last one left on the roof of the cloning spire, where so many awful and wonderful things had happened. Soon it would be gone forever. Tightening the collar around her bruised throat, she ran up the ramp and into the *Rogue Shadow*, vowing never to look back.

Darth Vader was standing in the crew compartment, domed head looming high above hers, seeming to fill the whole ship with shadow.

Juno reached for the blaster at her side, heart thudding hard in her chest.

With a flash of light, Vader disappeared.

"PROXY?" Juno lowered the blaster. Her hands were shaking. "What on Coruscant are you playing at?"

"I am experimenting, Captain Eclipse," said the droid, reaching up to tap the back of his head. "My Master suggested that I ask myself what the people I have been imitating have in common. The only detail I can discern is that they have a sense of purpose beyond themselves. They stand for principles, not just self-preservation—as I must, too, in order to be whole."

She remembered what Leia had said about their being a message behind PROXY's manifestations. "Maybe you knew that all along, on that deeper level of programming you talked about, and you've been trying to tell yourself about it."

"That is possible."

"But Darth Vader fits . . . how, exactly?"

"I am as yet unsure. This may be a residue from one of the chips I have salvaged."

"He serves a Master, too, don't forget. And if he has any principles, they're not anything you'd want to follow."

"Assuredly not, Captain Eclipse."

PROXY look pleased, and she didn't have the heart to argue the point.

"Well, good, I guess," she said. "I'm glad your primary program is finally fixed. We're going to need you in full working order."

"I exist to serve, Captain."

Juno brushed past him to the bridge, where Starkiller was sitting in the copilot's seat. A hit of déjà vu struck her as she crossed the threshold.

He looked up. "Anything wrong?"

"Absolutely nothing," she said, coming to sit next to him, at the controls. Although she hadn't been inside the *Rogue Shadow* for more than a year, the layout of the console seemed as familiar to her as the back of her hands. As the battered fatigue on Starkiller's face.

PROXY took his seat behind them. "All systems are fully functional," he assured her.

She placed her hands on the controls. A series of deft touches closed the ramp and brought the repulsors to life. Gently, the *Rogue Shadow* lifted off and rose into the sky.

Starkiller's expression was impassive, but she could tell that he was watching closely as the cloning towers receded below them. Barely had they lifted off when the first of the gutted Star Destroyers hit the ocean several klicks away. There was a flash like the rising of the sun as several megatons of water instantly vaporized. The shock wave radiated outward in a wave of steam hundreds of meters high. In seconds, the tsunami reached the towers, knocking them over and occluding the wreckage from sight.

Ahead, bright stars appeared through the thinning atmosphere. Dotted among them, the shining constellation of the Rebel fleet, all proudly marked with the symbol of the Alliance: Starkiller's family crest, with none of the soldiers or commanders aware that the one who had inspired it was among them again.

The *Rogue Shadow* joined twelve small freighters in orbit above the waterworld.

"You have your orders," said Commodore Viedas to each of them in a firm and steady voice. "May the Force be with you."

One by one, the freighters accelerated, each heading along a different trajectory into hyperspace.

Juno counted them off, double-checking the course for Dantooine. As their numbers dwindled, she glanced at Starkiller, who was still staring back at Kamino. The expanding circular shock wave looked like the pupil of an enormous eye.

He was difficult to read sometimes, and this was no exception. She reached out and placed a hand on his forearm, breaking his concentration.

"Ready for lightspeed," she said.

He managed a smile. "I'm ready for anything."

Her other hand pushed a lever on the console, and the hyperdrives kicked into life. The *Rogue Shadow* flung itself forward. Stars turned to streaks ahead of them. This time, Juno hoped, the past was left far, far behind.

Read on for an excerpt from

Star Wars: Fate of the Jedi:
Outcast

by Aaron Allston

Galactic Alliance Diplomatic Shuttle, High Coruscant Orbit

ONE BY ONE, the stars overhead began to disappear, swallowed by some enormous darkness interposing itself from above and behind the shuttle. Sharply pointed at its most forward position, broadening behind, the flood of blackness advanced, blotting out more and more of the unblinking starfield, until darkness was all there was to see.

Then, all across the length and breadth of the ominous shape, lights came on—blue and white running lights, tiny red hatch and security lights, sudden glows from within transparisteel viewports, one large rectangular whiteness limned by atmosphere shields. The lights showed the vast triangle to be the underside of an Imperial Star Destroyer, painted black, forbidding a moment ago, now comparatively cheerful in its proper running configuration. It was the *Gilad Pellaeon*, newly arrived from the Imperial Remnant, and its officers clearly knew how to put on a show.

Jaina Solo, sitting with the others in the dimly lit

passenger compartment of the government VIP shuttle, watched the entire display through the overhead transparisteel canopy and laughed out loud.

The Bothan in the sumptuously padded chair next to hers gave her a curious look. His mottled red and tan fur twitched, either from suppressed irritation or embarrassment at Jaina's outburst. "What do you find so amusing?"

"Oh, both the obviousness of it and the skill with which it was performed. It's so very, *You used to think of us as dark and scary, but now we're just your stylish allies.*" Jaina lowered her voice so that her next comment would not carry to the passengers in the seats behind. "The press will love it. That image will play on the holonews broadcasts constantly. Mark my words."

"Was that little show a Jagged Fel detail?"

Jaina tilted her head, considering. "I don't know. He could have come up with it, but he usually doesn't spend his time planning displays or events. When he does, though, they're usually pretty . . . effective."

The shuttle rose toward the *Gilad Pellaeon*'s main landing bay. In moments, it was through the square atmosphere barrier shield and drifting sideways to land on the deck nearby. The landing place was clearly marked—hundreds of beings, most wearing gray Imperial uniforms or the distinctive white armor of the Imperial stormtrooper, waited in the bay, and the one circular spot where none stood was just the right size for the Galactic Alliance shuttle.

The passengers rose as the shuttle settled into place. The Bothan smoothed his tunic, a cheerful blue decorated with a golden sliver pattern suggesting claws. "Time to go to work. You won't let me get killed, will you?"

Jaina let her eyes widen. "Is that what I was supposed to be doing here?" she asked in droll tones. "I should have brought my lightsaber."

The Bothan offered a long-suffering sigh and turned toward the exit.

They descended the shuttle's boarding ramp. With no duties required of her other than to keep alert and be the Jedi face at this preliminary meeting, Jaina was able to stand back and observe. She was struck with the unreality of it all. The niece and daughter of three of the most famous enemies of the Empire during the First Galactic Civil War of a few decades earlier, she was now witness to events that might bring the Galactic Empire—or Imperial Remnant, as it was called everywhere outside its own borders—into the Galactic Alliance on a lasting basis.

And at the center of the plan was the man, flanked by Imperial officers, who now approached the Bothan. Slightly under average size, though towering well above Jaina's diminutive height, he was dark-haired, with a trim beard and mustache that gave him a rakish look, and was handsome in a way that became more pronounced when he glowered. A scar on his forehead ran up into his hairline and seemed to continue as a lock of white hair from that point. He wore expensive but subdued black civilian garments, neck-to-toe, that would be inconspicuous anywhere on Coruscant but stood out in sharp relief to the gray and white uniforms, white armor, and colorful Alliance clothes surrounding him.

He had one moment to glance at Jaina. The look probably appeared neutral to onlookers, but for her it carried just a twinkle of humor, a touch of exasperation that the two of them had to put up with all these delays. Then an Alliance functionary, notable for his blandness, made introductions: "Imperial Head of State the most honorable Jagged Fel, may I present Senator Tiurrg Drey'lye of Bothawui, head of the Senate Unification Preparations Committee."

Jagged Fel took the Senator's hand. "I'm pleased to be working with you."

"And delighted to meet *you*. Chief of State Daala sends her compliments and looks forward to meeting you when you make planetfall."

Jag nodded. "And now, I believe, protocol insists that we open a bottle or a dozen of wine and make some preliminary discussion of security, introduction protocols, and so on."

"Fortunately about the wine, and regrettably about everything else, you are correct."

At the end of two full standard hours—Jaina knew from regular, surreptitious consultations of her chrono— Jag was able to convince the Senator and his retinue to accept a tour of the *Gilad Pellaeon*. He was also able to request a private consultation with the sole representative of the Jedi Order present. Moments later, the gray-walled conference room was empty of everyone but Jag and Jaina.

Jag glanced toward the door. "Security seal, access limited to Jagged Fel and Jedi Jaina Solo, voice identification, activate." The door hissed in response as it sealed. Then Jag returned his attention to Jaina.

She let an expression of anger and accusation cross her face. "You're not fooling anyone, Fel. You're planning for an Imperial invasion of Alliance space."

Jag nodded. "I've been planning it for quite a while. Come here."

She moved to him, settled into his lap, and was suddenly but not unexpectedly caught in his embrace. They kissed urgently, hungrily.

Finally Jaina drew back and smiled at him. "This isn't going to be a routine part of your consultations with every Jedi."

"Uh, no. That would cause some trouble here and at home. But I actually *do* have business with the Jedi that does not involve the Galactic Alliance, at least not initially."

"What sort of business?"

"Whether or not the Galactic Empire joins with the Galactic Alliance, I think there ought to be an official Jedi presence in the Empire. A second Temple, a branch, an offshoot, whatever. Providing advice and insight to the Head of State."

"And protection?"

He shrugged. "Less of an issue. I'm doing all right. Two years in this position and not dead yet."

"Emperor Palpatine went nearly twenty-five years."

"I guess that makes him my hero."

Jaina snorted. "Don't even say that in jest . . . Jag, if the Remnant doesn't join the Alliance, I'm not sure the Jedi *can* have a presence without Alliance approval."

"The Order still keeps its training facility for youngsters in Hapan space. And the Hapans haven't rejoined."

"You sound annoyed. The Hapans still giving you trouble?"

"Let's not talk about *that*."

"Besides, moving the school back to Alliance space is just a matter of time, logistics, and finances; there's no question that it will happen. On the other hand, it's very likely that the government would withhold approval for a Jedi branch in the Remnant, just out of spite, if the Remnant doesn't join."

"Well, there's such a thing as an *unofficial* presence. And there's such a thing as rival schools, schismatic branches, and places for former Jedi to go when they can't be at the Temple."

Jaina smiled again, but now there was suspicion in her expression. "You just want to have this so *I'll* be assigned to come to the Remnant and set it up."

"That's a motive, but not the only one. Remember, to the Moffs and to a lot of the Imperial population, the Jedi have been bogeymen since Palpatine died. At the very least, I don't want them to be inappropriately afraid of the woman I'm in love with."

Jaina was silent for a moment. "Have we talked enough politics?"

"I think so."

"Good."

Horn Family Quarters,
Kallad's Dream Vacation Hostel, Coruscant

Yawning, hair tousled, clad in a blue dressing robe, Valin Horn knew that he did not look anything like an experienced Jedi Knight. He looked like an unshaven, unkempt bachelor, which he also was. But here, in these rented quarters, there would be only family to see him— at least until he had breakfast, shaved, and dressed.

The Horns did not live here, of course. His mother, Mirax, was the anchor for the immediate family. Manager of a variety of interlinked businesses—trading, interplanetary finances, gambling and recreation, and, if rumors were true, still a little smuggling here and there—she maintained her home and business address on Corellia. Corran, her husband and Valin's father, was a Jedi Master, much of his life spent on missions away from the family, but his true home was where his heart resided, wherever Mirax lived. Valin and his sister, Jysella, also Jedi, lived wherever their missions sent them, and also counted Mirax as the center of the family.

Now Mirax had rented temporary quarters on Coruscant so the family could collect on one of its rare occasions, this time for the Unification Summit, where she and Corran would separately give depositions on the relationships among the Confederation states, the Imperial Remnant, and the Galactic Alliance as they related to trade and Jedi activities. Mirax had insisted that Valin and Jysella leave their Temple quarters and stay with their parents while these events were taking place, and few forces in the galaxy could stand before her decision—Luke Skywalker certainly knew better than to try.

Moving from the refresher toward the kitchen and dining nook, Valin brushed a lock of brown hair out of his eyes and grinned. Much as he might put up a public show of protest—the independent young man who did not need parents to direct his actions or tell him where to sleep—he hardly minded. It was good to see family. And both Corran and Mirax were better cooks than the ones at the Jedi Temple.

There was no sound of conversation from the kitchen, but there was some clattering of pans, so at least one of his parents must still be on hand. As he stepped from the hallway into the dining nook, Valin saw that it was his mother, her back to him as she worked at the stove. He pulled a chair from the table and sat. "Good morning."

"A joke, so early?" Mirax did not turn to face him, but her tone was cheerful. "No morning is good. I come light-years from Corellia to be with my family, and what happens? I have to keep Jedi hours to see them. Don't you know that I'm an executive? And a lazy one?"

"I forgot." Valin took a deep breath, sampling the smells of breakfast. His mother was making hotcakes Corellian-style, nerf sausage links on the side, and caf was brewing. For a moment, Valin was transported back to his childhood, to the family breakfasts that had been somewhat more common before the Yuuzhan Vong came, before Valin and Jysella had started down the Jedi path. "Where are Dad and Sella?"

"Your father is out getting some back-door information

from other Jedi Masters for his deposition." Mirax pulled a plate from a cabinet and began sliding hotcakes and links onto it. "Your sister left early and wouldn't say what she was doing, which I assume either means it's Jedi business I can't know about or that she's seeing some man she doesn't *want* me to know about."

"Or both."

"Or both." Mirax turned and moved over to put the plate down before him. She set utensils beside it.

The plate was heaped high with food, and Valin recoiled from it in mock horror. "Stang, Mom, you're feeding your son, not a squadron of Gamorreans." Then he caught sight of his mother's face and he was suddenly no longer in a joking mood.

This wasn't his mother.

Oh, the woman had Mirax's features. She had the round face that admirers had called "cute" far more often than "beautiful," much to Mirax's chagrin. She had Mirax's generous, curving lips that smiled so readily and expressively, and Mirax's bright, lively brown eyes. She had Mirax's hair, a glossy black with flecks of gray, worn shoulder-length to fit readily under a pilot's helmet, even though she piloted far less often these days. She was Mirax to every freckle and dimple.

But she was not Mirax.

The woman, whoever she was, caught sight of Valin's confusion. "Something wrong?"

"Uh, no." Stunned, Valin looked down at his plate.

He had to think—logically, correctly, and *fast*. He might be in grave danger right now, though the Force currently gave him no indication of imminent attack. The true Mirax, wherever she was, might be in serious trouble or worse. Valin tried in vain to slow his heart rate and speed up his thinking processes.

Fact: Mirax had been here but had been replaced by an imposter. Presumably the real Mirax was gone; Valin could not sense anyone but himself and the imposter in the immediate vicinity. The imposter had remained behind for some reason that had to relate to Valin, Jysella, or Corran. It couldn't have been to capture Valin, as she could have done that with drugs or other methods while he slept, so the food was probably not drugged.

Under Not-Mirax's concerned gaze, he took a tentative bite of sausage and turned a reassuring smile he didn't feel toward her.

Fact: Creating an imposter this perfect must have taken a fortune in money, an incredible amount of research, and a volunteer willing to let her features be permanently carved into the likeness of another's. Or perhaps this was a clone, raised and trained for the purpose of simulating Mirax. Or maybe she was a droid, one of the very expensive, very rare human replica droids. Or maybe a shape-shifter. Whichever, the simulation was nearly perfect. Valin hadn't recognized the deception until . . .

Until *what*? What had tipped him off? He took another bite, not registering the sausage's taste or temperature, and maintained the face-hurting smile as he tried to recall the detail that had alerted him that this wasn't his mother.

He couldn't figure it out. It was just an instant

realization, too fleeting to remember, too overwhelming to reject.

Would Corran be able to see through the deception? Would Jysella? Surely, they had to be able to. But what if they couldn't? Valin would accuse this woman and be thought insane.

Were Corran and Jysella even still at liberty? Still *alive*? At this moment, the Not-Mirax's colleagues could be spiriting the two of them away with the true Mirax. Or Corran and Jysella could be lying, bleeding, at the bottom of an access shaft, their lives draining away.

Valin couldn't think straight. The situation was too overwhelming, the mystery too deep, and the only person here who knew the answers was the one who wore the face of his mother.

He stood, sending his chair clattering backward, and fixed the false Mirax with a hard look. "Just a moment." He dashed to his room.

His lightsaber was still where he'd left it, on the nightstand beside his bed. He snatched it up and gave it a near-instantaneous examination. Battery power was still optimal; there was no sign that it had been tampered with.

He returned to the dining room with the weapon in his hand. Not-Mirax, clearly confused and beginning to look a little alarmed, stood by the stove, staring at him.

Valin ignited the lightsaber, its *snap-hiss* of activation startlingly loud, and held the point of the gleaming energy blade against the food on his plate. Hotcakes shriveled and blackened from contact with the weapon's plasma.

Valin gave Not-Mirax an approving nod. "Flesh does the same thing under the same conditions, you know."

"Valin, what's *wrong*?"

"You may address me as Jedi Horn. You don't have the right to use my personal name." Valin swung the lightsaber around in a practice form, allowing the blade to come within a few centimeters of the glow rod fixture overhead, the wall, the dining table, and the woman with his mother's face. "You probably know from your research that the Jedi don't worry much about amputations."

Not-Mirax shrank back away from him, both hands on the stove edge behind her. "What?"

"We know that a severed limb can readily be replaced by a prosthetic that looks identical to the real thing. Prosthetics offer sensation and do everything flesh can. They're ideal substitutes in every way, except for requiring maintenance. So we don't feel too badly when we have to cut the arm or leg off a very bad person. But I assure you, that very bad person remembers the pain forever."

"Valin, I'm going to call your father now." Mirax sidled toward the blue bantha-hide carrybag she had left on a side table.

Valin positioned the tip of his lightsaber directly beneath her chin. At the distance of half a centimeter, its containing force field kept her from feeling any heat from the blade, but a slight twitch on Valin's part could maim or kill her instantly. She froze.

"No, you're not. You know what you're going to do instead?"

Mirax's voice wavered. "What?"

"You're going to *tell me what you've done with my mother!*" The last several words emerged as a bellow, driven by fear and anger. Valin knew that he looked as angry as he sounded; he could feel blood reddening his face, could even see redness begin to suffuse everything in his vision.

"Boy, put the blade down." Those were not the woman's words. They came from behind. Valin spun, bringing his blade up into a defensive position.

In the doorway stood a man, middle-aged, clean-shaven, his hair graying from brown. He was of below-average height, his eyes a startling green. He wore the brown robes of a Jedi. His hands were on his belt, his own lightsaber still dangling from it.

He was Valin's father, Jedi Master Corran Horn. But he wasn't, any more than the woman behind Valin was Mirax Horn.

Valin felt a wave of despair wash over him. *Both* parents replaced. Odds were growing that the real Corran and Mirax were already dead.

Yet Valin's voice was soft when he spoke. "They may have made you a virtual double for my father. But they can't have given you his expertise with the lightsaber."

"You don't want to do what you're thinking about, son."

"When I cut you in half, that's all the proof anyone will ever need that you're not the real Corran Horn."

Valin lunged.

ABOUT THE AUTHOR

Sean Williams is the #1 *New York Times* bestselling and award-winning author of more than seventy published short stories and thirty novels, including *Star Wars: The Force Unleashed* and *Star Wars: The Old Republic: Fatal Alliance*. He is a judge for the Writers of the Future contest, which he won in 1993. He is also a multiple winner of Australia's speculative fiction awards and is the recipient of both the Ditmar and the Aurealis for *The Crooked Letter*, marking the first time in the history of the awards that a fantasy novel has won both. Williams lives with his wife, Amanda, in Adelaide, South Australia

www.seanwilliams.com.au

ABOUT THE TYPE

This book was set in Sabon, a typeface designed by the well-known German typographer Jan Tschichold (1902–74). Sabon's design is based upon the original letter forms of Claude Garamond and was created specifically to be used for three sources: foundry type for hand composition, Linotype, and Monotype. Tschichold named his typeface for the famous Frankfurt typefounder Jacques Sabon, who died in 1580.

ALSO AVAILABLE FROM TITAN BOOKS:

Star Wars: The Force Unleashed
by Sean Williams

Star Wars: The Old Republic: Fatal Alliance
by Sean Williams

Star Wars: The Old Republic: Deceived
by Paul S. Kemp

COMING SOON FROM TITAN BOOKS:

Star Wars: The Old Republic: Revan
by Drew Karpyshyn